ANGEL

An SOBs Novel

IRISH WINTERS

Angel, An SOBs Novel

Copyright ©2018 by Irish Winters

All rights reserved

First Edition

Cover design and author photo: Letitia Hasser, Romantic Book Designs

Interior book design: Bob Houston eBook Formatting

Editor: Darcy Fairbanks, editor

ISBN Paperback: 978-1-942895-88-6

ISBN eBook: 978-1-942895-54-1

Library of Congress Control Number: 2018931846

Irish Winter's websites: http://www.irishwinters.com and irishwinters.blogspot.com

Angel

An SOBs novel

Angel – Chance's story

Coming soon:

Assassin – Pagan's story
Damned – Kruze's story

You can find Irish Winters
On Facebook
&
On Twitter

Sign up for Irish Winters' Newsletter at:
http://www.irishwinters.com/newsletter.html

For more information about all Irish Winters'
books, visit:
http://www.irishwinters.com.

Prologue

It was an ordinary day. Weather was good and skies were clear. The operation was supposed to be hands-down easy. *Retrieve the package. Waste any and all tangos on the way in. Bust ass to the extraction point on the way out. Exfil in record time. Job over. Go home. Kick your boots off. Kill a few beers.*

Wasn't working out that way.

Chief Chance Sinclair and his eight-man SEAL team had been tasked to retrieve a kidnapped missionary, a woman, Gillian Enright, from a band of Shining Path guerillas outside Lima, Peru. Where once the Shining Path wanted world domination and communism, now they wanted control of the country's drug trade. Being converted to Christianity by bible thumping do-gooders from the heart of North America wasn't on their agenda.

Mrs. Enright's husband Reed had died fast and hard, but they'd taken Gillian hostage instead of hacking her to death by machete. They wanted three million from the Peruvian government for her release. Since the Enrights were Americans, the President of Peru contacted the President of the United States. In turn, he called an admiral friend.

When talks between the guerillas and the United States disintegrated, Chance's SEAL Team won the lottery—and a CIA escort to Peru. There hadn't been sufficient time to rehearse this extraction like they usually did, not with the woman's life on the line. Chance had done enough of these rescues. His team knew what to do. So why was his gut pulling a U-turn on him when they had maybe twenty yards left to engage the tangos?

Because he had yet to spot any.

One step on dry land, and he'd already fisted his hand, signaling his men to stand fast. They'd just climbed out of the murky, snake-infested river at their rear. Geared-up as only Navy SEALs could be, with grease paint, waterproof grenades dangling from their belts, enough weaponry to start a war, waterlogged and crawling with mosquitoes and flies, they snapped to and held position.

Chance popped one of the peppermint candies he always packed around with him into his mouth to negate the after taste of the dirty river. He couldn't shake the prickly sensation of spiders crawling up the back of his neck. He and his men were being watched. He was sure of it.

One quick look at the three POS shacks straight ahead made the sensation worse. No concertina wire. No lookout towers. No guards. Not even a curl of smoke from the fire pit to prove this band of Shining Path guerillas had recently been here. Yet this was the place.

"Something's up, Chief," Jimmy *Superman* Olsen whispered at his six, his voice of steel as firm as if this mess were just another bump in the road. "She was supposed to be here. A couple dozen assholes, too."

"Then where is everyone?" Gerard *Hot Shot* Rowe bit out. *Hot Shot* was forever short on patience, hence the nickname. Both men had served with Chance for years. They knew each other's moves, brews, and whether the other wore boxers or briefs. He owed them to do this right and to get them home safely, but Chance was no quitter like his old man. He owed that sister missionary safe passage out of Peru, too.

"Our fuckin' intel's wrong," Kevin *Chill* Frost advised. The blood ran as cold as ice in the team's best sniper's veins.

Possibly.

It shouldn't be wrong. It came straight from their missing CIA Agent Card, aka *The Dick,* not his real name. Assigned by higher-ups beyond CO Tom Bratton's pay grade, this op had been screwed from the get-go, once the spook got involved. Central Intelligence didn't play well with others. Neither did *The Dick.*

Like a privileged frat boy off-campus, he came and went as he pleased, offered random updates at the last damned moment, then ghosted when the going got tough. He'd been late for take-off, too. Made Chance's team wait two hours on the tarmac for his sorry ass like they had nothing better to do. Like now, when seconds counted. When lives hung in the balance.

"Where's Card?" Chance asked, his eyes still parsing the scene ahead.

"Said he had to take a leak a mile back," Merrick *Ears* Wong, his communications guy, reported. "You were underwater by then, or I'd have told you. Thought the shithead'd be back by now."

"What? He couldn't pee in the river like everyone else?" Darrell *Texas* Contreras grumbled.

Chance understood why *Ears* hadn't reported sooner. Helmet mics might be waterproof, but a man still couldn't speak underwater. It figured Card would wait until then to take off. "Contact him, *Ears*," Chance ordered. "I want his ass with us when we go in."

Ears adjusted his headset, and dialed *The Dick*. A grim shake of his head told Chance all he needed to know. Card wasn't answering. As usual. A man could only hope an anaconda or something just as lethal had swallowed the sniveling bastard whole for all the good he'd been. Not that it mattered. The primary goal of this mission was to rescue this lone woman from the Shining Path, not to save Card's ass. Chance didn't intend to deviate.

Superman cleared his throat, an outright question in spec ops lingo: *Are we going in or bugging out?*

Chance stalled, still quarterbacking the scene, second-guessing and not willing to risk his men for what sure as hell felt like an ambush. He damned well knew it, but this crap was what SEALs did every single day. The impossible.

"Move out," he ordered, "but keep it tight. We've got ten minutes to get in and get out. Keep your eyes open. This one stinks."

"To high heaven," came back from *Texas*.

Infiltration went as smooth as grease through a fully automatic, pneumatic grease gun on a hot day. While *Texas* and *Ears* circled the camp to intercept any strays, Chance and *Superman* took the hut at the far right, weapons drawn. *Hot Shot* and Stokes *Gun Powder* Remington zeroed in, center stage. Pete *Ducky* Newton and Walker *Crack* Martinez rushed left. Two shots rang out.

"All clear," *Hot Shot* reported.

"Targets neutralized," *Ducky* seconded.

Chance plowed straight through his assigned target with *Superman* on his rear. They'd encountered no dirtbags, but found Mrs. Enright beyond the hut, damn it. She'd been crucified, nailed to a dirty wooden cross and left in the open like a door prize. Blood still dripped from the palms of her punctured hands and feet. Chance's gut churned at this obvious trap. "They're still here," he growled. "I know damned well they are."

"Copy that," *Crack* hissed. "I can smell 'em."

"Just can't see 'em," *Ducky* growled. "Want me to shoot the trees to see what falls out."

"Or who," Superman said.

"Later," Chance growled. The package was in critical condition. Her open shirt flapped at her sides like a dirty rag. Swarms of black flies feasted on her bare, bloodied chest.

Superman spit to the side. "Fuck. They carved her up."

"Heads on swivels, boys," Chance warned as he and *Superman* eased the wooden beam holding Gillian Enright out of its hole and to the ground. Once down, Chance jerked the extra T-shirt he always carried from one of his many pants pocket. Ripping it from its sealed plastic bag, he draped it over her for modesty's sake. The poor woman's eyes flashed open. A wretched growl began deep in her chest and quickly graduated to a blood-curdling scream.

"Medic," Chance ordered even as his hands came forward to placate the traumatized woman. "Take it easy, ma'am. We're Americans and we're taking you home," he told her, keeping his voice low and his tone level. She was a tiny, blonde thing, no more than college student age. Shit. Just looking at her hurt.

She blinked as if she didn't trust her eyes. "A-Americans?" God, the torment in her voice.

"SEALs," *Superman* hissed. "We're SEALs, ma'am, America's best. You're going to be okay."

Chance wasn't so sure about her being okay or that they were America's best, but that was what SEALs did. They took out the bad guys and one-by-one, they gave the world hope when it needed it most.

Those words seemed to calm her, while *Ducky* administered a tiny hypo of morphine. He'd gotten his nickname because he was good with emergency first-aid, like some dude on some *NCIS* show. The moment she slumped into oblivion, everything got easier.

Chance scanned the immediate area for the hammer used to do this dirty work, but came up with nothing. "Find me something to pull these nails out," he snapped at his guys.

Hot Shot shook his head. "Told you. There's nothing here. Use what you've got."

Superman already had his Leatherman in hand.

"Jesus Christ, we don't have time for this," Chance hissed to himself. "Get it done."

"On it." *Superman* put one boot to the crossbeam, got a good grip with the multi-tool, and jerked a long rusty nail out of Gillian's left hand. He tossed the tool to Chance, who freed her right hand while *Ducky* began a temporary saline drip to keep her stable during transport. Once in the air, he could commence better treatment, but they were running out of time.

Carefully, Chance tugged the three vicious nails out of her feet, damned sorry he'd hurt her. If he lived to be a hundred, he'd never understand what drove some men to brutalize the fairer sex. It made no sense.

Getting her across the river and back to the Army Blackhawk was another problem, but *Ducky* was one step ahead. He wrapped her in waterproof plastic, then sealed the edges with duct tape to keep her wounds as clean and dry as possible.

"Contact Gleason," Chance ordered. "We'll be coming in hot."

Ears cursed under his breath. "Been trying, Chief. No answer."

That brought everyone's heads up. Without Chief Warrant Officer Gleason, the Blackhawk's pilot, they were screwed.

"Try again," Chance snapped. *Shit! Could anything else go wrong?*

While *Ears* complied, the others reported their findings. No beds or mats. No food on site. And no guerillas. "There's a shithole that direction," *Crack* chin nodded to the jungle north of the huts. "Smells plenty fresh. They haven't been gone long."

The targets he'd eliminated earlier ended up being two large rats the size of small dogs, which explained some of the wounds on the lady at hand. She'd been imprisoned with them, poor thing.

"Gleason's still MIA," *Ears* reported, his head cocked and waiting on Chance's order.

Shit! No tangos, no Card, and no Gleason. Didn't matter. Their ten minutes were gone. "Pack her up and let's roll," Chance told his men, his gut on fire with a steady *'get-the-hell-out-of-there-an-do-it-right-now!'*

Moving fast, *Gun Powder* cradled the package like a baby, his eyes wide at what was left of the woman in his arms. She'd been stronger than most to have survived thus far, but she'd have to be stronger still for what lay ahead. Chance had his doubts. Gillian was in obvious shock and she'd lost a lot of blood. He didn't want to think what those rats had infected her with.

Back to the river they went, then straight across with *Gun Powder* floating Gillian on her back in a lifeguard grip. *Superman* and *Hot Shot* hung close by to assist. In thirty minutes, Chance and his team stood on the opposite shore within sight of the Blackhawk.

Once again his men waited on his decision. The Army's stealth modified bird rested one klick ahead, its skids planted in knee-high grass, its rotors as still as the suffocating humidity. Chance had yet to receive a 'Copy that' from his calls to Gleason for assistance.

Jesus Christ, what now? Rescue Gleason and Card?

The muddy ground beneath their boots had been recently chewed up by heavy machinery. Metal track marks led everywhere, but they were old news. They'd been there when they'd landed. Chance hadn't cared then, but he did now. Logging trucks and tanks left those kinds of tracks, so why were no trees in this area cleared? He motioned *Crack* and *Texas* to scout right while *Chill* and *Ducky* went left.

Gun Powder knelt to Chance's right, Gillian secure in his arms, her head against his chest. Chance had to look twice. *Gun Powder* held her hands together with one hand so her arms wouldn't flop at her sides. That was thoughtful. He held the pistol in his free hand ready to protect her. That was smart.

"Get Bratton on the line," Chance told *Ears* while the rest of his guys waited on intel, their rifles ready. CO Bratton needed to know what they were up against.

"Look," *Gun Powder* hissed. "There. In the tree." He tilted forward. His knee barely slid forward in the mud when—

BOOM!

The Earth lifted beneath Chance, rag-dolling him end over end into a massive tree trunk. He hit hard. The leafy jungle toppled around him like dominoes. Stinging blood and gore splashed into his eyes. A blinding shockwave rippled over him as a swarm of killer bees nailed his face. Stinging the shit out of him. Biting. Chewing through his scalp.

His last thought? *'Mom!'*

Chapter One

That damned dog.

"Gallo! Gallo! Come here, boy!" Chance bellowed into the midnight swirl of wind-driven ice and snow, sleet and hail. *Before I wring your stubborn neck!*

Of all the times for his mother's *'I-know-better-than-you'* gift-from-the-grave to take off for a late night run. Gallo had better plan on sleeping on the porch tonight because Chance'd had enough of the German Shepherd's air-headed disobedience. Maybe a night spent outdoors in the cold would do the pampered beast good. Might make him think twice before he pulled this stunt again.

"Oh, hell," Chance cursed. He couldn't leave the dog outside, not with the first winter storm of the season busting through Northern Montana like a beast on steroids. Gallo wasn't a year old yet, and he hadn't a lick of sense. He'd probably freeze to death and—*what would Mom say then, huh?* Chance didn't need to be haunted by more ghosts than he already was.

"What were you thinking, Mom? A German Shepherd? You should've bought a poodle instead of a big-footed, air-headed moose that likes to run."

The reading of his famous author/mother's will five months earlier had left Chance a reluctant multi-millionaire as well as the owner of Gallo. He'd wanted neither. Wealth was an unfamiliar burden he had yet to acknowledge. Admitting it meant she was gone, and he plain wasn't ready to face that truth.

But damn. The number of digits currently preceding the decimal point in his new bank balance he could ignore until he got around to it. The dog was something else again. He cast a final threat out into the stiffening wind. "This is the last time I hunt your sorry ass down, you mangy mutt!"

Then, because there was no choice, he slammed his cabin door and prepared to go into the cold, cruel world to rescue a four-legged kid. Again.

"This is the second time today. You're going on a chain from now on," Chance grumbled as he shoved his feet into an old pair of combat boots, then jerked his Gortex jacket, a midnight requisition from Uncle Sam, off the hook by his door. "A damned short chain."

A gray wool hat went snug over his head and a thick scarf went around his neck. Flipping the jacket collar upright against the weather, he zipped up. Winters in Northern Montana were wicked, and this sudden storm was delivering one hell of a punch. Old Man Mountain to the north of his cabin would be thick with drifts and avalanche-worthy overhangs by morning—if the storm let up by then. It might not.

Chance had owned this property for three years now, and he'd visited often. Not one of those winters had been the same. The only hard fast rule? Once it settled in, it was here to stay.

Damn that dog. Still grousing, Chance snagged the twenty-foot windup leash from the box of dog toys beside the door before he stepped outside and into the blizzard that came with gale force winds. This was no snowfall, it was Snowmageddon, the sleet and snow coming sideways instead of vertically.

"Gallo!" he called, in hopes the errant animal had grown a brain during the time it took his master to gear up. No such luck.

Chance stomped through the drifts already turning his five steps to ground level into a treacherous slide. The light had turned dim, gray, and deceiving. Pausing at the last step with the enticement of the forest to his right, the granite wall of Old Man Mountain at his left, he debated. *Which way did Gallo go?*

Would he be chasing after a snowshoe hare into the trees or charging up the mountain just because the idiot loved to run? German Shepherds were working dogs, damn it. Why'd Mom have to have one?

With the wind scouring the countryside clean while it simultaneously frosted it thick with white, there were no tracks to follow. Even the deep, big-footed tracks of what would've made a decent Army/Navy/Air Force/Marines—whatever—K-9, were long buried.

"Shit, damn," Chance cussed when, for some reason he couldn't name, he turned left to the more formidable of the two choices, the mountain. "A six-foot chain, you mangy mongrel," he vowed. The wintery bluster seared his eyeballs because he'd left his Oakley goggles, the smart kind with lenses designed specifically for low-light conditions like now, on the hook back at the cabin. *Where it was warm!*

Ah, who was he kidding? Chance wouldn't have worn them anyway. The silicone-backed strap of those goggles dug into the recently healed scars on the sides of his head, his reward for an op gone sideways in South America. Besides, this midnight foray wouldn't take long, simply because it couldn't. That dunderhead dog would be dead if he didn't get out of this weather soon. What the hell was in that dog's head? Mustering an ounce of enthusiasm, Chance gave Gallo one last chance to straighten up. "Gallo! Here, boy! Come here!"

Did it work? He cocked his head, sure he'd heard a groan, but no. It wasn't Gallo. That would've been too easy. *Damn your sorry ass.*

Chance adjusted the punishment to fit the crime. "Maybe a three-foot chain." *A dog doesn't need much more room than that, not when he spends most of his days sleeping on my couch!*

Truth be known, Gallo wasn't the bother Chance had first anticipated when he'd been forced to adopt the pup after his mother's untimely death months earlier. Gallo was still young, and good company most of the time, especially now that days had grown shorter in the high country. He was something to talk to, and he made a decent bedfellow when he wasn't pushing his rump into Chance, shoving him out of his own bed.

Chance followed the narrow deer trail that dipped down from the barren field of shale surrounding Old Man Mountain and spilled above his log cabin like a final warning to trespassers. He'd bought this parcel of land just above the tree-line and built his home three years ago. It wasn't John Donne's *'no-man-is-an-island'* perfect, but its isolated location served Chance's need for solitude and separation from the world. Its exclusivity kept well-wishers, nosy ex-buddies, and non-combatants at bay. The local white supremacists, too.

Sturdy and fit from his years in the Navy, certainly used to marching in worse conditions, he made it through the shale bed to the edge of the now frozen pond in minutes. Nothing more than a hollow depression that filled with seasonal runoff, the pond might make a worrisome distraction to an adventurous pup on a night like this. The warm front that preceded the blizzard had dumped a good three inches of rain before it had turned to driven snow. For the first time, Chance admitted his worry.

After all, Gallo was just a pup, and a decent owner would watch over a young dog like him. He was a child by human standards, could fall into that pond, and... *what the hell is that kid doing out here*? Cougars frequented this stretch of the shale, though Chance had yet to spot one. Black bears were another story. He'd seen plenty of them last spring with a few cubs. A few gray wolves, too.

His ire transformed into fatherly concern. This night could go so, so bad, and Chance had already had enough *bad* in his life. Except for his two brothers, Kruze and Pagan, he had no friends left but this dog. The thought of burying a gangly pup so young...

"Where the hell are you, boy?"

Damned if a rowdy "Woof!" didn't come back to him this time, along with the sounds of a hard crack and a splash. Ice breaking. *God, no. My dog fell in!*

"Gallo!" Chance stepped one boot to the thin crackly ice at the edge of what he now knew was not a frozen-solid pond. But people weren't supposed to risk their lives for their dogs. *Like hell.*

He ran headlong toward Gallo's rowdy voice, all the while listening for the creak and groan of distressed fractures underfoot. All he heard was the ghoulish wind in his ear roaring that he was already too late. It would've helped if he could've seen where he was going, but tears ran down Chance's cheeks, tears from the words in the wind, and terror in his heart that the wind was right.

Too late. Forever too, tooooooooooooooooo late...

"I'm coming," Chance called out, needing this furry buddy to hang on for one more minute. One more breath. Needing his buddy to live.

Hypothermia. Drowning. Run faster, Sinclair, damn it. Run for your dog's life!

As he knew it eventually would, the ice gave way, and instantly, Chance went belly-deep into gut-wrenching, ice-cold water that sucked the air out of him. Why hadn't Gallo barked again? *Am I too late? The dog had to be hurt or... or...*

"No! He's not dead!" Thrashing against the jagged ice, shoving it aside with his bare hands, Chance elbowed his way forward. "I'm coming, boy. Hold on, damn you. I'll carry you home if you can't walk, and I'll stoke the fire, and I'll..."

God, I promise I'll go to back to church if you let my dog live. Then, as quickly as he'd beseeched heaven, he cursed it. "Goddamn it, Gallo. Don't you dare die!"

At last! The dark blur of his dog's head broke through the ragged blizzard. There he clung to the edge of a hole in the ice, his claws dug in, and struggling to climb out. Something long and angular hung from his jaws.

Chance ran, a slow-motion effort in freezing, waterlogged clothes, his boots full and the cold, dead weight holding him back. Frigid chills ratcheted up his spine. A bone-numbing burn settled into his legs and arms, but fear drove him forward. Gallo was a blithering idiot to be swimming in this storm, but he was also a youngster without an ounce of fat or bulk to his name. He'd be drenched and freezing to the bone. Or dying.

Minutes counted.

"I'm almost to you," Chance yelled as he dove for his dog, fast stroking to clear the distance. Ice slapped at his chin and face, instantly resuscitating the still healing nerve endings buried beneath his scars. Despite the pain, he didn't slow. This was what Navy SEALs were trained for. This was what they did. They fought as hard for their brothers, even the four-legged kind, as they did for themselves.

One stroke. Then another. With a solid kick into the muddy bed under his feet, Chance propelled forward. It took a second to wrangle a decent hold on the scruff of the frantic animal's neck, but by God, Chance was having none of it. He jerked Gallo off his four feet and into his arms with a heartfelt, "Gotcha. God damn you, hold still."

The dog had the nerve to growl. "Knock it off," Chance rasped, his lungs on fire now and his body long past numb. It was all he could do to curl his fingers into a tight enough grip to hang on. "Home," he growled at his dog. "We're going home and then

I'm chaining you up and you'll never run free again."
My heart can't bear it!

Gallo twisted then, something dangling from his grinning mouth. *Holy shit. An arm?*

Chapter Two

"Wh-what you got, boy?" Chance asked, though he already knew. Gallo had found a human body, and by the way his eyes glowed with wolfish pride, he wasn't about to let it go.

Chance gave himself two seconds of shock-and-awe before he grabbed that delicate forearm and came up with two handfuls of a still-as-death, waterlogged woman. He jerked her face out of the water, tucked her under his arm in a lifeguard's hold, and made for shore. Gallo followed, his jaws clamped on her other arm, helping transport her in his smiling, canine way, splashing out of the shallows and onto the frozen, snow-drifted shore.

H-h-holy shit. Shivers rattled Chance as he hunched over the prone body of a young woman, her legs sprawled like those of a forgotten mannequin out of a horror movie. Long, dark hair hid her facial features, not that they mattered. The dead weren't known for their good looks. Chance didn't want to leave her here, but if he didn't hurry, he and his dog would soon be just as dead. Time had officially expired for this poor gal—whoever she was—and it would soon expire for silly lost dogs and men foolish enough to go into the storm after them.

Still... he had heard a groan before. He damned well knew it. It might have been the wind or a tree. It could've been Gallo. But it might have been her.

Canting his head to listen better—in case she made another sound—Chance dragged the seaweed-style-hair off her face. Two wide-open eyes stared back at him, not that he'd expected anything else. *Damn, I'm right. She is dead.*

Peering upward into the swirling storm battering his mountain, he wondered back to that cracking sound he'd heard. Was it her? Could she have fallen from his mountain? No way. What were the odds of anyone surviving something like that? The southern face of Old Man Mountain wasn't particularly high, maybe thirty feet at the most. Nothing but a toothy, ragged ledge waited between the top lip of the cliff and the sheer drop to the bottom. The northern peak was the higher of the two, but no one could survive a fall from the south exposure. It just wasn't possible. Not on a night like this.

Still. Here she was. And old habits died hard. Chance rolled the cramp out of his neck. He wasn't one to leave anyone behind. He hadn't in all his service years; he wasn't going to start now. Stripping out of his waterlogged and frozen gloves, he pressed two icy fingers to her neck, hoping to find a pulse.

Nothing. Pressing his ear to her gaping mouth, he begged for the barest proof of life. A puff of frozen air. A wheeze. Anything! "Breathe for me, baby," he commanded the frozen corpse. "Give me a reason to stay." *Because I'm dumb like that. I'll stay.*

The woman lay lifeless, as stiff as a board and just as responsive. Frost already glazed the tip of her pert nose and her eyelashes, but not a ghost of frozen vapor whispered past her blue lips.

Chance turned to the sky. "Goddamn it! Give me something to work with here! I don't want to leave her, but I will if I have to. I have to save my dog." *And myself.*

God didn't answer any quicker than the dead body had. *Jesus H. Christ!*

Chance sat back on his haunches, as pissed at the Lord as he was the serial killer called Mother Nature. He couldn't walk away from this sad corpse, even in this wicked storm. SEALs didn't do that. The credo he'd taken into his soul resonated like a pulsing fire: *Never Quit. Never!*

Okay then. We do this the hard way. He steeled his nerve against the bitter weather. Interlocking his thumbs, Chance compressed both palms over her chest and pushed.

One-one-thousand. Two-one-thousand.

Her sodden shirt and bra squished under his hands. Shifting his knees, he pressed his mouth over her icicle lips and inflated her lungs with the last of his overheated air. Again and again, he pushed, counted, then exhaled into this dead body's lungs. She was someone's little girl. Someone, somewhere had to be missing her. Worrying about her. Her parents? Her husband? Maybe a baby?

One-one-thousand. Two-one-thousand. Refusing to give up, Chance gave her all he'd brought with him, his pig-headed heart and his last dying breath.

One-one-thousand. Two-one-thousand.

With each compression, water bubbled between her lips, but not once did she gasp, cough, choke, spit, or blink. Silly Gallo had taken up residence on her belly and thighs, the woman claimed and her left wrist still caught in his jaw. He held it gently though, not like a bone to eat so much as a—lifeline. Whether he knew it or not, his soggy body warmth had to be seeping into her, but was it enough?

Pursing his lips before he breathed into her one last time, he knew this was the end. He had no more to give. The wind tore the moisture out of his eyes as he labored to bring her back from the frozen dead, but nothing worked. This was yet another battle he couldn't win. He sat back, exhausted.

Facts were facts. *Shit. She's really dead.*

Swallowing hard at his failure, Chance rested as that bleak reality sank in, his chest heaving and his lungs on fire. Like that other time, he'd arrived too late to save this woman. She was gone, and he was a fool to think he could fight the odds. In a few minutes, his mother's pup would be as frozen as this corpse if they didn't start for home now.

A man can only do so much.

Yeah. Heard all that before.

But Chance was not most men. He'd made promises he refused to break, even now, at the worst of times. *I humbly serve as a guardian to my fellow Americans, always ready to defend those who are unable to defend themselves. I will never quit. I will not fail!*

"Goddamn it, you're going to live," he bit out, as the stiff wind stole Gallo's whine of encouragement. Chance risked a quick swipe across his brow, surprised that he was sweating. Like the downward end of a teeter-totter, he leaned back into the face of Death and told it to, "Go back to hell!"

Sheer willpower flamed back to life. With a jerk, he rolled the righteous wrath of too many losses off his shoulders. Compressions began anew. Solid strokes that might break her ribs, but she *would* live, damn it.

One-one-thousand. Two-one-thousand. Working on borrowed time now, he covered her mouth and inflated her lungs with the warm moist air from his body. *Breathe, baby. I know you can do it. Just try. You want to live. I know you do.*

Shaking from the cold, he tipped back to his haunches to catch his breath, out of his ever-loving mind to be working this hard on a dead body, but the thought of leaving this waif of a woman out here by herself ate at him. She had no business being on his mountain. She sure as hell wasn't going to die on it.

Gallo offered another anxious whine when—her chest heaved. *It did!*

The frozen lady sputtered. She blinked!

"Cough it all out," Chance ordered, even as the wicked winter sliced like a switchblade across both their exposed throats. "I knew you could do it." He tipped her up into one arm while water dribbled out of her mouth and down her neck. "Thank God, you're alive. I've got you now. Breathe. Just breathe. Keep it up. There you go."

She shook her head, just barely, but hell, yeah! She coughed and gagged and that was enough answer for Chance. Unzipping his sodden jacket and scarf, he pulled her onto his lap and tucked her against his chest, dislodging his faithful mutt from her legs.

"Let her go," he told his dog, and for the first time that night, Gallo obeyed. The crazy kid's black licorice lips stretched wide with a silly smile when he released his prize. "Good, good boy," Chance praised.

With her wrapped up as tightly as he could get her inside the life-saving Gortex, he zipped it up to her chin. Between the two of them, a wet jacket was better than nothing. Worried that he might have caused his victim permanent spinal damage while saving her, Chance struggled to his feet. Catching his balance, he hurried back to his cabin and the fire he'd left banked and glowing in his fireplace, his charge pressed tightly into his body. The blaze would be close to ashes by now, but the cabin would still be warm.

Every step chilled the hell out of him, but seconds. He had mere seconds to get her out of the weather, out of her wet clothes, and warmed, or he'd saved nothing. Whoever this gal was, she was the important one now. Only her.

"Are you with me?" he asked the four-legged buddy dashing through the drifts beside him as if this was merely a fun romp in the snow.

A hearty "Yap!" sounded over the stiff wind, and mentally, Chance promised Gallo a big slice off the venison roast thawing in his refrigerator. Mom's dog might be worth something after all.

Chance ran then, the icy snow pelting his cheeks, making it harder to see. The trail his boots made on his way to the pond was already well covered, but he didn't need it. He was the finder of lost people on SEAL Team Three. He knew how many steps would put him at his bottom step, and he cut that time by half, the find of a lifetime secure in his arms. But God! She was so cold!

Whoever she was, she was light. Maybe a hundred pounds. Maybe five foot nothing. Soft, blessed with curves, and full-busted—yes, he'd noticed—but hell. She wore nothing but jeans, boots, and a flannel shirt, foolish get-up for a night so raw. Where was her coat? Her hat? Her gloves. Her damned friends? She couldn't have been out here alone.

On his porch at last, his body thrummed with cold and adrenaline while his mind worked a ready list of imperatives if this stranger were to survive—and she would, by hell. *Strip her wet clothes off. Wrap her in my warmest blankets. Wrap a towel around her wet head. Stoke the fire. Keep it hot in the cabin. Boil water to cleanse any wounds. But mostly, keep her breathing.*

Angling her headfirst toward the door, he fumbled, one-handed at the icy knob. His fingers were numb, but he kept at it until it gave. He all but ran to deposit his sad guest on the leather couch facing his fireplace. Gallo took position on his spot, the rag rug at the hearth. Dogs were smart like that.

"Good, good boy," Chance praised him as he returned to shut the door. Back at the fireplace, he put three hefty pine logs on the glowing embers of what had been a stout blaze earlier. The spent wood crumbled to ash under the weight, but three fresh logs ought to do it. For now.

It took three minutes tops to scrape out of his wet clothes and boots in his bathroom. Once again in jeans and a T-shirt from the stack of dirty clothes near the foot of his bed, Chance collected an armful of supplies from the linen closet on his way back to the couch. He draped one bath sheet around Gallo's shoulders and back. "I'm sorry, but she comes first," Chance told his faithful companion. "Be good and stay by the fire."

Without waiting for an answer from a dog that was known to talk back in his grumbly German Shepherd voice, Chance stacked the rest of the supplies on the end table beside the couch. Next, he retrieved a deep pan of warm, sudsy water from the kitchen. Returning to the unconscious woman, he wrapped her head and most of her sodden hair, a deep scarlet shade, in another bath sheet until her face barely showed. He needed to keep her head warm.

While Gallo watched, the soggy Gortex jacket, her waterlogged boots and socks went into a pile at the other end of the couch. Her shirt and bra were next, lastly her jeans and panties. Even naked, she didn't shiver, and that was a bad sign. But worse? An ugly gash on the outside of her left thigh ran in a ragged line from her kneecap to her hipbone, widening near her hip.

"What'd you do, run into a sharp chunk of shale on your way down?" Chance asked his silent guest while he wrapped his most absorbent blanket around her, then doubled it with another. That assessment made sense. Maybe she'd fallen in increments instead of straight down. That might explain how she'd survived, though he was fairly certain it was a dead drop from top to bottom.

The highest cliff on this side of Old Man Mountain was a ragged granite edge with a ten-foot lip that extended over dead air. On a good day, a guy could see forever from that vantage point. The seasonal waterfall began its descent there. Considering where she'd landed, she had to have fallen from that cliff, then struck the second ledge farther down the sheer granite wall, a narrow overhang of last chances, before she'd hit dead center of the pool.

The runoff spilling over that cliff had earned the name Mother's Day Falls over the years, since May was the only season the snowmelt blossomed into an actual waterfall. Millennia of high snowpack years had hollowed the divot below the sheer granite face of that mountain, creating the pond. What the hell was she doing up there on a night like this?

Battle injuries he knew, but this woman's condition had all the earmarks of an attempted suicide—a first for his corner of the world. She'd jumped. That was all that made sense. His reasoning? No coat. What kind of person climbed to the top of a mountain in a storm without proper winter gear?

One who wants to die.

Chapter Three

I can't worry about that now.

Chance couldn't work fast enough. The wound on her thigh wasn't deep and it wasn't bleeding, but it would as soon as her blood warmed, and that was the kicker. It needed a good cleaning, stitches, and a pressure bandage, exactly what was in his first-aid kit. But if she came to while he treated her, she'd fight. He would if he were in her situation, but he had no anesthetic to offer other than the booze in his liquor cabinet, not what a person with compromised lung capacity needed.

"Sorry about this," he said as he went for a piece of nylon rope from the closet near his front door. "I don't usually tie ladies up, but…" It had to be done.

Looping the rope around her knee, he tugged her left knee forward and out of the blanket, careful not to stretch the painful looking wound any more than he had to. Fortunately, his couch came with three sturdy legs at the front of it, three more at the rear. Tucking one of the washcloths into the loop of the rope to cushion the rope against her skin, he tied the opposite end around the center couch leg to hold her leg taut and still.

With her still unconscious and sufficiently restrained, he dragged the coffee table from against the wall where he usually kept it, over to the couch and used it for a stool. The moment he dropped his butt to the table, training from his years on the teams took over. He disinfected the length of the gash with simple sudsy water. Using the sterile tweezers from his kit, he worked quickly, picking out a few rock shards, some as sharp as needles. She made no sound, not a peep, and he was seriously worried that brain damage might be her real problem.

What if I'm too late? A fall that far...

I can't worry about that either. Triage. He could only manage what he knew, and now that she was inside and, hopefully, growing warm, the oozing tear on her thigh took precedence. A person could bleed to death with an open wound that size. Her other injuries were guesses anyway.

Carefully, with steady hands and gentle fingertips, he closed the narrow end of the cut nearest her kneecap, spacing his sutures evenly and as small as he could. When the width of the laceration widened and he could stitch no more, Chance covered the rest of the gaping sore with a pressure bandage. Lifting her limb, he wrapped layers of flesh-toned stretch tape around her thigh to hold everything in place. He kept an eye out for broken bones and other injuries as he worked. Finding none on her legs, he rotated the hip socket.

Everything seemed to be in physical working order, but worry tapped at the base of his skull. She hadn't yet made a sound. She barely inhaled. He had to listen closely to detect any indication that she was still alive. Even a whimper would've encouraged him. A grunt. A shudder. But she remained unresponsive. It was as if he was treating a corpse. Chance swallowed hard, knowing he might be doing just that.

Gallo sat grooming his sodden fur at the hearth, for once doing what he'd been told. But the more Chance took care of his silent patient, the more questions begged answers. Suicide seemed too obvious. This woman hadn't been wearing a coat when he'd found her, yet her boots were top-of-the-line hikers with fur linings. Her socks were super-thick Thorlos, designed to prevent blisters while they delivered maximum warmth to mountain climbers and hikers. Nothing about the extra-padded flannel shirt he'd stripped off of her said I-want-to-kill-myself, either. He was fairly certain the cylindrical shape he'd felt in her chest pocket when he stripped her out of her shirt was lip-gloss or lipstick, not a live round. It didn't add up. Would a woman bundle up to keep warm and then worry about chapped lips if she'd meant to end herself?

And another thing, the bra and panties now laying in a pile with her boots and pants were high-end satin, a matching set of lace he would've lusted over given different conditions. Her jeans were sturdy denim, and new. They weren't the run-of-the-mill shabby fashion statements with holes and slashes that most young people liked these days, but pants that serious sportsmen and sportswomen wore. The knees were scraped and one leg was torn at the thigh, but that probably happened in the fall.

It wasn't until he'd decided his work was done that Chance caught sight of the black bruise on her left butt cheek close to her hipbone. "What the hell?" he ran his palm up her thigh and placed two fingers to the bruise. Softball sized, it throbbed at his touch, and he didn't know what to make of it. As swollen as it was, as angry looking...

Shit. An infection? Already? A shattered bone beneath the muscle, bleeding, maybe hemorrhaging? What do I do now?

He swallowed hard, intent on treating her while she was still out. "I'm sorry," he said again as he rummaged in his first-aid kit for the heavy-duty plastic sleeve that held a single surgical scalpel. "But whatever's in there has to come out. Hold on. This won't take long." *But it will hurt.*

Just to be safe, Chance opened another pre-packaged pressure bandage and lined up a few sterile wipes to disinfect the aftermath. He hedged his bets with a towel to catch any infection, held his breath, and—*one, two, three*— he pierced her hot-to-the-touch skin. A geyser of infection shot into the towel like a pressurized load. What the hell, indeed. There could be no stitches for a wound like this. This tender knot needed to drain until all the infection was gone.

Carefully, he pressed and probed her butt muscle to extract as much bloody fluid as he could. "How'd you do this?" he asked as blood and pus drained onto the towel, "and how long have you been dealing with it? Weeks? It had to hurt like a mother. Do you do drugs?" *What doper shoots up in their butt cheek?*

"You know what? I can't worry about that either," he told his big-eared sidekick. "She might not live through the night. All I can do, is do the best I can do. The rest is up to her."

Right on cue, Gallo's ears perked up as if he understood, while Chance taped a thick layer of sterile gauze over the latest discovery on his patient's backside and called it good. Moving on, he undid the rope and tucked her bandaged leg under the blankets. She should've been plenty warm by then, but her skin was clammy and still cold as ice.

He examined her more thoroughly then, keeping her covered as he went. Smoothing his hands over her ribcage, he moved quickly to her neck and collarbones. Whoever she was, she deserved to be handled with dignity and respect, especially now. No broken bones presented themselves. That much was good.

Moving his fingertips quickly over her shoulders, shoulder blades, and spine, Chance mapped as he went, diagnosing and hoping. She'd roused for a moment, but that moment was short-lived and amounted to nothing more than her taking a shuddering breath.

Moving to her lower extremities, he examined her ankles and tiny feet, her long legs and poor, scraped-raw knees. *She has pretty toes.* Not pudgy, but slender and elegant. Manicured nails. Strong calves and a decent, athletic build, too. Nothing seemed broken and he located no more open wounds or bruises like that one on her backside. For now, her life rested in his hands, but with every inch and curve his fingers mapped, he wished he was a smarter, wiser man who could more aptly help her. She needed a real doctor, not him.

Extending her right arm, he flattened her much smaller hand over his palm. Fury hissed out of him at the sight of her much smaller hand in his. Defensive wounds. The woman had definitely fought someone, and she'd fought hard. Every fingernail was broken. Her fingertips were bloodied and shredded into hamburger. The poor damned thing. Mottled bruises circled both wrists like ugly bracelets.

"Who the hell did this to you?" he asked, angry as a son-of-a-bitch that one so delicate had been treated so badly. A vicious kick could explain the nasty bruise on her butt. He'd seen bumps and bangs in the field lead to anaerobic infections deep beneath the surface of the skin. Was that what she'd been dealing with? Prior abuse? For how long?

The towel he'd wrapped like a thick turban around her head was soaked by then, and Chance still needed to inspect her face. Tucking her into the double layers, he shifted on the coffee table to focus on her head and hair. Cupping her head gently in his big palm, he unwrapped the wet towel. Burnished auburn tangles fell everywhere, but as they fell away from her face, a hearty "Oh, shit!" slammed out of Chance. *It can't be.* He knew this woman. The whole world did. He'd rescued Suede Tennyson, the wild-as-sin daughter of the governor of Oregon.

She didn't look so wild nor so temperamental tonight, not with her split lip, bruised cheek, and that vivid red mark high on her cheekbone. Shadows rimmed her sunken eyes, but the worst indignity? The boot print purpling at the center of her forehead. Compassion flared.

"You poor thing." Chance traced the pad of his thumb over the mottled imprint, pissed as hell. "What jackass used you for target practice, baby?"

Righteous rage lifted its weary head. This wasn't suicide. It was attempted murder.

*****

Suede came to at the edge of life and found herself on the Titanic, going down along with everyone else, sinking into freezing, frigid depths. Icy tentacles circled her ankles and legs like weighted shackles.

The frightened dying shrieked like banshees around her, deafening her sensitive eardrums. Waves of wicked cold whipped at any exposed skin, flailing her ribs and spine with a cat-o-nine-tails. Stinging. Biting. Death seemed a welcome friend. Breathing surely wasn't.

The noise in her ears threatened her slim hold on sanity. Her head reverberated from the pain. Stiff and numb, her fingers were useless. She couldn't make them bend to work. *I can't hold on because there's nothing to hold onto. Nothing, but all that noise. I'm dying.*

A woman can only fight for so long, and Suede Tennyson had been fighting all of her life. Why would death, with its alleged promise of freedom from misery, be any less a struggle, damn it?

Passing over wasn't supposed to hurt this bad, was it? Wasn't a big, bright light supposed to pull her upward and into a better existence, someplace peaceful where angels were real and some magnanimous entity had a big heart that loved even bad girls and boys? Wasn't that how death was supposed to work? Why'd everything have to hurt so fucking bad? She should've known better. Death was no different than life.

Lies. More lies.

Just when all seemed lost, just when hysteria edged up her throat, choking her, a gentle warm current slipped over and around her. The noise in her head ebbed, and she became aware of a persistent probing of her every last muscle and nerve. It moved over her battered body, parsing her in methodical sections. Some devil must truly hate her to inflict the torture she felt now. Someone strong and precise, who knew how to make lost souls suffer.

Resistance was futile. Suede couldn't open an eyelid or crack her lips, much less lift a finger to defend herself. *Fuck off,* she meant to declare with her usual snark. That never failed to get her noticed in the past. She meant to shrug this shadowy ghoul hovering over her away. He was every bit as evil as the others. Life was a fucking bitter disappointment, but death wasn't any better.

Let me be. Let me die.

Yet even as despair crystallized in her stubborn heart, the tiniest scent of pine and manly sweat breached the debris in what stung like a tender, broken nose. A persistent *'Not yet'* blurted out of her impetuous soul. She hadn't come this far, nor gone through all she'd endured in her short twenty years, to give up now. *Hell no.*

A mellow voice whispered down at her from far above, "All you've got to do is breathe for me, ma'am. I know it's hard, but I promise, if you'll concentrate on living, I can take it from there."

Breathe, huh? Like that's so fucking easy? Just snap my fingers and turn the dragon fire in my lungs into a springtime breeze? Yet want to or not, this stranger had evoked a long drawn inhalation from her compressed lungs. It wasn't deep and it hurt like a motherfucker, but it helped, too. Her lungs *had* expanded a tiny bit more that time. Oxygen *had* saturated her body. Something warm uncoiled at the center of her innermost self. Felt like—life.

The same warm wind sliced over her, whispering, "There you go. I knew you could do it," and for some reason, Suede was reminded of candy canes and childhood dreams, evergreens and Santa. *Almost* being like every other kid in her class. *Almost* being good enough.

Tender fingertips traced her shoulder blades, "I won't hurt you. You're going to live. I'll make sure of that."

The last thing she wanted was some strange guy manhandling her, but touch her, this idiot did. With efficient care and gentleness she hadn't realized that she desperately craved, he massaged and rubbed warmth into her chilled neck and shoulder muscles. Down her back and up her spine again he went, gentle fingers stroking past her hair, kneading luxurious comfort into her scalp.

Suede found herself leaning into that wide, masculine palm smoothing over her, gentling her as easily as if she were a skittish colt in spring. Damn, it felt good. This guy, this stranger, seemed to care that she was comfortable and warm. It mattered to him that she lived.

A tear stung the corner of her eye. Whoever he was, this new demon in her life made her want to believe again. *Almost...*

Chapter Four

Suede woke again in the midst of a suffocating fog, the searing desert wind in her throat and mouth. The place she found herself smelled of campfire and wet dog, and she was certain some kind of a knitted stocking cap covered her head. Her scalp felt tight. Weird.

It didn't make sense, but not much did when a woman woke with the throbbing beat of a nightmare behind her eyes, fire and brimstone in her lungs. Water. She needed a sip of cool water more than anything. Make that cold water. Now. Her vocal cords produced a barely audible "thurdie" instead of a distinct "thirsty," in case anyone was out there.

As quickly as she'd asked, a hulking shadow appeared out of nowhere. Steady, warm hands smoothed over the blanket wrapped around her head, and a male voice said, "Take it easy, kid. Here's a drink."

Lying on her side, she was more puddle than a human being. Barely able to move, her body ached down to the pads of her toes. Weirder still, she was fairly sure she was nude beneath the blankets. A hat on her head and no clothes on her ass? What asshole had dressed her like this? Not that she truly cared. Death had a way of making a vain woman humble. Her needs were simpler here in the dark. Warmth. Water. Air. A pain pill. Not necessarily in that order.

Mostly shadow, the orange glow of the fire backlit the guy who'd spoken. Suede didn't care about that either. The moment the straw hit her lips, she latched onto it and sucked in a mouthful of sweet cool bliss that felt like heaven going down.

"Easy," the guy said. Smoky baritone, his voice was smooth as bourbon on the rocks with a gentle sting of command embedded in it, something she had no use for. The bourbon, yes. The command, no. Suede Tennyson'd had enough of being jerked around by—jerks.

He eased the straw away after one paltry swallow. "Let's make sure that first drink stays down."

He must not know who I am or he wouldn't be so fucking nice. On a good day, she'd light him up with her vicious tongue, but now… Suede might be naked, but she got the sense that this guy meant her no harm. Besides, she was too weak to argue. "C-c-cold," she mumbled. *I'm fucking cold.* Frigid was more like it. Lionel would no doubt agree if he'd been there.

Speaking of the ass... A shiver rattled over her, jarring every last aching bone in her body. Her brain roared *'Lionel pushed me!'* even as this stranger tugged a thick blanket under her chin, tucking her in like a little girl.

It had been so long since anyone had done that—if ever—that Suede honestly couldn't remember the last time. She grunted, needing someone to know that Lionel tried to murder her, but nothing intelligent-sounding passed beyond her dry lips.

A hand that felt like the size of a platter cupped her trembling bicep, pressing warmth into her shivering muscles. "There are two bladders of hot water at your back to warm you, ma'am, but it'll take time before your body temp returns to normal." There was that *ma'am* again, an oddly reassuring gesture in the midst of her full-blown panic. "Take another sip, but take it slow. We need to rehydrate you as quickly as we can, I just don't want you throwing up what you drink. You're in tough shape and retching is bound to hurt your ribs, and you can't afford to lose more moisture. I'm afraid I was a little rough on you." The straw glanced over her bottom lip, and greedily, she snagged it before it got away. Talking about Lionel could fucking wait. She needed a drink.

But what did that mean? *A little rough on me?* Shivering tremors hit her hard, but she wasn't losing hold of that straw this time. Clamping it between her teeth, she took in as much as she could before she released it. At last she wet her lips. "You hurt me?" she asked even though she knew better. But still. Men did that to women all the time. What made this guy any better than the others in her life?

"Not on purpose, but I did do dozens of chest compressions and they've been known to break ribs. I don't think I broke any of yours, but tell me if you're having trouble breathing. I need to know."

Tears stung her eyes. "How... how would I know? Everything" —her body clenched as searing pain shot up from her thigh. Want to or not, she whimpered— "hurts."

That same warm hand cupped the back of her head, holding her steady. Gently. She leaned into this strange, kind man like a little girl, needing this odd new sensation of being cared for—just once in her fucked-up life—to last.

"Easy now. No sudden movements. All you've got to do is breathe. Just breathe." He seemed so familiar, and that voice. Growly low, but soft like velvet over steel. It caressed her soul as much as that big hand of his had caressed her broken body.

"W-who are you?" The words grated like the serrated teeth of a steak knife drawn past her tonsils and over her tongue. "And where the fuck am I? What..." She sucked in a searing, shivering gasp. "What'd you do to me?"

"Chance Sinclair at your service, ma'am." His voice tightened, but she didn't care why. Nice or not, this guy had some explaining to do. "I pulled you out of the pond below Mother's Day Falls tonight, and you're lucky to be alive. It's wicked weather out there. Right now, you're in my cabin in Northern Montana and you're safe. Now open your mouth and take these three tablets."

Another order. Did he think she was weak *and* stupid? *Why would I take any pills from you?* "You a doctor?" she asked stubbornly, her brain on fire from the headache crushing her skull. She'd meant to tell him something important, but it eluded her now. No hangover had ever felt this fucking bad.

"No, ma'am. I'm no doctor, but I am the Navy SEAL who pulled your ass out of frigid water, got you breathing again, and hiked home in a blizzard to save your life." He didn't say that with anger, more like it was a history lesson she needed to understand right here and now.

"Oh," was all she could come up with. She had been up on that mountain, but the why was lost in the fog in her head. It had something important to do with Lionel, but thinking took energy she didn't have. But taking pills from a stranger? A definite no-go. Smart girls and women didn't do that—she would know—not in bars and not wherever she was now. "W-what are they?" *And why the fuck should I take anything from you?*

"Sorry. I should've told you that. My bad. They're just two painkillers, Ibuprofen, each eight hundred milligrams. The other's an antibiotic. I'm not big on drugs, so it's all I've got on hand. I know it's not much, but" —his shoulders lifted— "you're in bad shape, ma'am, and these are better than nothing."

Suede hesitated. The direct honesty in his voice combined with that silky tone of command was wearing her down. What did she have to lose? Her body did feel like it had been steamrolled, and to be honest, the formidable strength reverberating inside Chance's tone quieted her suspicions. He sounded like he knew what he was talking about.

Why would he have saved her if he intended to dope her? Okay, erase that stupid question. She'd known enough sleazy guys in clubs and private parties all over the world who would've done exactly that to get at her. In between listening to her heart pounding in her poor head and this guy's steady breathing, a searing cough that felt like gasoline on fire squeezed out of her lungs in short, sharp barks. She'd never been sicker.

The man tipped his forehead closer to hers. "You can trust me, ma'am. I served with honor on and off the battlefield. Uncompromising integrity is my standard. My character and honor are steadfast. My word is my bond."

Wow. That sounded like an important oath or something. Better yet, not once had he called her baby or darling, just *ma'am*. It sounded as if he respected her. How bizarre was that? Respect was the last thing she expected from a, a guy. Hearing it spoken out loud gave her the sense that Chance

Sinclair wasn't a player. He was a serious man and he meant what he said.

I am sick. He is taking care of me. Maybe I can trust him.

She squinted to see if it brought him into any better focus, but his facial features were lost in a blur of shadows and the headache in her eyes. All she could make out was shaggy hair spiked in all directions. It circled his head like a rugged halo on a fallen angel with the orange burning glow of some kind of fire behind him. She was fairly sure that was a beard on his chin, not just more obscurity caused by her brain fog.

Still, she stalled, unwilling to surrender her hard-earned independence to another man.

He didn't force them down her throat. Instead, "Listen. If you won't take the pills, at least suck on one of the medicated throat lozenges I've got. Your lungs were full of dirty water by the time I reached you tonight, and your voice sounds like gravel, so I know you're in pain. Inhaling has got to hurt. I've also got an analgesic spray to deaden the pain in your throat if you'd rather. This storm could last for days, and I won't be able to get you to a doctor, so you need to use what's available."

It all came back to her. The driving snow. The bitterest cold. A shiver racked her from head to toe. Suede Tennyson didn't have amnesia or any of those damsel-in-distress fainting spells. Not any more. She remembered who'd shoved her off that cliff, and who'd kicked her while she'd hung on her fingernails. *That jerk-off, Lionel York.*

Tears stung her eyes, but this guy wasn't York, was he? Why did she feel like she could trust this Chance Sinclair guy, a stranger she didn't know, when life had taught her not to trust anyone? Not her mother or father. Certainly not Lionel and his guys.

But this mountain-man was different, and he seemed sure of himself. Better yet, he'd helped her. Who does that these days? Not accustomed to being treated with kindness or dignity jolted her paradigm of men in general. "Chance Sinclair, huh?" she asked, her throat on fire.

His head bobbed. "Yes, ma'am. United States Navy Former Petty Officer Chance Sinclair, at your service."

That was a lot of good stuff to know. The few military men she'd met at the Governor's mansion had always impressed her with their manners and sense of honor. So Chance was one of the good guys. He wasn't a politician and he probably worked for a living. Did she dare trust him? Suede caved. "The pills," whispered out of her dry, cracked lips. Might as well.

"Good choice." Chance cupped the back of her head again and tipped her enough to reach the straw. His fingertips grazed her lips as he tucked two smaller pills, then one larger on into her mouth.

Finished swallowing the meds, she ducked back into the plush nest she'd awakened in. Layers of blankets covered her and the water things at her back and backside were warm, so why couldn't she stop shivering? "My leg hurts," she murmured, her eyes brimming.

"I was afraid of that. Your left one?"

She nodded, biting her bottom lip to keep from crying like a baby. What a fucking bad day.

That gentle hand at the back of her head stroked over her skull to settle at the nape of her neck. "I'm sorry, but you've got a nasty cut on your thigh. I stitched it closed and bandaged it, but it'll hurt a while. If the pain gets too bad, tell me, and I'll see what else I can do. Do you remember what happened?"

Another nod. "He, he pushed me..." And the dam broke. Not one to show weakness, she squeezed her eyes to hold back the tears, but they ran like faucets turned on high, and she hiccupped like a baby. "I... I tried to hold on, b-but..." Every word sliced and diced her throat and her heart. "He kicked me. In the head."

A deep growl rumbled. Suede wasn't sure if it came from Chance or the dog she could smell but hadn't seen yet.

"What's his name?" Chance asked, his question reverberating with menace.

"Lionel York," she admitted. "My fiancé."

"The tennis player? Him? You're marrying that jackass? He's... old." This time she knew where the growl came from. Chance couldn't have sounded meaner.

"Just by ten years. That's all." Age didn't matter. All men were jackasses.

The pad of a callused thumb wiped the teary stream from her cheek. "Listen. It's late and you've had enough for one day. We'll talk more tomorrow or whenever you're up to it. Are you ready for that cough drop now? It might help." There was that caring tone again, melting her prickly defenses like honey on a hot buttered roll fresh from the oven.

"Yes, please." Suede would've bobbed her head, but it was shaking enough already.

The tips of his fingers tucked that tiny piece of instant menthol relief between her lips. For whatever reason, even the minimal effort to lift her head or work her jaw muscles hurt. Who would've thought that she, America's sassiest darling, could've been brought so low?

"Thanks," she rasped, sucking that cough drop as if he'd just given her a succulent bit of fresh king crab. Menthol vapors stormed her sinuses even as a soothing sting settled at the back of her throat. *Good. Oh, so good.*

A giant hand smoothed over the top of her head, and finally, the face that went with it came closer and into better focus. Worried, pinched brows first, then a manly nose, long and straight. She blinked to clear her murky vision. Thick whiskers covered his cheeks and chin, which added to the shadows. His head was much larger than hers, his brow wider, but the tenderness glowing in his dark eyes caught her in their trap.

"I'm sorry if I hurt you before, but I had to stitch your leg while you were out," he explained as the hint of peppermint wafted over her face, drowning out the menthol in her mouth. "I couldn't let you bleed to death. Are you hungry at all? Could you handle a couple spoonfuls of broth before you go back to sleep?"

Suede closed her eyes at the thought of warm soup sliding down her raw throat, but she shook her head. "Not now." That tiny slice of menthol heaven on her tongue, the warm wash of peppermint in her nostrils, and the gentle hand cupping her aching head already soothed like nothing had before. As awful as her broken body felt, and it had to be broken as much as everything hurt, these small acts of kindness brought another rush of tears to her eyes. No one was nice to Suede Tennyson. Not on purpose.

Tonguing the cough drop into her cheek, she tried to tell him who she was. A muffled "Suede" was all she got out before the tip of a warm finger sealed her lips.

"Shush," he murmured, his forehead nearly to hers, and his breath so delicious she wanted to lick his lips. "I know who you are, Suede. You're Governor Tennyson's daughter, and you're also one of Hollywood's hottest hotshots, now shush. Go to sleep. The broth will be just as good later. Rest easy."

She meant to argue. This man was so bossy, but "You're being nice to me" was all she came up with.

He cocked his head. "Why wouldn't I be?"

"Because... because..." A hiccup squeaked out of her. *No one's ever nice just to be nice.*

His head dipped closer. "You, young lady, are sick, and you're exhausted. Get some sleep."

No, I'm not. I'm... I'm saved. Overwhelmed by this gentle warrior's kindness, Suede grabbed onto his forearm sleeve and pulled herself into his chest. "Don't leave me," she cried, frightened and lost and so damned thankful for this one good man in her crazy celebrity life. "Please," she begged. "Please don't let go. Don't let me fall!"

He stiffened, his body taut as if he didn't know quite what to do with her, but gradually, his arms circled her nearly as tightly as she gripped him. She needed him so damned much.

"It's okay," he murmured, his lips in her hair. "You're going to be okay. You're safe. Honest. No one can get to you here."

"He... he..." She couldn't get a grip! "He k-k-killed me!" Where this sudden torment came from, she didn't know, but it rolled over her like a steamroller, pulverizing her tough bitch alter ego to dust, leaving her confidence shredded and bleeding in its wake. Never—NEVER—had she lost control like this. Not even all those times...

Fears bubbled up from her soul. Fears from long ago. Fear of shadows and of the dark. Fear of falling.

Of never—ever—being good enough for anyone. Not even herself.

Chance didn't let go. "He tried, but you're still here. You're still here, baby."

She felt like one. Suede couldn't stop her damned eyes from leaking. Her nose ran into his shirt. She sobbed and wept, coughed and shuddered, and still he held on. Rocking. Gently rocking until the hysteria released its death-grip, and she could catch a breath.

Shocked she'd come undone so completely, she sucked in a rasping gulp of air. It was his fault she'd unraveled, this strange caring man. She'd never dealt with anyone as kind nor as capable as Chance Sinclair before, not once in her life. It felt uncommonly, extraordinarily safe inside this circle of his big arms, his body wrapped around her like a last line of defense. Like a wall between her and the world. There was no censure here. No berating. Just strength and power and warmth. A steady heartbeat. A tender touch.

Her body quivered like a jar of apple jelly that hadn't set. "W-what's wrong with m-me?" she asked, another round of tears on its way. Her teeth chattered so hard, she bit her lip. Wishing she could leech some of the calm from Chance, her fingertips still clenched his biceps while the top of her head bumped under his chin.

He molded her to him, his fingers splayed at her back, his head, shoulders, and upper body curved around her like a protective shell. "You're dealing with shock and trauma right now, that's all. It'll pass. Give it time. Just breathe. Know that I won't let anything happen to you. You'll be okay here, I promise."

She rubbed her cheek against his shirt, believing him. Trusting for the first time in forever. Of all the people in her life, this stranger was the only one who hadn't let her down, and she didn't think he was going to. "I'm scared," she admitted. *Of everything.*

"Shush," he crooned, swaying back and forth. "I'm here. Go to sleep, Suede. Go to sleep."

Again with the ordering her around. What was with this guy? Yet the way he'd said those last words melted what little was left of her defensiveness. Warm and safe in the arms of this rugged angel was a good enough place to be. She'd leave as soon as she was able to, but for now, Suede closed her eyes, and with a sigh, she let the darkness take her.

Chapter Five

The hot water bladders and blankets weren't working fast enough, but Chance didn't want to take that last step, not if he could help it. He would *not* join Suede Tennyson in that big bed—his big bed. No way.

Earlier, he'd transferred her from the couch to his room because it was smaller and easier to heat, and she'd need privacy once she came to. His bed was softer, but the wood-burning stove in the corner produced so much heat he'd had to strip down to a wife-beater and boxers. That he'd added five-inch-thick steel plating between the outside logs and the inside framing of his cabin made certain no storm or enemies could get in, but neither could the excess heat get out.

Poor Gallo's long tongue lolled to the floor. He'd curled up next to the bed, panting like crazy, but not leaving the lady he'd found. Chance made sure his water dish was full, but tomorrow morning, that dog had a deer leg coming. Maybe an entire roast.

It was good that Suede talked when she'd come to, and taken the meds Chance offered, but she had a long way to go before she was back on her feet. That barky cough of hers worried him. He felt certain he hadn't broken her ribs, but her lungs were congested, her voice was weak and hoarse. Pneumonia and being snowed-in weren't a good mix.

Chance didn't think Suede was afraid of him. More likely disoriented. Maybe remembering who'd pushed her. But those eyes. They were too big for her face, and the fear radiating from those glimmering blue pools rattled him. She'd looked so much like a lost little girl about to cry. Not at all what he'd expected from her *girl-gone-wild* video.

It was no wonder the press went ape shit over Suede Tennyson. After he'd dried her hair, Chance tied it into a loose ponytail to keep it out of her face, but those tangled auburn curls were enticing. Wisps and tendrils framed gaunt cheeks, and when she'd finally opened her eyes, he'd turned away. It wasn't that he was intimidated, *well, okay, maybe a little*, but this woman was a looker, one of those *'I-just-stepped-off-the-glamour-rags'* types, and way above his pay grade.

Lionel York, huh? Chance clenched his fist into the hammer it could be. Known for his temperamental outbursts on and off the court, York had one helluva come-to-Jesus meeting in his future, and Chance meant to deliver.

"What do you think?" he asked his dog, as if Gallo had a clue what he was asking. As expected, the dog's gaze flitted up from the floor to Chance's face, then dropped to the feminine body in his bed. "Yeah, I'm worried about her, too," Chance admitted.

A canine whine came back as Chance ran his fingers through his own shaggy hair. "You might be right." Sunrise had come and gone, but the day was still dark, the hour burdened with the never-ending blizzard. The last time he'd checked, the drifts on his porch were two feet high and rising. At this rate, he'd soon be shoveling a path from his front door into the trees just so his dog could go take a leak.

Chance swallowed hard, not ready to take the final step that would put him in bed with a woman with an ungodly rep the size of Suede's—if the tabloids were right. Neither could he walk away. Leaving her on her own unsettled him as much as leaving her in that pond last night.

"Shit," he hissed, his arms crossed over his chest. She might need something, but he was a sound sleeper, and...

Should I or shouldn't I?

It was uncanny was what it was, but both he and his dog had sensed it the moment she'd gasped her first breath on the edge of the pond. In that split second, she'd changed everything, their priorities and their daily schedule, even their dynamics. Like it or not, Suede Tennyson had brought something intangible, nearly mystical, to his four square walls just by being female. It was that thing all women did whether they knew it or not, the balance and promise, the sunrise and the sunset all wrapped up in a feminine package of long legs and intriguing eyes. Women were the reason men fought wars, sang songs, and played guitars. Any guy knew that.

Chance intended to fight the instinctive male attraction that raged inside his body. Even half dead, she'd lit up the inside of his man cave and maybe a fraction of his weary heart. Why couldn't Gallo have found a moose or an elk in that pond? Even a bear would've been preferable. Why'd it have to be a complicated woman? *This woman?*

Suede Tennyson was a hot mess. She always had been. She'd grown up in the spotlight of her driven, very political parents, but at the tender age of sixteen, she'd sued for emancipation and won. Then she'd hit the public scene like a hurricane, dressed in nothing but skimpy, baby-doll negligees that took the world by storm and gave the paparazzi another target. Her publicity-grabbing stunts had quickly devolved into less and less clothing until a video surfaced. There she was up high on a Ferris wheel. In the nude. Flaunting her assets. She hadn't stooped so low that she'd licked a hammer yet, but she might as well have.

The official word from Oregon's state capitol after that display had declared the governor and his wife wanted nothing to do with their wayward daughter.

Suede was nothing but an outrageous embarrassment and their biggest regret. From that day on, she was dead to them. No more questions would be entertained on the subject. End of discussion.

As self-righteous as that official statement sounded, it struck Chance as parental betrayal the day he'd read the headline. Their *biggest* regret? *Come on. Get over yourselves.* Kids messed up. That's what they did. Regularly. They made mistakes, and sometimes those mistakes were flamboyant, dangerous, embarrassing, and illegal, but a press conference and a public disowning? *What kind of parent does that?*

Their self-righteous stand had reeked of Governor Tennyson choosing his career over his daughter. Chance never liked the guy. Charismatic and a fast-talker, the lawyer-turned-politician was currently making a bid for the White House. As crooked as he was, he'd probably get there, too.

Frozen in place at Suede's side, Chance waited, not willing to leave. Why couldn't he tear himself away and go catch forty winks while he had the opportunity? Probably for the same reason Gallo endured the heat. They were both dumb like that.

BANG! The storm picked that moment to hurl a blast of wicked weather against the east side of the cabin, reminding Chance that Suede could very well have stayed in that icy pond where she wouldn't have been found until spring. How sad.

The hot water bladders would help warm Suede, but body heat could warm her faster. If a man were brave enough...

Okay then. Chance felt better once he'd made up his mind. The hot water bottles he'd rigged up would cool too soon. He'd have to be up checking on them anyway. It made sense to stay with her in case anything, you know, happened.

Lifting the thick layers of blankets so as not to disturb his prickly, sleeping beauty, Chance eased his long legs onto the bed and alongside Suede's. Gently, he straightened her left knee and adjusted her bandaged thigh to make room for his bulky frame. A Lilliputian he was not, and that sealed his decision. The faster he got his big, wide body next to hers, the quicker she'd be back to 98.6.

Sounded simple enough. Facing Suede, he lifted an arm over her head and pressed down until she groggily accepted his bicep for her pillow. He wrapped that same arm around her shoulder, cupping his palm to her bicep instead of her breast where it naturally tended to stray.

That put them face-to-face and belly-to-belly. Still chilled to the touch, he smoothed his other palm down her arm, bending it at the elbow so her hand came to rest on his ribs instead of getting mashed between their bodies. Carefully, he tucked her head under his chin, which put her breath in his neck. She was still cold and so small.

There was no soft, sweet scent drifting up from her body though, a good thing given their intimate position. That would've done him in. Molding her against his pecs, abs, and thighs, he strove to keep his cock at a respectable distance, but arching his back made for an uncomfortable position, so he relaxed and went with the flow. Why not? She'd never know what she did to him, not as hard as she slept.

Chance held Suede as tightly as he dared while the whole man-to-woman heat exchange thing began. Shivering now, which was a good sign, she breathed in fast, short pants, her breasts heaving against him. "Don't get any sicker on me. I've only got that one pack of antibiotics, so you've got to show signs of improvement right away." A hot toddy might help her once she was up and moving. It might help him, too.

As fragile as she was, he held her tenderly and respectfully. This was no man shagging a woman when the opportunity arose. Chance wasn't made that way. His romance-writing mother, Scarlett Sinclair, might have written some spicy erotica during her life, but her three sons were most definitely not her heroes' role models. Chance knew that for a fact.

They'd each evolved from her loveless marriage to Anthony Sinclair, aka Deadbeat Dad. He'd bailed when Scarlett's first novel made the New York Time's best-sellers list. Chance was three and already more man than good old Tony the day the old man took off. Chance never knew him. Couldn't remember what he looked like. Didn't try to.

Where his mom's sexy heroes were balanced and cool in the ways of debonair movie stars and Captain-America-wannabes, Chance, his younger brothers Kruze and Pagan, were heroes on the broken side of life. All former SEALs, they'd done the dirty work for America, the impossible jobs. Scarred and beat up now, they were the guys who'd once pushed back at the monsters who went bump in the night, even if those monsters lived on the other side of the world.

He himself was no looker, but Scarlett Sinclair had been a truly beautiful woman, and each of her sons resembled her in one way or another. Kruze had her looks. He was the lady-killer in the family, and to prove it, he went through women like a kid in a candy store, tasting each on one-night stands, then moving on. Never dating the same woman twice. Always looking. Never finding. Whatever demon he had on his back rode him hard.

Pagan, another handsome Sinclair brother, had her keen eyesight and aptitude for reflective listening. He always would be Scarlett's baby boy, but he was one tough SOB and a paradox. Despite his chosen vocation as a sniper, Pagan desperately craved a family of his own. He missed his mom and he loved children, a double whammy. That was what sparked his need to set the world right. If there was a child threatened, brutalized, or suffering in the world, he was the man for the job. But like Scarlett, he wasn't lucky in love.

And Chance? He liked to think he had the same good heart as she had. He certainly no longer had her looks. During his last deployment to South America, his mission had been compromised and his team ambushed. He'd lost the woman they'd been sent to save, as well as two-thirds of his nine-man team. His friends.

That was months ago, and the day he'd learned the hard way not to stand next to the guy who'd inadvertently set off an IED. It was a simple mistake, but nothing was simple about the consequences of getting peppered with a wicked blast of four-inch spiral-shank nails. Those buggers tore through Chance's face, neck, and one shoulder like killer bees on a scavenger hunt for human flesh. He'd damned near died in the jungle that day, nearly bled to death. Lost what was left of his vanity, too.

The cocky, good-looking SEAL in the mirror was gone, replaced by a pockmarked freakazoid with a couple skid marks over his skull and through his once thick head of hair. Worse, he'd lost six of the men he called brothers. The only ones left were Walker *Crack* Martinez and Darrell *Texas* Contreras. All the rest lay in national or state cemeteries. Yet it could've been worse. *Everyone could've died.*

As if those losses weren't enough, on the same day back home in sunny San Diego, Death came calling. Chance found out when he'd come to in Walter Reed. Scarlett Sinclair had left without telling him goodbye. Talk about a sucker punch from hell.

While recuperating, enduring plastic surgeries, infection, and PT, Senator McQueen Sullivan had arrived one day with an offer Chance found hard to refuse. Sullivan wanted him and his brothers to come work for him and a clandestine federal organization called the Strike Back Force. That got Chance back on his feet and out of mind-numbing depression.

He'd wanted payback at that time. He'd just lost the only worlds he knew. He was hurting, but he'd also recognized that a benched SEAL was not the life for him. Yes, he could've easily coached BUD/S, the Basic Underwater Demolition/SEAL school, or tackled warrior counseling, but he'd wanted action. Hence, Montana.

He'd bought this specific parcel of land three years earlier, intending it as an investment slash retirement option. Once he and his brothers signed onto the task force, and with a little assist from the millions his mother left him, Chance turned the cabin into a command center and a right tight fortress Scarlett would've been proud of.

But guilt for surviving when others did not was a hard-earned price to pay for having served with honor. It was that survivor's guilt that truly made the decision for Chance. It came with one condition. Chance upped the testosterone in that lackluster moniker and changed the politically correct *Strike Back Force* to *Sons of Bitches*, SOBs for short. What'd Sullivan expect? He hadn't hired paper-pushing pansies. Not hardly.

Though he craved the salt spray in his face, and the foggy marine layer of NAS, the Navel Air Station on North Island off the Pacific Coast, that was also the day Chance accepted that his Navy days were over. There was no sense lingering where his presence could get other SEALs killed if this SOB concept panned out. He owed his good buddies and their families that much.

Now Chance ruled the Montana portion of the SOBs. Comprised only of the three Sinclair brothers, it headquartered out of this cabin. They might comprise Sullivan's first team, but it wasn't his last. He'd built a far-reaching network in the last few months. *Lone Wolves*, a team of former Army rangers operated out of central Wyoming. The *Panthers,* an elusive group of former CIA agents, targeted the bad guys deep in the Florida Everglades and along the southeastern seaboard. *Night Shadows*, a team of former FBI agents who'd seen too much and felt like they'd done too little, worked America in general, from sea to shining sea.

Then there was the *Dia de Muertos* out of New Mexico, an elite team of USA border guards who worked South American troubles all the way to the southernmost point of South America, Cape Froward on the northern shores of the Magellan Strait in Chile, when needed. Chance hadn't met them yet, but he looked forward to the day. He hadn't met the *Serengeti Apex* either, a South African team.

The Sin brothers were hands-down the best because, duh, they were former SEALs. Highly trained and finely honed, any one of them could put a double tap inside the Kremlin as easily as an armed drone inside the Forbidden City. No one was safe and no mountain too high when the order came down from Sullivan for one of the Sin brothers to end an injustice.

Pagan proved it last week when the latest ISIS leader filmed a DIY film of him training his six-year old daughter to participate in a grisly beheading. There he was in Syria, indoctrinating a baby into his brutal ideology online. The guy had the nerve to advertise it ahead of time so all the world could tune in as if it was just the latest reality show.

Double tap nothing. Pagan nailed the guy a full dozen times before the little girl knew what went down behind her back, and before her dirtbag father's body hit the ground. The sensational story of a mystery sniper in Syria lit up all the liberal news channels that day. But by the time it did, Pagan was deep inside Taliban territory, offing the bearded braggart called the Iron Fist of Islam, a child predator who raped little boys for sport, then killed them.

Suede whimpered, drawing Chance back out of his reverie. She sucked in a raspy breath, then released it with a terrified "Don't!" while she ground her face into Chance's chest. "Hate you. Lion. No. Stop! No!"

He cupped the back of her head and held her trembling body close, his nose in the beanie on her head. She was a tiny frightened thing, and everything she did, every move she made hit a chord inside of him as if she strummed his heartstrings with those shredded fingertips. The alpha male in him lifted its head, needing to protect and keep what he'd found. "It's okay, Suede," he murmured, "I'm here and you're safe now. Lion can't get to you. Relax. Sleep."

"Never be safe. Never, ever..." She coughed out those last words, her nose in his neck and her whine fading fast into slumber.

Chance growled softly. *Want to bet?*

Chapter Six

Suede came to slowly, groggy and weak, her cheek against a massive heartbeat that called to her with its strong, steady rhythm. The intoxicating scent beneath her nose was too luscious to pull away from. She didn't want to, even if she could. This man smelled as if he'd captured the wind and the sun, rolled them together with a sprig of peppermint, and tucked the combination under the covers with her.

Nuzzling closer, she swallowed a gulp of masculine warmth. Her nose rubbed along a stretch of cotton that gave way to crisp, manly chest hairs. *Mhmmm.* A woman could get used to waking up like this. It beat all the priciest hotels for bodily comfort, and she wanted to stay here. For the first time that she could recall, the hole in her psyche, the one that had ached most of her life, seemed full of something other than anxiety for being worthless. Her nervous stomach didn't pinch or cramp with unfulfilled expectations. She felt as if she belonged where she was.

I must be on my deathbed.

But waking came with a migraine that radiated down her spine to her toes. Even the simple act of stretching her neck brought aches and pains to vicious life in her body, ending with an exclamation point in the form of a jolting burn up one leg. She stilled to calm the agony, content to be alive and breathing.

A tiny nugget of the nearly dissolved cough drop had stuck to the roof of her mouth during the night, and a drink would be nice, but she was alive, and yes, grateful. At long last, her wayward, argumentative spirit had nothing rude or catty to throw at the world. She, Suede Tennyson, was simply—humbly—content to draw in one breath after another.

Lying there with a melting shard of menthol bliss in her mouth, she was frightened, but she was also suddenly *rich enough*. She didn't need anything but the warm body beneath her tender fingertips. Breathing without fire in her lungs was *good enough*. Yes, her throat was sore and her stomach muscles ached, but every last one of her pains also reminded her that a very hard lesson had finally been learned. Life wasn't meant to be squandered in the press. They didn't care about the media darlings they created, then tormented until the day they died anyway. No one did.

Life wasn't meant to be wasted on the riotous living that had left her soul bankrupt and sad at the end of every day, either. Nor spent on foolish thrill rides that rivaled the crass lifestyles spewing out of Hollywood on a daily, if not hourly, basis. Look where her previous decisions had gotten her. Thrown off a cliff like a half-eaten apple tossed from a speeding car on I-5. Not how Suede wanted her life to end.

It had been a long time since she'd entertained thoughts of changing, but waking up like this, enfolded against this mountain of a man who held her as carefully as if she were a baby, mattered. This guy might not like her, but at that moment he was giving her something she'd never had before. Himself. His body heat. His strength. To a mixed-up girl who'd nearly drowned, those few things were suddenly—enough.

Humility shivered over her warm shoulders. *I should be dead.* On the heels of that came, *I would be dead if this stranger hadn't saved me.* Chance could've walked away. He probably had better things to do last night, like getting out of the cold. Keeping warm. He could've minded his own business. *God knows everyone else would have.*

Instead, he'd risked everything. He'd given his life to her, his very breath, when he hadn't had to. He'd brought her into his home and he'd stitched her leg. How does anyone begin to repay unwarranted kindness like that?

Suede lifted her arm and pressed two bandaged fingers to the back of her neck, massaging the knotted muscles to get the blood supply moving to her brain.

"You're awake," Chance murmured to the top of her head. "How are you feeling?"

Better, she meant to tell him, but the answer died in her tender throat. In stretching to reach her neck, she'd rubbed her sensitive breasts against his chest, not that it did anything for her. Her body was too sore to be excited by that sensual contact, but men were men. She dropped her arm, plastered one hand against his chest as a barrier, and prepared to be groped.

Oddly, he didn't make a move.

"Alive," she corrected with a growly voice. *I think for the first time in my life, I'm really alive, but you'd better keep your hands to yourself.* Then, because no fingers strayed under her shirt to pinch her nipples, and because that simple inaction made him seem too honorable to be real, she asked, "We're sleeping together? When the fuck did that happen?"

His arms tightened like a muscular steel band over the blanket around her. "Yes, ma'am, but only until you're warm. You aren't dying on my watch."

Her silly heart fluttered at the certainty in his deep baritone. Who did this guy think he was, Sir Lancelot come to save the faint at heart Lady Guinevere? "Am I warm enough?" she dared ask.

"You tell me."

The sexy rumble in his voice was enough to curl her cold toes. "No," she whispered when his hands still hadn't moved from their original position. "I'm still cold." *On the inside. Where I've never been warm.*

It was easy to hear his heart rate quicken at her reply with her ear pressed to his chest like it was. Suede drew in as deep a breath of Chance Sinclair as she could muster without coughing. He smelled good enough to eat. The scent of wind, sun, and a hint of clean masculine sweat came to her nostrils. It soothed and it warmed. She nuzzled. This was one of those once-in-a-lifetime moments she didn't want to end. She would know. There'd been so few.

After the wreck she'd made of her life, now—while she wasn't full of anger— would've been the perfect time to die. Nothing could get better than this unique sensation of being cared for. It was better than an orgasm. Would probably last as long as one, too.

"So tell me what happened up there?" he asked quietly, his lips at the top of her head. "Why'd York push you? What were you guys doing up there in the first place?"

A note of despair crept out of her mouth. "I thought he loved me." *I should've known better. The Lion only loves himself.*

"Answer me." Command rippled in Chance's tone. "Why were you up there in this storm?"

She steeled her emotions. "Because..." *Don't let him see you cry.* "Because Lionel bet I wouldn't last one night camping. He dared me to tag along on a sports photo shoot with him and his guys, only there was no photographer waiting like he said there'd be. Only a big steel trailer he expected to spend the night in." *Just him and his guys though. Not me.*

"And?" Chance pushed for more.

Suede never thought of sassing him, but obedience? That was what he'd just extracted from her, and it was weird that she'd responded civilly. She stalled, caught off balance and genuinely distracted by the power this male held over her. "And my throat hurts. Got another one of those cough drops?"

Releasing her, he stretched an arm to somewhere over her head, and she was back in heaven, tracing her palm over a thick pec, loving the ripple of muscles at her fingertips and the flat disc of the manly nipple beneath his shirt. It took him a second to unwrap the menthol drop, and to ease it between her lips. She didn't mean to lick his fingertip, but once she did, she wished she'd sucked that finger into her mouth instead of the cough drop.

When he hissed at the contact, she knew she'd gotten to him. That should've made her crow. Inciting this response in a true alpha male would put another notch on her bedpost, so to speak, but Suede took no pleasure in arousing Chance. For once in her worthless life, she had something unique and rare within reach, and she didn't want to spoil it by being herself.

He'd physically pushed life back into her. How could she defile a noble gift like that? Time needed to stop right here and now, so she wouldn't go back to who or what she used to be.

Chance gave her seconds to moisten the cough drop in her mouth, then repeated his question, his arms once more warm around her shoulders like a security blanket. "Why'd he push you, Suede?"

"Because he's Lion." Just talking about the pompous ass squeezed her throat closed all over again. "He's got a temper. Everyone knows that."

"And?" Man, this guy was a bulldog. Chance wouldn't give up.

"I called him out for lying to me," Suede admitted. *Definitely not my wisest decision.* "I should've known better. Why would a tennis player need a sports shoot in the mountains? We were breaking up anyway, but the real reason I went up there with him was because he said he had a diamond ring, only I had to earn it to keep it and accompanying him on the photo shoot was the deal. Only once he gave it to me, he wanted it back."

"Why? Was he buying you off?"

"No," she croaked. *Well, maybe.* "But I didn't care if he was. Once he gave it to me, I thought that I... that I..."

"You honestly thought marriage would change an ass like Lionel York?" Disbelief and accusation shadowed Chance's question.

"N-no." *Not exactly*. Swallowing past the lump in her tender throat, Suede admitted, "I always knew he didn't really care about me, but once I had that ring, I could've disappeared, so his men couldn't find me."

Chance's fingertips tapped at her shoulder blades. "You were going to sell it?"

Suede nodded. Blinking furiously, she worked that cough drop between her tongue and the roof of her mouth to keep her mind off how desperate she had been for Lionel's attention, hell, for anyone's attention, from the beginning of their tempestuous relationship. He'd gotten her to do wild and crazy things she never would've dreamed up on her own. And this was where it had gotten her.

But at first, he'd been her ticket to good times, independence, and fun, like a joyride through the tunnel of love that had too quickly plummeted into a house of horrors. A smarter woman would've known better, but Suede had only been sixteen when he'd come into her life, seventeen when she moved in with him. Yes, she'd been star struck. What kid could've rejected the attentions of a celebrity at a time like that?

She'd just declared to the world she could make it without her parents, that she didn't need them. Pride had pushed her into his arms, and she'd gone skipping into the sunset. Yet, from the beginning, the signs were everywhere: his temper tantrums on and off the court, his vulgar tirades with reporters and sportscasters, and his very loud, very vocal disdain for anyone he considered beneath him. Like the rest of the world.

Suede shivered at the desperation that had driven her into Lionel York's circle of influence. She'd been in such a low place back then, not that things had improved much since. But even now, she wondered what she'd done to catch the eye of a dangerous man like Lionel York. She never could handle him, but he'd certainly handled her.

Chance must've taken that shiver as his cue to warm her up. His broad palms moved sure and firm down her back, nearly to the swell of her ass. But there he stopped, even as his heart rate kicked up. *Interesting...*

"I'm a mess," she told him honestly. "I've fucked up my—"

"Stop with the bad language, Suede. I'm a SEAL. I've heard it all." His fingers tapped the small of her back where they'd landed. "You don't need to impress me."

No one had ever told her to stop swearing before. She opened her mouth to tell him to go to hell, but instead, she murmured a hesitant, "Umm... well, okay. Umm..."

Does that mean that I impress you? Now? In this condition?

"I just meant that I've chosen poorly, and I... I..." Her excuses stalled out.

I what? Want this stranger to understand how much I hate my life? That I pushed Lionel's temper to the limit, and I don't know why? "Never mind. I'm really tired and..." *I don't want to talk about it.*

Chance shrugged out from under her, like she hadn't seen that brush-off coming. Men hated needy women. Lifting to his feet, he pulled the blankets nearly over her face and walked away.

Loser!

Burrowing her nose into the warmth he left behind, Suede let the tears come. All her life she'd been the odd one out, the unwanted child of an upwardly mobile couple who'd had higher aspirations than parenthood on their minds. Her parents didn't want her. Why should they? They had better things to do, more important things.

Her father planned to be president. Her mother was the nation's poster girl for feminine rights, not for the entire feminine gender though, only for the ones who believed like she did, that traditional motherhood was dead. Children were inconvenient and hindered a woman's social standing. That women's rights preceded everything and everyone else.

How Suede had hated living with them, being the child they'd never wanted, and listening to their steady pro-abortion arguments as to how much better off they would've been without her. So why had they kept their love child, if she'd ever, in her wildest dreams, been that? She'd never know.

At seventeen, she'd sued for emancipation, but they'd glossed it over when the press got hold of the story. Said it was all a misunderstanding. Like hell it was. Suede wanted nothing to do with two lawyers who could lie to each other as quickly as to the world and her. Only now...

A sob hiccupped out of her. *Now I'm sick and I'm hurt and I'm still alone. What else is new?* Her heart broke yet again. It was pretty bad when the Good Samaritan who'd saved her life didn't want anything to do with her either. Right now, Chance was probably washing his mouth out with extra-strength Listerine because he'd given her mouth-to-mouth, but why she cared what he was doing galled Suede. She was tougher than this!

The warm palm settling on her shoulder ended her hysterical internal rant. "Hey. Move it over. I'm back."

How embarrassing. Slowly, Suede turned her back on Chance, wiping the tears as she dragged her hurting legs along with her temper tantrum away from him.

The mattress flexed as he joined her. That big warm hand clutched her shoulder again. "Where do you think you're going? You're still cold. Get back here."

"Leave me the fuck alone," she ordered, her hackles up now. People thought she was a bitch and this was why. She hadn't a friend in the world, and she sure as fuck didn't need one now. Every time she'd put herself out there, every time she'd left herself vulnerable, this happened. *Every time!* She found herself spurned, used, or tossed aside. *Fucking enough!*

"You're sick," he reminded her, his tone as patient as if he were talking with a child.

"Guess again, asshole. I don't need you or your place, and I don't need your help either." She shrugged her shoulder to dislodge his grip, making up lies as she went. "So keep your fuckin' hands off me. I can sue you for assault. Don't think I won't."

He all but forced her back around to face him. "You're swearing again. What's wrong?"

"Don't your ears work? I said I don't need you," she spat, not brave enough to meet his gaze. "I don't fuckin' need" —a hiccup wrenched out of her raw throat— "anyone!" She meant to scream that last line to get him to back off, but she ended up coughing in his face, making her argument sound weak and petty. Like her.

Suede found her body tugged forward until her cheek mashed against a warm masculine chest. One manly palm cupped her head and held her fast. Jesus, for not needing anyone, she sure couldn't hold her own in this fight. Chance had a good hold on her, but his fingers were splayed and flexed as if he were holding someone who mattered instead of copping a feel.

The dumbass! She wriggled, too tired to fight but giving it all she had left. Her wimpy efforts didn't seem to matter. That massive hand at the back of her head didn't budge, and she was too weak to act upon her vicious words. "Let me go," whimpered out of her instead of another audacious lie she couldn't back up with action.

"You poor thing," Chance whispered into the cap on her head. "You've been fighting the world for a long time, haven't you? It's over, Suede. Let it go."

"Shut the fuck up," she hissed, her eyes squeezed tight against the tsunami of loneliness about to swallow her whole. "You don't know what you're talking about. I don't need you telling me what to do. I d-d-don't need—"

"Anyone or anything," he murmured. "I get that, baby. That's why you resort to foul language when you feel threatened. You don't need anyone, and you can't trust anyone, either, but you're here now, and you're safe with me. York can't get to you. Breathe, Suede. Stop trying to be someone you're not and just relax. Breathe." His chest expanded as if he needed to show her how it was done. "That's all you have to do right now, let your body heal. Know you can do that, Suede. Believe in yourself for a change. Trust me to have your back while you rest."

Listening to the intake and output of his lungs under her ear almost made her believe what he said was possible. It sounded doable, all that believe-in-yourself, warm-fuzzy crap. His hands and fingers weren't roaming her body for a cheap thrill. This damned guy was simply holding onto her like he meant to hold her together until she could handle living. He'd called her baby, but it felt like an endearment instead of the come-on she'd heard a million other times.

"You don't understand," eked out of her. "You have to let me go." *Or I'll fall apart. I'll shatter.* The pain of a lifetime still towered over her in one giant wave that could crush her if she ever let it go. *Who'd pick up the pieces then, huh?*

"Why should I?" If his voice dipped any lower, she'd melt right here in his arms.

"You already know," she told him honestly. She was so damned fucked up, and he was just some guy, and men always let her down, even the nice ones. They'd used and abused her, every last one of them. What good were they?

His answer for that came in a brush of warm peppermint and another soft kiss on her forehead. "You're tired and you're sick, that's what I know."

Suede didn't understand Chance. He had to be gay for not taking advantage of her. She'd certainly given him enough opportunities. "Liar. You've seen the videos. The headlines. I'm no fucking good."

A soft growl rumbled beneath her ear. "Then it's time to prove the world wrong. Everyone makes mistakes, Suede. Stop looking back. Get over yourself and move on."

Why didn't he get it? Why'd he continually look for something in her that wasn't there? Like goodness? Better question, why'd he see things in her worth saving when she knew damned well she had no redeeming qualities. *Just ask Mom and Dad.*

Wow, that came out of nowhere. Aching down to her toes, she couldn't bring herself to meet his eyes. "I am tired." Which she was, but that wasn't the whole truth. "And I'm sorry I've inconvenienced you," she added to prove she'd meant what she'd said. "I'll leave as soon as I can walk out of here."

"Trust me. You're no inconvenience and you're welcome to stay as long as you want. Do you need the restroom? It's only a few feet away. I'll help you."

That was why he'd left? Because Nature called? "No, I'm fine," she whispered, daring to hope for the first time in a long time that she and Chance could be friends. She'd never had a gay *guyfriend* before. It would be such a relief not to have to be sexually involved with a man for a change. Suede lifted her lashes to meet her savior.

"No, you're not fine," he whispered. "If you don't need the restroom, you're still dehydrated and I'm not doing my job. I need to make sure you drink more water."

The light was dim, but she could make out the gentlest eyes peering down at her. *This...this is Chance? This shaggy-haired god?* There were no words in the entire dictionary to define the handsome man who'd just tucked her under his arm like she belonged there. Her fingertips fluttered over a massive pec, and her heart flipped a backward somersault right before it climbed handstands up her sore throat.

"Ch-Chance?" she asked like a hoarse-voiced fool. Who else could he be?

Thick, ebony lashes blinked down at her, pulling her deeper into their depths. She wanted to know the color of his eyes. Rugged masculine brows joined in a gentle crease as his index finger steadied her shaking head. "Yes, ma'am?" A hint of warm peppermint drifted over her cheeks as he tugged her body into alignment with his side. His ribs. His hips. What had to be his—cock.

Oh my, my, my, Chance is definitely not gay, not if he's this happy to see me.

"It's n-n-nice to m-m-meet you," stuttered off her tongue.

His lips quirked into a half-smile as he arched his back, distancing that single piece of male anatomy as if he hadn't meant to make contact with his horny welcome wagon. "It's my pleasure to serve, Miss Tennyson."

Suede closed her eyes again. She had to be dreaming. None of this was real. It couldn't be. When she woke up, she'd be dead and drowned in that pond at the bottom of, what'd he call it, Mother's Day Falls? Stupid name.

The warmth of a massive male hand cupped the back of her head even as his lips landed on the middle of her forehead again. "Rest easy, Suede. Keep warm. I'll fix breakfast the next time you wake up."

No, you won't. You'll disappear, because none of this is real. It can't be.

Chapter Seven

Damn it, her eyes are blue. Not just blue, but tropical blue, one part turquoise and two parts azure, just like the ocean off the Southern California coast. Chance hadn't realized how much he'd craved that exact hue until now. Those colors and all of those lush curves hadn't been photo-shopped. Even bruised and battered, Suede Tennyson was Just. That. Gorgeous.

She'd knocked the wind out of his sails and Chance found himself in the doldrums without a rudder. The sad glaze in those vulnerable blues was enough to derail a man's purest intentions. This was no wily vixen skilled in the dark magic of seduction and sex, though. Not even close. There was no get-down-get-dirty gleam in those pretty eyes. More like fear. Panic. Calculated worry. More like the terror of a lost little girl who'd found herself face-to-face with the big bad wolf.

Chance cursed every last one of his scars for frightening her. The hero side of him wanted to save her all over again, to give her whatever she needed to feel good about herself, but the monster side wanted to shove off and run. Hide! There was no way short of copious amounts of plastic surgery that would restore him to a respectable sight pleasing to the feminine persuasion. Not like she'd stay if he did, and where that notion came from, he had no idea. He was only there to save her life. Who cared what he looked like.

He tucked his new, bitter reality down deep in his gut, took his own advice, and got over himself. This was about saving her, not him. Like a star-struck groupie, he wanted, no, he needed her to smile at him. Just him. But that wasn't going to happen, and he was dumb to think it could. He was Disney's Beast to her Beauty, a ragged man, face-to-face with a genteel woman of breeding and worth. Not a porn star. Not a tramp. If what his gut told him was spot on, Suede Tennyson was no porn star in the making. She wasn't even close.

He groaned when she settled her hips against him, but when she lifted her left knee onto his thigh, no doubt because of her wounded leg, his heart caught in his throat. It was all he could do to not grab the cheek of her ass and mold her tender body parts to his. Or fill her up with every last ounce of all he had to give, his manhood and the rest of his life.

Where these feelings and thoughts came from, he hadn't a clue, but this woman, this complex female, had changed everything the moment she'd taken that first frosty breath below Mother's Day Falls.

She edged in closer, one hand trapped between their bodies, the other as soft as a kitten on his chest, and like it or not, Chance was her slave forever. And that slave wanted inside of her body. How disgusting was that? He wasn't any better than that pig, York. Here she was, such a tiny little thing thrown to her death, and all Chance could think about was making her come. Putting a smile on her lips and a blush on her body. Every last inch of it.

Enough. Fighting the rowdy demands of his all-male body, Chance forced his mind off the broken yet seductive beauty in his arms. He sent his horny brain back to A-School, the fierce seven-week pre-BUD'S training. Then onto Coronado for another seven punishing months that ended in Hell Week instead of romantic fiction.

Not working.

He forced his stubborn mind to the twenty mile runs in full gear, then to scuba diving at all hours of the night. When those didn't work, he focused on the underwater long-distance transit dives he'd made in frigid weather, and from there, to rigging underwater explosives in the midst of prowling hungry sharks with rows of razor sharp teeth. He re-lived weapons training on every caliber, make, and model he'd ever touched.

Shit. He was hard as a brick. This wasn't working either, not with Suede's warm breath on his neck, melting his finely honed military mind into a bucket of galaxy slime. Closing his eyes, Chance forced his fingers to loosen their hold on her bicep. Naturally, the impulse to stroke his way down to the flare of her bare, lush hips remained, but he triumphed over the temptation and stopped at her waist.

He'd dressed her in his favorite T-shirt before he'd settled her into his bed. She'd been unconscious then, but her legs and backside were bare and inviting and... *my hell!* This woman was made for sin and sex. It was no wonder she ran with the pack of animals she did. Down to her painted pink toenails, Suede Tennyson was the Grecian goddess Aphrodite come to life, a curvaceous woman made to be loved and loved hard.

Thankfully, Gallo picked that moment to whine, and Chance flashed back to his senses. *Of course! He needs to take a leak too.*

Glad for the distraction, Chance whispered, "I'll be right back," in case Suede was still awake, which he doubted. Her breathing had evened out, a good sign she was plenty warm. Who was he kidding? Warming her wasn't the only reason he was still in bed with her, but damn. His fingers didn't want to let her go.

Another whine lifted up from the floor, and there was no choice.

"I'm coming." Gingerly, Chance eased one foot to the floor while he released his hold on the luscious woman in his bed. Moaning, she turned her nose into his pillow, so he drew the blankets up to her chin, made sure she was tucked in extra tight and warm, and left her to rest.

At his closet, he traded his nightwear for a pair of jeans and a black, long-sleeved Henley. A pair of warm socks completed his ensemble while Gallo waggled his body at Chance's knees for attention. Closing the bedroom door behind him, he ruffled Gallo's thick mane. "I know what you mean. She's something else, isn't she, boy?" He'd no more than closed his big mouth when his hackles lifted. They weren't alone.

"I'm back," a gruff male voice growled from the darkened room beyond.

"Pagan?" *What a relief.* "How the hell'd you get here?" *In a blizzard?*

"Easy. I was nearly to your place when the storm hit. It was either freeze to death in the timber or keep marching, so here I am. Coffee's on."

"Why are you here?"

"Apparently your cell phone's out again, or you shut it off." Pagan lifted a coffee mug in a half-hearted toast that didn't reach his startling green eyes, so much like his mother's. "We need to talk."

Chance pointed to the charging station on the end table next to his couch. Under the towel he'd wrapped Suede's head with. No wonder he hadn't heard the phone he'd plugged in there. Damn. Not good. *Was I that distracted? Guess so.* "Let me clear a path for Gallo to go take a leak first."

That proved easy. Pagan's incoming boot tracks still marked a semi-decent trail through the drifts of snow and into the trees. Chance sent Gallo off to do his business with a stern, "Stay close," while he waited at the door. Damn, it was still snowing and blowing. If this kept up, they'd be stranded for weeks.

A good dusting blanketed Gallo's rump when he returned, his big ears perked up, and a smile on his face. "Good boy," Chance told his buddy. Back inside, he stomped his boots quietly to not wake Suede before he joined Pagan at the kitchen table. "You're looking tired, Baby Brother. When'd you get in?"

Pagan stretched his long legs alongside the four-person wooden kitchen table as Gallo moved in for a quick pat on the head before he returned to his spot at the hearth. "An hour ago." Pagan nodded at Chance's bedroom door. "Who's your lady friend?"

Chance chuffed at the prying question. "You're not going to believe this, but Gallo found Suede Tennyson half-dead in the pond last night. I resuscitated her and brought her home."

Pagan's eyes narrowed to slits. "Say again?"

"That's right. She was camping up top when her asshole boyfriend pitched her over the cliff."

"That boyfriend wouldn't be Lionel York, would he?"

"Yeah, why?"

Pagan blew out a low whistle. "Because he's my next mark. Sullivan tried to reach you. When he couldn't, he tagged me for the hit."

"So that's why you're here. To off York?" Chance asked, not entirely displeased with this new mission. York deserved to die for what he'd done to Suede, but why had he hit Sullivan's radar, and why was Chance just hearing about it? He had a sat phone. Sullivan should've been able to reach him.

"You really don't know, do you?" With a head full of shaggy hair as black as his eyes, Pagan's lip lifted into a sneer. "Damn it, Chance, get your head out of your ass and re-engage, will you? It's been months. You've got to let it go."

Chance shut down, not going to discuss his feelings with his brother. Not yet. The months since he'd lost his team, his mother, and his career didn't equate to a man being ready to jump back into work that could get other good men killed. Chance wasn't hiding from life as much as trying to figure out where he fit in the equation. Or if he still fit. Losing his men had hurt, but losing his mom the same day? Karma had dealt him an unforgivably tough hand. Chance hadn't processed much past the anger stage of grief. Didn't think he could.

Pagan was right, but he made it sound easy. Chance knew better.

"The snow must've knocked out the satellite," he told his brother, "or I'd have talked with Sullivan and put York down already. Now, I'll ask one more time. What'd York do to piss Sullivan off?"

"There's a reason York goes to Cuba every month, and it's not to play tennis. He's balls deep in the drug trade. Cocaine. He gets it out of South America and he's opened shop in Oregon. You'd know this if Sullivan could ever reach you."

Chance rolled the pinch out of his neck. "I just talked with Sullivan two days ago. He didn't say anything about York then, but if he wanted me to off the guy, why'd he wait until this storm rolled in to assign the hit? He knew it was coming."

A shadow shifted over Pagan's already dark countenance. He looked away and flicked his middle finger off his thumb like he was brushing away a gnat. "Hell if I know, but I'm tired, Chance. Back-to-back overseas flights are ball busters."

So were back-to-back hits. Pagan shouldn't have had to accept two tough jobs in the same week, and that foul was on Chance. Now that the cabin was finished and safeguards were set in stone, he needed to step up and go active.

But something else was going on here. Leaning into his brother's face, Chance peered closer. Pagan didn't usually suffer over the loss of a few lowlifes in the world. He was known to throw back a few drinks and ask for another assignment, not drink. "What's really going on? You're not just tired."

Pagan's square head rotated on his thick neck. His fists clenched. Still wearing his boots and Gortex jacket, he'd present a formidable adversary to folks who didn't know him. His fist hit the table, upsetting his mug. Coffee went flying. "Do you even know where I've been? Did you see what I had to do? Do you even care?"

Enough said. The Sinclair brothers had never fought each other. Chance didn't want this to be the day they did. He cleared the table. Grabbing his brother by the nape of his neck, he jerked Pagan forward and into his shoulder. "I know, brother. I know. You were in Syria then straight onto Afghanistan. Trust me, I know, and yes, I care."

"I had to kill him, Chance, in front of his little girl!" Pagan shoved back, but not getting out of his older brother's grip. Anguish shuddered off him like heat off a radiator in August. "Shit, I had to off him before he made her take the first cut. Damn him!" He kicked at the tiled floor, the torment in his tone loud and clear. "I hate myself as much as I hate that bastard father of hers. Why couldn't she grow up like any other little kid? What is wrong with those people?"

"They're fucked up, man. Really fucked up," Chance gave him the only answer he knew while he hung onto his over-wrought brother. Bad language was one of those things his mother abhorred, in her writing and in her home. Hence, the brothers grew up learning other ways to express themselves intelligently. Most of the time...

But this was the brother who'd buried Chance's '48 Willey's Jeep to the floorboards in the sand dunes at Ocean Shores, Washington, on a joyride with his friends the night he'd graduated high school. This was the crazy-assed guy who'd jumped off the Narrows Bridge in Tacoma, Washington, on a dare, and who'd nearly broken his neck surviving the one hundred eighty-seven foot drop. Pagan could be bat-shit crazy, but he deserved respect. Most of all, he deserved a safe place to come in from the storms of this warrior's life they both lived. No one said this after-five job would be easy, and by God, it wasn't.

"And you're right. It's time I take my share of the assignments. Consider this one mine. I'll take it from here."

"Shit," Pagan hissed, "I'm beat."

"You need breakfast and a week of R&R," Chance decided. That much he could provide, but what was truly eating at Pagan was unsolvable. Ideologically, the Sinclair brothers were cut out of the same cloth, but for whatever reason, Pagan came with a bigger, softer heart. Maybe because he knew what it was like to be his mother's favorite son, to be the youngest in a family of three boys, to be loved and spoiled rotten, he wanted to save every child in the world. It just wasn't possible.

Chance let his resistant brother go. "Bacon and eggs, then a twelve-hour rest. How long can you stay?"

"You tell me," Pagan muttered. "You're the boss of this chicken shit outfit."

"You know the house rules. Stay as long as you want—"

"Just don't leave a trail behind you when you go," Pagan finished. "Yeah, yeah, is my room clean?"

Dragging his iron skillet to the stove, Chance fired up the front burners, threw on a side of bacon, and tossed together a quick batch of breakfast biscuits. He held off answering until the biscuits were in the oven and a dozen scrambled eggs sizzled alongside the bacon, filling the cabin with the best aroma in the world. "It's as clean as you left it. I'm thinking either Sullivan's got a mole on his staff who leaked my twenty, or York knows something we don't. What do you think? Why else would he decide to toss his girlfriend off the mountain in my backyard?"

"My thoughts exactly," Pagan agreed from his place at the table. Calmer now, he peeled out of his jacket and boots, creating a pile on the floor next to his chair and gear bag. That was Baby Brother for you, a born *pilot*.

"That or he's making a point, that he thinks he's untouchable." By then the oven timer declared the biscuits were done, and the last of the bacon was extra crispy. "Which means he's onto Sullivan and the SOBs. Orange juice? More coffee?"

Pagan held his mug out for a refill. "You got any of the good stuff?" He meant *Bushmills,* the pricey, single malt Irish Whiskey Chance kept on hand to warm his coffee on cold nights.

"You know where it is, help yourself," Chance said as he transferred breakfast to the table. "But keep it down. Suede's had a bad night. She needs to rest."

"Suede, huh? Does Kruze know she's here?" Pagan grunted from his haunches at the lower shelf of their mother's cherry wood liquor cabinet, one of Chance's prized possessions and the only real thing he'd wanted of her estate. Scarlett Sinclair might be gone, but her good taste in liquor lived on. Chance stocked it with nothing but the finest for moments like this. A brother come home from the wars was enough reason to celebrate.

"Not yet. You're the first one I've talked to since Sullivan called."

"That's another thing. Why'd he call me instead of you? You're already here."

"Not sure." Chance and Pagan settled back at the table, Pagan with the Bushmills at his plate. "When we talked, he asked if I was ready to come back online, and to be honest, I said yeah, in another week. It's not like I've been slacking, you know. I pay the bills and I keep you guys safe while you're out. I keep track."

"I know," Pagan admitted, the bottle between his knees as he popped the lid, then poured a stream of amber heat into his coffee mug. "You keep us safe. Forget what I said."

"No worries." Silence reigned as forks were lifted and the men ate. Gallo traded his favorite spot by the fire for one under the table, just in case. After five solid minutes of chewing and refilling coffee cups, the bacon was gone and the eggs were history.

Pagan stabbed the last biscuit, slathered it with butter, and eased back in his chair. He rolled his neck, the vertebrae cracking as he popped the flaky morsel into his mouth. His eyes closed. "Damn, I'm glad Mom taught one of us how to cook."

"You ought to try it sometime," Chance said pointedly, more to tease than to scold. Patting his thigh, he invited Gallo to come take the slice of crispy pork fat he'd set aside for him. "I'll get in touch with Sullivan for more intel on York. In the meantime, take a load off and for hell's sake, take a shower." Chance guessed Pagan hadn't had time for the simple amenities on his whirlwind week of plane hopping.

"Not 'til you tell me about your lady friend." Pagan's chair thumped all four legs to the floor. His eyes turned dark beneath his brows. "Did you consider this might be just an act to get inside our team? Inside the SOBs? Jesus, Chance, she could be a spy for York."

Chance shook his head, amused at his brother's suspicious mind. Kruze wouldn't have asked that question. Forever the ladies man, he'd have been hands-on treating Miss Tennyson by now, holding her while she sipped a cup of broth and massaging her aching muscles as he regaled her with his adventures. Why that mental image irked the hell out of Chance floored him, but it did. No one needed to be putting his dirty mitts on Suede.

"Man, you're cynical. She was as blue as a *Smurf* when I finally got her inside last night, and that was after I did chest compressions and mouth-to-mouth on her for a good five minutes. For all purposes, she was dead. If it hadn't been for Gallo, I wouldn't have known she was out there. He's the hero. He found her, not me. And there's no way she's a spy. Poor thing's got an ugly tear from here" —Chance stabbed his index finger in a line on his left thigh from knee to hip— "to here. This isn't a ploy by Suede Tennyson to get inside the SOBs or to get at us. I think it's a coincidence."

His gut twisted the moment he said that word out loud. Was there any such thing as a coincidence? Pagan grunted, not believing it either. "Where'd you find her?"

"Dead center of the pond below the falls. She'd dropped through the ice. Again, it was Gallo who found her. He helped me drag her to shore, didn't you, boy?" Chance tossed his companion the last crumbs of bacon. "She owes this dog her life, and I owe him a venison rump roast. All of it. Huh, boy?"

Gallo snarfed the tidbit, his tail thumping and his eyes bright.

Pinching his lips together, Pagan nodded. "You might be right, but it's mighty odd she showed up at the same time I get called to off York. Damned odd."

"I am right," Chance declared, "and you're too tired to think straight, now take off. Get some shuteye. I'll take first watch."

"That's another thing." Pagan's eyebrow lifted along with the back legs of his chair. "The beacons weren't on when I came in."

"Duly noted." Chance stared his stern brother down. The beacons were an early warning system of interconnected laser beams at the perimeter of his one hundred acre tract. Intended to alert him of any large animal's approach, they emitted an ear-piercing, ultrasonic shriek that discomforted animal and man alike. At best, they were a redundancy to the security cameras he'd also installed along the perimeter. Both alerted him of incoming visitors/enemies, one with visuals, one with noise, but the beacons would've worked during the whiteout while the cameras would've been rendered useless. Pagan was right. If not for Suede, they would've been on.

"I was a little busy making sure our visitor survived," Chance bit out. "My bad. It won't happen again."

His brother offered a chin nod at the closed bedroom door. "It's not like you have a lot of visitors up here anyway, not in this weather. Guess it's no big deal. How is she?"

"She'll live." But it was a big deal and Chance was worried. Pitching a woman, any woman, off that mountain might not be a ruse to infiltrate the SOBs, but it had created a distraction. Only Chance had been plenty distracted before he'd found Suede, so much so that he'd left his cabin unlocked and his defenses down when he'd gone after Gallo. He'd gotten lazy and lax over a dog and a woman. Things had to change.

Tired of the argument, Chance pointed at one of the two spare rooms. "Shower. Now."

The Sinclair brothers' bedrooms punctuated three of the four corners of the massive cabin. Each included an en suite bathroom, a wood-burning stove, and trap door that led to the escape tunnel beneath the cabin. Dug seven feet below surface, the tunnel held an armory of weaponry from guns and knives to flame throwers and gas masks in a vault at its entry. Its exit lay a half-mile due west and beyond another shale bed.

At the best, unexpected and unwanted company would be hard pressed to get inside the fortified cabin, but by the time they did, Chance, his brothers, and any guests would be long gone, if the beacons had been turned on. He rolled one shoulder, irritated at his lapse in judgment in the fury of locating Gallo and ultimately, of saving Suede's life.

A sloppy SEAL was a dead SEAL. It wouldn't happen again.

Chapter Eight

"It'd behoove you to watch your step, Miss Tennyson. Mountains can be dangerous this time of year." *Lionel sneered as he shoved her shoulder, pushing her back step-by-step. Then another.*

At the edge, she slipped and lost her footing, stumbling over the cliff she hadn't known was so close. Paralyzed with terror that the man who'd claimed he loved her could do such a despicable thing, she clung with all her strength to the gravel edge. "Lion! Save me!"

Instead, the waffle-tread of his boot came at her like a cannon ball shot from two feet away. Stars exploded inside her head, but Suede refused to let go. All ten fingernails shredded as she dug into rock and ice, hanging on for her life.

"Stop," she told him through weak, teary eyes, snow and wind pelting her in the face. "Please don't do this. H-help me." She cocked a knee and dug in

with the toe of her boot, sure she could still scramble to safety if he'd just offer a hand up.

"You've been a thorn in my side long enough, Suede Tennyson. So's your goddamned father. Now fall, damn you!" Another kick came at her, but she ducked to the left at the last second. If he wasn't going to help her, then damn the fucker. He could fall with her.

Wrong move.

She caught nothing but a handful of air and the mountain let go. For a dozen feet or so, her fingernails grated against sheer granite, frantically seeking any crack or root to prevent the plummet she knew lay in store for her.

"I'm falling!" she told the wind.

"See you at the bottom!" Lion yelled from above.

Suede was that cartoon mouse scrambling in super-fast-motion for purchase on rocks so slick that it seemed, for a moment there, she was suspended in space. Then—nothing but the disoriented sensation of falling through falling snow. She lost all sense of direction. There was no up. No down. No help in sight. Just a drawn out "No-o-o-o!" thrown into the heartless world.

I'm falling! I'm falling!

BLAM! Suede jump-started to her hands and knees, her scream pounding in her veins and shaken to her core. She licked her chapped dry lips, afraid of the dark for the first time in her life.

He pushed me. He kicked me. He... he killed me. Her heart felt ready to explode through the top of her head. The sheet knotted beneath her tender fingertips. *Me! Suede Tennyson! He killed me...*

There was no recollection of impact, only the gut-wrenching terror of the drop and the futility of ego, pride, and all that hard-earned independence. Only the degradation of life ending at someone else's cruel hands and brutal boot. The soul-sucking knowledge that Lion hated her enough that he wanted her dead. Suede couldn't wrap her head around any of it, not even the flailing and praying when she'd fallen to what should've been her death.

So why am I alive? Where am I? It took seconds to blink herself awake enough to remember. *Chance's cabin. Oh, yeah.*

That was his fire in the stove in the corner of his room; his cough drop on her tongue. She remembered now. He'd breathed for her, and she clung to that shred of human decency like a life preserver. York meant to kill her, but Chance meant to save her. It mattered. Damn, how it mattered.

Tremors set in and she buried her face in his pillow, her wounded thigh on fire and her left butt cheek throbbing so hard that she didn't dare lower either of them to the mattress. Here she was, at someone else's mercy again. *How fucking humiliating.*

The questions of the ages assaulted her pulverized psyche. *'Why am I still alive? I don't deserve it.'*

Followed immediately by, *'What have I done with my life? I've wasted it. All of it. What do I do now?'*

She knew to her soul she wasn't devious enough to plot revenge, and neither did she have the resources to level the same degree of terror on Lion that he'd caused her. York was a wealthy sports legend, a celebrity who lived a secretive life surrounded by burly bodyguards who had, even on her best and bravest days, intimidated her. Until recently, she'd once been part of his inner circle. He'd proposed and bought her a three-carat diamond. He'd talked to her of marriage and a lavish wedding in Berlin, Germany, his hometown.

And then he tried to kill me.

A sob croaked out of her moisture-deprived throat. Unloved and unwanted for too long, she had to think. What was the best revenge? *Living.* For a woman with nothing to her name and less to show for her time on Earth, Suede meant to get her act together and start that living, as soon as she stopped crying.

But truth was a bitter pill to swallow. This was all her fault. Everything she'd done had led her to this low point. She was the one who'd alienated her friends until the only one left in her pathetic life was a creep like Lion. *What a joke, huh? Just when you think you don't need anyone, you—do.*

A big palm came out of nowhere and landed over the blanket on her right butt cheek. She hadn't heard the bedroom door open, but apparently, Chance was back, and there she was, ass up and head down.

"Hey. Are you okay?" he asked, his tone filled with worry.

Stupid, stupid question. She wasn't okay. She was as stupid as that question. "No..." she whined like the petulant child everyone thought she was, her face still in the pillow. At this precise moment, depressed and foolish were better descriptors. The fall was Lionel's fault, but Suede was no dummy. She owned every step of the way to the pit of despair she was now in.

"I suck," she admitted hoarsely, her face still buried in Chance's pillow. "I've been an idiot my whole life. I got myself into this mess. I just don't know how to fix it and my leg hurts and my butt hurts and... I'm the biggest loser!" Didn't that make her sound like the diva she was trying not to be? Apparently recreating herself was going to be harder than she thought.

That big warm hand smoothed over the blankets and up her spine to her shoulder. When he reached the edge of the covers, Chance tossed the blankets aside. For a brief moment, the blast of cool air on her bare backside reminded Suede that all she had on was his shirt, and she was showing more skin than she wanted.

But he seemed not to notice her southern exposure. Handily, Chance lifted her into his arms and curled her to his lap as he sat on the bed. Almost fatherly, he pulled the blankets up and re-covered her. His lips pressed to her forehead. "I was afraid of this. You're running a fever."

See? He doesn't want me either. The only reason he put his lips on me was to check my temperature. Suede couldn't believe how pathetic she felt, how miserable or how easily she'd slipped back into the role of being a whiner. *Wah!*

"There, there," Chance soothed as he popped the plastic tops off two small bottles on the nightstand. He refilled her glass from the bottle of water setting there and lifted it to her lips. "Drink."

Suede obeyed, swallowing the cool liquid past her sore teeth and tongue. Her mouth felt coated and thick with infection.

"I brought toast, bacon, and eggs if you're hungry. Would you like coffee?" he asked as he touched the pills to her lips.

Opening her mouth, she swallowed again. "Thank you, yes. You don't have to do any of this, but you are, and... and thank you for everything."

He drew the blanket up to her shoulders, wrapping her tight and rocking as if she were a little girl instead of a grown woman. This strange man had a way of getting past her prickly defenses, and maybe it was just that he'd saved her life, but being with him made her feel safe. Protected, maybe. She didn't trust it, and yet she did.

"Your only mission is to heal and get back in the game, Suede. Unless you develop complications, a couple days downtime ought to do it. That leg will heal. Then you'll be back to your old self in no time. You'll see."

She shook her aching head against his massive shoulder. "I'm not going back to my old self," she said, her voice more growl than whine. "Ever. I've been..." She gulped, not sure if he truly knew what an awful beast she'd been. Her parents deserved her leaving them, but everyone else she'd stepped on, trash-talked, or backstabbed since then hadn't deserved the nastiness she'd dished out. She had a lot of forgiveness to ask for, and she knew it. "I've been bad." *And dumb. I can't go back to being who I was. I want a new me.*

"You have been a firecracker," he agreed.

Wait. Is he laughing at me? Suede snuggled deeper into the warmth of his body and the blanket, embarrassed but a little pleased he knew something about her. "Which YouTube video did you see?"

He didn't laugh, but he did admit, "The one on the Ferris wheel is your all-time best. I think every red-blooded male in the civilized world has seen it maybe, oh, a thousand times."

She closed her eyes, ashamed at what Lionel had talked her into. Yes, she'd exposed herself with sass and flare, but the idea was his. He'd said it would make her parents look bad, and at the time, that was all she'd wanted, to embarrass them. To pay them back for the neglect at their hands. All he'd needed was an idiot to command, and she'd certainly stepped up to the plate, shook her ass and tits like a brain dead cheerleader and said, *'Ooooo, ooooo, pick me! Pick me!'*

"Like I said, I've been dumb, but I'm not going to be dumb any longer." The alcohol she'd drunk the morning of the *'Ferris wheel incident'* hadn't helped. She'd passed out after her gaudy performance and woke up in her bed at York's place, not sure how she'd gotten there and afraid to ask. The raunchy display, she remembered though. How could she forget?

Chance tilted back to peer down at her. "I hope you mean that, Suede. People can change, but only if they want to. The toughest hurdle to overcome is always the one in our own minds."

The ibuprofen must've started working. Suede nodded, sleepy and warm and finally feeling like she was on the right track.

"But it will be hard. You'll have to put blinders on and shut the world out for a while. You'll have to be determined and fierce, no matter what people say about you. You'll have to be brave. Can you do that?"

No one had insinuated she could be brave before. Ever. Her mom called her a nuisance and her dad said she was a sycophant. Suede cringed. She'd actually consulted Merriam Webster that day, she'd been so naive. Imagine the kick to her heart when she'd realized her parents thought she was a bootlicker and a flunky. A brown-noser. A parasite.

She scrubbed a quick hand over her face to hide behind, just for a second. So why had Chance Sinclair's words rung with inspiration? Why'd he make her think she could be brave when she'd never been courageous before?

Suede gathered her best intentions and answered as truthfully as she knew how. "I can be brave." *I think.*

Yeah. Had to be the meds.

Chapter Nine

Talk about the pot calling the kettle black. There Chance sat with a very seductive woman in his lap and he was telling her to be brave and courageous? Him? The guy who'd been licking his wounds for months while his brothers took up the slack?

Not any longer. Like fear, courage could be a wildfire that burst to life inside a man's gut, compelling him to action when he'd rather sit back while others did the dirty work. The unlikely soldier in Chance's lap had awakened someone he'd been hiding from. Himself. If Suede Tennyson, with her wild, sordid reputation could change, he could certainly get his ass back in the saddle and go active again. His heart kicked up a lively beat, and damn it. His old self emerged with its cocky swagger, ready to take on the world and Mr. York with it.

Suede lifted her chin, eyeing him as she licked her lips. "If you were me, what would you do first?" she asked, her voice timid.

The sincerity in her eyes melted his resolve. This was not what he'd expected in a diva. It threw him off balance and Chance Sinclair caved. There was life in this woman and an energy he needed as much as she did. "I'd kiss me." He took her mouth, tenderly because of her fat lip.

Suede blocked him at first, but softened with a sigh, just enough to mold her lips to his. Yet when he pressed for more and teased the seam of her mouth with his tongue, she resisted. Saturated and content with just the feel of this woman inside his arms, he let her win this round. Chance licked his way to her earlobe instead and whispered, "'*To thine own self be true*', Suede. Stop trying to please the world. Trust me, they're not worth it."

A tiny whine sounded deep in her throat. "You make it sound easy, but it's not. I've done so many things..." Her voice trailed away, but her lashes lifted, and he was lost in the ocean of her incredible blue eyes. He'd never fallen so hard. Tears glimmered like rainfall in a tropical island forest, and, damn it. *What the hell am I doing?*

Chance eased back from his patient. That was all she was, not a lover and not a friend. Just a woman he'd rescued like so many others from combat zones and perilous situations. Whatever this was between them, it was downright radioactive and he needed to back off. He'd overstepped his bounds because he thought he'd recognized something of himself in her, but it wouldn't happen again.

The drill instructor stuck forever inside his head kicked in. "The change has to come from inside. No one can want that more than you."

"I do, but—"

"But you're tired and sick." He eased her off his lap and onto the mattress, covering her tempting but wounded body before he got any more bright ideas or out of control impulses. "Breakfast first, then if you're up to it" —he quirked his head toward the open bathroom door— "maybe a shower or bath. Come on, let's get it done."

No response. Suede sat there with the blanket tugged up to her chin, her big blue doe-eyes glimmering. It wasn't hard to read what was going on in her head. Rejection. Maybe even betrayal. She was right. He'd led her on, then dumped her in a sixty-second reach for what, he wasn't sure. His natural male instinct to protect the females of his species he understood, but the fire in his gut was something else.

The second she'd come to, Suede had lit his cabin with a light no male on Earth possessed. Even near death, she was that sputtering candle glowing in a very dark room. She was ground zero, the epitome of what men lived and died for. The light in her deep blues threw him off balance as much as it grounded him. Suede was unexploded ordnance, nitroglycerine in its most volatile state, and he was that unstable environment where anything could happen. He couldn't get caught in her frag zone. It just Would. Not. Happen.

"How's that sound?" he asked, keeping his tone crisp and businesslike. Formal. A complete one-eighty from the passionate kiss he'd initiated that, oh yeah, like a smart woman, she'd initially resisted. But she'd wanted it, too. He damned well knew that much.

Her lashes fell. "Fine," she murmured to the blanket.

His hard head bobbed with relief. "Yes, ma'am. Coming right up."

The moment he lifted the lid off the tray at her bedside, ahem, his bedside, she sniffed at the breakfast aromas trapped under that aluminum dome. Her head lifted. "Bacon?"

"That's the spirit." Chance brandished the cloth napkin he'd stuck on the tray at the last moment on his way out of the kitchen.

"No, wait. I can scoot over to the edge..." Her long legs stretched out from under the blanket. "Ouch. Maybe not." She tipped to the right as she smoothed a hand over her left hip. "What happened to me? Why all the bandages?"

"Like I said before, you've got a nasty tear on your thigh," he reminded her. "Cream? Sugar?"

"Yes, please." Her head bobbed as he doctored her coffee.

"And to be honest, I had to lance a swollen bruise on your butt. I'm not sure how you got that, but it was seriously infected." He cocked his head as he handed her the mug. "Do you? Know how you received that nasty bruise?"

Her nose twitched, and for the first time, Chance noticed the red sprinkles over the creamy skin on her cheeks. Cinnamon sprinkles on sugar. Man, she was a delectable dessert from her toes to her nose. *How the male mind does wander...*

Suede cast him a sideways glance as her lips met the rim of the cup. She sipped, then sighed, and his heart thumped at the contentment she derived from a simple cup of coffee, Folgers at that. *Yeah, I'm in trouble.*

"Lionel likes to be..." She paused, but Chance caught the way her throat muscles worked extra hard to swallow that tiny sip. "He gets, umm, rough sometimes."

"He hit you?" Chance canted his head, daring her to lie.

Suede didn't look at him, but she nodded at her cup, her thumb tucked through the loop of the handle, her fingers clasping it firmly. The ponytail trembled. "Actually, he kicked me, but he said he was sorry and..." Again her voice faded to nothing more than a whine.

Like a damned white knight on a prancing steed, Chance caved. He dropped to one knee, needing to see her eyes. "Look at me, Suede. How long's he been abusive?"

She met his gaze with the same indifference he'd masked his feelings with just moments before. "Always, but he won't do that again, will he? It's not like you care, do you?"

Chance smiled. He'd nearly forgotten. Suede Tennyson had claws. She seemed to fluctuate between sweet and sassy, but she was wrong. He did care.

"Don't laugh at me," she spat. "I've had enough assholes in my fucking life and—"

"Enough!" He cut her tirade against the entire male gender off before it got started. He'd heard it before, maybe not from her, but he doubted her variation was much different than the others. "Rule number one: We don't swear in my house. We listen and we communicate with real words. We argue, but we keep it civil. It's called discourse, not character assassination. Understood?"

Her brows slanted together and her lips thinned. Chance touched his index finger to the center of that mean looking line before she could retaliate. "You're sick, Suede. I had no right taking advantage of you before, and I'm sorry I kissed you like I did. I got swept away by the moment because I do care, but this visit is temporary. Once you're well enough to travel, you'll be gone. You've got a life to get back to. You're a celebrity."

Her chin came up and she pitched forward, her eyes ablaze. "Why don't you follow your own damned rules and listen? What about *'I'm not going back'* don't you fucking understand?"

She had him there, but that mouth. Chance wrapped his hand around her coffee mug and took it from her without breaking eye contact. Once it was safely on the nightstand, he cupped his palm to her jaw, his heart pounding like a freight train.

Like it or not, healthy or not, Suede was about to get what she had coming to her.

Chapter Ten

What now? Another high-handed rule? Another goddamned order!

For two cents, Suede would've poured that cup of hot coffee over Chance's fat head just to prove she had some fight left in her. If he thought for one moment he could bully her after what she'd lived through with Lion, he had another—

Chance moved like he'd bounced off a spring-loaded trampoline. One minute he was at her knee, the next his hands were in her hair and his mouth was fastened to hers, and... *Oh, my, my, my.* Every last bit of her snark melted. The man moved like a mountain cat, fluid and lethal, his knees now on the bed as he dragged her along with him to the pillow. She could smell the coffee and bacon he'd eaten for breakfast on his breath. She could taste it on his lips. In his mouth. *Mmmmmm...*

I don't want you, her heart screamed, even as her poor bandaged fingertips dug into the massive shoulders hulking over her like a life preserver on a raging ocean and made her a liar. With every fiber of her shredded heart, she clung to this one last— Chance. Heaven knew she needed someone in her life, someone who at least pretended he cared.

One manly palm slid to her right hip, mapping the jut of her hipbone before it cupped her ass. "I'm not him," he breathed, the salty, smoky flavor on his lips a delightful mix of flavors on her tongue. "I'll never hurt you."

I know. I know!

Sucking that whisker-rimmed lip into her mouth, Suede threw everything she was into the sensual assault of this male. This was no boy masquerading in a man's body and acting tough. This guy was massive power and ripped muscle backed up by intelligence and experience. He knew how to hold her. Where to squeeze. When to let go.

Chance made two of York, but he was considerate, and unlike the bully she'd lived with, he was gentle in his possession of her mouth. *A SEAL, huh?* The thought flitted over her unsettled brain like a butterfly on a spring breeze that couldn't decide where to land. The time for thinking had passed. Too much fire boiled in her veins to hold back now.

Chance plundered her mouth with finesse, tangling his tongue with hers, nipping at her lips, bumping teeth, and growling as if he hadn't eaten in days. Her body responded with wanton delight, lust popping under her skin like sparklers on the Fourth of July. The slut everyone thought they'd seen in the media, the one the press portrayed as willing to fuck any guy in sight, was actually a frigid klutz in bed. She had no skills, but this man seemed to know how to light her fuse. He was enjoying this. She could tell by the way he purred low in his throat. Best of all, he knew exactly what to do with that amazing mouth of his.

The scruff on his chin and around his mouth scraped her tender lips and her chin, but still she wanted more. When a powerful knee wedged its way between her thighs, she widened her knees, but damn. She couldn't go down that road. Not again!

This firestorm had to end before she got caught in the same trap. This time around had to be different—*had to*—or it would end like all the others. *Slam. Bam. Thank you ma'am, and out the door you go, yesterday's news. Good for nothing but sex.*

Her palms slid to his chest to push him away, and there they stopped, full of the throbbing, bulging muscles of a man who worked out. A lot. *Impressive.* Chance was as solid as the granite mountain behind his cabin. Bunched and corded, his chest flexed as he supported his weight on his forearms. A woman had to linger at the massive pecs pressed so adamantly into her palms and against her breasts and...

Oh, my, my, my, yes, yes, yes. All man. To hell with being a good girl. I want you. But the shirt in her way had to go. Growling like Chance now, Suede tugged it loose from his jeans and—

"Uh-uh," he groaned in her mouth, his arms trembling as much as her fingers.

A smile quirked her lips at the power she seemed to hold over this honorable man. "Are you sure?" she whined, just to be certain she'd heard right.

"No," he said, his breath in her mouth as delectable as the lips and tongue lathing hers. "I mean, yes. I'm sure. I'm not here to use you, Suede. I won't do that."

You won't? Those words took a minute to sink into her overheated brain. Despite wanting to change her life, she'd done it again, spread her legs out of habit. Men used her. It was what they did, and she'd let them, only now... Chance said no. *What the fuck?*

Fragments of the oath he'd spouted earlier came back to her. *You can trust me, ma'am. I served with honor... Uncompromising integrity... My word is my bond.* Therein lay the difference. Chance might be caught up in the heat of the moment—*who wasn't?*— but his intentions were different from the other men who'd used her. The ones she'd used in return. God, what a rotten life she'd led up to this point. This had to stop. She had to change.

Swallowing her passion and her pride, Suede eased back to maintain her thin hold on control. That was a mighty difficult first. Breathless and speechless, she decided it wasn't enough to be just another temptress. Until this impulsive moment, Chance had treated her like a lady. Once upon a time, she'd been one. She could—she would—do it again. *Maybe I can stop cursing, too. For him. Just for him. As soon as he moves his hot, hot body off me.*

Confused and out of her element, she kissed her way to his impressive chin, then settled her lips out of temptation's path at the hollow of his neck. He'd showered this morning, and the alcoholic drift of pine and cedar aftershave on his clean skin wasn't helping her turn this all-important corner in her life. But if he could control his passion—*and it was so, so hard*—she'd follow his lead.

Suede closed her eyes and moved her wandering fingertips far away from his zipper to his heaving sides, his safe zones. Her palms settled to his waist, and slowly, his palms settled at her hips, his nose in her hair and his heartbeat a throbbing hammer in his chest.

"I don't want to use you, either," she told him, keeping her voice devoid of the coaxing, come-on tones that worked on York. She had some skills as a slut, but she put them aside, and for once Suede meant to deal with Chance reasonably. Logically. With real words like he'd said. He was different from York in every way, and if she acted like she had before, she'd end up with nothing to show for her near-death experience but a roll in the sack with a stranger.

Sex with this man—if ever—would be incredible, but it had to come last, not first. After friendship, not before. Once they knew each other better than they did now. At the moment, they were barely acquaintances without much restraint, much less friends with benefits. If only she could stop the zany butterflies that had taken flight in her chest.

A manly chuckle vibrated up his throat. "I'm the guy here, remember. Isn't that my line?"

She shook her head. "No," she replied, still working on ignoring the tempting male body poised over her. Nature was a cruel mother to instill such wicked automatic impulses in her male and female creatures. Even now, the tip of Suede's tongue lifted to lick his neck, to taste the salty flavor of this magnificent man. She resisted the temptation. "I'm pretty sure it takes two. Every time. I'm not a victim. I'm as much to blame for this predicament as" — gulp— "you are."

It had taken nearly dying to realize that her life was a fucked-up, umm, a big mess, but Suede knew it now. Change had to come from within and it had to start right now.

"I think I care for you," she told her savior honestly. Resolutely. Chance might as well know what he was up against. Forewarned was forearmed, and all that stuff. That way he could push her away while the leaving was still easy. No strings. No happily-ever-afters. She didn't believe in that crap anyway.

He rolled to her side, but took her with him, his long fingers splayed like a catcher's mitt in the middle of her back. "I'm here to help," he whispered, his chest heaving as much as hers and his voice as tight. "Just ask."

Suede nodded, but didn't dare tell him how much his unexpected kindness meant. Anything she said now would only add fuel to the fire she needed to tamp down, the bright fire that was already burning out of control in her heart.

Chapter Eleven

Twice! I've kissed her twice, and damn, I want to do it again. Chance lay breathing hard on his back, one forearm draped over his eyes, his other still around Suede, and his fingers aching to do more than massage and medically treat her delightful body. Even as banged up as she was, he knew a real woman when he held one, and Suede Tennyson was a luscious, tempting armful.

But damn. He couldn't believe how easily he'd lost control. He swallowed hard, his throat dry and his body humming. She was injured, no doubt had whiplash from her fall, yet he'd been on the verge of taking her. Right here. Right now. Like a pig in rut. And she'd responded, melting that luscious body to his. Molding herself. Moaning into his mouth. Yeah. None of this was right, and he knew better. They were both running on emotions and this was sheer torture. It had to stop.

Chance drew in a deep breath to steady his physical reaction as much as his mind. The worst—or the best—was yet to come. He still had to help Suede into the shower, and change those dressings. The thigh wound would be easy enough. He had latex-free waterproof coverings to tape over the packing to keep it dry, but that hole on her hip was another thing. He hadn't stitched it on purpose. It needed to drain, and that, in and of itself, was no big deal. But it was On. Her. Ass. And that ass was fast becoming a problem.

She said she cared for him, but he knew better. Females tended to crush on the guy who came to their rescue. It happened a lot during and after hostage operations. The females got dewy-eyed and flirty. They sent thank-you cards and left their phone numbers once they were home safe, ones Chance had never called. He wasn't going to start now.

It'd be—hard. Just thinking the word sent his palm to his pants, needing to choke the little brain lurking there that overruled his good intentions. He wasn't a bastard who used and abused women, but Suede brought the animal in him to the surface in a quick way. He didn't dare think of her in a dress or when she was on her A-game, intentionally flirty. He'd lose.

Mind out of the gutter. Back to business. "Your coffee's getting cold," he said, clearing his throat when his tone sounded harsher than he intended. "I'll let you eat. Be right back."

Settling her back against the pillow, he set the breakfast tray on her lap and her cup of coffee within reach on the nightstand. He lingered just long enough to press a chaste kiss to her forehead, more to assure her that he wasn't deserting her than anything else. *Nothing more.*

Chance cleared the bathroom of his towels and dirty clothes, then vacated his bedroom, intending to make a quick call to Sullivan before he started what looked to be several loads of laundry if he counted Pagan's. His heart pounded as he shut the door quietly behind him.

"You kissed her," hissed out of his brother's big mouth. Pagan stood there by the fireplace, his thick hair wet from his shower, one forearm on the thick pine mantle, his other hand in his pocket. Gallo waggled at his knee. "Didn't you?"

"Shut the hell up," Chance shot back at him. "You're supposed to be resting." *So mind your business.*

"And you're supposed to be on the wire to Sullivan."

"On my way," Chance replied without meeting Baby Brother's sharp eye. "Now back off."

Pagan followed him down the east hall that led to their communications room and his office, the workout room, laundry, and Kruze's room in that order. "I knew it. You're in love with this chick. Shit, Chance. It's only been one night. What are you thinking?"

Chance growled as he dropped the load into the rolling laundry basket and backtracked to his desk to make that call. "I'm *not* in love, dumbass. She needed help. I helped. End of story." *Not.*

"I call bullshit," Pagan insisted as Chance sank into his leather chair. "I know trouble when I see it, and you're in trouble. Big time. It's written all over your ugly face. Admit it."

Two monitors lined the desktop. One keyboard. Deftly, Chance brought up Sullivan's private line and turned his back on Pagan. Baby Brother needed to learn when to shut up. Now'd be a good time.

The Senator picked up on the first ring. The monitor flickered to life as Chance acknowledged his supervisor. "Good morning, Senator."

"Not unless you know something I don't," Sullivan replied, his lips set in a thin line as his gaze drifted out the window of the car he was riding in. Back seat. Behind the driver. Most likely his limousine. Tall as a Texas fence post and just as weathered, the silver-haired giant of a man was a cattle baron in his home state and a miracle worker at compromise in D.C. The man hardly ever smiled. His fingertips worried the ends of his handlebar mustache when he turned to his in-car monitor and stared Chance down. "What?"

"Permission to speak frankly, sir."

"Cut the Navy bullshit, son, and stop calling me sir. You got something to say, spit it out. Make it quick. I'm busy."

"Is this line secure?"

Sullivan's bushy brows dropped as he leaned forward and activated the privacy screen between his driver and the rear seat. He flipped another set of buttons and said, "Is now."

"Pagan arrived early this morning with the assignment from you to end York," Chance declared brusquely. "Not sure why you didn't contact me first, but I'll be taking it."

"What else?" That was interesting. The busy senator's head bobbed once, but he'd offered no explanation as to why he'd tagged Pagan. Whatever was going on, Sullivan was playing hardball.

"I have Suede Tennyson in protective custody after she was thrown off my mountain late last night in the middle of the blizzard. You know the one I mean." Chance gave that a second to sink in before he reinforced it with, "You've got a mole in your staff."

"The bastard chucked her over the edge? I'm surprised she's alive. How bad is she?"

"Nothing's broken, but she'll be down awhile. She could use a change of clothes, a decent winter jacket, and boots before I move her to a hospital in the valley."

Another nod told Chance those supplies would be delivered to his front door via drone once the weather cleared. "I knew York was in Montana, but I didn't realize Miss Tennyson was with him. So the wedding of the century is off." Another evil-eyed squint and Sullivan's lips pinched to the side. "Which begs the questions, why your mountain and who knew what, right? That why you're calling me out, son?"

"Yes." Chance bit his lip at the automatic 'sir' that nearly tumbled out of his mouth. Navy habits died hard. "My question is how York knows where I am, and if he also knows he's at the top of your hit list. This can't be a coincidence. Someone on the SOB Force had to have fed him that intel."

"I'll check into it." Those silver brows collided like two Rocky Mountain rams in spring rut.

"Just to clarify, I'm taking him down because he's trafficking drugs?" Chance asked. It wasn't often Sullivan went after drug dealers. They were plenty worth the effort, and Chance would gladly wipe every last one of them off the face of the planet, but for the most part, they were no more bothersome than mosquitoes in a world gone crazy with the more dangerous suicide bombers, unprovoked attacks on civilians, and the continual threat from the Mideast.

Sullivan had set up a strict protocol to this federally funded, blackest of black ops worlds. All the teams he'd assembled operated outside the law, yet all were comprised of men who'd honorably served America as spec ops guys while in the military, CIA, or FBI SWAT. After witnessing man's depravity to man and various nations' failures to protect the people, the men Sullivan had tagged pledged allegiance to the SOBs to make a difference. They wanted to turn the tide of evil in the world while it was still doable.

None took their assignments lightly, and each decision to end a life required a unanimous vote from each individual team leader before any job. From that point, the team leader decided who did the actual hit. No reports were filed afterward, nor was forensic evidence collected at any scene. Once the selected agent reported job complete, the SOBs moved on.

Surprisingly, among men who'd seen what most combat-hardened SEALs, Green Berets, Rangers, PJs, and SWAT officers had, there tended to be more unanimous votes than not.

Discussion, when it surfaced, was brief, punctuated with acronyms, and buried in code. But decisive and final. Predators existed. The SOBs vowed to end them, and one by one, they were.

Were the SOBs a behind-the-scenes organization to exact justice for crimes against man and nature? Hell yeah. Was it legal? Authorized? Moral? In a redacted, change-the-names-to-protect-the-innocent kind of a way, yes. Could the men who stood up and answered another call to serve their country be termed super heroes? Chance nearly grunted at the notion that he or his brothers were anything like Iron Man, Superman, or Thor. He'd heard the banter amongst the other team leaders. If anything, they were *supper* heroes. Just ring that dinner bell and see who came running. But this time was different. Something bigger was going on. Chance tried again. "Was there a vote I missed since the last time we talked?"

"York's involved with some cartel out of South America, but it's not just the drugs..." Sullivan slow-rolled that lead-in, his gaze out the window again. "This is out of my hands, Chance. Can you do it or do I need to get someone else?" That stung. Sullivan knew Chance's demons, but he also knew his record as a SEAL. And Chance knew what he was really asking. *Are you fit for duty or not?*

"I can handle York," Chance replied evenly. *Especially since he's in my territory, but man. This guy had to be high on somebody's radar to force Sullivan's hand. What's really going on?*

"How long will it take?"

Chance rolled his neck as he mentally sized up and calculated climbing Old Man Mountain in this weather. It'd be tough, but he'd climbed tougher in worse conditions. Winter ops weren't any different than others, just a helluva lot colder. Slippery. "Forty eight hours, tops. Can you confirm York hasn't heloed out of here yet?" There was no sense wasting time going after a man who wasn't there. A satellite image would be helpful, but that wasn't happening in this storm.

Sullivan's silver head bobbed again. His eyes narrowed. More lethal bear traps hadn't yet been made. "He was there an hour ago. Give me five to ensure he's still on-site." The mute button flashed to vivid green in the lower right corner of the monitor as Sullivan switched frequencies and double-checked his intel.

"You need to know who else is up there with him," Pagan added from the doorjamb where he lounged, his ankles crossed. "You can bet he's not alone."

"Copy that," Chance agreed, "but I've only got the green light to off York. By the way, you're grounded. If I'm going up, you're staying down here with Miss Tennyson."

Pagan grunted. "So it's *Miss Tennyson* now, not *Suede baby*?"

"It'll always be Miss Tennyson to you." Chance made that clear. "Do me a favor. Pull the black ops file on York, and there had better be one. We need to know what's really going on. Sullivan's not acting like himself."

Pagan's chin hit his chest in an affirmative. Lifting the ruggedized laptop from its docking station, he headed to the kitchen as Sullivan re-engaged with more bad news. The wrinkles etched on his forehead hadn't let up since he'd taken the call. "Sorry, Chance. The timetable's been moved up. We need York out of play, the quicker the better. I can only give you twenty-four hours."

"Roger that."

"And Chance," Senator Sullivan cut in. "Make it hurt."

"Yes, sir," Chance snapped back, wincing as he did. "Keep your ears on." He ended the call. Shoving out of the chair, he headed to his room.

"One last goodbye kiss?" Pagan taunted from the kitchen table where he'd set the laptop.

Chance let him think what he wanted. "Check this place for bugs while you're at it. Do it now. It's just possible our guest is an unwilling pawn in a bigger game, that she brought something in with her. Sullivan's too antsy. Something's up."

"Will do." Pagan might growl and complain, but he snapped to when needed.

Chapter Twelve

At his bedroom door, Chance knocked. Her shower, bath, whatever had to wait. "Suede?" he called out, his ear cocked for her reply. He didn't want to wake her, but he would if he had to. He needed answers.

A soft "Come in" answered. Entering the room, he shut the door behind him and settled his back to it instead of crossing the room. Facing her brought the same feverish rush of emotions back to him. The breakfast tray was now on the nightstand with the cup. Even hurt as badly as she was, she was a beauty, but that wasn't what drew him. It was that tiny hand she'd stuck between them during that kiss, her fingers spread over his chest when she'd drawn the line. A man had to respect that and he did, but it told him a lot about her, too.

Right now it rested at her throat. Suede's delicate brows lifted over two blue eyes that were quickly turning black and blue. "What's wrong?"

"Tell me everything about York's camp. How did you get up top? Did you hike in? Fly in by helo?"

She nodded, her eyes wide. "Early yesterday morning while the sun was shining. A chopper dropped us off, but there was already a camping module in place. On skids. I guess another helicopter dropped it off earlier. Two of his guys came with us. There's an old cabin up there too, but it was empty, and we only peeked inside. The photographer should've arrived at noon, but the weather turned and no one showed. Why? What's going on?"

Chance shook his head, not willing to provide answers she wasn't ready to hear. "Is he armed?"

Blink. Blink. Blink. "Yes. He carries a pistol in a holster inside the back of his pants and a smaller one on his ankle, but that's no big deal. Everyone does it."

Maybe in her world that was true, but it smacked of underworld ties. "What kind of pistols?"

A dimple tweaked her cheek. "I don't know. They're... black. One's big. One's small." This woman needed a lesson on guns in the worst way.

"Did you ever see him use them? Has he killed anyone in front of you?"

"No."

"Did he bring luggage? Did you?"

Her bandaged hands smoothed the wrinkles out of the blanket over her lap. "He said we weren't staying long, only until the light changed, you know, for the photographer, so I only brought what I had on."

"What did you two talk about?"

"Stuff. Our engagement. My ring." The cords of her neck visibly tightened as she swallowed. Her fingers stiffened on the blanket. "My dad."

"What about your father?"

She stalled, her brows turned into delicate arches. The light in her stormy blues had turned grayer with every question. "What's this about, Chance? You're scaring me."

He pushed for more intel instead of comforting her, his first inclination. "Answer me. What'd York want to know about your dad?"

Her cheeks puffed with a deep breath. "He asked me how many bodyguards Dad employs these days, but how would I know? I left home four years ago, and I haven't been back. It's not like we ever talked much when I lived there anyway."

"What did you tell him?"

Her tongue made the rounds again, moistening her lips, and Chance wished he were taking care of that personal chore for her. "I told him five as far as I knew, but Dad might have hired more since I left."

"What'd he say to that?"

"He grunted and said, umm..." Her eyes narrowed as if she were trying to remember. "He said that jived, but then he clammed up, and he wanted to see my ring again. He took it off my finger and... and..." Her eyes brimmed.

"Don't cry, Suede," Chance said quietly. "York isn't worth it."

"But he took my ring and shoved me, and I didn't realize how close we'd gotten to the edge, and he kept shoving me, and when I stumbled, he... he kicked me, Chance. Can you believe that?" She leaned into her words, her fingertips fluttering over the swells of her breasts. "He. Kicked. *Me.*"

It took every last ounce of strength Chance had not to run to her, enfold her in his arms, and promise no one would ever hurt her again. Despite the sex-kitten allure of her, there was no denying the innocent disbelief radiating in those stormy, tropical blues. For the past years, she'd trusted York to some degree, and he'd betrayed her in the vilest ways possible. He'd stamped more than just that waffle-tread bruise above her blackening eyes.

"I know, Suede. I know. He's lived outside the law long enough. It's time he answers for his crimes." Chance clenched his hands behind his back, knowing that if he took one step toward Suede, she'd be in his arms. It was time to confess what little he could. "Your ex has been under investigation by the outfit I work for. He's more dangerous than we suspected."

That didn't explain why Sullivan had blown past all protocol stops for this particular hit, though. That by itself plagued Chance with enough doubt to call the senator back and demand NOT to be treated like a hired gun without scruples or honor. The rules were clear. Every sanctioned hit had to be vetted by all team leaders in this *chicken shit* outfit, Pagan's words, not Chance's, before Sullivan gave the green light.

True, it wasn't often team leaders turned down a sanctioned job, but it happened. Pagan had better find more than bureaucratic redacted roadblocks in York's file or this mission was going nowhere.

Suede's eyes widened. "He's dangerous? You think I don't know that? What are you going to do? Kill him because he tried to murder me?"

Bingo. Chance kept his game face on and his expression blank, but her eyes lit up with enlightenment. "You are, aren't you?" She leaned forward, her bandaged fingers cupped together on her lap. "You're going to kill Lionel York. It's impossible. Don't go. Chance, please don't go."

He froze. It wasn't fear shimmering in her eyes, it was outright terror. What on Earth had this poor woman lived through at York's hand? Chance softened his tone. "For all he knows, you're dead, and I'm not certain he knows I live in these parts. I'm willing to confront the bastard and make certain he never comes after you again."

"But... but he's a black belt and he plays dirty." Her voice pitched higher. "I've seen him fight with his guys. They never won."

"Then he's about to meet his match, isn't he?"

She tugged the blanket under her chin as if she needed to protect herself from him now, too. "W-w-who *are* you?"

Truth or dare. He stared her down and gave her what he could. "I'm the guy who keeps ladies who've just been shoved off mountains safe for the rest of their lives." That begged another question. "What happened to your coat, Suede? Why weren't you wearing one when I found you?"

Blink. Blink. "He... he..." Her lips thinned and her teeth clamped down on the bottom one. "He... he wanted me to undress. Up there. In the storm. He likes to play games, but the way he said it scared me, and I said n-n-n-o, that I wasn't a c-complete idiot."

Humiliation radiated between Chance and Suede the second she said that word—*idiot*. The degradation she'd endured lifted up her neck like a red wave, coloring her cheeks before her lashes dropped to hide her shame.

It broke Chance's heart when she rolled the blanket beneath her bandaged fingertips into a small line of defense. Suede believed herself an idiot. Damn the bastards who'd made her feel this way, and that included her self-serving parents and any high school jock who'd ever minimized her. Chance wanted to beat the shit out of every last one of them—after he killed York.

Focus!

"So he took your coat in the middle of a raging blizzard? He wanted you naked?" *The asshole.*

Her head bobbed. "He wanted everything," she said to the blanket beneath her fidgeting fingers. "My coat. His ring. My—"

"Suede," Chance barked loud enough to bring her head up. "Eyes on me. This isn't about you, so stop with the pity party." *Now I'm being a total ass, but I can't tell her I care because, damn it. I do.*

She looked at him then, her gaze desolate. "You don't understand," she said, her voice as small as a whisper. "I have nothing. I am nothing. He owns me. My clothes. My shoes. Everything. That's why he threw me away. I was just another—"

"Bullshit!" burst out of Chance before he could call it back. "He might want you to believe that, but you know better. You're beautiful. You're smart. You're..." *Digging yourself a deep hole here, buddy.* Chance changed the subject before he waxed any more complimentary with this particular lady. "Listen. I have to take off for awhile, but my brother's here. He'll stay with you until I get back, so if you need anything, yell at him and he'll get it for you."

"Wh-what's his name?" The outright fear in her tone rattled him. "When did h-he get here?"

"Pagan Sinclair. He's my baby brother, so don't worry. He'll mind his business unless you need something." *Or I'll break his neck when I get back.* To make certain she felt safe, Chance opened the door and called, "Here, boy."

Gallo slinked into the room, his head down and his tail between his legs as if he'd done something wrong.

Suede let out a tight little chuckle that caught in her throat. "Oh, a dog." Her lips pursed with a puff of relief. "I thought you, umm, called your brother, 'boy'."

"If I was calling him, I'd use stronger language," Chance teased to lighten the mood, "but no, this guy's Gallo. Pagan's more of a cocker spaniel type. I'll introduce him before I leave, but this guy'll be better company. Protect," he ordered.

That brought Gallo's ears up as quickly as Suede's. He took his place at her side, his big radar ears pitched forward and the guilty look wiped off his funny face. For a minute there, Gallo almost looked like he knew what he was doing.

"Protect?" she asked. "He's a guard dog? Can I pet him?"

"You bet, and no, he's not a guard dog yet, but he's learning. On the bed, Gallo. Keep her happy while I'm gone." It touched Chance to see the affection Suede lavished on his crazy hound. Gallo didn't look dangerous at all lying on his back with all four paws in the air and getting his belly scratched by her taped fingers.

The tension in the room dropped to zero until Suede lifted her face from the full body hug she'd bestowed on the dog. "Tell me. Who are you?"

He blew out a stiff breath of certainty. "At the moment, I'm your best bet against guys like York. Get some rest while I'm gone. I'll help you with that shower tomorrow. Promise."

"Kiss me goodbye?"

He sucked in a long draw of uncertainty. It'd been awhile since he'd been this close with a woman he couldn't resist. The SEAL flies and ex-wives hunting for wedding rings and pensions in Coronado were easy to spot, but this gal had gotten under his radar in a big way, and she'd done it in less than a day. Better yet, Suede seemed unaware of her natural charms. That moment she'd stuck her chin at him and told him she cared was an unexpected bonus. It was a dare, plain and simple. A truthful dare he had to handle with care so he didn't mislead her. A little finesse wouldn't hurt. Too bad, he didn't have any.

Despite her notorious rep, he liked Suede, but the last thing she needed in her life was another jerk. He wasn't finished with his wars yet, and when she found out that he'd offed her ex—if he did—well, Chance didn't want to go there. At best, they were two ships in the dark of one, maybe two, bad nights. It'd be best if they kept sailing in opposite directions.

If his feet would only move.

Her lashes dropped. "I want to do things with you," she whispered.

Heavens, me too. Kiss you. Fondle you. Make you scream when you come and—

"Like a picnic. Maybe go for a walk. Get to know you better."

Oh, that. He swallowed hard, his horny mind on a completely different agenda. She was no pure little angel, but Suede Tennyson was no hardcore tramp either. She deserved better than the cards she'd been dealt, and if she wanted a picnic, Chance could do that.

He walked to his bed and took a knee at her side. Cupping her jaw between both his callused hands, he leaned in and kissed her forehead instead of her tempting lips. "Rest easy, kid. I'll be back by morning."

Chapter Thirteen

"Did you find it?" Chance asked as he stepped out of his bedroom, his gear bags in hand. He kept a couple packed for moments when he needed to make a quick exit. All SEALs did.

Pagan rocked on the back legs of his kitchen chair, another cup of coffee in his hand. "Yes, but there's not much in York's file we don't know. I've tagged Halen Diego, boss of the *Dia de Muertos,* to see what they have on York since most of his illegal business has been south of the border."

"There's got to be a reason Sullivan wants York put down, no questions asked."

"Agreed, but whatever it is, there's nothing in the dossier, and I didn't find any bugs in this cabin, either. I did find a link between Sullivan and Tennyson when I was snooping around Sullivan's email, though. They went to Yale together. Same frat house and all that bullshit."

Interesting. That piece of intel went in Chance's rear pocket for later scrutiny. He had somewhere else to be. "Make sure Suede stays hydrated and gets her meds. All I've been giving her are the antibiotic and anti-inflammatory on her nightstand. You got anything stronger?"

"Just what I usually carry."

Chance shook his head. "Not whiskey. Her lungs are already compromised."

"Then I'll just keep her warm and fed. Half of recovery is rest anyway."

"True." Chance nodded at his closed door. "I'll introduce you before I go. Gallo's already in there."

The chair scraped as Pagan shoved to his feet. His big hand threaded through his thick dark hair like he thought he needed to look good, and that irked Chance. He rolled his shoulder and let it go. Now was not the time to get possessive over a sick woman who wasn't planning on staying once the weather cleared anyway.

Chance knocked softly as he re-opened the door. Sleepy and snug, with Gallo lying alongside, Suede offered a weak wave. "Hey, Chance."

He nodded at her, shocked at how much he liked his name on her lips. "Suede Tennyson, meet my brother, Pagan Sinclair. He's here to wait on you hand and foot until I get back, so keep him busy." Chance turned to Pagan. "A bowl of soup for lunch would be a nice start."

Pagan nodded, but the big ox seemed tongue-tied. His head kept bobbing, and there went that hand again, brushing over his head as if he could begin to tame his outrageous hat-hair.

"It's nice to meet you," Suede said. "Pagan, huh? That's an interesting name."

"Yeah, well..." Did Pagan just blush?

Chance knuckled his brother's meaty bicep. "Say something."

Pagan cleared his throat. "Howdy," came out of nowhere.

Wasn't that something, a big guy like him flummoxed over meeting a tiny thing like Suede Tennyson? Chance would've enjoyed the moment more if he hadn't been leaving said lady with his horny brother for the next twenty-four hours. "Okay then. I'll see you tomorrow."

"Don't go," whooshed out of Suede as Chance turned to the door.

"I'll..." Pagan pointed beyond the bedroom door just before he exited, stage left, "be out there."

Chance shot him a look for bailing, the coward. "I have work to do," he told Suede in no uncertain terms.

"But I have a bad feeling, and I... I don't want you to go. It's too dangerous."

Chance went to her bedside, sat down and gave her the talk he imagined thousands of SEALs gave their wives right before they deployed to places unknown. "I have work to do for our country, Suede.

That's the way I was made and the path I chose. I told you I'll be back, and I will. You have to rest while I'm gone. Can you do that for me?"

She nodded. "Be very careful up there."

"Yes, ma'am," he replied, his tone firm, "and you do what you're told. By the time I get back, maybe you'll feel good enough to join my brother and me in the living room. There's a larger fireplace out there. It will do you good to be up on your feet."

"I do feel better now that I'm warm."

He placed a palm to her forehead. "Not today. It's too soon. Pagan will make sure you get your meds on time so just stay put."

Her lips pinched to a thin line, and Chance knew he'd better leave before he kicked Gallo to the floor and crawled into bed beside Suede. "You're stronger than you know," he told her.

A twinkle flittered from beneath her lowered brows. "I am."

Chance pushed to his feet, meaning to walk away and let whatever was meant to happen, happen. Until he returned, she'd have to rely on Pagan. Chance would never intentionally jerk his brothers around, but things happened. The heart loved who it loved, and all that crap. If Pagan fell for her charms while Chance was gone, well, good on him.

Liar.

At the door, Chance glanced over his shoulder. Suede had straightened in the bed, and yes, by hell, she was watching him. There wasn't a man alive who could miss the hope shining in her eyes. Of course, Pagan would fall for her. They'd make a handsome match, one of those fairytale endings. He still had his looks. What was not to love about the big teddy bear?

Big, fat liar.

Suede lifted one hand and blew Chance a tiny kiss from those poor ragged fingertips. In return, he winked. That was all. It was just a wink. A guy thing. Winks didn't mean anything.

Bull. Shit.

He closed the door on the woman he now knew for certain he'd lay down his life for. Damn. Leaving her was nearly impossible.

"You didn't tell me she was gorgeous," Pagan accused from his kitchen chair, all ten of his fingers drumming the closed lid of the laptop like a piano keyboard.

"She's not," Chance shot back at him in a whispered growl. *She's stunning. Sexy. Out of this world.*

"And she needs lunch? Shit man, what'll I fix for a woman like her? A can of Campbell's soup won't cut it. She's used to caviar and fancy stuff."

"She'll eat whatever you put in front of her, but yeah. Some kind of soup would be best." That was what Scarlett had always fixed her boys when they were sick, right before she told them, *no, you're not staying home from school because of a little sneeze and a sniffle. Good try, but drag your butt to class.*

A smile teased Chance's lip remembering his spitfire mother. She would've liked Suede, and why the hell that notion popped into his hard head, he hadn't had a clue. All these thoughts about obedient wives and bossy mothers had to stop. Suede was leaving, not staying. THAT was the way it was.

At his front door, he paused long enough to gear up. He stripped down to his boxers and donned a pair of synthetic thermal underwear from his supply closet. A light woolen sweater and pants combo came next, then another all-in-one thermal suit, a heavy breathable jacket and pants. The key to surviving winter ops began at the fundamental level of knowing how to keep warm and dry even when a guy sweated up a storm.

Settling down to the bench next to the closet, he donned two pairs of woolen socks and knee high gaiters to keep the snow out of his boots. He rolled the gaiters up his shins, then stuffed his feet into a pair of ruggedized hiking boots with built-in cleats meant for glacier climbing. Chance topped his outfit off with a gray bandana tied at his neck, an insulated winter camouflaged jacket, and a gray woolen beanie for his head. UV-protective snow goggles went inside his chest pocket.

Winter camouflaged pants, white snow boots, climbing gear, his usual dozen or so weapons and supporting ammo. It either went on him or into his bag. Lastly, he grabbed a couple coiled ropes for the trek ahead. His gear bag already contained enough energy bars and several liters of water to see him through the next twenty-four, as well as a decent supply of foot warmers and a thermal pad if forced to sit a while.

Before he zipped up, he ran a wire from the fully charged transmitter in his pack to the receiver in his ear and stuffed a gray balaclava in his hip pocket. The nylon back rifle holster went next, then his AR, fully loaded and ready to mince meat.

"Can you hear me now?" Pagan asked, tapping the mic he always wore on his collar just to irritate Chance.

That earned a glare. "You know damned well I can hear you. You're standing two feet away. Comm check me once I'm outside, why don'tcha?"

"Here, you'll need this" —Pagan slapped a tube of lip protection in Chance's open palm— "to keep those manly lips ready for action when you get back."

"Shut the hell up." Chance slapped the tube away, pissed Pagan reminded him that he was going and she was staying. "Keep this frequency open. If you find anything more on York, pass it along. Or Tennyson and Sullivan, too. Got it?"

Pagan grinned. "Trust me. I'll take care of everything while you're gone."

Not what Chance wanted to hear, especially if too much of that *care* extended to Suede. "And don't forget to feed Gallo. Can you do me a favor? I still owe him for finding Suede like he did. Give him a chunk of that roast in the fridge after I leave. He'll like that, but chain him on the porch, so he doesn't come after me. He'd like that, too."

"Aye, aye, Cap'n," Pagan growled. "Now take off. I've got work to do."

Chance thumped his brother's wide bicep, stabbed his hands into his climbing gloves and opened the door. "Until tomorrow," he signed off.

Pagan turned serious then. "Any trouble, any at all, you 9-11 me."

"Roger that," Chance agreed. "Keep your ears on."

Pagan tapped the side of his head where his twenty-four-seven earpiece rested deep inside his ear canal. "You got it. And Chance..." He turned earnest then. "I will take good care of Suede. You know that, don't you?"

Chance nodded. "Later, brother."

Chapter Fourteen

Chance had always knocked first, but Pagan just opened the bedroom door and whistled for Gallo like invading a woman's privacy was no big deal. The big dog bounded off the bed without so much as a goodbye glance, and Pagan slammed the door without saying a word.

Suede fidgeted, wondering if Chance was already gone. Tired and sleepy, she couldn't settle down knowing he might be on his way into a vicious storm to confront an even more vicious man.

No one knew Lionel York like Suede did. The man was heartless. He claimed he'd been faithful since they'd hooked up, but she had her doubts. He knew too many models and celebrities, and he spent too many unexplained nights away from his penthouse suite. Who'd Chance think he was to take on York all by himself, *Superman*?

He just might be.

She leaned back into the pillow where only an hour ago Chance had lovingly kissed the hell out of her. Touching her tender fingertips to her lip, she sent a prayer to the God she hadn't spoken to in years. *I know I don't have any right to ask favors, but could you please keep him safe? For him. For me too.*

That should've settled her nerves, but it didn't. Tired of lying in bed, she eased both feet to the floor, determined to be up and moving by the time Chance returned, if she was still here.

Suede lifted to her feet, bound and determined to be mobile. She took a minute to stretch her arms over her head, her back muscles protesting all the way down to her butt. Her bones popped and cracked, or maybe those were her muscles. Wow. That fall could've ended her. Surprised it hadn't broken anything, she arched backward, clenching her shoulder blades to determine how she felt. Except for the burning sensation in her thigh, not too bad.

With no clothes to change into, she shuffled over to Chance's closet like an elderly woman, her soles flat to the floor and using the mattress, then the footboard for support. As much as she was beginning to care about Chance, he didn't need someone like her. The quicker she got out of his life, the better off he'd be.

Now that she'd used it, her thigh hurt like she'd been burned with a red-hot poker, but she persevered. Her lungs were still tight with congestion, but she wasn't about to waste time lying around healing.

Opening his closet revealed your every day basic wardrobe for a guy who liked flannel, denim, and, *umm, gear bags?* He'd taken two with him, but three more packed and zippered canvas bags lined the far back corner of his closet behind a row of polished boots lined up as if for inspection, their laces stuffed down their throats. The funny guy had a touch of OCD. Jackets, sweatshirts, and hoodies hung neatly on the clothes bar at her right; jeans were straight ahead on pants hangers, and shirts were to the left. Funnier still, everything looked clean and ironed.

A drift of his manly scent—wind and sunshine—tickled her nose. For a moment, Suede closed her eyes and inhaled, thrilled to have some small part of him in the room with her, one she wished she could take with her. If only. She'd learned long ago that life was one disappointment after another, and this man? Tempting, but Chance Sinclair was clearly heartbreak in the making. He wasn't York, but she was still Suede Tennyson, and love stories were fucking fairytales. *Umm, damn. Darn.* Not swearing was going to be harder than she'd realized. But hey, Chance wasn't there. He hadn't heard her. This time.

The time to leave was now before he returned. She didn't need a hero. She needed a new life. *Yeah, I've got it bad, only this time I like the guy.* Which meant she needed to go. Yes, she'd liked Chance enough to kiss him, but that was all the more reason to get out of his life before she ruined it. Wasn't that what Mom always said? *Before you came along everything was perfect?*

An overflowing wicker clothesbasket in the corner of his closet completed the intimate picture of the man who'd rescued her. Suede lifted an olive drab flannel shirt to her nose. Since none of his pants would fit, this single shirt would have to do until she located her clothes and laundered them. But the scent of Chance clung to the weave in her hands. Suede couldn't help but bury her nose in the shirt and take a deep, make that two deep breaths of his masculine scent. God, it was addicting. Her heart thudded at the memory of his body wrapped around hers. His pepperminty breath in her face. His big warm hands. And this smell...

Suede took one last sniff of his shirt. Turning slowly so she didn't fall down, she headed into the bathroom. Leaving him was going to be just as difficult as not swearing.

*****

The thing about owning the mountain in your back yard, which Chance did, was that he'd climbed it plenty while working alongside the crew that built his cabin, dug his basement, and excavated his escape tunnel. None of the hardhats he'd hired knew they'd worked alongside the picky owner of this land and the cabin they'd built back then. He'd liked it that way.

For the most part they'd been blue-collar, honest hard workers, his kind of people.

Still recovering from the injuries of his last mission and his abrupt departure from the TEAMs, he'd found that sweat labor was best eased at the end of a long, blue-collar day by a good stiff climb to the highest peak on Old Man Mountain. A man could breathe there. The air smelled cleaner. Purer. It cleared his head.

It was during one of those climbs when he'd taken the face without safety gear, hand-over-hand and toe-to-toe with the mountain, setting anchors and pitons as he climbed. On the reverse climb, he'd laced a network of black nylon ropes, hammering more pitons where needed. On another evening, he'd networked another fifty or so anchors and ropes at intermittent angles until he'd created a nearly invisible interlocking escape grid to fall back on if needed. A man couldn't have enough alternate getaways the day his enemies caught up with him, but now? He could move experts and novices up these cliffs in record time.

Chance snowshoed to the base of the frozen falls in the middle of the storm that wouldn't quit. He stowed the showshoes on his back, pulled his balaclava over his head, donned his goggles, and up he went.

The sturdy ropes held fast. The roughened grip of his climbing gloves made certain of that. In less than an hour he was topside, sweating like a beast but warm. The wind at the peak crested around forty knots per hour, fresh gale force on the Beaufort Wind Force Scale. If he'd been out on the sea with this stiff wind, waves would've been choppy and running between eighteen and twenty-five feet high. The foam off those waves would've smacked his face and watered his eyes.

As fierce as it was now, the snow came sideways in hard-driven pellets, not flakes. He leaned into it, fighting Mother Nature's northwesterly attempt to shove him off the mountain. It was, after all, hers.

The old hunting cabin stood due north of his position, its windowless backside against the storm. Chance took that direction to keep his bearings. At fifty yards, he paused. The cabin was within reach. No lights glowed from within, not that he'd expected York to use the place.

Drifts banked up to the low roof on the windward side, making it resemble a Hobbit's hovel from Middle Earth instead of a fifty-year-old foursquare hunting cabin. What was left of the chimney on the roof was buried as well, and ice caked the windows. Leeward wasn't much better, but the doorway was passable.

Cocking his head to listen for any animal life inside, Chance gave the door a good shake, certain that any noise he made would be lost to the wind and would go undetected by York. The handle broke free in his hand, but that was just as well. He'd fix it later.

Ducking inside, he surveyed his only shelter. Cold. Barren. Good enough. The table he'd hauled up in pieces during the summer still stood under the window to his left. He'd chopped and stacked the cord of split pine logs to his right, but there'd be no cozy fire tonight. The snow on the chimney made certain of that.

His snowshoes went on the inside hook beside the door for easy access. He wouldn't leave them outside to give himself away. The broken door handle would do that if York's men came looking, which Chance doubted. His gear bag went to the floor by the nearest table leg.

Chance spent all of five minutes de-icing the windowpane before he got serious. His tripod and rifle took up residence in the center of the table, aimed out the now clear-as-a-bell port in the window. Visibility was still zero in the storm, but the only clearing on top this mountain lay twenty-one yards straight ahead. That was where York would be holed up in a heated modular unit, waiting out the storm. Chance planned to be ready if Mother Nature cooperated and the storm died down. He only needed one shot.

To make certain his gear stayed put and undisturbed, Chance stepped out in the blizzard and paced off ten feet from each corner of the cabin. He doubted York's men, probably all city boys, would be inclined to check the perimeter of their camp on an afternoon like this. North, south, east, and west,

Chance placed one of those pesky beacons. The shriek it emitted wouldn't have bothered Pagan had he broken the beacon's beam because he knew the shutoff code to disable them.

Animals would run the other way, frightened for their lives, but these smartass city guys? Chance doubted they were that bright. Their ears would be bleeding in seconds. By then he'd be on them, and York would be short a couple bodyguards.

Chance rubbed his gloved hands together, warming his frozen fingers. It was OK Corral time. He armed himself with the two pistols out of his bag, a six-inch knife in his boot sheath, and a back-up pistol up his sleeve. Brass knuckles went under his insulated gloves. Hand warmers and the thermal pad went into his jacket pockets.

He stuffed three bottles of water inside his flannel shirt and against his skin to prevent them from freezing. Dehydration was the biggest killer on arctic ops. Eating snow made it worse. Not only did it chill a guy's body from inside, it denied precious moisture. People died when they made greenhorn mistakes.

As an added precaution, he tied one end of one of the ropes he'd brought up with him over his jacket and around his waist, the other to the table leg for a lifeline. He wasn't normally directionally challenged, but the whiteout could mess with a man's internal compass and he didn't take unnecessary risks. With his back to the wind, Chance headed due east to the only place York could be.

Modular shelters were the ideal set up for rough terrain. Chance wasn't sure which he'd find, the heavier trailer-sized kind or a tent, a fiberglass igloo or, knowing York, a micro-camper unit with plumbing and heating, caviar and bubbly in the fridge.

It was interesting York had lied to Suede to get her all the way up here, though. The missing pieces of that puzzle irked Chance. What the hell did Sullivan have to do with this creep? What was so urgent that Sullivan broke his own rules to end the guy? Why here?

Chance paced off nineteen yards toward the clearing, then twenty before a black shadow evolved out of the driven snow and turned into a cylindrical overnight unit on tripod legs, not unlike a semi-trailer minus the semi. The unit had one point of egress and a silent generator, both portside. Interesting layout, but adequate for the weather, if that generator had been up and running. Heavy-duty hooks stood like giant eyes at the top of the rig, testifying that a chopper had transported it, but the generator was oddly silent. Didn't make sense.

Getting inside would be a definite no-go, but Chance hadn't planned to. Instead, he unwrapped the acoustic amplifier listening device he'd concealed inside his inner jacket pocket. Wiping a circle of frost from the wall of the aluminum-shielded rig, he attached a listening device with a built-in amplifier, the ceramic head of the microphone at its core, to the smooth surface. Trading one of the two earpieces that linked him to Pagan for half the stereo headset, he hunkered against the rig and out of the wind to eavesdrop.

Hell, it was cold as a witch's tit up here, and getting colder. He planned to be back inside that ugly little cabin by sunset. Chance tugged his bandana over the mouth of his balaclava for extra protection and adjusted the volume of his *'ears'*, his senses focused within the trailer.

Between the whistling wind and the moaning trees, it was a difficult listen at best. Finally, a deep male voice growled in Spanish, not a language Chance understood but for a few colorful swear words. Another voice, this one more alto than baritone, responded, but both were muffled. Chance set the device to record for later translation when another voice lifted above the others. "In English. You know I don't understand that crap."

Must be York. The German super star had hired muscle from South America. Interesting.

"I said I hate snow," Baritone complained with a rich Hispanic accent. "It's cold in here. Why can't we turn up the thermostat?"

"This storm can't last forever." York again. "We have to conserve what fuel we have in case things get worse."

A light bulb flashed over Chance's head. *Freezing to death would certainly take care of Sullivan and*

Suede's problem, but Sullivan had been clear. Make it hurt.

"Jesus Christ, how long before the chopper comes to get us?" That from Alto, the other whiner and another Hispanic. "I'm wearing two jackets and I'm still cold."

You should've hired help from the motherland, not the southland, mused Chance.

"You have her ring." York sounded pissed. "What more do you want? A Jacuzzi to bask in while we wait out the storm?"

Chance snapped to attention. *Alto had Suede's ring? What'd York do, divvy up her things with his posse? Good to know.*

"And you." York must've turned on Baritone. "If you're so damned cold, put her jacket on. You're small enough. It should fit."

Alto snickered, but neither man argued. Didn't matter. Chance canted his head, cracking the vertebrae in his neck at the mention of Suede's winter jacket. Suede. Forced to undress. Up here in the bitter cold? He needed to hit something as the image of the nearly lifeless body he'd so recently pulled from the pond came to mind. Baritone and Alto might live the day, but York? *No way.*

Chapter Fifteen

Showered and shaky, Suede limped out of Chance's bathroom a new but exhausted woman. Why he had a blow dryer in there she didn't know. He surely didn't use it, but it was a godsend for a woman fighting what felt like bronchitis settling in her lungs. Wet hair would only make everything worse.

Her plan to escape had been put on indefinite hold. All she wanted now was to climb back into his bed, pull the covers over her head, and feel sorry for herself.

The steam from the shower had loosened her lungs, but man, standing to shampoo, rinse, lather, and repeat was a lot of work. She'd removed the gauze on her fingers, which stung at first. By the time her knees were about to give out, she'd used his body wash, rubbed a dab of toothpaste over her teeth when she couldn't find an extra toothbrush, and left her damp towel on the counter. Enough was enough. She had to sit before she fell down.

The waterproof wraps he'd left on the counter to keep her bandages dry were helpful, although she hadn't used one on her backside. Too gross to save, she'd ripped that bandage off and tossed it. The open wound stung, but the burning lump she'd dealt with for days before this debacle, was gone and that was relief enough.

Damn. That big bed of Chance's looked enticing and safe. Trembling, she rested her hip to the edge of it. She'd brought a hand towel to catch any infection still draining from her left butt cheek, but other than that, she felt better. Tired as hell, but clean. If only he were there. She wouldn't mind his help. In fact, she might enjoy watching his reaction to her request to re-bandage her derriere. He embarrassed easy, not what she'd expected from a guy his size.

"Are you okay in there?" Pagan asked at the closed door. That was nice of him NOT to barge in when she was still wrapped in a bath sheet and holding onto her rear. Chance's clean shirt waited on the bed for her to shimmy into it. One thing at a time.

"I'm good," she called out. At least she tried to call out. Her sore throat didn't have the volume she'd intended.

Sure enough, Pagan either hadn't heard or chose not to. The knob turned, the door opened, and he about dropped his teeth. At least, his mouth fell open so wide he could've lost his teeth when he gaped at her.

"Do you mind?" she hissed, drawing up to every last bit of her five-foot-one-inch indignant height. She snugged the towel up to her chin. This was not the Sinclair brother she wanted ogling her.

"Ah, ah, yes, I mean no, ah... shit." Red-faced, he slammed the door.

"I'll be right out," she called as she dropped the towel and drifted Chance's shirt over her arms and head. The hem of it settled at her knees, but the smell of it. *Ahhhh.* Suede closed her eyes and hugged herself, imaging those were his arms around her.

Wouldn't you know? When she opened her eyes, Pagan was standing at the door again, still red-faced. Gawking.

Suede dropped her arms, embarrassed he'd caught her acting foolish. "What do you want?" she asked, her nose in the air. She refused to be intimidated by another man for as long as she lived.

His head jerked to the side once, then again. She nearly laughed. Pagan looked like he had a bad tick or was having a minor seizure.

"Umm, lunch is served." His palm came up as if to placate her. "If you're hungry, that is. Unless you want me to bring it in here. I could do that, you know. I'm here to serve, and you should, umm, probably get back into bed. To sleep, I mean. Just to sleep." His head kept bobbing like he needed her to agree with one of his more than kind options.

Suede couldn't help it. He was as handsome and as shy as Chance, but his shoulders were wider. Dressed in comfortable looking faded jeans and a white short-sleeved T, Pagan waited. His wavy hair was the identical shiny, ebony black, but longer, and his eyes were green, a deep crisp emerald green instead of warm amber. If anything, he was endearingly cute. Best of all, he hadn't been rude. "How about if I eat with you instead of by myself?" she asked.

"With me? Ah, sure. You bet." He spun on the ball of his foot, then turned as if he'd forgotten something. "You'll probably need help walking, huh?"

"Just a strong arm to lean on, that's all." Chance's arm would've been better, but Pagan's would do.

He flew to her side, his elbow cocked and an impressively inked forearm presented for her to hold onto. She clutched it as a wave of dizziness swarmed up from the floor. By then, she'd been on her feet a whole thirty minutes that felt more like hours. "I'm just a little unsteady," she assured the gentle giant at her side as she shuffled through the door and out into the real world. *I will not faint or fall down. Only sissy girls do that.*

Suede took a moment to take in the rustic, male appeal of Chance's magnificent log home, at least the massive overhead timbers and joists were constructed of logs, although the wall looked like any other wall. Wow. For a cabin, this place was breathtakingly huge.

One hallway stretched to her left, another to her right, both lined with floor-to-ceiling windows that framed the still snowing blizzard quite perfectly, if you liked frigid, wintery pictures. The rich burnished glow of hardwood floors combined with partially peeled logs beckoned her into a lavish family room with several leather couches, a high chandelier of deer antlers or... She squinted at that amazing piece of art in the rafters. Those clever things could be moose antlers for all she knew about North American wildlife.

A stone fireplace dominated the wall just outside her door, umm, Chance's door. A kitchen filled with copper pots and pans hanging over a stainless aluminum range glowed beyond. A huge black bear, stuffed of course, stood in the far corner near the entry with its claws raked high and a butterfly on its nose. *Cute.*

Cabinets and closets lined the double doors at the entry, itself a carved masterpiece of bounding deer, bears, and pine trees set in a thick rough-hewn frame. The entire room had been done in evergreens and browns, mimicking the décor of Mother Nature's forests. *Delightful. Simply delightful in a masculine, guy sort of way.*

Gallo lay on a rug by the fire, completing the cozy picture. He opened one eye, thumped his tail a couple times, then went back to sleep.

"Here you go, Princess," Pagan murmured as he stepped lightly around her, seating her in the corner of the couch. He took a minute to tuck a plush blanket over her lap before he stepped back and nodded as if he agreed with himself. "Are you warm enough?"

"Yes, thank you." She smoothed the wrinkles out of the blanket. "This place is, wow, really nice for a cabin."

"It is," he agreed, rubbing his hands. "Umm, lunch. I made lunch. Broccoli cheese soup. I'll, um, get a bowl for you. Toast tips?" he asked on his way past her to the kitchen.

"Yes, please," she called over her shoulder, projecting her squeaky, scratchy voice so he wouldn't think she was close to passing out. Exhausted was more like it. Suede curled her knees to the couch, careful of her hip and... *Oh damn.* She'd lost track of the towel for the open sore on her ass. By now, it had to be seeping through Chance's shirt and the blanket and onto this beautiful leather couch and...

Unsteadily, she lifted to her feet and twisted around to see what was going on back there. Wrong move. The cabin tilted and down she went, only she didn't get far. Strong, capable hands lifted her off her feet before she hit the floor. Suede found herself pressed against a warm chest, the heart beneath it pounding like a jackhammer.

"I've got you," Pagan murmured, gulping so hard she could hear the muscles in his throat constrict. "Are you okay? You didn't hit your head, did you? Chance will beat my ass if I let anything happen to you while he's gone."

She shook her head, embarrassed at her quandary. *Do I tell him? But if I do, I'll have to show him my bare butt and...* Suede stalled, worrying her bottom lip while she weighed her options.

His brows clenched when his gaze hit the red streaks on the leather cushion. "You're bleeding," he said, his voice quavering with male trepidation. Silly man. He thought it was *that* kind of blood, when it was only—blood.

"I couldn't reach the hole on my ass to bandage it." Okay, that didn't come out like she intended. "I mean" —Suede drew in a deep sigh and confessed— "I had a bad infection, and Chance lanced it, and I took the bandage off when I showered, but now... but now..." But now tears brimmed at yet another helpless predicament. "Can you help me?" *Without ridiculing me or making me feel worse than I already do?*

"You need a pressure bandage," he said like he knew what he was talking about.

"Okay. Sure." That sounded good. He hadn't called her '*dumb bitch*' or '*stupid cow*'. "As long as it won't leak, and..." One tear got away, and that was all she-wrote. Suede lowered her lashes, tired of being the damsel in distress. *This is so not me! I refused to cry in front of York. Why am I falling apart with these guys?*

The answer seemed obvious. York bullied her. Chance and Pagan didn't. They treated her with undue respect, and she didn't know what to do with that.

Pagan eased her back down to the couch. In two seconds, he returned with a first-aid kit, a fresh T-shirt, and a clean blanket from Chance's room. "Don't worry. I've dressed plenty worse wounds in my time. I'll be gentle."

"That's not what I'm worried about," she breathed. "It's just that…"

'Way to go, loser,' her mother's voice snapped to life as if she were there in Chance's log cabin. *'Act like a worthless child and you'll always be treated like one.'*

I'm not worthless! Suede screamed at the domineering witch in her head.

"Of course you're not worthless," Pagan muttered, his brows pinched in dismay and his eyes on the backside he was about to treat. "I never said you were. Are you okay?"

Did I say that out loud? Suede bit her bottom lip and nodded, her cheeks flooded with heat. "Sorry, umm, yes. I'm good." *Just fucking great. I mean, oh hell, darn!*

Embarrassed to death, she hooked her palms over the wide leather armrest and looked away while Pagan lifted the blanket and took care of her south end. He didn't say another word, just swiped her butt cheek with an antiseptic wipe before he pressed a squared bandage over it, which had to be easy to find as quickly as he finished. He tugged the soiled shirt back over her rump and stood. "I'm going to the kitchen. While I'm gone, change shirts, and when I get back, I'll clean the couch and trade blankets, deal?"

She nodded, embarrassed for having treated him like he was an imbecile before. Pagan had a soft touch and he seemed to care. And he'd made soup! *What guy does that for a woman he doesn't know?*

Tears glimmered again, and she swiped a quick finger under her eyes before they fell. "Thank you," she said, and this time, she meant it from the bottom of her heart.

He retreated to the kitchen. She traded shirts. Before she knew it, the smear on the leather couch was wiped clean, the soiled blanket was replaced, and she was warm and cuddled in another plush blanket. Talk about an exhausting morning.

Pagan served her a small cup of rich, creamy soup. He'd cut the broccoli into tiny niblets and the toast tips were done to golden perfection. He settled into the easy chair at her right, his long legs eating up the real estate between his chair and the coffee table.

The Sinclair boys were both out of some men's magazine where bodies were wide and rough-cut, muscled and massive. His boots had to be size twelves, at least, and his hefty biceps stretched the sleeves of his short-sleeved T. Like Chance, he wore the uniform of a man used to hard labor outdoors. Jeans. Calluses. A deep tan.

But Suede's ears were tuned for the stomp of another man's work boots on the porch. No matter how she fought the inclination, her traitorous eyes stole to the front door at every creak of Pagan's leather chair.

"Can I get you anything else?" he asked, his much larger and empty soup bowl on the table, his hands on his knees as if he'd spring to his feet at her bidding.

Suede startled, her mind up on that mountain again. "No, I'm good," she said. What a lie. She wasn't good. She was in trouble once more, only this time it felt different. This thing she felt for Chance seemed real. Solid. The difference between junk food and meat and potatoes. She swallowed hard and set her soup spoon in her empty bowl.

"You like him?" Pagan asked out of the blue. "My brother. Chance."

"No. He helped me. That's all. I'm just very grateful." She shook her head, then added. "To the both of you."

His head nodded, but his lips pursed. His brows slanted as if he was thinking. "He's my older brother, you know. There's three of us, Chance, Kruze, and me. Mom had us eleven months apart, then she stopped."

Hadn't that woman ever heard of birth control? "Sounds like a smart decision."

"Yeah, that's when Dad skipped out on us and got himself killed." Pagan shoved his long legs forward as he toed out of his boots. "Mom had just hit the big time with one of her books. New York Times bestseller. Guess it pissed him off. Big ego, small brain, you know the type. He went on a three-week drunk. Never came back."

"I'm sorry," Suede murmured. She surely knew that type of male.

"Don't worry. It's not like any of us miss him, but Mom..." A sigh escaped Pagan as he interlocked his fingers behind his head, his eyes cast up to the ceiling. "We all miss Mom. She was unforgettable."

Suede's heart clenched. Pagan's voice had mellowed at every mention of his mother. These rugged men weren't so rugged after all. They loved their mom. "Chance said she was an author?"

The dark curls at the top of his head trembled as he nodded, still looking up. "She was. We lost her..." His Adam's apple bobbed. "The same day Chance..." Pagan trailed off. "I don't know why I'm talking about this. It's not like you're interested and—"

"I am interested," tripped off of her tongue before her common sense could rein it in. "I care. I mean, it sounds like you and your brother were close to your mom." *Wouldn't that be something?*

He nodded. "She told us stories when we were kids. She took us camping. We lived in San Diego then. It's a big Navy town, so I guess it's no wonder we all joined up."

"You and Kruze and—"

"Yeah. Chance. He started it, no, that's not right. Mom started it. She was one of those dyed in the wool,   don't-step-on-my-flag,   love-it-or-leave-it patriots. She and a friend of hers taught us to shoot before we hit kindergarten, then taught us to stand up for truth and justice. The American way. All that stuff."

His gaze hadn't moved from the ceiling, so naturally, Suede's eyes were drawn to the heavy wooden rafters overhead, too. She hadn't noticed the rustic metal stars decorating them until then, nor the pinecones carved into the polished timbers. So much time and effort spent on beauty most people would never see. "It's lovely," she whispered.

"That she was." Pagan slapped his palms to his thighs, misunderstanding, yet saying the right words.

Suede gulped, afraid to ask. "What happened to her?"

His chin dropped and his lashes fell. With his longish hair hiding his eyes and his heavy brows, he looked more sinister than sad. Until glimmering eyes peered out through all that shaggy hair and said, "Stage four bone cancer. We never knew she'd already had breast cancer when she was younger or that it came back in her bones. 'Course we never knew she wasn't supposed to have children either, but she did a lot of things they said couldn't be done."

"I'm sorry," Suede said. How awful to actually *love* your mother only to lose her so early.

Pagan cleared his throat. "Yeah, well…" His voice trailed off until his eyes scrolled back to her.

Wait a minute. "Your mother was Scarlett Sinclair? *That* author? The one who wrote *My Enemy Tryst*?" What were the odds that Suede would now be in that famous woman's son's home?

He nodded, a tender glint in the corner of his eye. "That's the one. She would've liked you, 'course she would've kicked your butt for some of the stunts you've pulled, too. Mom was a stickler for education and reading. For amounting to something in the world. For doing good even when no one's looking." His index finger lifted off the armrest, pointing straight ahead to a massive set of bookshelves built out of the same gleaming wood as the rest of the cabin. "Chance keeps her books over there if you need something to read while you're here. There's no TV this far north."

Suede followed the direction he'd pointed. "I might just take you up on that."

"You do that," Pagan agreed, smoothing his hands over his thighs as he eased to the edge of his chair, the leather creaking with the shift of weight. "But right now, I've got to give Gallo his treat, and it's time you rested. May I help you back to bed, or would you rather stay out here by the fire?"

"Here," Suede answered. She might be exhausted, but she'd had enough of being alone.

He paused at the edge of his seat, his eyes narrowed. "You're nothing like I thought you were."

She grunted. "What was that, a slut?"

His head shook. "No, I wasn't thinking that, but you're..." He seemed to be searching for the right word. "Soft," he ended up saying, "not hard and coarse or bitchy like most hookers. Not trashy."

Wow. Most hookers. So that was how he saw her. What an ugly comparison. A quiet huff escaped through her nostrils. "Thanks, I guess."

"So what changed?" he asked, his gaze piercing. "You went from zero to sixty, then back to zero pretty damned fast."

Suede had the grace to squirm. He thought she'd done drugs. That's what he'd meant, and he was right to think that. Her behavior had been wildly erratic the last year, even to her. It was difficult to put into words the jolting conversion she'd so recently experienced. Her fingernails were suddenly easier to look at than her handsome benefactor, only they were as shredded as her past. Where to begin?

"I guess, umm, everything changed when I should've died last night," she murmured to herself. "Until your brother resuscitated me and brought me back to life, I was a skank, Pagan. I know that. I was nothing but throwaway trash, but he..." *God, it was true.* "He saved me." *In more ways than one.* "He made me realize I could go back to being what I used to be, or I could move forward and be someone better. I could change. He made me believe in myself again."

It was strange. Suede had thought of herself as nothing most of her life, but to finally have someone believe in her was—she swallowed hard—*life altering*. She should've been strong enough to make those changes before, but all that enlightenment hadn't come until she truly was at the end of her worthless life. Only now she knew better. She had never been worthless. Just lost. Just searching.

Pagan slapped his thigh, grabbing her attention. When she made eye contact, he winked like he knew a secret. "That's Chance for you. Sorry to break it to you, but Big Brother's got a savior complex. He's always saving the world. Guess it comes from being the oldest and having a crap dad like we did. He's got this idea in his hard head he has to take care of Kruze and me like we're still little boys, that he's the man of the house" —this was said with considerable swagger— "especially since Mom passed."

"He's a good man," Suede whispered.

"He's a pain in the ass, is what he is, "Pagan teased, "but I'm glad he found you. You're good for Chance. I can tell."

A huff of *'who me?'* nearly snorted out of Suede's nostrils. She rolled her eyes instead. "I doubt that, but thanks for saying so."

A genuine smile lit Pagan's rugged features, changing him into Chance's kid brother. For a split second, Suede glimpsed Scarlett Sinclair's baby boy. How strange. The more she got to know these guys, the more she liked their mother.

"Want me to get you one of Mom's books to read? That'll keep you busy."

He almost made it sound as if she were staying. Wouldn't that be a fairytale come true? Suede decided to play along. She wasn't up to leaving at the moment anyway. "Sure. That would be nice."

"Which title?" His brow lifted, and Suede nearly laughed. Pagan knew she'd never read any of his mother's works. She could tell by the way he'd just baited her. She'd only known who wrote *My Enemy Tryst* because it had hit the jackpot last year as a blockbuster movie. And wasn't that sad? Scarlett was more famous now that she'd died, now that she'd left behind the boys she'd loved, the boys who still grieved for her. It didn't seem fair.

Suede spiked a brow back at Pagan, but knew it couldn't match his in ferocity. "Bring it on, Pagan. I want to read them all. How about we start at the beginning?"

His face cracked into a teasing smile. "You do know she wrote over two hundred novels, don't you? They're not exactly short little fairytales. You might be here a while."

Wouldn't that be nice? She rubbed her hands together, her plans to leave indefinitely postponed. "Then you'd better get cracking, hadn't you?"

He cocked his head at her. "I know what Chance sees in you, Suede. You're... nice."

She bowed her head at that simple compliment. These Sinclair boys had a way of getting to her. Their wonderful mother, too. It seemed as if Scarlett hadn't left them behind, but lingered in this cabin and those elegant stars overhead. "I didn't used to be, but where there's a will, there's a way, right?"

Pagan sent her a sly wink. "You got it, sister."

A tear came out of nowhere. Suede dashed it away, her heart unexpectedly So. Damned. Full. Pagan had just made her feel like family.

Chapter Sixteen

Shit, it's cold up here. Chance jerked the thermal pad from his pocket, gave it a snap to activate the chemicals, then shoved it under the frozen cheeks of his ass. All he'd heard from inside so far amounted to nothing more than backbiting, pacing, and snoring. If these yahoos didn't start talking more, Chance was headed back to the empty cabin. It might not be warm, but it offered protection from the wicked wind biting at him.

"You should never have listened to Tennyson," Baritone muttered.

"Shut up," York shot back at him, his voice low and filled with menace.

The snoring stopped. "Whose idea was it to dump her all the way out here?" Alto asked. "We're in the middle of nowhere for Christ's sake."

"Mine," York ground out.

"Shit man, why?"

"Because I needed her to die like everyone thought she lived, in the nude and strung out on drugs."

"You could've accomplished that in LA, where it's warm."

"Too many investigative reporters in that town. It had to happen here."

"Yeah, but that chick never did drugs like your other girls," Baritone muttered. "She was different, know what I mean?"

"I don't get it. You drugged her when you wanted her to look like a porn star, but she was a good girl," Alto added. "All she ever did wrong was try to please you."

Chance forgot the cold. *Don't stop talking now, you bastards.*

"But nobody knew that, did they?" York bit out. His hired help's taunting was obviously pissing him off. "They only saw the hysterical celebrity preening every chance she got."

"So what did you get out of this shitty deal?" Baritone asked. "Tennyson has what he wants, but..." He coughed and Chance could imagine him covering his mouth to maybe hide his amusement. "'Scuse me, boss, but it seems all you got is the shaft."

"I was supposed to get free access to all Oregon ports," York hissed. "From the confluence of the Willamette and the Columbia Rivers, I should've been the boss, but now..." Something thumped, possibly his fist on a table. "Why don't you shut your fuckin' mouths? You work for me! You're not my buddies. You're not even good enough to lick the soles of my boots!"

Ah, here it comes, the much-televised berserker behind the suave playboy façade. It was surprising York had held onto his control this long.

"Sorry, boss," Alto said. "We don't mean nuthin'. We're just cold and hungry and—"

"How'd I know there'd be no food in this goddamned rig?"

No food? Well, well, well. Chance grinned. Except for what York had done to Suede, this guy was a joke. These three were stuck up here during one of the worst storms of the century without heat or food? His eyes strayed to the generator again. *Karma can be such a nasty bitch.*

But wasn't that interesting? The smiling, backslapping Governor Tennyson had off-loaded his independent, and once upon a time headstrong daughter, to York in exchange for free access to all Oregon ports. *What an asshole.* So far, Chance had yet to see anything in Suede to validate the media's vicious portrayal of her. *Drugs, huh?*

All this time, she'd been trying to get her father's attention, but what'd he do? Disowned her. Of course, she'd disowned him first when she'd sought and was granted emancipation, but shit. She was a sixteen-year-old kid when she'd pulled that coup. It wasn't hard to see what had propelled Suede to this point in her life. She needed to be wanted. But now Chance wondered. Who gave her that emancipation idea? Who helped her find a lawyer? Who the hell set her up with York? Was Tennyson responsible for all of that, too?

More pacing came from inside the rig, then York muttered, for once his voice loud enough. "She was a pain in the ass from the start."

"But you got what you wanted, right?" Alto asked. "You got her gone and the footage to prove it to Tennyson?"

"Oh, yeah," Baritone spoke up. "I filmed her from where she couldn't see me. I got a nice clear shot of her falling, but with the snow and all, that's all I got. Couldn't see her land. That woulda been sweet."

Sweet?! Watching a twenty-year-old woman falling to her death was sweet? Sons-of-bitches! Chance gritted his molars loud enough they cracked.

"It would've been better if you'd got her falling in the nude like you were supposed to, but guess it'll have to do," Alto said, his voice oddly soothing. "You think Tennyson will buy it?"

"He will if he knows what's good for him. I'm tired of the bastard. He's not getting the tapes, and I don't care if—"

"It's on a USB drive," Baritone interrupted. "Not tapes. We don't use—"

"I don't give a shit if it's on the moon!" York bellowed. "Julio Juarez is coming in Tuesday. If I'm not there..."

Chance couldn't make out York's last words. *What tapes and who the hell is Julio Juarez?*

Baritone grunted. "You'll be there, boss. Tennyson ain't so big you can't shave him down to size. Once he sees what happened to his kid, he'll straighten up. You'll get what's coming to you. You'll see."

So, York's threatening Tennyson? Was that what this was all about, killing Tennyson's daughter to prove York meant business? Was Juarez a hit man with a contract on Tennyson now that Suede was, as far as York knew, dead? Then what? Who had a good shot at the Oregon governorship once Tennyson was gone? York? One of his buddies? Tennyson's wife?

The earpiece in Chance's ear canal came to startling life as Pagan said, "Comm check," loud and clear.

"You're a little late, Baby Brother," Chance teased.

"I've been busy. I made soup. Homemade soup. It took time."

A grin tugged at Chance's lips. Imagine that, Pagan in the kitchen with an apron on. "How's Suede?"

"Good, real good. She ate a small bowl of soup and a piece of toast, but she's tired. She's had a busy day."

That spiked Chance's brow. "Oh?"

"Yeah, she took a shower, and she's been out in the living room with me and Gallo. I had to change the bandage on her rump though, so don't go ballistic for me touching your woman when you get back. She couldn't reach it, and it was bleeding, and I could, and..." Pagan trailed off.

Chance let the *'your woman'* comment slide. He could see his brother raking his fingers over his head, embarrassed that he'd been even a tiny bit intimate with a woman like Suede. Pagan was a mystery. As much as he wanted and needed a good woman in his life, Chance doubted he'd know what to do with one when he caught one. It just had better not be Suede, damn his handsome ass.

"So she ate? Have you kept up with her meds? Don't forget to give her the antibiotic at bedtime." The thought of Pagan putting Suede to bed irked Chance. He blocked what might be a tender goodnight scene from his mind. York needed to start talking.

"Of course," Pagan replied. "She took two pain pills at lunch, and I think they put her to sleep. She was reading one of Mom's books, but now she and Gallo are snuggled on the couch. You should see them. Gallo likes her."

Almost as much as I do. "So why'd you call?" Chance asked to get his mind back on the job.

"I've been checking for a connection between Sullivan and Tennyson."

"And?"

"Well, this is where it gets interesting. I came across an email..."

Chance rolled his eyes. "Don't tell me you hacked the boss's server."

"No, oh, hell no."

"You lying son-of-a-gun. You did!" Chance hissed. Pagan never could lie.

"Yeah, okay, so I hacked Sullivan's server. He's not being square with us. Do you want to know what I found or not?"

"Spill."

"An email from Tennyson to Sullivan, dated three days ago. Tennyson sounded desperate. He outright asked Sullivan to rescue his daughter from Lionel York. Said he didn't want her involved with a known drug lord. Said he'd pay anything if Sullivan could make York disappear."

Which might explain Pagan's current assignment, the one Chance had taken over. Even as Chance thought that, a prickle of unease skated up his spine. Would Sullivan act on an old frat buddy's request for help just because he had the means? He couldn't believe the man he respected would stoop that low.

"Not buying it," Chance said. "Why would Tennyson ask that of anyone, Sullivan in particular? That's conspiracy to commit, plain and simple. Tennyson might have been trolling for insider information. What was Sullivan's answer?"

"Haven't found one yet. Hang on a sec. That you Kruze?" Pagan bellowed to the side.

Great. Now both his horny brothers were warm and snug at his place with Suede while he froze his ass off on the mountaintop. If that didn't add a shot of nitro to his already thrumming need to protect her, nothing did.

"Come back to me, Pagan," Chance prompted, tapping his mic to get his brother's attention.

"Chance, Kruze just showed." Pagan again. *Like I couldn't hear that?* "And I just discovered we've got another player in this mess, Victoria Hex. Ever heard of her?"

"Wait a minute. One thing at a time. Did Sullivan respond to Tennyson's request or not?"

"Not by email, but he could've called him. Two good old boys, you know. I can't track that."

Chance shook his head. "No. Sullivan's not one of the good old boys, and I can't see him undermining the SOBs by not following the protocol he himself established. That would unravel the teams from the inside out. Something else is going on here."

"I'll keep digging. You want to hear about Hex yet?"

"Yeah, the mob's number one assassin, straight out of Sicily. Go ahead."

"Right, and a Class A weapons dealer on her day job. She just arrived in Portland."

Chance blew out a puff of frustration. That was all he needed, one more player in this convoluted game of one-upmanship between Tennyson and York. This had all the makings of a major drug war brewing. "What the hell is going on in Oregon?" he bit out.

"Trouble, huh. Listen, I'm tied up here so Kruze is going on ahead of you to keep track of Hex. He'll spend the night here resting, then meet you at the usual tomorrow, once you off York." The usual being the Mount Hood Lounge off River Street, a local dive on the Portland waterfront. "You think you'll be there?"

"Not unless this storm lets up."

"Jesus Christ!" Kruze's booming baritone joined the fray. "That could be next week the way the front's stalled over Canada."

"Hey, Kruze. I'm pressed for time or I'd talk more, but I'll be there if I can. Once you spot Miss Vicky, don't lose her, okay?"

"You know I won't. Fly safe, Big Brother."

"One more thing." Chance cut in while the cutting was good. "I need to know who helped Suede file her petition for emancipation. I want the names of her lawyer if she had one, the judge who decided in her favor, and the nine commissioners who currently regulate the Port of Portland."

"That's four things," Kruze, always one to point out another's errors, grumbled, "maybe twelve."

"And you," Chance shut him down. "Find out who the hell Julio Juarez is before I get to town."

"Julio? JJ? What's he got to do with this?"

"You know him?" *Unbelievable.*

"Sure, if it's the same guy I went through BUD/S with, that's Boomer. He rang out the fifth day."

What a small damn world. "Did you two stay close? Can you get in touch with him?"

"Not really. He took some job back east, but why? What's he been up to?"

"Don't know, but he's supposed to meet Lionel York in Oregon on Tuesday, and we know for certain York's after control of Portland docks. I need to know if JJ's part of the cartel out of South America that York's distributing for or if he's an enforcer on someone else's team. Could be either. York's into some heavy shit."

"Can't be the same guy," Kruze replied. "The Julio I remember was a straight up hero back then. He wouldn't have gone rogue."

"Then find out if he's the same hero he used to be. Get back to me as quick as you can."

"You bet. I'll reach out to him now."

"What else?" Chance asked his brothers. He still wanted to know why Tennyson felt comfortable asking Sullivan for an assist in making York disappear. Did the guy have balls or what?

"Well, since I didn't feel comfortable hacking Sullivan's files..." Pagan let the insinuation that he might've done something illegal trail away.

"Don't tell me. You hacked York's." *This ought to be good.* "What'd you find?"

"That York's got a contract on Governor Tennyson."

"You're kidding."

"That's not the only hit he's paid for, but yeah. The man's proud of himself. He keeps good records."

"Which might explain Julio Juarez. He could be the hit man. Kruze?" Chance snapped. "You make that call yet?"

"I'm getting a disconnect. Let me try a few of my buddies. Someone's bound to know where he is. I'm telling you, Chance, JJ's one of the good guys."

"Not until we know for sure."

"York say what airlines Julio's flying?" Pagan asked.

"Give me a break. 'Course not," Chance answered. Grumbling ensued from inside the trailer rig. He leaned in to hear better as the grumbling escalated to what sounded like a brawl inside York's home away from home.

"There's something else," Pagan murmured. "York's not the only one keeping bad company. You ever hear of the Rio Brothers? The twins? Juan and Jorge?"

Aw, shit. Not the boys from Colombia.

Chapter Seventeen

"Yeah, I've heard of them." Chance held his breath, hoping that Tennyson wasn't that stupid, that he hadn't enlisted foreign thugs to end York. The Rio Brothers were nothing but stone-cold killers.

"I did not!" Baritone squealed from inside.

"Shhh," Chance told Pagan. "Something's up. Hang on."

"You did!" York roared.

The door to the rig burst open as a thin, olive-skinned male ran into the weather. He wore two jackets, the top one pink with a fur hood and cuffs. No boots. Gray socks on his feet. He pivoted, his palms raised and forward. "I didn't tell her nothin', I promise."

"The Rio Brothers will be in Portland on Tuesday, too," Pagan whispered.

"You want to bet this is all about Tennyson taking over York's Colombian drug business? That he's setting York up for a hard fall?" Chance asked, keeping his eyes and his weapon on the shivering man who had to be Baritone. "That's why he cozied up with York to take Suede off his hands. He didn't care about her. Check all incoming flights. Put tails on all these guys as soon as they hit US airspace."

"Yes, you did, Philip!" York snarled from the rig. "You told her how much the ring cost. That was why she was leaving me! To sell it! To run home to Daddy."

"No, boss, no, I swear, I—"

One shot boomed from the rig. Philip, aka Baritone, dropped in the snow amidst a misty red shower. The door slammed and York stepped into the open, a black pistol in his hand.

"Chance!" Pagan roared. "Chance! Are you—?"

"Calm down," Chance whispered as York stalked to the man he'd just killed and fired again. Point blank. In the back of the head. It would've been so easy. Chance had the shot of a lifetime. A single round at this range, and, poof! Suede's problem would be solved, but not Sullivan's.

If Pagan was right, Tennyson was behind not only York's Old Man Mountain campout and possibly Suede's attempted murder, but Sullivan's order to eliminate York as well. If Tennyson couched it right, and if the press played along, American hearts would be moved to vote for the *'poor Governor who'd lost his only child to drugs and hard living'*. The fact that she'd acted out and he'd responded by publically disowning her could certainly be window-dressed during his bid for the White House as a beleaguered father doing the best he could for an out-of-control adult child.

Not that America hadn't seen its share of crooked governors from Arkansas to New York and all the way to the Golden State, but damn. This took balls. Great big, hairy balls.

And this guy wants to be President? Jesus Christ, he's dirty enough. He just might win.

"What the hell's going on?" Pagan demanded.

Chance hunkered his shoulder into the side of the rig, for the first time praying for more wind and snow. The most he could do was send his brother a double click over his mic to signify he was still alive. The second York turned to go back into the rig, Chance would be out in the open, still winter camouflaged in shadow and snow, but visible if a smart man knew where and how to look.

Of course, York wasn't trained and he wasn't expecting company. He turned and the gun lifted in his hand, his dark eyes intent on the rig. The man looked more wolf-like than human. He swiped the long blond hair dangling into his eyes out of his way, his lips twisted in a grimace and his eyes sharp. Sinister. "Pablo!" he called to the last man in the trailer rig. "We need to talk."

"Y-y-yes, boss?" came a quavering reply from within.

"Get out here! Now!"

"C-coming." Squeak. Click. Alto must've opened the door, the fool. He'd have been smarter if he'd locked himself inside and York out. "Y-yes?"

York waved his pistol for Alto to come closer. A beefy man in a plaid hunting vest, the kind with plenty of pockets, stepped into the weather. All Chance could see was the guy's back and his trembling, raised hands, but he scanned those pockets, wondering which held Suede's three-carat diamond. She would be getting it back.

York pointed the gun and Chance hunkered with his back flat against the rig as he watched. He was officially in York's backstop. If that bullet went wide or through Alto...

Yeah, not thinking about that either.

Pagan's voice broke through the tension. "I'll bet Tennyson's just using his friendship with Sullivan. He's probing. He must suspect Sullivan has something to do with the SOBs. That's why he asked for help rescuing Suede."

Chance caught the tenderness in Pagan's voice. *So now she's Suede, huh?* "You may be right. Listen. Sit tight and—"

Another gunshot roared through the snow and Alto fell alongside his baritone partner. Chance cringed knowing now how much danger Suede had been in with York. He waited, not daring to breathe until finally, York kicked a boot full of snow onto Alto's prone body and stomped inside, grumbling with each step. The door slammed shut. The generator came on, which was just plain interesting. Had York baited his men into talking, withholding heat until they'd thought they could speak their minds? *The calculating son-of-a-bitch.*

"Talk to me, brother," Pagan pleaded. "Tell me you're still—"

"Alive," Chance finished for him. "Take it easy. I've done this once or twice before, remember?"

An audible sigh hit his eardrum. "Yeah, but last time" —Pagan cleared his throat— "Damn it. I knew I shouldn't let you take this job. Did you get him? Did you end York?"

Yes, last time I got my guys killed when I should've been home with Mom. I know. God, I know. But this time's different.

Chance shook his head. There comes a time in every black operator's life when he truly is an island, when he's all alone on the top of a mountain staring down his rifle sights with a man's life in his hands. No one can make the ultimate decision to squeeze the trigger to end that life. Chance owed it to himself to not only follow protocol, but to do what was right. Sullivan might make the calls, but it was Chance's soul on the line.

Could he have saved Alto and Baritone? Possibly. Should he have at least tried? Absolutely not. This mission had begun to end the threat against Suede and Sullivan, not to protect men who by their own admission were complicit in and seemed amused by Suede's attempted murder.

"The way I see it, Pagan, York didn't push Suede off the cliff because he hated her. He was sending her father a message: *'Renege on our deal and this happens. It's just business.'*"

"Yeah, so? Did you kill him, damn it?"

"No, Baby Brother. I've got a better idea."

"What?"

Chance ignored the disbelief in Pagan's question. The wind had died, but not the snow. It fell steadily. Too quickly, Alto and Baritone's bodies would be under a drift of the white stuff, so Chance broke cover. He worked fast as he rifled Alto's pockets until his gloved fingertips hit the stone that belonged to Suede. Lightening Alto's load by three carats, he tucked the ring inside his jacket pocket.

"I think Tennyson and York deserve each other," he said as he eyed the closed door to the rig. "Call Sullivan and tell him I'll need a lift to Oregon as soon as York's chopper arrives and he's out of my way."

"You're shittin' me?" Pagan's angst vibrated against Chance's eardrum like the wings of an angry hornet. "Sullivan's going to be pissed and what the fuck do you want me to tell Suede? You know she's sweet on you. You told her you'd be home soon. I didn't come home just to babysit."

"Are you swearing at me?" Chance asked quietly as he crouched out of sight beside the rig again.

Pause. Silence. Then a perturbed and grumpy, "Maybe."

Chance could imagine the cocky chin nod that went with that reply. He might be one tough son-of-a-bitch, but Pagan always was a spoiled brat. "What's Mom's rule?"

"Shit," Pagan hissed before he recited what the Sinclair boys had heard hundreds, maybe thousands of times, "'*Anyone can swear. Only real men understand the importance of honest discourse and open dialogue in the world today.*' Blah, blah, blah. There. Are you happy now?"

Chance smirked as Scarlett Sinclair lived again. She had to be rolling over in her grave—laughing. The thought of her smile brightened what had become a dismal day. "Suede isn't sweet on me, Little Brother. She's been treated badly by her parents and the guy who asked her to marry him, then I happened along. That's all. Nothing's going on between us, so knock it off. As far as what to tell her, I explained before I left that this is what I do. Get her healthy and on her feet, then take her wherever she wants to go." *It'll break my heart, but it'll be better this way.*

Pagan scoffed. "Tell me another lie. She's been watching the front door like a hawk since you left. She's waiting for you. That girl's got feelings, Chance. You can't do this to her."

"I can't do this to her or to you?"

Another stretch of silence ensued. "Fine. I'll tell her you'll be home as soon as you can."

"Tell her to trust me," Chance suggested. That much was true. She could trust him, to do what was right. Even if it meant letting her go.

Chapter Eighteen

Suede woke in a snarky mood, edgy, but she didn't know why, other than snarky was her normal. Embers glowed red and orange from the fireplace, but Pagan and Gallo were nowhere in sight. Pushing up from the couch, she stopped at the edge of the cushion with her feet to the floor. It seemed odd she'd be tired after sleeping, but bed. She wanted back under the covers in Chance's bed and she wanted to be there now. Her head pounded, and he needed to get his butt back here and kiss her forehead while checking for a fever. Then she wanted a stiff drink, a big box of tissues, and a good long cry while she lay there and felt sorry for herself.

Feverish, crabby, and achy, she'd slept the day away. The romance she'd started reading now lay on the floor beside the couch with a bookmark tucked within the pages of the first chapter. Pagan must've eased it out of her hands. That was thoughtful.

Quiet male voices drifted from the hall to the right of the kitchen. It was dark outside, lending a cave-like feeling to the dimly lit cabin. One of these days she needed to explore the rest of this place. Suede hated not knowing the layout of where she was, but that day would wait.

"Pagan?" she called. Then she called again, this time without the poor-me tone dripping all over her voice. "Can I help fix dinner?" Or something? Her only other option was to go back to bed, but that meant she was still sick. Which she was, but admitting it reduced her to a weakling, which she wasn't, and... *Oh hell. Where was I going with this?*

Her stomach growled. *Oh yes. Dinner. It's late. I'm hungry.* "Pagan?"

His head popped around the corner. Dressed in workout pants and a white T-shirt, his hair was damp and curlier than before, his forehead glistened with sweat. He must have a weight room on site. That explained the physiques of these guys. "You rang?"

By then she'd made it all the way to the end of the couch, a whopping six steps. Suede leaned her butt to the armrest before she fell down. "Yes, I'm hungry, and I can help fix some—"

"Want to chat with your boyfriend?"

"Chance?"

Pagan flinched as if he'd just been pinched. He shook his head and tapped his index finger to the wire leading to his ear. "Will you stop bellowing?" he bit out even as he grinned at Suede. "Yeah, I hear you just fine. She's not your girlfriend, ah-huh. Whatever you say." He winked and nodded toward the phone set charging on the end table. "Pick up. He needs to talk to you."

"He's not my boyfriend," Suede stated clearly as she sank back to the cushions.

"Yeah, yeah. Just pick up the phone and talk to him so I can sign off."

"Chance?" she asked, the receiver at her ear and Pagan gone to who knew where.

"Hey," a deep voice rumbled over the line, along with a whining whistle in the background. "Baby Brother been taking good care of you?"

"Yes. Is that the wind? Are you outside? Did you, you know?"

"No, I didn't kill York. He's still alive, but yeah, I'm in the cabin and the wind's strong up here. Still snowing, too."

"When are you coming down?"

"Pagan didn't tell you?"

"Tell me what?" Only the wind whispered in her ear. "Chance? Are you still there?"

"I'm not coming down tonight, Suede. If I can, I'll be flying out of here as soon as the weather clears. I've got to see this through. York's got evidence I need. This might be my only chance."

She nodded, not sure what to say, but not going to whine to a man who was toughing it out in a ferocious blizzard while she lounged by a fire. "Well, okay."

"He might be here awhile. Least until the storm blows over."

"It's been snowing more than a day, Chance," she reminded him. "Did you take enough food and water with you? Are you okay? How are you keeping warm?" *What are you thinking?*

She could've sworn he purred. "You're worried about me?"

"Yes," she blurted. *Strangely, I am.* "You're up there because of me. Of course I'm worried." *Make that terrified. You'll freeze to death and then what will I do?*

"I'm up here because this guy's up to his neck in murder and mayhem, not just because of what he did to you, though that's enough in my book. Pagan was just telling me that my brother Kruze got in. Hope you can stand another Sinclair hanging around for the night."

Suede fingered the hem of the blanket she'd wrapped around herself. Sinclair brothers seemed to be climbing out of the woodwork, all except the right one.

"Hey, I've got a question for you. What's your mother's personal assistant like?"

"Mitchell Franks?" Her hands went to her belly at that creep's name. Cramps clenched at the memories she wanted to forget. "He's nice enough, I guess," she said, hoping the quaver in her voice didn't give her away. "Kind of a brownnoser, but that's the type Mom hires. Why?"

"Does he always go on vacations with her?"

"Yes, he organizes her daily schedule and itinerary when she travels."

"So he's her press-agent as well?"

"Yes. He is." Suede nodded as Mitchell's stern insistence that she make an appointment to see her mom came back to her. *'Your mother's time is more important than you are, Miss Tennyson. You know that. We've been over this before.'* That time Suede had needed one of her parent's signatures since the high school dance was being held out of town. She didn't go.

"Do you like him?" Chance asked.

What a question. She met him head on to deflect her nerves. "No. He had no use for me. I was just a kid that bugged him. I got in his way." *Unless he wanted something from me.*

"How so?"

Suede rolled her eyes, masking her true feelings on the subject. "Mitch is..." *What's a good word for two-faced? Despicable? Pervert?* "...different. He caters to Mom, and he's protective of her." *Just not her daughter. She was fair game.*

Chance must've heard the hesitation in her voice. "Suede...?" He drew her name out. "You don't like Mitch. Why?"

She pinched her lips and told part of the truth. "H-he lies, Chance. He tells my Mom what she wants to hear, then he treats Mom's secretary like she's stupid behind Mom's back. He blames her when things go wrong, and…" Suede swallowed hard, remembering the den of snakes she'd escaped. "He lied about me." *Worse, Mom believed him.*

"Specifics, Suede. Give me details."

The room closed in, and it was suddenly hard to swallow. "It's nothing. It happened a long time ago and…" *I don't want to think about—that.*

"You're safe now, Suede," Chance murmured in her ear. "Whatever you say stays between you and me."

She nodded, sure of that singular comforting bit of knowledge even as her eyes filled with tears. But to tell Chance this? To admit she'd been used by Mitch, too? Crap, by every male she'd ever known until now? "I'm reading one of your mother's books," she said to change the subject.

Static crackled over the line. "Whoa. Now we've got lightning and thunder. Crazy weather up here. One of Mom's books, huh? I'll be—"

Snap. The phone went dead. Suede shifted the receiver from her ear, staring at her chance to share the thing that never should've happened to a fifteen-year-old girl. A daughter, for hell's sake.

"You lose him?"

She looked up into Pagan's green eyes at that well-meaning question. *I never had him.* "It's storming up there," she told him for lack of anything better to say.

He nodded. "Montana blizzards can get wild."

"Will he be okay?" *I am not going to cry. Of course he'll be okay. He's invincible. He doesn't need* me, either. *What am I thinking? I almost told him. Everything.*

Pagan nodded. "This is what we do, Suede. We get into places others can't. We do the impossible without the press being in our face, and we do it without fanfare or recognition. He'll be home before you know it, you'll see."

"I'm not leaving until he does." Why that popped out of her mouth, Suede hadn't a clue, but it felt right. Where else could she go? Back home to Salem? To her parents? Like they'd care.

For the first time in her life she found herself surrounded by a family that watched out for each other. She heard their love for each other in their voices. Little things defined it, like Chance calling his brother a cocker spaniel. Like Pagan fixing lunch for her while Chance went to confront York.

Worry lines crinkled Pagan's forehead. "You don't feel good, do you? Your cheeks are red."

I'm not sure I'll ever feel good again. "No, I'm fine." *I just need to sleep for a week and then leave.*

There was no fooling Pagan. "No, you're not. Go back to bed and take your meds. Dinner's in half an hour. I'm making chicken stir-fry. Would you like soy sauce with that?"

Suede replaced the phone in its charger. "I can help with dinner," she offered one last time.

"Are you kidding? Chance would kick my ass if I let you do anything but rest while he's gone, now off with you." Pagan canted his head toward Chance's open bedroom door, his emerald eyes aglitter.

A lump caught in her throat. "Thanks Pagan," she murmured, biting her lip at the helplessness swarming into her eyes like a flood.

Up went both dark brows. "For what?"

"For treating me like family. It means a lot." *More than you know.*

He shrugged. "Blame that on Mom. Chance too. They're the ones who kept us together when things got tough."

Suede lifted her chin, *not going to cry, damn it.* "I am tired."

Pagan let out a soft whistle as he offered his elbow. "Gallo, come. Let's take your girlfriend back to bed."

Claws scratching up the wooden hall floor announced the dog's enthusiastic arrival. She hadn't noticed he wasn't in his usual spot.

"There, now you'll have company," he said at the door. "I won't be long. Just need a shower after my workout. Go on, get."

"Come Gallo," Suede told Chance's dog. "Let's go back to bed."

Darned if the happy-go-lucky pup didn't beat her to it.

*****

"You disobeyed a direct order."

Chance cranked his neck to the side, stiff from the cold and pissed at the unhappy reception his call to Sullivan had gotten. "Not yet, I haven't. York is still in my sights, but I'd appreciate a candid answer while I wait. Did you conspire with Mitch Tennyson to end York or not? Is that why you sent Pagan here without vetting this mission with me? To do your dirty work?"

"Goddamn it." Something banged on the Senator's end. Might have been his fist.

Chance waited. He'd poked a hornet's nest, but damn it. The bullshit ended today. If Sullivan was dirty, the SOBs were nothing but a hit squad, and the Sinclair boys were out of there.

"Son-of-a-goddamned-bitch!" Sullivan hissed this time, apparently seething mad. *Well, good. That makes two of us.*

"You know I'll follow you to hell and back, Senator, but you didn't hire me because I'm a brainless killer. Level with me. What's York done to merit execution, and why didn't you go through the channels that you set up?"

The silence stretched and Chance let it. He'd said his piece. The ball was now in a Washington D.C. court.

"He's got Tennyson's wife," finally hissed out of Sullivan like the air out of a flat tire.

Like hell he does. "Then why doesn't Pagan know that?" Chance snapped, tired of the run around. "From what he just told me, Mrs. Tennyson boarded the Gusta Marie, a cruise ship headed to Puerta

Vallarta. Pagan double-checked her ID and confirmed her presence aboard ship with the captain. Vera Tennyson is on vacation and her personal assistant Mitchell Franks is with her. Here's another thing, Tennyson withdrew five million from his Swiss bank account late yesterday afternoon. Explain that. Is he paying you off?"

"He what?" Sullivan barked. "That lying son-of-a-bitch."

"Level with me, sir. How close are you and the Governor?" *Close enough to kiss his ass without verifying his story? Close enough to do his dirty work for him?*

"I thought we were friends, not that we've seen each other much over the years. He's been busy."

Sick of the double-talk, Chance called, "Bullshit! Tell me right damned now what's going on, or my brothers and I are out of here!"

A grunt rumbled over the connection. "'Bout son-of-a-bitchin' time. Now, you sound like the man I hired. I've been waiting for you to pull your head out of your ass." Sullivan almost sounded pleased with himself.

"Excuse me?"

"What's going on, Chance, is that Lionel York's taken over the Portland Port Authority, one by one." The senator's West Texas drawl was back, too. "The authority is comprised of nine commissioners, each appointed by his buddy, the Governor. Their responsibilities range from overseeing the daily operations to playing softball with international shipping conglomerates, enticing them to ship into and out of Portland. It's big business and it's political as hell. The man who gets the lucrative job of running the show is the Port Commissioner. He's the one who controls what comes into and out of those docks, what foreign shipping lines he wants to do business with, and who he leases terminals to."

"Keep talking," Chance ordered.

"Just so you know upfront, I've already acquired the go-ahead from all the other SOBs as far as terminating York and a few others. You're the only hold-out."

"And?" Chance bit out. He wasn't ready to capitulate just because Sullivan said that everyone else had blackballed York and his friends. Some deaths were worth waiting for. So was the truth.

"And the FBI has been watching York weasel his way into Oregon politics step-by-step. As soon as one of those commissioners resigns, or dies, as in two recent instances we're aware of, Tennyson's filled those vacancies with York's associates: one with North Korean ties, another associated with the cartel in Colombia. Sound fishy to you?"

"Sounds illegal. That's what this is about, York's strong-arming Tennyson? That's why Suede Tennyson's attempted murder?"

"I wish it were that simple. We believe there's someone behind the scenes pulling the strings, someone with more clout that either Tennyson or York. Remember Pablo Escobar?"

The name from the eighties and nineties rang a bell. "The Colombian drug lord? What's he got to do with anything?"

"Nothing, but this guy, whoever he is, is on the same fast-track today as Escobar was back then. Since York decided he liked Portland, more of the city's police officers, judges, and local officials have been murdered. Last month, Homeland Defense lost two agents tracking weapons at the Portland International Airport, another one over at the Troutdale Airport."

"You do know Miss Hex is in Portland," Chance said, baiting his friend to reveal more. "What's her stake in this?"

"Wish I knew, but the Rio Brothers are already there. That means their boss, Viktor Patrone wants in. Be advised, both Miss Hex and the Rio boys are now sanctioned hits." He cleared his throat. "Pending your concurrence, that is. I don't need to tell you that we're looking at an all out drug war in the Northwest if we don't step in now."

"Do you know Julio Juarez?"

Sullivan hissed. "Shit. That's Wilhelm Gonzales' personal body guard. How's he involved?"

"Not exactly sure, but York's supposed to meet with him and—"

"Juarez is Gonzales's muscle. If he's working with York, and if Patrone's in league with Tennyson, Jesus H. Christ—"

"We've got a drug war coming to Portland," Chance finished. Gonzales was the only upstart drug lord in Colombia not under Patrone's heel. They'd battled plenty in South America, and it looked like their gruesome, bloody war would soon be on American shores.

"You've got my agreement, Senator, but why didn't you tell me this up front?" Chance asked.

"Because you're right..." Sullivan let out a sigh as deep as the Grand Canyon. "I do have a mole in my organization. I had to make sure it wasn't you."

Chapter Nineteen

When dinner didn't materialize as promised, Suede took matters into her own hands. She never could ignore her grumbling stomach. Back on her feet again, she aimed for the hallway Pagan had taken, then thought twice. She knew her way around a kitchen. "Let's make dinner, shall we?" she asked the gangly puppy at her heels.

The kitchen was a surprise. Snow peas, bean sprouts, shiitake mushrooms, broccoli, and bamboo shoots had been rinsed, sliced and drained and now rested in a large colander beside the sink. Pagan planned to make stir fry from scratch? Interesting, but not what she'd expected. Most men ordered out. This guy actually cooked with real food?

She checked for a steamer full of rice or a pan of rice noodles at the ready. When she found none, she got creative. This was right up her alley. To protect her tender fingers, she snooped until she found a box of nitrile kitchen gloves under the sink. Then she went to work.

In no time at all, thanks to Pagan's astute preparations, Suede had a wok full of the diced, marinated chicken pieces she'd found in the refrigerator, now sizzling on the front stove burner. The vegetables went into the wok next. To that she added her own mixture of fish sauce, soy sauce, egg, and rice wine, then drained the linguine-size rice noodles that took her five quick seconds of prep time in boiling water.

By the time she garnished her masterpieces with slivered scallions, toasted almonds, and sliced boiled eggs, again courtesy of Chance's brother, Suede was tired but content. Her thigh was killing her, but she'd proved she wasn't a complete drain on this family. There was a small measure of satisfaction in that.

Dizzy from being on her feet for so long, she took a break to survey her handiwork. This meal wasn't equal to the gourmet dishes by some of the great chefs in Hollywood, but it would feed two hungry men, hopefully three if Chance showed. Better yet, the guys could grab what they wanted buffet-style. She wasn't up to setting a grand table with the pricey cutlery she'd spied in the drawer, though it was tempting. Rest. She wanted back in Chance's bed and a quick nap before dinner.

The Sinclair kitchen was a foodie's dream, stocked with utensils and culinary equipment a master chef would use, enticing for a woman who'd rather be behind the counter whipping up a batch of sour cream and onion pancakes than dealing with the drama of the celebrity world. Just the thought of all she'd endured with York, soured her empty stomach.

"Why ever did I stay with him?" she wondered out loud.

Gallo sat patiently under the table watching, his soulful brown eyes so expressive she thought he might actually talk. "What do you think, Gallo? Did we do good today or what?"

The dog's big ears flopped with his one quick nod and a growly whine.

"You talk, don't you?"

Another floppy-eared nod and a whine and he slid to his belly, his gaze fast on her.

Suede couldn't resist. She'd never owned a dog, and this guy was too cute to resist. Off came the gloves. As carefully as possible, she eased to her knees and joined him. "Can you shake hands, I mean paws?"

His ears flopped as one big paw landed in her extended palm.

She squeezed his paw. "What else can you do? Roll over?" *That would be so cool.*

Gallo's long nose twitched and over he went, scrambling to get back on his belly and feet, his eyes wide and expressive and... Expectant?

"Ha!" Suede nearly squealed. "I'm supposed to reward you when you do good, huh? That's what you're waiting for. You're still learning tricks, but you've learned about treats, haven't you? I know just what you'd like."

She pushed to her knees, then jumped to her feet, going for a slice of that chilled roast in the refrigerator. Too fast. The kitchen spun like a tilt-a-whirl and down she went. Falling to the floor wouldn't have mattered, but she landed on her left hip, and... ouch. Her forehead collided with the edge of one of the wooden chairs, and stars... Suede saw bright, spinning stars that weren't connected to the overhead rafters.

The sound of deep male voices approaching worried her, but there was nothing to be done. Her energy had left her high and dry.

Chance's brothers found her on the floor with Gallo sitting on her lap. "Gallo! Off!" Pagan roared as he dropped to his knees. "Did he hurt you?"

"No, no, he's a good boy," Suede said as she tugged Gallo back to her side. "St-stay b-boy." Wow, that one little fall took the wind out of her. She lowered her head, sure she might still pass out, but swallowing hard so she didn't throw up. "You were busy and I... I fixed dinner."

"What were you thinking?" Pagan asked as one big hand cupped her shoulder. "You're trembling, woman. I told you to go to bed."

Suede lifted her chin at the caveman rationale. "I did, but I was hungry, and you were busy, and..."

"She did a right fine job," another male spoke. That had to be Kruze. Suede could barely stand to meet his appreciative gaze. My goodness, Kruze Sinclair was as handsome as his brothers with that mop of black hair and those deep green eyes. He stayed at the door, his arm sprawled over his head while he gripped the doorjamb. Where did these guys get those massive shoulders and biceps?

Just great. Why look like a simpering female in front of one Sinclair brother when it was more embarrassing to fall on your ass in front of two? Could this day get any worse? Yes. Just lifting her head to look at these guys caused rolling, boiling chaos in her stomach.

Suede swallowed hard and pushed away from Pagan, not going to ruin her perfect dinner by hurling in the kitchen. Instead of getting out of her way so she could crawl, he hoisted her off the floor like a sack of potatoes, and she landed in his arms. He cradled her against him, the last place she wanted to be, if and when her stomach won.

Too much motion. *Not helping!*

"No," she grumbled. "You don't understand."

"Be still. I need to look at that cut. You're bleeding and Chance will—"

"I'm going to throw up. You have to let me down," she croaked, her belly muscles already retching from the double whammy of being dizzy and the sudden change in altitude.

Pagan was a tall man, but he could run. Suede made it into Chance's bathroom before she lost her cookies. By then, all she wanted was to be left to die alone from embarrassment.

"L-leave," she ordered, already face down and choking over the porcelain throne.

But did he listen? *Does any man listen to a puking woman?* She lost track of him as her stomach ruined the end of what would've been a good day. Everything came up and out. By the time her traitorous body finished making her look like the weakest, most helpless woman on the planet, Suede was just that. To make matters worse, she started to cry, and once the tears started, Suede was done.

Kindly Pagan was still there, holding her hair like a loyal boy scout who didn't know when to quit. He didn't say a word as he flushed the toilet and ran the faucet. On one knee now, he tugged her against his leg, smoothed her hair and wiped her face. At least he'd used cool water to wet that cloth. Warm wouldn't have done a bit of good.

Suede closed her eyes at his gentle care, weary of her life and the mess it always turned into. "Thank you," she whispered so he'd know she wasn't a complete ass.

"Shush now," he whispered back. "You're running a fever, and you've done too much for a woman in your delicate condition. I'm going to lift you now. Do you think you can handle it this time?"

"I'm not in a delicate condition." That made her sound pregnant.

Pagan growled. "Don't argue. I just meant you're still recovering."

Oh, that. She nodded, ashamed that he meant to carry her, but crawling would've been so much more demeaning. "I'm not pregnant," she told him as he settled her butt on his knee, then lifted to his feet as easily as if he were lifting a child.

"I never said you were, but you're not one hundred percent either, are you, Suede? Christ, you fell off a cliff yesterday. It's a wonder you're not broken."

In no time, she was tucked into bed, leaning heavily against Chance's pillow, and her adventure helping in the kitchen was over. Pagan pulled the blanket up to her chin as he sat at the edge of the bed. "You're bleeding again."

"I know," whined out of her. *Floor, just swallow me now!*

Black eyes peered out from under his brows. "I meant your hip, not your head. I need to change the bandage."

"Okay," she whimpered as she rolled to her good side. *Get it over with.* "I just wanted to help." What was that saying about good intentions? That they paved the way to hell? *Taxi!*

Pagan was as swift at changing the dressing this time as he was the last. In minutes, Suede was on her back again and exhausted. While he dealt with the cut on her forehead, she kept her eyes closed. Maybe he'd go away if he thought she'd fallen asleep. No such luck.

"If you'd like, I could braid a few cornrows on this side of your head. Maybe add some colorful beads. An eye-patch."

Suede peered up at him. "What are you talking about?"

He winked down at her through his arms since both of his hands were busy, one cupping her head to hold her steady while the other smoothed a butterfly bandage over her latest injury. "You look like a pirate with your black eyes and bruises. Aye Matey?"

He almost made her smile. "I'm a fucking idiot," she confessed in case there was any way possible that he'd missed that incredible talent of hers. Some people were piano or math geniuses. She apparently was best at messing up her life.

His brows collided in the same way that Chance's did when she'd cussed. "Now Suede, my mother always said, if you can't say anything nice, then—"

"*'Don't say anything at all,'*" she whispered the last of that well-known axiom. "I forgot. I'm trying not to cuss, but I don't get it. You're obviously former military. So's Chance, but you guys don't use bad language. What's up with that?"

Pagan's big shoulders quirked upward and his eyes stayed fastened to his fingers as he closed the first aid kit. "Now, don't go turning us into saints. You haven't heard me when I bash my finger with a wrench or when Chance drops a pine tree on his foot. We know the same expletives you do. Maybe more."

"But you strive to be better."

He winked at her then. "I don't know about Chance, but not cursing is my way of keeping Mom alive in my heart. You would've liked her, Suede, and I have no doubt she would've liked you."

There was something incredibly dear about these Sinclair boys who missed their mom. "You really loved her, huh?"

"Sure. That's what kids do. No matter how big they get, they always love their mothers. Don't you?"

Wasn't that the question of the century? "I don't know," Suede answered truthfully. "My mom never had time for me. I don't have warm memories of her."

Pagan set the kit to the nightstand. "What you need to do is rest, Suede. Are you hungry at all? I've got to be honest, the dinner you fixed looks better than what I had in mind."

She shook her head. "No, thank you, but save some for Chance, would you? He might show."

Pagan cocked his head. "That's what you're hoping, isn't it? That Chance comes back tonight. Didn't he tell you he had work to do?"

She nodded, her eyes heavy and fading fast. "He did, but a woman can always hope."

"Aye, aye Matey," she thought she heard Pagan whisper from the doorway. "And it's high time Chance stopped running."

Chapter Twenty

"She's what?" Chance couldn't believe his ears. Suede had taken a turn for the worse? How'd that happen?

"You heard me, brother. The antibiotic isn't working. She's delirious and she keeps asking for you," Pagan insisted. "Kruze just left to get a doctor. You'd better get back here. I'm worried."

There was a catch to Pagan's tone that Chance couldn't decipher, but the thought of Suede failing after all he'd gone through to ensure she lived, sent a stabbing pain to his gut. Losing a bright and shining star like her was akin to being thrown overboard and keelhauled. He wouldn't survive in a world without her in it. Not that he expected to marry the woman. That was most definitely not what this was about, but knowing that she was alive and happy somewhere out there...

It didn't have to be with him...

"But the mission always comes first..." Chance let his words trail away. That was what he'd thought the last time he'd lost someone important in his life, while he was on an important mission. If he'd been in San Diego where he should've been, if he'd been with his mom, he wouldn't have lost his team.

What would it hurt? He'd been waiting a day now for her highness Mother Nature to finish the high-handed blizzard that wouldn't seem to end. So far, that had left him cold to his bones and biding his time until who knew how much longer? The soft peppermint candies he'd brought with him were nearly gone. There might be enough time to rappel down Old Man Mountain one last time. Just to see Suede. Just to make sure.

It wasn't that far of a drop. *Think about it. You'll be back in an hour or two. Three tops. What could happen in that amount of time?* York wasn't going anywhere, and if Suede was that bad...? Chance raked a hand over his balaclava and beanie covered head. *If she's that bad, I'll fix it. I will. Then I'll be back on duty. I will.*

"Be right there," he told his brother, but why wasn't Pagan still hanging on the line? That he'd hung up without an answer spiked a burst of adrenaline like Chance had never known before. He jumped to his feet. His hyper vigilance red zoned. Suede must've taken a turn for the worse. She could be dying, and Pagan was too busy caring for her to waste time convincing his hardheaded older brother to man up. *Well, I'm manning up now.*

It took Chance seconds to pack his rifle and gear. Before he knew it, he was out of that rustic cabin and running into the wind. The pistol in his hand was the only reminder that York was still a man to be taken seriously, just not enough of a deterrent to prevent Chance from getting to Suede. If York got in the way, he was dead.

At the edge of the cliff, Chance set his bag down and strapped in to his rappel gear for the trip down. With his rappel device secured to his belay loop, he jerked enough rope for the slack needed. By then he was anchored and ready to drop his line over the edge at what might have been the exact spot where York had shoved Suede to her death. *The flaming bastard.*

Chance glanced back at the direction of York's rig, seeing red. *For two cents I'd...*

Was leaving this murderer to live another day the right decision? For the first time he questioned his rationale. Another man might have offed York without a second thought, but damn it. As much as Chance wanted revenge, he wanted the best for Suede more. She needed a second chance at a decent life.

Bottom line: there wasn't time for York's come-to-Jesus meeting. Not right now.

Chance double-checked his weight against the rappel anchor and the setup, fighting for composure. This wasn't the time to make an amateur mistake and fall, not with Suede's future in the balance. Not with her murderer a mere yards away. If York were out and about, Chance doubted he'd have a clue what the snow-camouflaged shadow was standing at the drop point anyway, but a smart man didn't take unnecessary risks.

Jerking the ropes one last time, Chance made certain they were threaded through the device correctly. He set his auto-block, his backup in case the unexpected happened and somehow, he was knocked unconscious. With this wind, anything could happen once he stepped over the edge. A man in a hurry made mistakes. Chance Sinclair didn't want to be that man.

Bouncing on pure adrenaline now, he secured his gear bags over one shoulder with a bungee cord, turned his back on the blizzard whipping at his six, and over he went. Kicking away from the sheer granite face to give himself more room, he jackrabbited his descent, his boots hitting the granite wall in steady jumps instead of one long fall.

The hardest lesson he'd brought home from all of his deployments was that there were no second chances. The guys you roomed with, fought side by side with, and were prepared to die for, too many times didn't come home at the end of a long, hard day. And no, by God, seeing them for the last time when they were laid out in flag-covered coffins aboard a C-130 loading platform didn't count. It worked the same for those you left behind. That one last goodbye at the guard shack at whichever naval base you deployed from had better be good because it might be your last. And if you were dumb enough to procrastinate telling the ones closest to you that you loved them? He swallowed hard. *Then you were a fool.*

Shit, the wind was bitter and brisk, nipping at his exposed skin, which wasn't much due to his balaclava. Distances were difficult to determine when your whole world was moving, blustering snow, so Chance took his time. He let his harness hold his weight. At the next anchor, he repeated the process and wondered yet again how Suede had survived such a fall.

Because of the odds against her, it was easy to jump to the conclusion that she was a spy, but Chance knew better. He still hadn't a clue why York had chosen this specific location, but he knew Suede's heart. She wasn't who the press or York had portrayed her to be.

The only thing that made a lick of sense involved the capriciously wild storm that seemed to have set up camp over Northern Montana. It was just possible that Mother Nature's relentless assault that night was what slowed Suede's fall. Maybe an updraft. Maybe it was just that Suede weighed no more than a downy fluff in comparison to Mother Nature's massive power. Maybe she'd been tossed around on her way down instead of falling like a stone.

It sounded like one too many maybes. Chance had no idea what really happened, but the notion of

Suede's billion-to-one survival played at the edge of his keen mind. He didn't believe in coincidences, and his mom had always said everything happened for a reason, even the bad things. Suede was like the dog Scarlett had left her oldest son, an unexpected gift Chance had no idea how much he'd want at the end of the day.

Christ, if the antibiotics hadn't worked, what choice did Pagan have but to send Kruze for a doctor? *What are you trying to tell me, Mom? That you're watching over me? That you always know better? Well, knock it off already.*

At last! His boots touched down. Home was less than a mile away, an easy hump on a good day. He made it in ten minutes despite the accumulated snow, his only goal to reach Suede before she coughed her last breath.

Damn it, Pagan. All you had to do was keep her safe and get her well. What was so hard about that? The answer, of course, was York. He'd meant Suede to die, and she was, damn him to hell.

Shoving his heavy wooden front door open, Chance inhaled the heated indoor air and shook the snow off his shoulders and head. The cabin was dark and no fire burned in the central fireplace. Gallo didn't come running to meet him. *Where is everyone? Shit. Am I too late?*

He slammed the door and ran for his room, shedding his gear as he went. The eerie silence of his mansion in the mountains whispered, *'You're always too late. She's gone and you've lost her, too.'*

Like hell, Chance thought as he laid an open palm to his door, but bowed his head instead of shoving it open. "I need this one in my life," he murmured to himself. Really. He wasn't praying to God or, or anyone—up there. He didn't believe in that stuff, not after the last six months. Those words were for him and him alone. No one else. Certainly not a higher power that might actually be real and waiting on him to call out for an assist, like a kid to a father.

Regardless of what Chance thought he believed in, the relentless plea spilled out of him and flew heavenward. "This one's different. Please. Let her live."

Enough! Silently, Chance propelled himself into the darkness. He could've sworn he heard a shuffle and the hiss of a door closing behind him, but there she was, as still as a corpse, her head on his pillow and her body motionless. That Gallo had chosen to sleep on the floor at the end of the bed confirmed Chance's worst fears. Even the dog knew...

Chance choked as he fell to his knees at Suede's side, his head bowed and his worst nightmare come true. "Mom, no. Not fair."

Gentle fingers threaded into his hair caressing his scalp. "Chance?"

His head jerked up. "You're not dead?"

Suede coughed that awful, barky cough, but shook her head. "I don't think so."

He hadn't a clue how he got up off his knees, but the next thing he knew he was on the bed and holding her frail body in his arms, her poor backside on his lap as he shook with relief. He buried his face in her hair. She'd washed it, and by God, his cock stood up and took notice, but for the first time in years, it wasn't enough. He let his tears loose. This sweet, gentle person was alive. There'd be no coffin or funeral this time. No last regrets either. *I'm not too late.*

The sweetest fingers traced his cheekbones, wiping at the emotion running like a river into his beard. "What's wrong? Did York hurt you? Are you okay?"

Ah, where to start? "Nothing," was all he could choke out, his heart and soul on fire for the lady in his arms. "Pagan said you were ill, and I thought…" He swallowed hard and tried again, "I thought…" *That I'd lost you like I'd lost my mother. That I'd arrived too late to tell you goodbye, or that I care, or that maybe… God! So many maybes!*

"I have had a bad day," Suede admitted hoarsely, smoothing her fingers over his beard, tugging at it in her gentle way and ending with her palm over his thrumming breastbone.

So have I, but I'm okay now. Chance pressed her head under his chin and lowered his nose to the sweet perfume in her hair, needing to catch his balance before he fell apart. He hadn't been this emotional in months, six to be exact. It had never been made clearer. He needed a woman in his life. Not just any woman, but this one. Only this one.

He planted a kiss in the deepest, sweetest smelling tangles against her warm scalp, breathing her back into his soul where he wanted her to stay.

"But I feel better now," she whispered, her fingers stealing up his bicep to his shoulder, and from there, to the curve of his stiff neck.

"Me too," he said, meaning it from the darkest corner of his tattered soul. His lungs expanded with a welcome rush of relief. The wicked buzz of regret in his head cleared. For the first time in months, Chance Sinclair felt better.

Chapter Twenty-One

It seemed surreal, holding Chance in a full embrace like she was, but Suede didn't care. This was what she'd wanted since he'd left to go after York. To have him safe and sound in her arms after all the terrible things that could've happened, warmed her like nothing else. He'd come for her and that made twice she owed him. Once for saving her life, this time for saving her soul.

Her fingers wandered up the back of his neck to tangle in his shaggy hair. He smelled of wind and snow mixed with manly sweat, and that epithelial-filled combination was fast becoming her favorite fragrance. Lifting her chin, her nose grazed his bearded chin.

"What's wrong, Chance?" He seemed distraught, but why he'd thought she'd died was a puzzle she didn't have the answer to. "And don't tell me *nothing*. I'm not stupid. You're upset. Talk to me."

She had been sleeping extra sound after her debacle in the kitchen and puking her guts up in the bathroom with Pagan, but she didn't look that bad, did she? She'd brushed her hair, and she'd finally found a toothbrush. Her breath was decent again. Okay, so maybe she had a bad case of bed-hair, but what'd he expect from a woman who was lucky to be alive?

He tilted his upper body away from her but kept his hands on her biceps. "Pagan told me you weren't feeling well, and I thought—"

Canting her head, she got into that space between them where he had no choice but to look down at her. "You thought I was dying?"

A nearly imperceptible quiver was her only answer.

"You called me Mom," she whispered. He'd sounded so desperate then, as if he were beseeching his mother for help.

"No, I didn't, I... I..." He rolled his neck, drawing his gaze away from her as he huffed, struggling with something that seemed to be tearing him apart. "It was just that... Shit. I mean..." One hand stabbed into the dark shadows of his hair like a rake in a pitch black haystack.

Suede tapped her index finger to his lips, tracing the lower lip because it was so full and soft. So inviting.

Chance blew out a tremendous sigh, feathering the tangles that had fallen over her forehead with a gentle peppermint breeze. She closed her eyes and took it in, promising to remember him for the rest of her life by this simple fragrance. Peppermint and evergreen would forever bring back memories of Chance Sinclair and the time he saved her life.

"Mom died when I was out of the country on my last deployment, Suede. I wasn't there and I should've been. Pagan and Kruze made it to her bedside in time, but I was... I was—"

"On an important mission, right?" she finished for him. "You couldn't get home to her in time, and you haven't forgiven yourself for not being there, have you?"

His eyes closed and Suede was afraid she'd ruined the tender moment. No man had ever confided in her like this before and she wasn't quite sure if she'd responded correctly. This was a new and rewarding experience to be allowed an intimate insight into a warrior as fierce and as locked up tight as Chance Sinclair. Compared to him, Pagan was a big fluffy teddy bear and York was an empty scarecrow, stuffed full of BS.

"That's the thing. The Navy would've sent me home if they'd known, but I thought I had more time. My mission was important, and I thought she could wait until..." Chance blew out another sigh. "Shit, never mind. I don't know why I'm telling you this. You sure you're okay?"

His voice had grown thin and tight with every word. He still suffered for what had happened to his men and his mom. His grief was a living, breathing monster on his back, and Suede wanted, somehow, to make it go away.

She nodded, bumping against his scruffy chin in the process. "Like I said, I am now that you're here." But she wasn't about to let him change the subject. "Did you know how bad your mom was? Did you know she was dying?"

He shook his head. "None of us boys did. We didn't know she'd had breast cancer before then either. Damn. There were a lot of signs we missed."

Suede found it endearing that he still referred to himself and his brothers as boys. "She sounds like a normal mother, shielding her boys from the ugly side of life." *I wish mine was more like her.*

"But I thought we were tight. Why'd she keep that from us? We weren't babies. We deserved to know."

Suede bit her bottom lip. She had no experience with the behavior of a caring woman like Scarlett Sinclair in her life. The closest she could relate was her high school girlfriend, Karen Singleton's relationship with her mom. They treated each other like girlfriends, like best friends. They confided in each other. Shared things. Went to movies together. "I don't know, but I'm a little jealous for the time you did have with your mom. I'd give everything to have had someone like her in my life, even if it was just for a couple years."

"I lived with her, Suede. I lived with her, and she still kept that from me."

Her eyes widened. She'd assumed he'd been divorced, or something the way he'd tended to her. "You weren't married?"

"No way. Deployments are tough on married guys. I've watched plenty go through divorces. Why would I do that to a woman?"

She had no answer, but wow. A man like Chance still living at home with his mom. You didn't hear that every day. "You, umm, lived with your mother?"

His brows slammed together. "In the same gated community, not the same house. Not like either of us was home much, but she wanted to stay close. Said it made her feel safer. I didn't mind. Lots of SEALs lived there with their families."

Oh, good. It was her idea. Not his. That helped. An older woman on her own deserved someone she could trust within driving distance. For a moment there, Suede thought he might have been a mama's boy. It was time for another change of discussion. "So you were injured during the time you lost your mom?"

A groan eked out of Chance. "Yeah. Same time."

Her fingers lifted automatically to his cheek, threading through the scruffy beard there, wishing she knew how to make him feel better. "So you were distracted when you got the news, weren't you? That's when you were hurt."

"No, I didn't get the news she'd passed until after I was rescued. That wasn't why I lost most of my team. We hit a piece of bad intel and ended up in the middle of an ambush. The only things that saved us were the Little Birds on our six that day."

She cocked her head, her hand not breaking their link. "Little Birds?"

"MH-6 light helicopters. We were working with the Night Stalkers on that mission and—"

This man spoke in code. "Night Stalkers?"

The tension eased out of his body while he explained. "I forget, sorry. You're not one of the guys. The Night Stalkers are the 160th Spec Ops Aviation Regiment out of Fort Campbell, Kentucky. They fly us black ops guys into tight places. It's called an insertion. That day we went in by Blackhawk, but lucky for us, we had four baby birds on stand-by. While one laid down suppressive fire, the others pulled us out. So, yeah. Same fucking day."

Oh, oh, he'd cursed. "The same *day*?" Suede swallowed hard. *Not the same week?* "So your team was hit the same day that... you nearly died the same day that..." She couldn't say it, so she cupped the back of his head, pulling him in closer, so damned sorry that he'd lost his sweet mom the same day he'd lost his team and almost his life. "I'm so sorry, Chance. You didn't know she was gone until you finally called home, did you?"

He shook his head, blinking, but not meeting her gaze. "I never got the chance. My CO gave me the news when I came to in the hospital." Chance cupped her chin, rotating her head to one side then the other, studying her from what angles he could, given the lack of much light in his bedroom, but still not making eye contact.

She wasn't certain if he meant to hit her or kiss her. York would've told her to shut up long ago. He would've punctuated that order with a smack or two, and she would've run to her room to escape the prying eyes of his *'friends'*. But then, he never would've shared this much of his heart in the first place.

Chance met her eyes then. "Let it go, Suede. I can't change what happened six months ago. What's important now is that you're not dying. You never were, were you?" His fingers traced her still swollen bottom lip, seeming to need to make certain.

She allowed the change of discussion. Some things were too hard to talk about. "I did too much today, and I wore myself out. I should've listened to Pagan and stayed in bed, but I'm definitely going to live."

She would've sung and danced to prove her point, but her eyes had finally grown used to the dark and Suede couldn't look away. His face was dark and fierce. Predatory at an instinctual, elemental level where animal impulses ruled at a glance. Where anything could happen.

"I'm going to kiss you," he said, a gruff growl to his tone.

Every last one of her resolutions vanished into thin air. "Ah huh," she said, her tongue already moistening her lips in preparation and her heart singing its happy song, *'Yes, oh yes, oh yesssssssss!'*

Chance closed the distance by one painfully slow centimeter at a time, not taking his gaze from her. Suede lifted her arms and circled his neck. But where she'd expected rough handling and frenzy, he took her with the most reverent kiss she'd ever tasted instead. There was no biting or mashing of teeth to this peppermint flavored encounter, just a gentle connection that sent shivers racing up her spine and over her scalp. He drew her against his massive chest, pressing her breasts where she wanted them pressed, molded her to him like she belonged *Right. There.* Like a shirt or a coat or his—heart.

A quiet, sad groan wound up and out of his throat, sparking a maternal instinct inside Suede she had no idea she possessed until then. This gentle man needed something from her, and it wasn't sex. There was no foreplay to this contact, no wandering male fingers probing her feminine defenses or roaming under her shirt. No pinching. Rubbing. No fondling.

If anything, he seemed intent on absorbing what was left of her wounded soul into his, offering his strength as he took something, she wasn't quite sure what, from her. Whatever it was, he seemed to need it as much as she needed him, so she relaxed into his embrace like a lover.

For the first time, Suede was aware of the hard balance of his musculature against her soft curves. Her heart awoke to the easy give and take of the male and female forms. He wasn't using his strength against her. He didn't have to. Puzzle pieces. They were two lost puzzles pieces that had found each other compatible, and were interlocking in a physical way that defied all the frenzied, smutty, sexual lies ever told. Man and woman weren't created merely for the sake of a good fuck. They weren't play things for the other's basest needs. No. This was different. There was something magical about the respectful way Chance held her. He wasn't groping, stroking, or petting. It felt more as if he were—praying. And she was the answer to that prayer.

Suede let him own her mouth and her lips, arching backward as she surrendered to the spirit of the moment. If this man was her other half, the part of her she hadn't realized she'd been searching for, was this—she dared think it—*love?*

Can't be. Love's another one of those lies. Isn't it?

Yet the need to offer every last bit of herself, such as it was, swelled within Suede until there was no holding back. The time was now, and Chance was her reason for breathing. She wanted him to be happy with her and for her. It was enough. It truly was.

Carefully, cautiously, he broke the link, but didn't go any farther than her nose. Nuzzling her cheek, he whispered, "I should let you rest."

No, you should let me love you, sprang to her lips, but she caught the words before they leapt the distance between Chance and herself. If this thing was real, she meant to become the woman he deserved first, not some spineless tennis player's discarded toy of the month. Chance was too good a man to be reduced to a rebound.

As hard as it was to dampen the tempting fire bubbling in her veins, Suede swallowed her lust and did just that. The day would come that Chance Sinclair would look at her with better eyes than the raw, emotion-filled ones tonight. If he could see past the woman she was yesterday to the woman she planned to be tomorrow, then she'd know she was good enough for him. Until then...

"I am tired," she admitted, the blankets now puddled on the floor.

Like the gentleman she knew he was, Chance extricated his body from hers and ended this extraordinary encounter by climbing to his feet, tugging the blankets up and tucking her into his bed like he cared. "Sleep tight, Suede," he whispered as he dipped low to plant a warm kiss in the middle of her forehead. "Goodnight."

One thing was very clear: she'd never get enough of this man. Suede lifted to her elbows. "Will you be here in the morning?" *Because if you're not, I'm not going back to sleep.*

"That's the plan. My brothers took over my operation without so much as a by your leave. Do you believe those jerks telling me you were on the verge of death?" He raked a quick hand through his beard, but she could tell he wasn't as mad as he let on. "Sweet dreams," he murmured.

A sigh escaped her lips at that affectionately spoken command. Little did he know that was exactly what he'd given her: a reason to dream. Suede sank into the pillow, her hands clasped over her breastbone. If this was love, it had all the earmarks of a terrible, wonderful, frightening thing. Chance Sinclair now had the power to hurt her worse than her parents or Lionel York ever had.

Chapter Twenty-Two

"You dogs!" Chance ground out, as pissed as he'd ever been. "You guys let me think she was dying." *And I fell for it!* "You turned the beacons off until I was home, then turned them on after you left!" If that didn't make Chance feel like a love-struck hound dog, nothing did.

"It was either that or let you run off and be noble again," Pagan growled back as the helicopter he and Kruze had hitched a ride in zipped south-by-southwest to Portland, Oregon. "Kruze and I got this op, man. We'll be in touch when justice is done."

"Wait!" Chance barked. "Don't you dare hang up. Why aren't you topside with York? I thought you wanted him dead. You were sure ready to end him last time we talked."

"I had time to think and you're right. 'Sides, Portland's filling up fast with assassins. Kruze and I want a ringside seat. Revenge aside, Sullivan gave me this job first, so stow the righteous wrath routine and take care of your woman.”

The connection went dead and Chance's mouth went dry before he could say, *'She's not my woman.'* What a lie. Suede Tennyson was precisely that and he knew it. He'd never felt this way about a woman before. Beneath the foul mouth and her crude public image, an innocence that he hadn't seen coming lay hidden in Suede. As brash and snarky as she could be, he sensed an inner vulnerability, and that surprise discovery had triggered every last one of his male receptors. He wanted to not only protect her, but to support her and provide for her. *Love her.*

He dropped his headset to the desktop, shaking his head. No way. This wasn't *that*. Had to be that whole hero/damsel-in-distress syndrome, but damn it to hell. He was a goner. All it took was that one call from Pagan, and like an idiot, Chance had nearly fallen down the mountain to get to Suede in time. Baby Brother knew how raw he was after losing his team and their mother, and he'd used that weakness against him like a damned pro.

Chance had been well played by the two men he respected most—until tonight. He'd made a fool of himself. Kruze and Pagan had set him up, and if anyone knew precisely how to do it, it was the men who knew him best. *The dogs!* This was Pagan's underhanded idea. He had a smack-down coming. Kruze too, for going along with him.

Chance pushed away from his laptop, not as angry as he let on, but still. There should've at least been a civil discussion before they'd hoodwinked him into leaving his post. What kind of a man does that? *Apparently a lovesick SEAL, that's who.*

Nope. Not lovesick. Emotional, maybe. Brain-damaged, certainly.

Retracing his steps, he went back to his room, the beacons on and the storm in his heart calm for the first time in months. The room was dark and Suede had already fallen asleep. Chance didn't need to do anything more than tend to his unexpected patient until she was fit for travel. Try telling his heart that.

Carefully, he climbed under the covers behind Suede. She moaned when he wrapped an arm around her tiny waist and slid his legs alongside hers. When she bowed her head, that was enough invitation to bury his nose in her hair. And there he stayed for the next days and nights, tending to her instead of saving the world. Making certain she took her meds. Carrying her to the bathroom when she needed to go. Standing guard when she showered, so she didn't slip and fall. Fixing breakfasts and lunches, snacks and dinners to keep her on the mend. Watching her sleep and marveling at the tender beauty who'd fallen into his arms. Wanting her to stay.

Finally her bruises faded to yellow. The tear on her thigh healed and the five-day antibiotic cleared her lungs before they had a chance to get worse. All she needed now was rest. In the wee hours of day four, with her asleep in his arms, he let his mind return to duty.

He'd already informed Sullivan that Pagan and Kruze were now on task; that he'd stayed behind to guard Suede Tennyson. Sullivan didn't need to know the particulars of how that came to be, only that the single most powerful piece in this game of cat-and-mouse between Tennyson and York now lay sound asleep in Chance's bed without a care in the world. No one but the Sinclair brothers and Senator Sullivan knew she'd survived, but even two-faced Governor Tennyson would soon believe the despicable piece of evidence York had carefully captured before he'd offed his own men.

If Tennyson were in on Suede's murder attempt, the video would no doubt make him happy. But if this were the game of comeuppance Chance feared it was, the war between Tennyson and York would escalate. Tennyson would strike back using Viktor Patrone's brute force. York could counter with his buddy Juarez and the Gonzales cartel. The innocent folks of poor Portland, Oregon, would be caught in the middle of gang warfare.

One burden lifted even as another settled like a heavy mantle over Chance's shoulders. Suede was also the key to ending this war before it began, but he and she were alone now in this wild and rugged wilderness called Montana. If anyone came looking for her, if anyone thought for a moment to dredge the pond beneath Mother's Day Falls for her body and didn't find what they were looking for, things could turn ugly.

A tremor ran up his spine. Chance ran a hand over his head and down the back of his neck, sure of two things. He needed to pound out a good workout to get his brain back in the game, and he needed to keep Suede Tennyson safe. Okay, make that three.

Chance shrugged at the unheard, yet always-with-him prompting from Kruze that while Chance declared one discussion point, he always had more. So make it a dozen or two, but Suede Tennyson would also learn how to handle a weapon while she was here. She needed plenty of rest first, but she also needed practice knocking down man-sized targets at the practice range in his basement. She had to learn to protect herself, and Chance was just the man for the job.

Maybe there was a way Suede could draw those two bastards into the open. Wouldn't that kill the buzz York and Tennyson had going, to come face to face with the woman who could end them both during a well-orchestrated press conference? Once they knew she was still alive, all hell would break loose. They'd react, maybe over-react, and hopefully, do something stupid. Homeland Security and the FBI could take it from there.

He scrubbed a hand over his face at the inherent danger in using her to bait men the likes of Tennyson and York, Gonzales and Patrone. The workout was cancelled. He needed to pass these latest insights onto Pagan, Kruze, and Sullivan. A war was coming and the quicker they prepared for it, the better.

Chapter Twenty-Three

Suede woke to the scent of a freshly showered male body sliding into bed and under the sheets behind her. Her heart skipped a beat, but she held her position on her side facing the door, feigning sleep. Even though her entire body, down to her toes, thrummed with an irrepressible need to roll over and touch him, now was not the time to maul Chance Sinclair. She clenched her fingers into fists, fighting the itch to smooth one hand up that toned muscular thigh that had just come to rest behind her leg, so close yet so far away.

His knees bent, aligning themselves with hers, but her thigh still ached from the tremendous wound. Not as badly as before, but enough to keep her aware. As long as she got enough rest, her lungs seemed to be clearing. The antibiotic was working, as was all the bed rest. But damn. She had on nothing but his shirt, and he was wearing only boxers.

And that chest. That marvelous, muscled chest. A woman shouldn't be tempted like this. Squeezing her eyes tight, she let a trembling sigh go. As broad and powerful as Chance's chest was, it was also her soft place to land, and damn, had she landed. She'd never grow tired of rubbing her nose through the dusting of chest hairs across his pecs, or the way his nipples hardened when she accidentally-on-purpose let her fingers wander. It didn't seem to take much to get his attention.

But she needed to be the strong one in this bed tonight. She was the one who needed to change, not Chance. *Where there's a will, there's a way, remember?*

He must've thought she'd fallen asleep, since he picked that moment to align his body more fully with hers. Chance cupped one warm palm to her shoulder, his thumb light and easy on her shoulder blade, gently massaging like he'd done the first night. The scent of peppermint from his breath spilled through her hair, delighting her nose. He seemed to enjoy burrowing his face into her messy locks, and that was fine with Suede. She loved the unique intimacy she shared with this man. There was no roughness or cruelty involved. No bullying and no name-calling.

Like a gentleman, he kept his cock away from her backside, but there was no way to pretend sleep, not with her soul vibrating to be let loose and free. Every nerve ending in her body wanted Chance. If he kept this simple contact going, she'd be glowing in no time.

"I know you're awake."

Thank Heavens! Suede rolled over to face him, carefully adjusting her bandaged thigh as she rotated her body. The wound had healed considerably. "How could you tell?" she asked in the dark, waves of excitement coursing up from her belly. *How could he not?*

"I've known all along. Your breath hitched when I opened the door."

He had her there, but honestly, how could she sleep with him in the same room? The same bed? "Where's Gallo?" she asked, still avoiding the elephant in the room. "I haven't seen him much tonight."

A lighthearted rumble purred out of Chance. "He's sound asleep at the foot of the bed. The mutt never made a peep when I came in. What'd you do? Put a spell on him, too?"

"I'm no witch," she told him. Wiggling one arm out from under the covers, Suede snaked it around Chance's shoulder, letting her fingers come to rest at the back of his neck, her thumb aligned at his ear. *What's this? He shaved? Oh my.*

This man had a delightful neckline now that he'd reduced the beard on his face to mere scruff and tidied up his shaggy hair. Her nostrils flared with the coconut-lime scent of a clean male body. The outdoorsy scent of wind and sunshine that was unique to Chance still lingered, but if she wasn't trying so hard to be a better woman, she would've licked his neck and kept going over his chin and all the way to those warm, manly lips. Damned if her tongue and lips didn't jump to the challenge and bathe each other, just in case.

I'm trying to be better than that, she reminded her aching physical self.

Then kiss him and get it over with.

Oddly, that worthless piece of advice sounded perfect. *I want to,* she admitted despite her wavering resolution.

And he wants you to or he wouldn't be back in bed with you now, would he?

"Chance?" she asked, her fingers threaded into the soft curls of his hair. "Just one goodnight kiss?"

"Thought you'd never ask," he growled as his mouth covered hers, and Suede forgot that other woman she was trying to be. Who cared? Heat flared between her body and his, but he gave her no quarter. With one broad hand splayed to the small of her back, he pulled her against his bare belly, and she knew where they were headed.

It had to stop, but how does a woman with no moral compass stop a man she truly cares about at a time like this? How does a girl who'd never said 'no' to a man in her life, say 'no' now? Chance was unlike any other she'd been with. Okay, so there'd only been two, and Suede was sure that nerd in high school didn't count. York didn't really count either, but Chance was—oh wow, he was worth waiting for.

His fingers dipped down her spine to her backside, squeezing life into yet another wound even as he slowed his own freight train. "Am I hurting you?"

'No! Not at all!' sprang to her lips, but Suede forced a reluctant, squeaky, "Maybe we should stop."

Shifting his hand from her ass to the flare of her waist, Chance shuddered. "I'm sorry. I'm no better than my dog when it comes to you."

"Not true. You're just..." *Everything.* "...tired, and it's been a long day and..." *I'm rambling.*

"You do things to me, Suede. When I'm with you I want to be a better man," he breathed into her face. "I know we just met, but there's something about you that gets me. I'm sorry. I'm not making sense. I'll shut up."

"No, don't. I love listening to you," she said earnestly, wishing there was a nightlight in his room so she could watch the way his eyes sparkled and how the skin between his brows pinched into three distinct lines when he frowned. Little things like that. *But mostly, I lo... I like you.*

"You shaved," she told him, her fingertips on his chin and her wayward heart up high in her throat at the word that had sprung to her mind. "At least, you thinned," she corrected, her voice uncommonly hoarse and her pulse pounding.

"About time," he admitted with a hard swallow. "I keep it on the long side to conceal a couple scars. You know how it is."

"What scars?" Suddenly nervous, she let her fingers tiptoe through what facial hair was left, just enough to distinguish a couple ridges. Several marked his chin. One ran from high on his cheekbone to his ear and along his skull. Long and thin, it was as if a metal claw had raked him. Some were just as long and thin while others were shallow divots where flesh had been carved away. "What happened? Tell me," she urged.

"IED," he hissed. "Nails and explosives. Plastic surgery. All that crap."

"Did this happen when—"

"Yeah. My last deployment. The day Mom—"

She couldn't let him say it. Suede arched into him, aching to kiss every one of those scars away, to make the pain disappear with them. "I'm so, so sorry."

"Yeah, well..."

Smoothing her fingertips through his scruff and over his face, she mapped his rugged features, growing more aroused with every subtle nuance defining this gentle warrior. He held still while her fingers skated gently over the ledge of his brows and eyelids. His straight nose. His lips. She'd never known a man who'd fought for his country and still lived by its code. There wasn't a soft or feminine thing about him.

Pride swelled in her heart for him. "I don't feel scars, Chance; I feel badges and medals of honor. Each tells me that life tried to kill you, but that you're tougher than you know. You survived. You're still here."

His eyes narrowed. "That's it? You're not disgusted with the way I look? The way my skin feels?"

Suede pressed her forehead to his lips, inhaling the scent of him, aroused at this intimate exploration he'd allowed. She had no business caring about this man like she did, but how could she not? He'd cut himself off from the world,andt he was just as alone as she was. Maybe more. He needed her. She knew it to her soul. "You're like a Timex watch, Chance. You might have gotten run over, hammered and dented, but you're still ticking." *And I'm so thankful you are.*

"That's something Mom would've said. Who told you that?"

Her shoulders lifted, but Suede kept her nose in his neck. "Pagan. Your baby brother."

That earned a delighted masculine chuckle. "Guess he listened to her more than I thought he did."

"You guys had a very unique relationship with your mom. You know that, don't you?" Suede whispered, relishing the heat from his body. His gentleness. Her hands slid to his chest, and she couldn't help but turn her head to listen to his heartbeat. To the steady in and out of his lungs as he inhaled and exhaled. That particular miracle from

Mother Nature held a special fascination for her now. The breath he'd given her had become a gift she could never repay.

"No, we didn't. It was pretty much the normal mother/son relationship," he said, his voice rich and rumbling under her ear. "We gave her a run for her money, but she always knew how to get each of us to turn around and listen up."

Suede sensed that talking about his mom was Chance's favorite subject the way he wrapped his arms around her. "How was that?" she asked to keep him talking.

"Well, with me, all she had to do was take away my bike-riding privileges. A kid on a bike in San Diego could ride forever. I used to ride down to Mission Bay, when I could get away with it." He inhaled, filling his lungs. "There's nothing like the ocean breeze in your face and an ice cold Peach Nehi in your hand when you're twelve and think you know it all."

"A Peach Nehi?"

He arched back from her, so she looked up. Peppermint wafted over her face like a blessing. "You've never had a Peach Nehi? What's wrong with you, girl?"

Now it was Suede's turn to laugh. "I guess I didn't have any brothers to get in trouble with. I'll bet you guys had great times together."

He nodded. "We did, but we fought a lot, too. The whole *'boys-will-be-boys'* thing. We were competitive little guys, but Mom had a way of turning us into a team without us knowing it. I credit her with instilling that skill set into all of us. Knowing how to get along with others, how to work together, helped me become a SEAL."

"So you're the oldest?"

Another nod. "Kruze is eleven months younger, then the baby came along eleven months later."

"Pagan. He's at least as old as I am."

"Nope. He's twenty-five and Kruse is twenty-six. I'm the oldest at twenty-seven."

And I'm twenty. Seven years difference. For some reason, that number seemed like a sure sign that she was in sync with the universe, or something. "What'd she look like?

Another deep sigh wafted over Suede before Chance said, "Mom was beautiful. Black hair. Long. She liked to let it dry into natural curls. Happy. That was Mom to a T. She always found a way to make lemonade out of the lemons life gave her. She had the prettiest green eyes."

"Like Pagan's?"

"Like both Pagan and Kruze. I'm the only one who got stuck with my dad's eyes."

"Where is he?"

Another sigh. "Don't know and don't care. He left after Mom hit the big time, just walked out on us after dinner one night. He had the guts to sit there and eat what she'd made before he hauled his sorry ass up and told her to get a divorce on his way out the door. I was three at the time. Can't remember one damned thing about him but that."

"He never kept in touch?" *How dreadful.*

"Some guy told us he moved to Hawaii. I heard he died, but I never confirmed the story. Seemed like a waste of time tracking the jerk down."

"Why'd your mother marry him?"

"He was another writer. She thought they had a lot in common. Didn't work out that way."

Suede had nothing to say to that. She'd never had anything in common with York. If anything, he was just another distorted father-figure in her life. The only difference between him and Dad was she'd slept with York. Even that was blasé. Sex had been exciting at first, a forbidden taboo for the young woman she was, but during the past year or so, it had devolved into an endurance test she dreaded. Once he'd stopped coming to her bed, she'd been relieved.

"What would you say to holding a press conference once this weather moves out?"

Whoa. That came out of the blue. "Me? Why would I do that?" Just the thought of more public humiliation sent icy ripples of terror up her spine. "York would know where I am. So would my parents. They'd..." A shiver wriggled up from her toes. "They'd all come for me." *And not in a good way.*

"No, they won't. You'd be with me and I wouldn't let anyone get near you," Chance explained, his fingers splayed at her waist. "I'll keep you safe, and by then you'll know how to shoot and defend yourself."

"I will?"

"Sure. We've got a practice range downstairs. I'll show you. It'll be fun."

"Hmmmmm," was all Suede could come up with. *Me with a weapon? In my hands?* The notion terrified her, but it came with a tiny shoulder bump of empowerment, too. No one could slap her around if they knew she was qualified with a gun. She wouldn't have to take crap from York ever again. Better yet, the next guy who tried to throw her off a cliff would be in for a big surprise. "I would like to learn about guns," she admitted, swallowing hard at this brave direction her new life had taken. "You'd teach me, and you wouldn't yell at me when I missed the bull's head or whatever it is I'm supposed to aim at?"

The hug she found herself enveloped in was pure heaven, especially when he dipped his head and chuckled in her ear. The joy in that masculine sound went straight to her core, dampening her when she was trying her best to be a good girl for the first time in for-evvvvv-er.

"It's called a bull's-eye, Suede, and no, I won't be angry if you miss. That's why it's called practice. When you're up for it, we'll spend as much time at the range as you want. Trust me, once you're comfortable handling a pistol, and as long as you follow gun safety, you'll do fine."

"What kind of gun? A six-shooter?"

"Most likely a nine-millimeter. I have a couple others that would fit your grip. My .44 Magnum's probably too heavy for you, and it packs one helluva recoil. It'll knock you on your rear if you're not careful, but whatever's mine's yours, babe."

Did he have any idea what he'd just said, or how he'd said it? Suede froze. Was he this generous with all his girlfriends? On second thought, was there another woman in his life besides his mother? Her mouth opened, but she hadn't any idea what to say, so she snapped it shut.

He made it worse then. He leaned his forehead to hers and bumped noses. "I mean it, Miss Tennyson. As long as you live in my house, you're welcome to anything except what's in the control center, my office. I keep it locked, but when I'm in there, you're welcome to join me. Any time. Understood?"

This man was too good to be true. "I have a bank account," blurted out of her big mouth before she could stop it. Like proving she wasn't a complete sponge made her Chance's equal.

"Good, so do I." He cocked his head. "This isn't about taking over, Suede. I'm only here to help you get back on your feet. You know where the door is. Anytime you've had enough of us Sinclairs, just say the word."

"I didn't mean that, I just meant..." She chewed the inside of her cheek, not sure what she meant. "I can pay you back for taking care of me, and I will."

"That's up to you. It's called personal power. Money in a bank account certainly helps you feel empowered, but being able to stand on your own two feet and defend yourself goes a long ways, too. You told me York made you believe he owned you, but that crap doesn't go 'round here. You don't owe me anything, and if you've got a problem, I'm here to talk it out, but in the end, the decisions are all yours. Like this press conference. Think about it, but if you don't want to do it, then it's a no-go. No pressure. No hype. Got it?"

"Got it." Suede relaxed in the arms of her knight in shining armor, his hand tangled in her hair as he cupped her to him. "Chance?"

A warm breath of peppermint skated down her arm. "Yes," he asked, his voice gone rough and hoarse.

"Shut up and kiss me," she begged, her soul on fire for this incredible man.

He tipped her chin up with one finger and swallowed her mouth, and this was wrong on so many levels. She'd just escaped York's clutches. Why was she drawn to Chance? They didn't know each other. Not really. And love at first sight just Did. Not. Happen.

A deep-seated fear niggled at the back of her mind that all men were dogs. They chewed on a woman for a while, and then moved on. But could she break away from the tenderness he'd ensnared her with? Not tonight.

He was the one who broke contact first, his pulse racing beneath her fingertips. "Get some rest," he growled, "or I'll take you nine ways to Sunday."

Then do it! her heart cried, but her mouth whispered, "Okay."

A groan lifted out of him, but he muttered, "Goodnight, Suede."

"Goodnight, Chance." To prove she could do it, that she could wait for sex until she was a better woman, Suede rolled over, her back to Chance. Liquid fire still sizzled in her veins, but now she knew for sure. He was that one in a million. She could wait.

Chapter Twenty-Four

Distraction, thy name is woman, Chance thought as he steadied Suede's right arm while she took careful aim at the paper zombie fifty yards down range. Last night he'd barely slept with the feel of her warm body snuggled against him. Spooning was torture, pure torture! But this morning she'd awakened bright-eyed and eager to get on with her life. At the moment, she was working with her newly acclaimed favorite weapon, a sweet little 308 Ruger that fit her palm perfectly.

The girl turned out to be a damned good shot. Her fingers had healed enough that she'd discarded the bandages, and she paid attention to everything he'd told her, from how to cup her left hand under her right to steady her aim, to marrying her thumbs like lovers at the left of her piece so they didn't get in the way. She cleared the chamber of her pistol like a pro, racked it without pinching her fingers or the heel of her palm even once, and already she'd killed more bull's eyes than Chance had on hand. Hence the zombies. They were Kruze's idea of a joke and the only targets left.

Suede's lungs had cleared. She'd taken the last of Chance's wonder drug and was up on her feet. She still moved a little slow, but if anything, she had cabin fever. The promised delivery drone had come and gone, gifting her with a feminine wardrobe that she promised she'd pay Sullivan back for. He'd even sent all the delicate necessities that went on under those clothes too, along with toiletries, several pairs of athletic shoes, and new hiking boots. Everything a woman could want, he'd sent on the taxpayers' dime.

The problem was the smile on her pretty face after she'd showered and climbed into those jeans that fit just right. That was all the payment Chance needed. Her new T-shirt could've been a size larger, not that he minded how it accentuated her lush curves in all the best ways. The woman had been blessed with a full figure and bounce, plump in all the best places.

But the flowery scent drifting up from those messy tangles? The way his nose twitched to draw her into his soul? This woman was enough to drive a sex-starved man insane. All morning Chance had fought the urge to grab a handful of that gorgeous auburn hair, bend her over the set-up tables behind the gun stations, and go down on her. If she twitched that sweet ass one more time, her tell that she was ready to fire, it might happen.

He forced his thoughts to the mission. By the time the storm had cleared out of Northern Montana, Pagan and Kruze were tucked in a room at the Mount Hood Motel and Lounge on Portland's waterfront, a dive that catered to clientele who rented rooms by the hour, as well as a few transients. No one slept in that joint, unless a man was dog-tired or deaf to wall banging.

Portland found itself hosting an assassins-from-out-of-town convention. Kruze hadn't yet crossed paths with his buddy JJ since Kruze was on Vicky Hex's tail day and night, keeping up and keeping on. The woman was an active runner, so that kept him plenty busy. He had yet to see her without earphones, running shoes, or her sleek and sexy athletic gear. But Chance knew better. Some snakes were beautiful, but they were crafty, and Miss Hex wasn't in town to compete. She already knew she was the best assassin in the world. No doubt she packed a pistol even when she worked out.

Pagan still dogged the Rio Brothers religiously, but Juan and Jorge had yet to take in any of Portland's lavish sights. They ate in their room or the hotel restaurant, and no car service attended them because they didn't go anywhere. Neither did maid service enter their suite to freshen sheets and towels. Odd, but most cold-blooded assassins were odd ducks to begin with. They worked in shadows and misdirection, which kept Pagan on his toes.

The first time they'd eaten breakfast in the hotel's restaurant, he'd B&Eed their room, planted two bugs, then ducked out before they'd returned. But video surveillance only confirmed what Pagan already knew. The lethal brothers weren't doing anything but catching up on television. By all appearances, they seemed to be waiting for someone. Had to be Patrone.

So yeah, nothing much going on in Portland. On the East Coast however, Senator Sullivan had cleaned house. He'd replaced most of his staff when it became apparent that several of them had accepted hard-to-resist job offers from an as yet unnamed benefactor whose slimy grasp seemed to be everywhere.

Sullivan hadn't been able to put a name to the actual person who'd made the deals with his employees. The guy was savvy enough to have enticed non-disclosure statements from them. None would share his identity with Sullivan, but they'd certainly shared what little they knew about the SOBs with the bastard, hadn't they?

Not that there was much to share. The only one with complete access to confidential information was Sullivan. Didn't matter. After a long hard week of *'goodbyes'* and *'good-riddances'*, the beleaguered Senator's much smaller staff had been thoroughly re-investigated and their names cleared. Most had worked with him on previous Senate jobs. His secretary of ten years cried when she'd passed muster. He felt confident in them once again.

As far as the integrity of his other teams? Sullivan had played the same type of Russian roulette with them as he'd played with Chance, feigning that he had a job so urgent that SOB protocol no longer mattered. Funny thing. Every single one of those team leaders told him to go to hell, that they weren't paid assassins and if he couldn't play by the rules he'd set up, they wanted out of the SOBs. Enough said.

Twitch, twitch went Miss Tennyson's backside as she shifted her weight from her right to her left foot. Either she knew what she was doing to Chance, or holding a loaded weapon made her nervous. This time, her luscious, plump derriere brushed against his zipper just enough to incite the steel rod crammed beneath it. Weapons practice with Suede had taken on a whole new dimension. Chance had never been so turned on by a woman holding a gun, and why, oh why did that thing in his pants spring to life every time she touched him?

God, help me now, he thought, his body stiffening from the wayward surge of red, hot American blood. She touched him in places he'd denied for so long they'd turned into fortresses with locked dungeon doors and battened hatches. Damned if she didn't seem to be the one holding all the keys.

"Practice is over after you make this shot," he said, his throat as tight as his jeans.

"Who says I'll make it?" she asked out of the corner of her mouth, her eyes still on target like a good girl.

"Oh, you'll make it all right." *Because you're already making me.* This woman drove him stark raving crazy with that streak of innocence wrapped up in her sexy body. She knew damned well she was taunting him, yet to her it was play. To him? Deliciously unbearable.

Suede Tennyson was a sight to behold, well endowed from the flare of her sexy hips to the T-shirt stretched over her plush breasts. He couldn't take his eyes off the way they pushed together when she trapped them between her biceps while taking aim. His jaw cracked from the tension radiating up his spine from his tailbone. If the lust between them didn't ease off, he'd soon be upstairs under another cold shower.

She aimed. *Twitch. Twitch.*

Chance crossed his arms over his chest and took a full step back from the danger zone. *Just kill the damned zombie.*

Twitch. Twitch. Then—BLAM! Another paper zombie blown to smithereens. Even they couldn't survive twenty closely ranked headshots.

He wiped his brow before she pivoted with that sweet smile of accomplishment on her lips. "I did it!" she squealed, jiggling her girls. "Did you see that?"

He forced his eyes off her bouncing cleavage to the joy on her pretty face. "I'm not telling you what you already know."

"Are you just saying that?" Her lack of confidence overwhelmed him. Why didn't she believe him when he said she'd done good? Had no one praised her before? Not even a teacher or a close confidant?

"We're done here," he said as firmly as he knew how. She didn't need a fat head and he didn't need to repeat himself. "You already know you're good, now stop looking for *'attaboys'*. The only one you need to impress is yourself, Suede. Do better tomorrow. Beat your best time. Be so damned good with that weapon that it becomes an extension of your hand instead of a tool. It's called muscle training. Learn it. Rely on it. You're in this fight to win, not just to look good while you practice. Now" —he smacked that sweet ass to get her moving— "back upstairs for drills."

Her nose wrinkled, but she didn't fuss as she holstered her piece. Drills meant push-ups, sit-ups, pull-ups, and lunges followed by simple weightlifting and toning in his gym. He'd explained the need for her to get back in shape as quickly as possible. She started today. Her thigh wasn't ready for the heavy weights, and she didn't need to look like a muscular male. He liked her curves where they were, but she needed the workout.

"You like me," she purred, her head canted as she peeked out of the corners of her sparkling eyes. Damn, the girl had mischief written all over her face.

Once coiled with enough hyper vigilance to power a freight train, now she'd relaxed enough to tease him. Being safe and protected will do that to a woman, but she wasn't out of danger yet. Chance wanted her prepared for any and all things.

"You're a fast learner, I'll give you that," he answered, dropping his eyes to the brass shell casings strewn at his feet. "Now sweep up. Let's take a break, then we'll reconvene in the exercise room upstairs." *After I take a cold shower.*

Her shoulders lifted and he couldn't resist looking. Damned if the brat wasn't smiling to herself, her eyes on the floor. "It's okay, you don't have to say it. I know you do."

Chance swallowed hard, but didn't join in the playful banter. Suede was fast becoming the temptation he couldn't resist, and that set-up table would work just fine. He tossed her the broom and ran for his life.

Chapter Twenty-Five

Stalking upstairs from what Chance called a basement, but which was more like an armory that trailed off to who knew where, Suede cocked her head at the sound of water running. *Again?* That man took more showers than anyone she'd ever known. Either he was locked up in his office or under the showerhead, yet he wouldn't let her take over the cooking. What was up with that? She didn't care about the whole politically correct thing or what everyone thought about gender specific roles. She liked to cook and he liked to eat. Get over it.

Now's my chance. Her lips cracked into a smile at that incredibly clever pun. *My Chance. Get it?* Not like he was hers, but they certainly seemed compatible. They even slept together, though not in the marital sense like most of her generation. *What was up with that?*

At the refrigerator, she pulled out another slab of peppered bacon, his favorite, a dozen eggs, green onions, and the last of the tomatoes. He liked her salsa, so he was getting a Spanish omelet with four slices of artisan toast along with a hearty helping of salsa. How he'd arranged with a company to deliver fresh groceries by drone amazed her. What a novel way to live in the middle of nowhere.

Suede whipped up her specialty, lit the front burner on the gas stove, and breakfast was on the table by the time Chance arrived with a towel around his neck. She froze at another mouth-watering sight. Him. With his hair wet. His eyes bigger and blacker than usual. That funny half-smile quirking at his lips like he knew something she didn't.

Just like every other time he'd caught her in the kitchen, and there had been many because Suede Tennyson was nothing if not persistent—he winked. The funny guy. Chance filled the doorway. He was a paradox of bottled-up angst glossed over with the charm of a playboy, what had become a lethal combination, and her fatal attraction.

If she hadn't promised herself to a higher standard this time around, she'd run at him and jump into his arms. He'd catch her and she'd wrap her aching legs around his belly and let his sexy mouth ravage her neck and breasts with those hot, steamy kisses he'd given her before. She'd give him the best breakfast of his life was what she'd do, only...

I'm not that person anymore, she told herself even as her heart fluttered with a million butterflies that seemed to be calling her a liar. *I'm not.*

His brows lifted. "You're not what?"

She rolled her eyes at her big mouth. Apparently she'd said that last bit out loud. "Umm, I'm going to be a better marksman by the time we're through." *And I'm going to learn to keep my thoughts to myself and my big mouth shut.*

His mouth quirked as he offered her one of those manly *'attaboy'* chin nods guys gave each other. "Tell me something I don't know, but I'm sure you meant markswoman."

Her head bobbed because she didn't dare speak. She didn't want to be Mark's woman, whoever Mark was. She wanted to be Chance's woman, just... not... yet. She had to prove herself first. Snuggling under the covers with him at night was one thing, but commitment, that was what she wanted, out of herself first, then out of the man who could stand to live with her.

Suede swallowed hard. She wanted more than just a guy tolerating her this time around. Was she destined to be the slut she'd portrayed herself to be, just a good time, party-girl, easily discarded and just as easily forgotten? Was that how life worked, you made one mistake and were branded with a big scarlet 'S' you couldn't escape the rest of your life? Her father hadn't wanted her. York certainly didn't. How could Chance?

Breakfast didn't smell so tasty any more.

"Aren't you joining me?" Chance asked from where he already sat at the table.

She nodded, no longer sure of herself. Her life felt like a yo-yo. One smile or a sexy wink from him sent her flying, but too soon, self-doubt wiggled into every happy moment and spoiled it. She couldn't shake off the stranglehold that York wasn't done with her yet, that he waited just around the corner. Or that Chance was too good for the likes of her. That she'd be smart to leave the protection of his cabin before this fairytale crashed and burned. Before she got him killed.

Chance cocked his head. "I'd give anything to know what's going on behind those big blue eyes of yours right now."

Suede sat stiff as a board at the lovely kitchen table she'd set for two, her throat gone as dry as the paper napkins she'd found in the cupboard. "Just, umm..." *Wishing I was someone else. Someone better.*

His brows slammed down over his eyes, hooding them until he was looking at her through thick, ebony lashes. "Something's bothering you. Come on, spill. You can tell me anything."

Do I dare? Suede took hold of the table edge at each side of her empty plate, wishing it were that easy. Maybe that was exactly what she should do. Spill her guts, then leave and go somewhere else to become that better woman. Separation was good for the soul, wasn't it? Didn't it make the heart grow fonder? Would time away from Chance give her what she needed to be good enough for him?

His head moved slowly from side to side as if he'd read her mind and disagreed. The napkin in his fingers dropped to his plate. "No," he said, his jaw clenched. "Damn it, Suede, no." He jumped to his feet and came around that table like a bull in a china shop. Silverware tinkled to the floor and poor Gallo scrambled out of the way. "You're not leaving me."

But I never said that. Thought it, yes, but I'm still here. Kind of. Worried now, she tilted into the back of her chair, fully expecting to be slapped for challenging him, even though she hadn't. Not really. Thinking about leaving didn't count.

He dropped to one knee instead. "I can't do this anymore," he ground out, his shoulders bowed and his face pressed into her lap. "I can't pretend I don't care, that I..."

Suede ran her fingers through his thick, wet hair, loving the way it curled around her fingertips, trembling at this sudden outburst but needing to comfort him. York would've knocked her flat by now. He would've screamed and cursed, belittled her until she would've wanted to crawl under a rock. But Chance seemed angry with himself, not—*me.*

She drew in a deep breath and believed enough to trust that he wouldn't hurt her.

When his head lifted and his chin came up, she was drowning in pools of tormented amber. "Stay," he commanded, his voice raw and deep. "I can't teach you to protect yourself if you leave me now."

She nodded because compliance had always worked in the past. Agreement bought time. Every abused woman knew that. *Stall. Say whatever he wants to hear. Then run and hide.* Only Chance wasn't threatening or hurting her. The thought of leaving him was.

"You don't believe me," he ground out. "I can see it in your eyes. You don't trust me, do you?"

"It's not you..." She let her answer die in her throat. *It's me. I don't know who I am yet. Not really, and if I'm not good enough for me, how can I be good enough for you?*

"How can I prove I'll never hurt you? Tell me," he begged, his eyes so deep and dark she felt as if she were falling into wells of melted maple syrup.

Like the fool it had been from her birth, her mouth whispered, "Kiss me."

Chapter Twenty-Six

Chance dragged her off the chair and onto his lap. She landed with him on the floor, her healing hip against his belly and his fingers caging her face in a gentle hold. Suede swallowed hard, wanting his kiss more than her next breath, but worried things were going too fast. That none of this was real. That this dream would shatter, and she wouldn't be able to put this beautiful thing with Chance back together again once she lost it.

"I will never hurt you," he murmured, his voice as sad as she'd ever heard. "I've fallen for you, Suede Tennyson. Let me kiss you. Let me love you."

There was that word again—*love*. An impossible universe of wonder and safety lay within its four letters. Tears blurred her vision of the honorable man she wanted more than anything in her life. Was she brave enough to trust him? To believe him? He'd given her no reasons not to, and yet...

"I want you," she admitted, her voice a strangled whisper in her dry throat. "I shouldn't, but I do. It's too soon, but I'm weak, and I'm scared, and—I need you just to... to breathe."

Wasn't that the acidly bitter, yet blindingly beautiful truth? If not for York's sin, she would never have come to know Chance, and if not for the breath he'd feely given—to her, a total stranger—she wouldn't be in his arms now. She wouldn't feel as if she were falling off yet another dangerous precipice that could inflict infinitely more heartache. York and Chance, the two polar opposites in her life, were inexorably linked by her near death. Both were etched on her heart in very different ways. York offered the worst cruelty, yet Chance had only, always offered life. Was she brave enough to be all that he needed? Could she accept the love she wasn't sure she deserved?

He shook his head as if he'd read her doubts. "It's never too early when it's real."

Not waiting for a reply, he shoved off the floor, taking her with him. In seconds they were in his bedroom, and he'd locked Gallo out. Orange embers glowed in the wood-burning stove. The blankets hit the floor and with extreme gentleness, Chance laid her on his side of his bed. He wasted no time climbing over her, caging her with his knees locked at her thighs. Cradling her head with one hand, he circled the back of her neck with the other as hot kisses bathed her forehead.

Instinctively, her palms went to his chest, not to shove him off, but to absorb the breadth and power of his massive pecs and soak up the wild energy pouring off him. The man was as tense and as big as a battleship, yet his tongue and lips left starlight wherever they touched her skin. Tiny kisses turned into sparks trailing from her forehead to her eyelids, and straight to her heart.

One knee drew up alongside her hip as he straddled her, still fully clothed, but so damned hot and gloriously beautiful Automatically, Suede arched into his body, rubbing belly to belly, breast to chest beneath their clothes. Friction. She needed friction or the pent-up heat she'd stored for too many days would burn her to cinders where she lay. There'd be nothing left of her but ashes. She growled at Chance to step it up.

"You want more?" he asked, a sly smile in his voice.

"I want you," she whined like a spoiled brat. "Naked, Chance. I want you naked and climbing all over me."

"You're bossy," he purred. "My kind of woman."

Instantly freed from anxiety, Suede tossed her head back and giggled. She had nothing to worry about, not with this man. What was it about this sexy beast that brought out the devil-may-care kid in her instead of the sultry sex demon?

He eased his feet to the floor and turned sideways. His boots went first. The beast he unveiled as he stripped out of his shirt was nearly her undoing. His prominent shoulders gave way to rock solid biceps as thick and as wide as her thighs. Maybe wider. Chance Sinclair was an impressive work of chiseled art. The man's chest was one big *Hot. Damn!* Tanned and taut, she wanted to touch every last bit of him.

Fingering his zipper, he glanced sideways. "I've got a few scars," he warned, like that would stop her now?

"So show me what you've got." Suede lifted to her elbows to watch the show, her heart pounding in her veins. Her tongue slid over her lips at the mere thought of tasting all that man flesh. "You're killing me," she whined. "Can't you undress any faster?"

That sparked a wicked grin that deepened the laugh lines at the corners of his eyes. The heated look he gave her was enough to melt the Arctic. If he didn't hurry, Suede was sure she'd detonate at this handsome display of eye candy alone.

His pants dropped. Then his boxers. Scars, yes. He hadn't lied. Chance had plenty of scars. Most punctuated his upper torso though. His arms. Some decorated his skull. His shaggy hair covered those and his eyes were clear. No scars had left him disfigured where it counted. She would know. She'd checked all he'd revealed.

If anything, every one of those scars declared that a warrior had met the enemy and that he'd survived against all odds. They declared a hero who'd faced the fires of hell and won. No woman should be this lucky.

"C'mere," she whimpered, knowing what she wanted to do next. He'd make a scrumptious mouthful.

"No, little girl," he said as he climbed up her body. His forearms landed beside her head when he straddled her again.

Trapped. Suede was deliciously trapped and on fire for this glorious man. Her arms barely reached around him, but she clenched that massive back with all ten fingers, hanging on for whatever came next.

"You asked for a kiss, and you're going to get one."

She had no time to answer as his mouth covered hers, swallowing her moans and groans. Yes. This was the breakfast she'd wanted. Her bones turned fluid as he mapped one hand over her shoulder and tugged her T-shirt aside.

"This won't do," he growled, then pushed the shirt up to her chin and out of his way. The man was quick with his hands. Her bra slid up next and his mouth came down, suckling her breast, and sending a mind-wrenching shot of molten lust straight to her core. He eased back long enough to push her breasts together, lathing her nipples, worshipping at each, then blowing soft breaths over them as she mewed and wiggled beneath him.

The harder he worked on her, the stronger the tension rose within her worn body. Explosive lust roared though her veins. The pleasurable rush of her climax started in her toes, then bottle-rocketed up her legs to her spine, and then... and then...

"Chance!" she screamed as his skillful mouth on her breasts detonated mind-blowing fireworks at her dripping core. "Chance, Chance, Chance," she whined, the pleasure he'd given her body surging in searing waves and ripples that wouldn't stop. The more he suckled, the more she responded. The more she needed. The more she cried.

"Don't cry. Breathe," he whispered, his lips wet and warm from the assault her breasts had barely survived.

She gasped as every muscle in her body clenched again, gripping him as if she couldn't bear to let him go. Was this what an orgasm was supposed to feel like? *Wow. Wow. Wow!*

His lips trailed to her mouth where he buried his tongue and claimed her all over again. Teeth and lips and tongue, they wrestled like kids who'd never made love before. Suede felt precisely so. Nothing with What's-His-Name had ever been this intense, this passionate, or this goooooooood.

Chance licked one final lap around her mouth before he pulled back to his haunches, his hands on her knees, hopefully ready to spread her wide and make her scream again. But first...

"Your turn," he growled, his baritone ragged and rough. Delightfully needy. "Drop 'em and assume the position."

Chapter Twenty-Seven

I did not *just say that, did I?* Chance rolled his eyes at the less than romantic come-on he'd shot at Suede, but the woman was obediently peeling her shirt over her head. She couldn't seem to get out of it fast enough. Reaching behind her back, her bra went next.

He stopped the show with a hiss. He'd seen her naked before, but she'd been beat up and at death's door. No decent man in his right mind would've been turned on then, but now? He was ruined at the gift she eagerly offered. Utterly, desperately ruined to his core.

Aphrodite, take a freakin' number.

A smug shot of pure masculine joy quirked his lips. If he were a betting man, he'd bet that orgasm was Suede's first. Humbled to have been the one to give her that experience, Chance bowed his head to inhale the plump breast that fit his greedy hand like a ripe cantaloupe, fresh off the vine and smelling just as sweet. Round and firm with a rock-hard nipple the color of a dark pink sunset, he leaned into the scent of that sweet fruit, so damned hungry for all this woman offered. Her tender flesh hardened at the touch of his callused thumb.

Easing away, his gaze dropped to her flat tummy, wanting her to take this tantalizing strip show as slow as possible even though he wanted her out of those jeans. It had only been a week. He didn't want their lovemaking to hurt her, but neither could he wait.

Once her pants hit the floor, her panties followed quickly. There was no way to last with this lovely lady laid bare, not as tight as his body ached to enter hers. Past the point of coherent speech, he drew in a deep breath of sugar cookies. That combined with sultry sweet smell of her arousal made self-control impossible. With a growl of anticipation, he wedged his knees between her legs and prepared for lift-off. There was no hesitation on her part, just two pointed feminine heels dug into his ass and a whimpering, moaning female at his fingertips.

Still... He was no pig in rut. Chance bowed his forehead to hers, the need to be seated deep within her body a relentless taskmaster that whipped up his spine like the devil, urging him onward and inward. He held it at bay for one last, breath stealing moment. More than anyone else in his life, she deserved all the respect he could muster.

"I can't hold back," he ground out as a drop of sweat fell from his brow to her cheek and landed near the corner of her mouth. Twisting her neck, she caught it with the tip of her tongue, her eyes bright, glittering with the act they were poised to commit with each other. Not to. *With.* Chance had never wanted anything more than to be *with* this saucy woman in every imaginable way.

"I don't want you to hold back. Hurry," she whined in her adorable petulant way. "I'm on the verge of—"

"Not without me, you're not." He met her challenge with a plunge into the hottest, tightest sheath on Earth. This wasn't sex. This was Heaven.

With a writhing wiggle, Suede climaxed after just a few thrusts. Her breath quickened and a scream whined out of her, "Chance, oh, oh... Chance!"

He found his release while the aftershocks rippling through her feminine muscles tightened. *So good. So damned good.* After these last excruciating months, Suede was that journey to the stars he hadn't known waited for him. Better yet, she was—home. His and only his home.

"I'll never hurt you," he told her just to be clear, still catching his breath at the pleasure of mating with this woman. Still seated inside her body, as deep as he'd never been before, Chance wanted her to know this was no one-night game of slap and tickle. This was the rest of his life, and she was that life. Yet even as he opened his mouth to utter that binding word, his unbelieving brain told him it was too soon. That modern women just don't—

"I love you," she breathed against his neck. Suede rubbed her nose over his chin, purring. "I really, really do, Chance Sinclair. I've been dying to tell you for days, but I was afraid. I'm not afraid anymore."

Right on cue, his phone buzzed from his pants pocket on the floor. "It can wait," he told her, needing to give her the same dedication she'd just given him.

Suede smoothed her fingers over his face, tracing the ugly scars he'd hid from the rest of the world. There was no recrimination in those tropical blues, just love shining there. Love and a dizzying kind of light. Suede was pure sunshine, and he was head over heels.

"You're happy," she told him, like he didn't know.

"I am," he admitted, his voice more growl than not.

Then say it!

"We have a lot to talk about, young lady."

Then start now. You already told her you want to love her. Tell her that you do! Say the words!

Her shoulders scrunched just as his phone reminded Chance he had to end this tender get together to reach for his pants. He stalled. There'd always be black ops, but this precious thing with Suede couldn't wait. Shouldn't wait. Lowering his mouth to hers, he pleasured himself one last time with a kiss that tasted like candied apple wine. Desire sparked strong and hard, and once again, he was ready. "I—"

His phone buzzed again. *Damn it to hell!* "I should get that," he told her. *And toss the damned thing out the window!*

Suede grinned and he was drunk on the light in her pretty blue eyes. "Then get it. I'm not going anywhere."

Easing to his knees, he bowed his head in remorse. He'd done the unforgiveable. He'd run like a coward instead of telling her how he felt, and to make matters worse, he hadn't used a condom. If the phone hadn't buzzed again, he'd have that important conversation with Suede right now, but first things first.

Leaning over Suede, he wrangled his phone from his pants pocket. Thumbing accept, he answered the damned call. "Yeah?" he bit out, tired of the intrigue that ruled his life, and for the first time, wanting less of it and more of her. To prove it, he dropped a kiss to the end of her nose.

"Where the hell have you been?" Pagan all but shrieked in his ear. "Where's your earpiece? You pulled it out, didn't you? You're... Shit! You're in bed with her, aren't you?"

Damned if that didn't spoil the mood. Chance rolled his feet to the floor. *When the hell had Pagan gotten so perceptive?* "The day I answer to you is a long ways off, baby Brother," Chance growled as he ran a hand over his head. "Why'd you call?" He could've sworn he heard high-fives smacking in the background. *Was that Kruze there with Pagan? Had they bet on him doing just this? Were they laughing at him? Brothers!*

Suede sidled up behind Chance, her sensually pliant body warm and molded against his spine, her fingers smoothing over his bare shoulders and down his biceps. She trailed kisses up the center of his back and between his shoulder blades until he shivered. Through it all, Pagan kept talking. "Kruze and I have a question for you, Romeo. You seen York recently?"

"Why would I? He and his rig should've been lifted off my mountain by now." Chance stiffened. "Wasn't he?"

"Apparently not. Kruze finally made contact with his buddy, JJ. York was supposed to meet Benito Garcia last week, only York never showed, and get this. He's not answering his cell. Garcia's only in town because York and his boss, Wilhelm Gonzales, share some kind of German connection. And you know Miss Vicki? Kruze caught up with her. She's waiting on York's ass, too."

Holy shit. It all made sense now. Benito Garcia was Colombia's latest wannabe drug lord's right hand man. His boss and one evil son-of-a-bitch, Wilhelm Gonzales, hailed from the loins of a German Nazi who'd migrated to South America after World War II. He ruled his kingdom with an iron fist that included despicable beheadings after brutal murders, all of which he filmed for posterity's sake. Were he and York related? Man, the implications.

Suede's gentle fingers smoothed up Chance's spine, reminding him that there was beauty in this ugly world.

"You talked with Sullivan yet?" Chance asked.

"That's your job."

"This op's gotten out of hand."

"You got it. The real question now is who do we off first? Everyone? Or do we sit on our thumbs and wait on York like everyone else?"

"He could be dead by now," Chance said as he lifted his eyes to the ceiling in the direction of the mountain where he'd last seen York alive. The perfect solution would be if York died of exposure, but Chance doubted Karma would be that accommodating. "I've got a mountain to climb," he told his baby brother.

"Call Sullivan first. Kruze and I can still take out these vaqueros before things get out of hand here in Portland."

"Copy that," Chance answered, weary of the job he'd signed onto. He had nothing to lose before, but now he had Suede. He didn't want her caught up in this. Yet she already was.

"Talk to you soon." Pagan signed off.

"What's wrong?" Suede asked, her luscious breasts plump against Chance's shoulder blades, her nose at the back of his neck, tickling. Warm and soft, so tender that he was certain no man on Earth deserved a woman like her. Certainly not him.

Chance snagged her and rolled her over his hip and onto his lap. "I have to go topside," he said when she lay flushed and completely naked, yet at ease in his arms. "There's a strong possibility Yor's still up there. This has to end."

Her eyes widened, but the real tell to her fear was the deathly pallor that replaced her sexy blush. "He's... here?"

"No, he's up on the mountain, Suede, not down here." Chance tightened his hold when she moved to sit up. "You've got nothing to worry about. Trust me on this. That guy's not smart enough to know how to stock a rig with food and water, much less how to climb down the south face." Although he might've figured it out by now, what with all the ropes and rigging Chance had fortified his mountain with. No need to tell Suede that. "It'll be easy. I'll go take care of business, and I'll be back by sunset."

"You said that last time," she whispered, "but you didn't come back until your brothers tricked you into returning. What if you get hurt? What if York's not as stupid as you think he is? What if—"

Dropping his head, Chance sealed her lips with his mouth, needing to end this downward spiral she was caught in. The more he kissed and tasted, the more their tongues tangled, the more he knew. Suede was right. A smart man never underestimated his enemy, not when he had this much to lose.

He didn't come up for air until he was sure what his next words would be. Setting her upright and back far enough on his thighs to meet her worried eyes, he admitted, "You're right. York isn't stupid, but he doesn't know you're alive, does he?"

Suede had that dazed, just been kissed light in her dewy blues. She shook her head, her swollen lips wet, and her lovely breasts heaving from anxiety instead of lust for him, damn it. His hands should be full of those pert babies, pinching her nipples, not planning how to end a murderer. They should be lying in each other's arms in his enormously expensive bathtub by now, the one she didn't yet know about.

Chance gave her the only answer he had left. "Gear up. I'm going hunting, and you're coming with me."

Chapter Twenty-Eight

Where there's a will, there's a way, Suede chanted over and over as she tried to keep up with Chance. But stepping into the deep prints left by his man-sized boots was a chore all by itself. The snow came up to her knees and each step took deliberate care and time. It didn't help that he'd fitted her hiking boots with a pair of traction cleats before they'd started out. They might work for rock climbing, but walking in deep snow turned those rugged straps on her soles into grabbers and all the snow they'd accumulated turned into dead weight. Her calves were screaming.

Dressed in identical gray snow pants and jackets as Chance, she hadn't thought she'd need the winter goggles now strapped over her eyes. But one step outside and the bright winter white convinced her. Apparently being able to see without tearing up was a good idea. But the burn in her legs...

With every step, Suede wished she'd stayed behind with Gallo. She'd still be warm, and her hamstrings wouldn't be stretched to the limit and burning like someone had set her ass on fire. The ragged wound of her thigh complained, but her calves? A hundred lunges couldn't have hurt this bad.

The weak winter sun shone directly over her shoulder, casting a pale thin shadow that reminded her of a scarecrow's next to Chance's heftier, wider one. He had no trouble outpacing her, but every couple paces, he'd turn to make sure she kept up.

She bit back every complaint that lifted to the tip of her tongue, determined to match him for endurance and camaraderie if not skill. This was the first day of the rest of her new normal, and by the end of it, she would prove she was a woman of worth. She would!

Thinking of the way he'd made love to her kept her warm even though an icy winter breeze sifted over the powdery flakes, cutting into her jacket and biting at her nose. He'd offered a balaclava to protect her face, but he had none on hand that didn't need serious alteration to fit her properly. Man, the Sinclair boys' heads were big. She'd settled for a knitted beanie that still hung into her eyes when it unrolled, but it would do. *Where there's a will, there's a way, right? Man, I hope so.*

Suede kept her focus on the back of her man, loving the view of his wide shoulders and taut ass, looking forward to more lovemaking. Never had she known sex could be so—fulfilling. So tender. So. Damned. Hot.

Just knowing it was him entering her body, that the hulking male over her had saved her, breathed life into her, and doctored her... Wow. The mere thought turned her into a quivering puddle of female hormones that went up in flames at the first touch of that glorious, rigid cock. And that orgasm he'd given her? Phenomenal. And a first.

She'd always faked it with York, and Mitch had been an entirely different story. No woman in her right mind found fulfillment during rape. But Chance? Her core clenched recalling the way her body had simply detonated under his expert tutelage. Intimacy had never thrilled her the way it did now.

She licked her lips thinking about that all-male instrument of pure pleasure he'd used on her. He was impressive, larger and thicker than any man she'd seen before. The way he'd entered her cautiously at first, as if he didn't want to hurt her, resonated to her core, even now. He'd been exquisitely gentle. They had to do it again soon. *Tonight.*

Oomph!

Apparently Chance had stopped, but she'd been daydreaming and tripped. Down she went, spreading her hands wide to catch herself.

He flew to her side in a heartbeat, tugging her to her feet as she puffed snow out of her nose and wiped it off her face. His hand swiped over her forehead even as she shook her head to dislodge the clumps in her hair. "I must look like Frosty the Snowman," she told him, stifling a giggle. Then she added, "Ho, ho, ho," just because she had to be the biggest klutz in Montana.

His breath hung over her head like a cloud of fog. "You okay?"

Suede nodded, smiling at her mistake. "Yes, but let's spend a day playing in this white stuff soon. I had no idea winter could be so much fun."

That merited the sweetest *'are-you-daft?'* look. "I take it you didn't get much snow in Oregon?"

She shrugged her shoulders as icy drips worked their way under her collar and down her back. *Brrr.* "Uh-uh. I went to Alaska with my mom once, but there wasn't time to just go for a walk and make snow angels. We were on a schedule. Time is money, don't you know?" *Besides, Mitch was there. Mom and he had things to do. Thank heaven none of them included me.*

Before she could brace herself, Chance lifted both gloved hands and bumped Suede's shoulders. Down she went. Backward. Into a drift that cradled her like a baby.

"Hey!" she squealed as she fell, tickled he'd do such a crazy thing when they probably didn't have time to play.

He stood over her with the sun at his back and his hands on his hips. "Make your snow angel, baby. I'll stand guard, so spread your wings and fly."

Awwww. Tears welled up and Suede honestly needed a hug and a kiss. Chance did have romantic bones in his body, well, at least in his pants. Squeezing her eyes tight, she spread her mittened hands to the side and made the best snow angel she knew how, or as Chance put it, a *snow angel baby*.

He stood there looking to the right and then the left, a frosty blue sky for a backdrop, and her heart took wings again. "What are you watching?"

His head tilted down at her, but she couldn't see through the dark black goggles perched on his nose. "Just some tracks."

That brought Suede to her knees and back to her feet in record time. Bumping into Chance's side, she latched onto his forearm. "Is he here?"

Chance tapped a finger under her chin to get her to look up at him. "Wolf tracks, not human."

Like that made her feel better? "Are you sure? I don't see anything moving," she advised with her extreme lack of knowledge of wild animal behavior. But if animals were out there, York could be, too.

"They travel at night," he said, "but winter's tough on wild animals and they're all hungry. Who knows what we'll find. Just stick close. I'm armed, remember?"

She nodded. She was armed too, she just didn't plan to shoot anything with the nine millimeter holstered on her hip. That was Chance's job. She was there for moral support only. Maybe today wasn't the best day for fun in the snow after all.

"Thanks for pushing me down," she teased, dusting her backside off. "I never would've done that if you hadn't helped." Suede let her smile speak the feelings of her heart. Trusting Chance became easier every day. "How much farther?"

She couldn't tell for sure, but the way his cheek tweaked, she was pretty certain Chance had just winked at her behind those reflective goggles. He chin nodded at the granite wall on her right. "Mother's Day Falls is straight ahead. The pool you fell in is just below that edge," he said as he pointed upward to a craggy set of five rocks in the granite face. They almost looked like a giant's toes sticking out of the wall like they were. All they needed to do was wiggle.

"I figure you struck that ledge on your way down. It possibly slowed your descent enough that you didn't fall as hard as you could have. Do you want to see where you landed?"

"Okay." Suede gulped, her lips dry from the cold, but her throat had gone drier. The mountain loomed tall overhead, and this exact spot was where York had meant her to die. Nothing humbled a person as quickly as coming face-to-face with the site of their death. She took hold of Chance's gloved hand, needing to stay close to him for this awful side trip.

He stopped and wrapped one arm around her shoulders, pointing a finger to the flat fluffy drifts of glittering snow several yards ahead. "See that stick pointing up? That one right there?"

She nodded. It might have been a little tree, but it was dead now. Like she should've been.

"That's where Gallo found you. I think I actually heard the ice crack when you touched down, but he's the one who dragged you to the surface."

Glancing up, she crossed her arms over her chest, shivering even as she bumped her butt into Chance's thigh. This side of the mountain was tall and frozen. So damned high. "Why... why didn't I die?" *I should have.*

"Not sure," he replied, enfolding her against his chest with his arm around her neck and his chin on her shoulder. "I think it's because you're an angel from heaven. You were sent to me, Suede. You're a miracle."

No, I'm not. Suede couldn't make her gaze move from that dead branch. It looked like a witch's finger, the end of it sharp like a long, dead fingernail, pointing skyward. Condemning. All at once, her past mistakes were too much to bear. Suede twisted around and buried her face in his jacket, breathing hard and drawing in the warmth and smell of the man who'd run to her rescue and saved her life when he didn't have to.

"Why were you out here that night?" She had to know.

He wrapped her up tight, smothering her against him. "I told you already. I couldn't find Gallo. He'd taken off and when I went looking for him, I found you. I couldn't just leave you here, could I?"

All Suede could think was: *One man's trash is another man's treasure.* Gallo might have found her, but without Chance's lifesaving skills, she would've been nothing more than a cadaver Gallo dragged home. A piece of garbage York hadn't wanted to deal with.

"I want to go home," tumbled off her lips.

Chance stood there in the pale winter sun and rocked her. "Do you mean California or Ore—?"

"No, here. Your cabin," she cut him off before he said anything crazier. California was nothing but a deathtrap waiting to slice her to ribbons. She didn't belong in Oregon either.

"Good answer," he murmured into the top of her beanie. "Come on, snow angel. We've got us a mountain to climb."

Chapter Twenty-Nine

"When a man loves a woman..." With every touch and every sigh, the lyrics sung by Percy Sledge spun round and round in Chance's head, taunting him to tell her. To say the word that mattered. It was past time.

He'd caught the hint of a shadow flicker through her pretty blues when he hadn't returned her sentiments. It wasn't that he didn't care deeply about her, because he did, but what would a woman like Suede want with a banged up guy like him? What would she get out of the deal? Lonely nights while he was off in some dark corner of the world fighting more bad guys? Never ending worry that he wouldn't come home again? Heartache? A flag-draped coffin and a white marble headstone in Arlington? It didn't seem fair and he wasn't that selfish.

Suede deserved more. Man, she was adorable. She made it hard to stay focused on the dangerous job at hand, and damn it. He had to get his mind back to zero or this op would fail before it got off the ground.

He'd purposely set the beacons to safeguard the cabin while he was away, and to reinforce, at least to himself, how risky this trip topside would be. Suede was no trained operator. She'd never climbed before, and he was pretty certain that if all went as planned, rappelling down the south face of Old Man Mountain would be extremely difficult for the woman who'd been shoved off of it just days earlier.

Yet one look at her, one frosty hint of her minty breath, and he was lost in space. Hitching her into her climbing gear hadn't helped. A certain protectiveness had filled him with every tug at her harness, especially the strap between her legs. It had to be the caveman in him, but there was something about tying a woman up that teased the erotic beast within. Not that he'd ever been into all that BDSM crap, but the instinct to dominate her was there, nonetheless. So was an intense need to control everything around her, so she didn't get hurt today or ever again. Yeah. Had to be the caveman in him.

Chance bumped her chin with his thumb to make her look up at him. Wearing the same style of tinted goggles he wore, he couldn't see her tropical blues, but her brows were arched, and he knew she was worried. This would be a difficult mission for a novice, but there weren't a lot of choices. It was York or Suede, and Chance chose Suede every time.

"It's not a tough climb," he told her. "Keep your head up and your eyes on the ropes in front of you. I've set enough anchors along the way, and there are plenty of footholds, you'll be okay. It's south facing granite, so the sun's melted what snow the wind didn't blow away. If you get in trouble, stop and breathe, but do not look down."

Suede had a habit of jerking her head to the left when she was stressed, like a nervous tick. She was plenty nervous now. She nodded, jerked her head, but pressed her lips into a tight line.

Chance intended to help her relax in his extra-large bathtub once they got home. A good deep massage ought to loosen her up. A little bubble bath filled with the fragrant delights that Sullivan had included in the drone delivery wouldn't hurt, either. That man certainly knew a lot about women.

See what I mean? Lost. In. Space!

Averting his gaze before he succumbed to the urge to kiss her into submission, Chance cocked his head to squeeze the tension out of his neck, and they were off. She'd already swapped her mittens for the rugged, leather climbing gloves. When Suede took the first step up Old Man Mountain, he followed a bit to her right, coaching and encouraging. "Good girl. That's right. You're doing fine."

With every step up, her timidity changed into confidence. The rappelling gear would be heavier coming down, mainly because he toted most of it in his backpack going up, but a person could fall on the way up just as easily as on the way down. Like firearms training, Suede was a quick study. Not once did she slip, always a plus when you're teaching a greenhorn. Better yet, she wasn't afraid to try, and that was most of the battle right there. Attitude.

He smiled as his first impression of her came to fruition. Her right foot slipped and for a split second, she dangled over thin air, her only hold on the rock ledge overhead. The crazy woman turned to him and grinned. "Look at me! This is fun. I'm doing it, huh?"

His face cracked with joy. Suede was no victim. She'd meant what she'd said about turning over a new leaf, and she was doing it. *Look at her go.* His heart swelled with pride and a little lust, too.

"Don't be a smart ass," he told her as he stifled the urge to reach out and pat said ass. Still grinning, she secured her footing, stuck that cute backside out, and up she went. Right behind her, Chance smiled. Near the top lip of the cliff, right where it hung over the edge offering nothing but airspace and a long drop down, he shifted to her side and put a hand on her wrist to slow her.

Suede turned to face him. "Am I doing it wrong?"

"No, babe, you're fantastic at this, but we need to traverse to your left about twenty feet. See those anchors over there? I studded this entire face with plenty for just this purpose. Take it slow and easy, one step at a time. Make sure your footing's solid before you lift your other boot. Hold onto the grips.

They're just above eye level. They'll keep you on track."

She maneuvered to her left like a pro, kicking the snow that had packed into her cleats when she couldn't get a solid grip on the anchor still buried in ice. Mountain climbing in winter was tough, but this granite face absorbed heat like a mother. It'd be the first bare face come spring and all that solar energy proved beneficial now. Chance followed her lead until she stopped where he'd told her to stop.

She turned expectantly to him, and he wanted to kiss that cocky pout off her face. She knew she'd done good, *the brat.*

"If York survived this last week, he could be waiting for us," he warned.

Her head ducked into her shoulders as she looked up. "Right here? Now?"

Chance nodded. "It's truth or dare time. One of us has to look over the edge to get a bead on him. Are you game?"

Suede angled her shoulders to the side, giving Chance the go-ahead, as if he'd let her take the risk? *Silly girl.*

He nodded in agreement, then gripped the handhold directly over his head. This edge of the cliff put him closer to the empty cabin than to York's rig, but the biggest vulnerability to this plan was the sun shining behind him. It was broad daylight and Chance hadn't worn snow camouflage. He and Suede were dressed in identical light gray snowsuits, right down to their matching beanies. *When in doubt, always go Navy gray.*

Taking a deep breath, he paused, then bobbed up for a quick look-see. A look that fast wouldn't give York, if he happened to be facing the exact direction, enough time to focus on what he thought he'd seen. He'd most likely dismiss it as a shadow from some bird overhead. Maybe a rabbit. And in this sun, even as weak as it was, he'd still be snow blind—if he were even outside.

Chance took a second look with more deliberation until he was a full head above the edge. "Looks quiet. I'll go first, then I'll give you a hand up."

She nodded like a good troop should. "Be careful," she murmured, and didn't that warm him up on the inside like someone had just lit a fire inside his rib cage.

Focus!

Chance palmed the icy ledge and rolled topside. He kept his head on a swivel and both eyes on high alert, scanning for any sign of York and quartering the snowy landscape for animals or other trouble. Those two dead bodies outside York's front door had to have attracted some wildlife, but Chance detected nothing from his prone position. Drifts now blocked the cabin on all four sides. The fancy rig that York had airlifted for his convenience was in the same shape. Snowed in.

Without shifting his focus from the rig, Chance swung his right hand over the edge for Suede to grab onto. She engaged, and he hung on tight. If anything went wrong now, he could easily swing her topside with him.

She came up breathless, hunkering low on her belly into the snow beside him. "Is he here? Did you see him yet?"

The tremble in her voice about did Chance in. He smoothed a hand over her back and left it between her shoulder blades to settle her nerves. "Not yet, but I'm not seeing any tracks either. He's got to still be inside that rig, but look. The door's snowed shut."

Her head bobbed. "I see it and you're right. He hates the cold. I doubt he'd be outside, but it'd be nice if he was. Frozen. Like a *Popsicle.*"

Chance smiled at her choice of deaths for the man who'd viciously tried to kill her. But a *Popsicle* fate was too good for a bastard like York. If Chance had his way, he'd strip York's hairy ass and dangle him over the edge of this mountain to bait the bald eagles that lived in these parts. What better end to an ignoble man's life than to be gutted and have his eyeballs ripped out of their sockets by the noblest of birds in the sky?

Chance tugged his sat phone up from his jacket pocket, tense as hell. He'd expected a confrontation from the dangerous man who planned to take down a city as large as Portland, not some simpering coward in a can.

"What now?" Sullivan bit out.

Chance grinned. *You've got to love working with a guy who has zero tolerance for small talk.* "I'm topside with Suede. Looks like York never left Montana. I'm going in unless you want to send a chopper, take control of his rig, and have him your way."

Sullivan grunted. "End him, Chance. Then tell Pagan and Kruze to end the Rio boys. They've got no business stepping foot in my country. I want them gone, and yes, I've got everyone else's concurrence, damn it."

Chance ended the call with a clipped "Copy that." He stashed his phone and flexed his fingers on Suede's back. "Don't engage York and don't say a word to him, understood?"

She turned her goggle-covered eyes on him. "No, I don't understand. He hurt me, Chance. I want him to know I'm still alive. I want him to know he's the biggest asshole in the world, and that I'm fighting mad."

"Not going to happen, Suede. Assholes hurt good people like you, and this one's already tried to kill you once. Stay behind me."

She bit her lip. "And let him hurt you? Why should I?"

Chance dropped his forehead to his wrist in the snow. He should've known this part wouldn't be easy for Suede. Telling her to stay put was an option Chance had already rejected. Suede needed closure and she was about to get it. The hard way.

Canting his head, he stared her down. "Trust me. York's not man enough to hurt me. I'm the black ops guy here, remember? He's the prick. Now keep behind me, and let's get this done, so we can go home where I can lick every inch of your naked body, okay?"

That did the trick. At least, she bobbed her head and said, "Copy that. I won't get in your way, but I'm going with you."

"Good girl," Chance told her honestly.

"Just don't get shot," she bit out just as he pushed forward to finish the job.

Damned if that didn't make him smile.

Chapter Thirty

I don't get it. Suede kept blinking, but her eyes brimmed and overflowed anyway. Chance meant to stand between her and a known killer. He meant to protect her even if it meant taking a bullet for her. What kind of man does that? None she'd known until he came along.

He'd tugged her to her feet when he'd stood, and now they were beside York's rig. The generator was running. Not good. Just like he'd told her he'd do, Chance stood like a solid wall between her and the door, and she was afraid. He thought York would be plenty hungry by now, maybe dead, but Suede had her doubts. York was too big of a snake to go out with a whimper.

She'd already racked her pistol and pointed it skyward, but kept her trigger finger alongside the barrel like Chance had taught. Her nerves were strung tight. When he placed his gloved fingers around the doorknob, it was all she could do not to cry out and tell him to wait, that York wasn't worth dying for.

Chance never quavered. Once he set his hand to the knob, entry was swift and frightening. She'd stayed frozen outside the door with her eyes squeezed tight, expecting to hear at least one shot. But none came.

"You can come in now," Chance called to her.

Swallowing hard, Suede forced her boots to move, at least enough to peek around the corner. York was in there, but he didn't look anything like the monster she remembered. He wasn't even in one of his scary martial art poses. Dressed in his black down-filled jacket, black jeans, and hiking boots, he sat on the narrow side bench shivering, his fingers at his mouth as if he'd been blowing on them to keep them warm.

His eyes were bloodshot and rimmed red, but fixed on Chance like a kid who'd been caught with his hand in the cookie jar. Wispy thin whiskers dotted his cheeks, chin, and neck. The guy never could grow a decent beard, certainly nothing close to Chance's thick scruff.

Suede entered York's frozen mountain hideaway, her pistol ready in case Chance needed her. Not likely. He took up most of the space inside York's, *umm, refrigerator.* Even with the generator running, this place was c-c-cold.

At the moment, Chance searched the cupboards and drawers, chuckling. "The idiot's got water but no food. He's starving."

"Where are his guns?" Suede asked.

Chance patted his chest. "In my pockets. Already removed the magazines. His knives too. You're safe."

York cocked his head and looked her way through greasy blond hair. His upper lip lifted in that snarky sneer that used to make her blood run cold. It didn't work this time. "S-S-Suede?" he asked.

Gathering her wits, she lowered her pistol to her side, and took a brave step into his line of sight. "Yes, Lionel. It's me."

His eyes followed the weapon she carried, one of the many SIGs Chance owned, and because York couldn't seem to take his gaze from the gun, she tapped her index finger along the barrel. He needed to know she could end him if it came down to him or Chance.

The thought flittered through her mind that she ought to be grateful to this creep. If he hadn't tried to kill her, she wouldn't have met Chance. She'd still be York's scared little bunny, trapped and slowly dying in his LA penthouse.

"Boo!" she spat, needing him to jump for a change. When he did, she took a breath of freedom. This guy was nothing but a scrawny bully. Certainly not smart. Not even remotely masculine, now that she knew had a real man in her life.

York jerked his head to the left, his greasy blond hair dropping into his eyes. He didn't seem able to move very fast. The man was suffering. *Good.*

"All clear," Chance muttered, but Suede wasn't done.

Squatting at York's knees, she told him to, "Get up. You and I have a date."

He shook his head, quivering like a little girl. Chance came to her aid then, grabbing York by the elbow and hoisting him to his feet. "You heard the lady. You're on Suede's dime now. What she says, goes." He jerked York around to face the woman he thought he'd killed.

She nodded at the open door. "Outside. I want a good look at you."

"I need him to answer a couple questions before you use him for target practice, ma'am."

Suede blinked at what sounded more like an endearment coming from Chance than just a term of military respect. Ma'am. It made her lady parts quiver.

"Five minutes," she clipped as if she were in control of this operation.

"Where's the video your asshole friends made?" Chance asked York, a deadly edge to his voice.

A video? Of what? She cocked her head. *Oh crap, of me?*

York's chin came up. "D-d-don't know what you're t-t-talking about."

"Wrong answer." Chance didn't ask again, just pretzeled the high and mighty jerk's arm behind his back.

Grunting with surprise, York thrashed against the bulk of a man who'd barely moved during the two-second contest. After another tweak, York kicked the floor, sweat beading on his forehead. "Alright, alright. S-stop! It's on a USB drive in my money belt. Christ, take it. Take everything!"

"I intend to," Chance growled.

York twisted enough to glare over his shoulder at the massive man who towered over him, pulled his jacket and shirt out of the way and ripped the money belt off his waist. Chance fingered it, searching for the USB drive, then tossed it to Suede. "Here. Hold onto this."

"Copy that." She caught the sweaty thing with her free hand, then stuffed it into one of the many zippered pockets on her jacket. There was no telling what was on that video, but if it was of her, it had to be bad. York wasn't one of those family-home-movie kinds of guys.

Without warning, Chance jerked York nearly off the ground by that same elbow. "Who paid you to kill her, asshole? Who wanted her out of the way?"

"Her father," he bawled, jumping to get away from Chance, but not going anywhere. "That jerk-off Tennyson wanted her dead so he'd have a clear shot at the White House."

Suede's heart ground to a painful halt in her chest. She could barely draw in a gulp of air at that ugly revelation. "D-d-dad paid you to kill me? M-m-my Dad?"

"You're lying!" Chance grabbed York in a chokehold this time, turning York's face an ugly shade of blue. "Tennyson wanted her out of the way, but he didn't want her dead. That's why the video clip. That was all your idea. You're blackmailing him, aren't you? You want to be Port Commissioner, don't you?"

"N-n-not me. Not me," York wheezed, his dirty fingernails digging into Chance's thick forearm. "It's not l-l-like that. I'm just the little guy in this scheme. I'm nobody. You've..." Gasp. Sputter. Hack, hack, hack. "Y-you've got to believe me!"

"Tell me another lie, and I promise you'll fly," Chance growled, his head ducked low and his mouth at York's ear. "Now, why the damned video clip, you bastard?"

York blew out a tight raspy breath before he wheezed, "You're right, it was blackmail, all right?" Chance's elbow loosened, allowing York to continue. "Tennyson's hired some big guns from South America. They're, shit! They're already in Portland. You gotta let me go. You gotta help! If I don't show, there's gonna be a war."

"So now you're the hero. Sounds like you need a flying lesson," Chance growled as he dragged York to the door.

"No! You can't! You gotta believe me!" York screamed, kicking and fighting all the way. "I'm nobody, but I know people, and, shit! I didn't know Tennyson would go straight to Patrone! Nobody did. So I bought myself some insurance, that's all. I thought if he saw what I could do, that he'd back off."

"You killed his daughter to reason with him?" The veins on Chance's neck and forehead bulged he was so angry. "Then you cozied up with a bastard like Wilhelm Gonzales to fight Patrone and Tennyson! Are you out of your mind?"

"I had to," York spat, his face as red as his eyeballs. "He's got someone more powerful than Patrone on his side, you motherfucker! Don't you get it?"

Chance grabbed York by his jacket collar and jerked him off his feet until they were nose to nose. "Talk. Who's more powerful than Patrone?"

York gasped, barely able to breathe. "Don't know his name," he wheezed. "Only know some asshat keeps ruining my plans. Why the fuck do you think I'm still up here? He must've cancelled the work order to come get me. Next time I see him, I'll kill him!"

Chance spun York around and slammed his face to the inside wall beside the door. "Give me a name!"

"Chance," Suede said that one word quietly.

His face came up grim and determined, his jaw tight and his lips thin. She knew he could see her, but the goggles made him look like *RoboCop* instead of the gentle man she knew.

"Yes?" he asked, his voice monotone, and the veins on his forehead dark and rigid with barely controlled fury.

"My turn," she said quietly. There'd be time to ask more questions later. This moment was between her and York, but it was also between her and Chance. If he was the man she knew he was, he'd listen to her, not as in obey her, but as in hear her out. He might even defer to her. Wouldn't that be a once in a lifetime event? A male the size and power of Chance actually caring what she had to say?

"No, please! Christ, no! Not her." York whined, but Chance gave him no choice. He hopped the arrogant tennis player out of the frigid rig and into the late afternoon sun. Suede followed. She wasn't in charge, but Chance had deferred to her, even though he was the baddest badass up here. But in that moment, she knew precisely who she was. She was his woman.

A brisk winter breeze had come out of nowhere. It wasn't anything close to a blizzard, but it was enough. "Strip," Suede barked at York, her recollection of another night, painfully crystal clear in her mind.

Chance still had hold of York's back collar, but York thought he had a choice. The idiot kept shaking his head until Chance drew his pistol and shoved it under York's chin. "Do it, wise guy," he growled, "and maybe she'll let you live."

The man who'd belittled tennis officials, ball boys and girls, reporters, and spectators alike, now stood with his knees knocking in his skinny black jeans. Why she'd ever thought him appealing galled Suede. She snorted. "Should be easy enough, Lionel. That was what you wanted me to do, wasn't it? Put on one last show? Do it. Take your clothes off. All of them. Now!"

He drew in a deep lungful before he peeled out of his goose-down jacket, one turtleneck sweater, three T-shirts, and his boots. Standing there bare-chested in just jeans and socks, he finally lifted his gaze to Suede. "Don't do this," he begged, his head canted for dramatic effect, his hair in his face and blinking those lying eyes for effect.

He always had that blond-haired, charming-little-boy-thing going for him, but that time was gone. Suede used her weapon for a pointer, her index finger still alongside the barrel, not on the trigger. That'd be too much temptation. "All. Off." She gestured down to the snowdrift York stood in. "Socks too. Do it quick. It's cold out here. I wouldn't want you to freeze to death like I nearly did."

"Nearly, nothing. You *were* dead when I got to you," Chance muttered. "Trust me. I know dead."

Didn't that warm her heart? He hadn't given up on her even when she was clinically dead, and he had her back now. There was that warm feeling in her chest again. Had to be her heart.

York's arrogant chin came up then, daring her, but Chance beat her to it. "Either you do it, smartass, or I will, but I promise, you won't like how I'll remove those name brand pants off your hairy ass." A seven-inch blade snapped to life in Chance's palm where just seconds before his gun had been. "Your call, *Lionel*. Me or Suede?"

She shot him the barest smile. There was something incredibly sexy about the power of Chance Sinclair. Bigger than life, he stood for something, and right then, she wanted to strip him naked and lick every inch of his hard male body until he screamed her name.

York whined, forcing her salacious thoughts back to the problem at hand. He'd dropped his jeans and stepped on them, like that little bit of cloth comfort would matter in a few minutes. Suede grunted. Not hardly. Not for what she had planned.

"You want to dance, buster?" she asked the freezing man in his sporty *Calvin Kleins,* who now jumped from one foot to the other, slapping his biceps to keep warm. She aimed her pistol at his feet, yet kept her trigger finger where it was, not certain she could actually shoot when it came down to it.

That earned her a suppressed smile from Chance. The way his sexy lips curled nearly made her lose focus, but she had a bully to taunt. She refused the answering smile that threatened to blossom over her face.

"What do you want, darling? I mean really, Suede?" York asked, his hair still hanging in his face. "If it's money, I can—"

"Here we go again." Suede rolled her eyes. "It's always about money with you, isn't it? I don't care about your money, Lionel. News flash. I never did. Where's my ring?"

"The ring? You want the ring? I don't know," York whined as he glanced around. "I lost—"

"This guy doesn't have it, Suede," Chance declared. "Sorry, but I do. He gave it to his buddy Pablo after he shoved you over the edge. Philip got your jacket. Pablo got the ring. I meant to give it to you, but we've been a little busy."

Pablo and Philip? I thought they were my friends. Suede felt the blood drain from her face at that awful revelation. York had divided her belongings with his buddies? *Who does that?*

There went his last chance. "Get your ugly ass over to the edge, *Lion*," she ordered, her finger shifted to the trigger and her tears rising. *God, I hate you.* "Now!"

He stalled, but once again, Chance strong-armed the guy, hotfooting him toward the fast way down.

"You can't do this!" York shrieked at every frantic step forward. "It's inhumane! It's... it's wrong!"

"You're right. It is," Chance replied, his voice as calm as a summer day, and York's hands twisted behind his back.

Suede kept up with Chance as much as she could, but the snow was deep and the drifts were crusted over. It took her a couple minutes to catch up. By then, Chance had her ex-fiancé leaning over the edge while York tried not to. It was comical how he thought he could resist a man as big and as solid as Chance.

She'd barely stepped to the edge when a sickening wave swept through her. Bile pitched up her throat. "Is this where he... he shoved me over?" she asked Chance, hating the tremor in her voice.

"Yes, ma'am. This is where he kicked your face." It was so hard to know what Chance was thinking behind those goggles. He looked like a stone-faced robot, not a speck of emotion showing on his handsome face. If this was him holding his rage in check, he was plenty scary.

"I need to do this," she told him, blinking hard to see through her goggles. They'd gone steamy.

He nodded. Solemn. Stiff. "Understood, ma'am. Totally your call."

He hadn't argued. At all. *And he called me ma'am.* Did that mean he agreed with her? Was he behind her all the way? Should she go through with what she'd intended when she'd started this risky game of cat-and-mouse with a murderer? Could she really kill a man in cold blood? Was she just as evil as York?

Suede gulped, no longer sure that she hated York enough to sacrifice the woman she'd so recently become. *York meant to kill me. I'm not dead, but he deserves to die the same way he wanted me to die. Doesn't he?*

Chapter Thirty-One

Chance stood there with his heart in his throat, willing to go along with whatever justice Suede meted out to this conniving bastard. York deserved to die for all he'd done to her, and Chance didn't have one speck of trouble with the eye-for-an-eye philosophy, not after what he'd seen in the world. Predators like York were nothing but rabid dogs that preyed on innocent, trusting people. Every last one of them deserved a righteous comeuppance, and what better way for this jerk to go down than at the hand of the woman he'd damn near killed?

For two cents, Chance would've twisted York's neck and been done with him, but true justice now rested in the hands of the woman Chance loved. Yes, loved. He knew it to his core. He just didn't want Suede to off anyone, not even this dirt bag, and it had nothing to do with gender assigned roles. Not one bit.

Chance knew plenty of female snipers who were better shots than he was, but this was Suede, the lady of his heart. He kept his mouth shut. He'd said what he knew she needed to hear, but he didn't want this for her. Murder was a soul-sucking last resort kind of act that left a hard man broken in ways normal people couldn't understand. Women were certainly capable of the lethal act, but *please, not Suede.*

That was why he hadn't revealed what was on the USB drive. He couldn't even make eye contact because of his goggles, but if he did, he'd send her every last bit of his trust just like he was doing now. She'd do the right thing. He knew she would.

Suede faced him then, her lower lip quivering.

He nodded one last time, for what it was worth. Who knew? He might have just signed York's death warrant.

With a whimper, Suede twisted the goggles off her head. They fell into the drift at her feet. The beanie went next, spilling all of that gorgeous hair over her shoulders. Setting her spirit free. The sun drew a halo of golden highlights behind her head, transforming her into the angel Chance knew she was.

"Look at me," she ordered York, her pistol raised and on target. "I want you to know who killed you. I want you to know it was me, Suede Tennyson, the woman you used and abused for years. I want you to know that I lived despite everything you did to me! I'm finally happy, Lionel. And I'm strong enough!"

Her voice pitched higher at every word, but her hand didn't waver, and Chance prepared for the inevitable. *Yeah, she's mad enough. She could do this.*

When the bastard refused her order to look at her, Chance lifted York's left arm until it tweaked his shoulder socket. "Hard way it is. You will obey this lady or I'll throw you off myself. And I won't waste a bullet before I do."

York turned his prideful head to Suede. "That bitch is no lady. Tennyson's little girl spreads her legs for any creep who comes alone. Guess it's you now, asshole. That's how she is."

Chance sucked in a deep breath of patience and let Suede do what she needed to do.

"I loved you," she told York, her chin quivering, but the pistol in her hand still straight and true.

She blinked, and Chance's heart melted at her feet. Those were tears in her eyes, and not from the wind. She was crying for this douche bag? *Don't, baby,* Chance sent her. *Cry for men of valor, not creeps who abuse women. York doesn't deserve a single one of your tears.*

"No, you didn't!" York shrieked. "You wanted a good time and I gave it to you. High-end clothes. All the best booze. Designer drugs. Who do you think bought that crap for you? Your daddy? Guess again!"

"I never did drugs," she said with a proud toss of her mane, her blue eyes gone hurricane dark.

York didn't know when to shut up "Yeah, you did, you just never knew it. I put 'em in your booze.

Christ, you've been nothing but a pain in my ass since your old man talked me into babysitting. I had to do something to loosen you up, you frigid whore." He had the nerve to lean forward into Suede's face. "I can get a better piece of ass in any back alley, anytime, any day."

Chance had heard enough. He tweaked York's shoulder a stiff one rather than let him disrespect Suede one more time. "It's time," Chance told her. *If you're going to do this, get it done.*

"Ouch! Damn it. Stop! You're hurting me!" the bully cried.

Her pistol sank to her side, her finger off the trigger. Her lips pinched as if she wanted to say something but couldn't, and Chance released the breath he'd been holding. *That's my girl.*

"I knew you couldn't do it!" York shrieked, grinning like a fool and hopping on his frozen bare feet like he'd won the contest. "You're nothing but a cock-blocking tease, Suede Tennyson! You're just like your old man said you were. You'll never amount to anything. I knew it! You can't do it!"

Enough!

"But I can," Chance growled.

That was all it took. York jerked out of Chance's grip and screeched like the devil had just twisted his balls. Too late he realized his mistake. Overcorrecting and panicked, he flapped his arms as his fatal mistake hit home. He fell, sliding backward over the same edge he'd shoved Suede off, clawing at the icy edge for purchase he'd never find.

"Help me!" he ordered, one hand stretched to the woman he'd tried to kill.

"Hang on!" Suede screamed as she lurched for him, her fingers stretched wide to save him.

But it was too late. Chance grabbed her before York could pull her over with him. He fell screaming to the now frozen pond at the bottom of Mother's Day Falls. Only there was no happy-go-lucky pup playing in the snow to find him today, and the shallow pond was frozen rock solid. He'd hit the ground hard. There'd be nothing to rescue. Ask Chance if he cared.

But Suede collapsed to her knees at the edge, her pistol flat in the snow beside her. Gut wrenching sobs choked her. "I.., I wasn't going to shoot him. Honest. He knew that. I tried to reach him. I did, I really did."

Chance couldn't take it. He dropped beside her and dragged her onto his lap. "It's okay," he told her as he started to rock the woman he loved there on the edge of his mountain. "I'm sorry you had to see that. Shush. It's okay."

"He k-k-killed me," she cried, her teeth chattering and her heart broken all over again. "Right here. This is the same spot. He shoved me, and he thought he *killed* me, but I didn't want him to die. Not really."

"You're tougher than he was, baby. You just proved it by trying to save him. Please don't cry." Chance pressed her ear to his heart, scraping his own goggles away so there'd be nothing between them. If she'd only tip that pretty face up and see him. "God, you were amazing. You stood there and faced him down. I'm so proud of you. Most guys wouldn't have the balls to do that. Then you let him live, when he didn't deserve it. You gave him every chance to be a man, and guess what? York wasn't one to begin with. In the end, he got what he deserved."

"He killed me," she whimpered. "Right here on this spot. He kicked me like I was a piece of garbage that he didn't want to look at anymore. In the face, Chance!" *Like I don't already know that?* "Then he gave his friends my stuff like I was... like I was n-n-nothing."

She sobbed harder as her voice ramped up, and this had to stop. They still had a tough climb down and Chance didn't need a hysterical woman on his hands, not while rappelling where one mistake could end a person. Yet he kept quiet. He'd said his piece. It was up to Suede to make peace with what had just happened.

She lifted her chin and looked at him then. "W-w-was he right? Did my dad make a deal with him to t-take me off his hands? Did he pay him to kill me?"

Chance nodded. "I'm sorry. I should've told you all of this before we came up here today, but yes. From the evidence we've gathered, it looks like your father intended York to take over Portland's Port Authority."

"Why?" she ground out, her voice sad and empty. "What did I ever do to my dad but try to stay out of his way? I was a good girl. I got good grades, and I excelled in most of my classes. Six universities accepted me even after I moved out of the Governor's mansion. I could've gone to Willamette U! Gonzaga wanted me. What more did he want?"

"Just because a man makes a baby doesn't make him a father. Look at my sperm-donor dad. He walked out on Mom and us boys when I was three."

Suede buried her face in his chest, sobbing so hard that her shoulders shook, and he sat there and took it. Life shouldn't have to be this difficult, but there were plenty of people across the world in worse conditions than hers. He just didn't love them the way he did Suede Tennyson.

Man, she was tough. He'd expected her to wail because York had taken flight, but that wasn't what this meltdown was about. Her last week had been one wretched revelation after another, and all the betrayals had finally overwhelmed her. His gut clenched. Damned if he didn't have another unsettling truth to tell her. "You still have that USB?"

Patting her chest pocket, she nodded. "Right here. You want it back?"

He shook his head, his mouth gone dry. "No. Do you want to know what's on it?"

Her face scrunched into adorable wrinkles he wanted to kiss. "I don't know. Do I?"

He nodded once. This had to be done and it had to be done now. She needed to know. "York's buddies videoed your death. Your murder."

Her breath hitched as her mouth formed a silent *O*.

Chance swallowed hard. "We need to watch it when we get home. Just you and me. Then we need to decide what to do with it."

"You... you knew?"

"I overheard them fighting last time I was here, so yeah, I knew."

"God," she breathed, her palm over the pocket where that despicable piece of evidence rested. "W-why?"

Why what? Why didn't I tell you what I knew? Why did I keep it from you? Why am I so scared to tell you I love you that my chest hurts thinking of what I'd be without you?

As if she'd read his hesitation, Suede rephrased her question. "Why'd he film what he did to me?"

Oh, that. "York filmed it, so he could force your father's hand," Chance told her, though he wasn't convinced Tennyson hadn't been in on Suede's attempted murder all along. Chance just didn't have the heart to tell her that.

Her hair whipped into a curtain, hiding her face. Her breasts heaved. "I don't understand any of this."

"Don't try. We'll never understand men the likes of York and your dad," Chance told her as he circled her tender body in his arms and vowed to protect her as long as he lived.

Governor Tennyson was a pig not to have recognized the brilliant woman living under his roof before he'd thrown her to a dog like York. That was a thought. Maybe the esteemed governor and his wife recognized something in Suede years ago that they couldn't compete with. Maybe her brand of courage and honesty threatened their tidy, selfish little worlds. That would explain a helluva lot.

At last, she calmed. Her breathing leveled out. He stroked her back and shoulders. "It is pretty up here," she murmured sadly, her head turned to the west, her ear still against his heart.

Tell her.

Chance wanted to, but this didn't seem the right place or the right time. A bastard had just died, and marking York's death with tender words meant for Suede alone seemed sacrilegious, if not downright obscene.

Instead, Chance looked out across the valley where he lived. Smoke curled from the scattered chimneys of all the neighbors he didn't yet know. The sun was low in the sky, painting the landscape with all its yellows, oranges, and hints of purple. Dusk would come soon, and with it, the first of the evening stars.

They needed to be down before then. Gallo would be waiting. But for now, sitting with Suede was an extraordinarily pleasant respite in a world gone bat-shit crazy. Chance had chosen well. This mountain and the valley below were beginning to feel like home. So was the woman hugged up against him.

"You ready?" he asked, tipping back, wishing she'd look at him now that she'd witnessed what he was capable of. Worried that he'd see recrimination.

He didn't. The prettiest tropical blue eyes peered up at him, her thick, lush lashes rimmed with tiny tears that looked like diamonds. "Thank you, Chance" —she swallowed hard— "for believing in me."

He nodded like the lap dog he was turning into. For Suede, anything. "I do believe in you. You're the strongest woman I know."

Her lips curled into a tired smile. "All this time, I thought I had to change who I was to make other people happy, only I never could."

"You make your own destiny, Suede. It's not about the family you're born into. It's what you decide to do with the life you've been given. You find your real family along the way. Sometimes they're SEALs. Sometimes..." He let the words go unsaid. *They're angels who fall into your heart when you least expect them.*

She nodded. "I know that now. The thing is, the more I tried, the more fu-, umm, I mean, the worse things got."

He sealed her lips with his index finger. "Wait a sec. Was that you not swearing?"

Suede nodded, scrunching her shoulders like an embarrassed kid. "I still slip sometimes, but yes. I'm trying."

Why that mattered, he wasn't quite sure, but it seemed as if Scarlett Sinclair was smiling over his shoulder.

Suede continued. "I've only had one real girlfriend in my life, Chance. Her name's Karen Singleton, and she lives in Salem with her mom, but you know what? They get along, and they like each other. They really do, and when I was with them, I'd look at their happiness, and I'd be jealous because..." Suede swallowed hard. "I wanted what they had."

"You don't have to change a thing," he told her honestly.

"Not even for you?" she asked, peering up at him with those big, dewy eyes again.

"Never for me," he promised her, gathering her in for one last hug. "I like you just the way you are." *Chicken! Say it.*

"I love you, Chance," she whispered, her index finger on his lip, lighting him up even there at the edge of what now was a murder come full circle. York had truly reaped what he'd sown. "Do you have his ring on you?"

Guilty as charged. Chance swallowed hard. "I do," he said as he fingered the weighty diamond up from an inner jacket pocket. "I always planned to give it back to you, but I had other things on my mind once I thought I'd lost you. I forgot about this." He handed the three carats over. "I need to make a call."

Suede's chest heaved with a long deep sigh, the diamond catching the sun's rays as it passed from his fingers to hers. "I can wait."

Chance thumb-dialed Senator Sullivan and said the words his boss waited to hear. "Justice is served." His caller ID would tell the rest of the story.

In a way, he regretted York falling like he had. The man needed to be questioned, but Suede also needed closure, and she would forever matter more than the man who'd tried to murder her. Chance stuffed the phone back in his pocket. "Now where were we?"

A mischievous smile quirked the corners of Suede's lush lips. "Do you know what I'm going to do with this?"

He shrugged. "Throw it for all I care."

She bounced to her feet, tugging him to join her. "Exactly."

Before he could protest, she cocked her arm over her head, and...

Zing! The diamond ring flew in a sparkling arc over the crystal clear icicles of Mother's Day Falls. Chance lost sight of it then because the lady of his dreams circled his neck with both hands, tugging his mouth down to her lips. "I hope you don't mind, but I had to do that. It was bought with blood money, Chance," she breathed against him. "It's cursed. It had to go."

Good girl.

Up on her toes, she laid a scorching French kiss on Chance's mouth, tangling her tongue with his, breathing hard, and it was all he could do to not lay her down and eat her up. But he'd never look at Old Man Mountain the same way if he did.

When she'd had her way with his mouth, a resolute smile replaced the gloom. She winked, nodding toward the granite ledge they needed to drop over before dark. "Take me home?" she asked slyly.

Chance grabbed her into his arms and spun in a slow circle away from the edge as he said what he planned to say for the rest of his life, "Yes, ma'am."

Chapter Thirty-Two

Chance looked ruggedly handsome by candlelight. After he'd taken care of Gallo, fed him, watered him, and let him outside to take care of his business, they'd settled in Chance's office to watch York's video clip. It reduced her to tears. Chance had been compensating ever since.

Suede lay facing him now in his stylish extra-wide hammered-copper bathtub, the one she hadn't known about until tonight. Guess those other doors in his bedroom weren't all closets.

She'd never seen such a lavish thing, nor had she ever seen a more glorious male in the nude. After he'd filled it, she'd lit the array of white candles on the windowsill. He thought his scars were ugly, but she had no problem with any of them. If anything, she loved them. They'd made him the man he was right now. What a sight.

He took up half the seventy-eight inch long tub, and his bulky male-body made her feel delicate. Like a lady. Like a treasure. She needed that since they'd viewed York's disgusting video. The jerk who'd held the camera, Pablo or Philip, had filmed the show from the edge where she'd fallen. They'd planned it, all of them, and the camera had caught everything. The terror in her eyes when York knocked her down. Her desperate scream when she'd slipped over the edge. The raw fear when she knew he meant to kill her. The stupid hope in her eyes when she'd reached for him, begging him to save her. Thinking he would.

The camera had even caught York's vicious kick and the way her head had jerked back on her spine upon impact. The clip ended with York leaning over the edge, his hand cupped to his mouth, bellowing as she fell, "See you at the bottom!"

If that wasn't ugly enough, York had then turned to his men, dusted his gloved palms together and said. "Anyone hungry?" Like he hadn't just murdered a woman. Like she'd meant nothing.

Chance had taken over then. He'd scooped her up and smothered her with kisses before she dissolved into tears. He'd wiped her eyes so tenderly, and he hadn't let go of her since, not even when they'd made love. Twice. Both times he'd used a condom, which made her smile despite the gloomy mood she hadn't quite shaken. She needed to tell him she was on birth control. He'd just seemed so earnest in protecting her that she hadn't had the heart, but she planned to. Any minute now.

Being with him like this freed Suede in ways she was just realizing. Smiling became a tiny bit easier now that the whole truth was finally out. Well, most of the truth anyway. And love really did cure a person's soul. Suede could feel her heart thawing. How could it not with the care Chance lavished on her? He hadn't said *the word* yet, but his feelings showed in everything he did.

But who knew rappelling down a granite mountainside could be so scary or so fun? He'd shown her a whole new world today, and it was clean and bright and safe. Like him. He didn't do drugs, not even the prescription kind, and he believed in honor, his mother, and his country. His brothers. *Me.*

It wasn't until they were halfway down the mountain, right at the edge of the stone ledge that looked like giant toes from below, that she'd solved the mystery of her lack of more serious injuries. It wasn't the wind that had saved her that night. It was one of Chance's guide lines, now stained with her blood from where her leg had hooked it on the way down. Somehow, it had slowed her momentum but it had also ripped her jeans and her thigh. The moment she'd spied the bloody evidence, the horror of her fall came back in a rush. Thank God for Chance. He hadn't left her side all day, and that was—enough.

Tears threatened yet again at how much he cared for her, but Suede dashed them away before they got out of hand. It had been a long day, and her body wasn't in shape for the endurance test she'd put it through.

"We need to talk," he murmured, his arms stretched along the edges of the tub and his fingertips tapping.

What a sight. If she lived to be a hundred, she'd never get tired of looking at this man's body. Rock solid muscle stretched from his shaggy head to his bare feet. The calves on this man! And that glorious chest—all male muscle and all power.

"About what?" she asked as she sunk to her nose in the already twice-heated water. They'd started out with bubbles, but that was an hour ago.

"Protection. I didn't use a condom the first time." He ran his fingers through his wet hair, carving trails that dripped water onto his shoulders and into his brows. "All my fault. I got carried away."

Suede lifted her lips above water level. "I'm on birth control. We're safe."

His brows knitted together over eyes turned more chocolate brown than caramel amber in the candlelight. "Don't get me wrong. If we're pregnant, I'd be thrilled, but I'd like to make life-changing decisions together, preferably when you're healthy. Babies and mothers deserve a man who can control his impulses. Since you've come along" —he shook his head, spraying her with droplets from his hair— "I'm not that man."

Back under the water she went, blowing kisses at him that morphed into bubbles. He'd said 'if *we're* pregnant', not 'if *you're* pregnant.' That was another reason to love this guy. He took children seriously. He'd make such a good dad.

He had yet to say he loved her though, and Suede understood why. He'd already told her. *'Deployments are tough on married guys. I've watched plenty go through divorces. Why would I do that to a woman?'* So she waited.

This thing between them was a rare treat in her emotionally impoverished life. She wasn't ready to walk away from it. Not the way lust simmered in his amber eyes, the way they turned dark and needy when he wanted her. The way he held her in both of his big hands like a treasure. With him, she felt like a gift, not garbage, and maybe it was selfish, but she needed this connection with an honest man for once in her life.

Cupping his fingers Chance splashed her, and the fight was on. At the end of it, she wound up giggling on his lap, her back pressed to his chest, and another round of hot water gurgling out of the tap. She rubbed the side of her head against his cheek, her breasts cupped by his slender fingers and her nipples hard knots of lust. She had it so, so bad. Yet she knew he was troubled. "Something's bothering you."

His grunt percolated through her body. "Aye. This isn't over yet. I hope you realize that."

She nodded, snuggling into him for more warmth, more of the *'I belong with you'* feeling she'd found in his arms. "Dad's behind all this, isn't he?"

"I'm not sure how much, but yes, Mick Tennyson's involved. I talked with my boss. He okayed me telling you what I know since you're intimately involved with a couple of the players."

Wiggling her ass against him, Suede purred, "I beg your pardon. I'm only intimately involved with one player. You."

Chance sank lower in the tub, groaning enough that she felt the vibration to her core. "Ready again?"

"Always. For you." Suede leaned the back of her head against his collarbone, relishing the way her body sprang to life at his touch. Her fingers drifted alongside his massive thighs, petting what she could reach while he cupped, pinched, and rolled her nipples, driving her back to the edge of passion as the water lapped at their bodies. "So tell me. Who is your boss?" she asked hoarsely.

"McQueen Sullivan," Chance muttered, his voice thick with desire. "What you do to me, woman." He nuzzled the crook of her ticklish neck. "What was I talking about?"

She giggled, secretly thrilled at the power she had over this giant of a man. "You were telling me about your boss, and that this mess with York and my dad isn't over."

"Right. So..." Chance must not have been as distracted as Suede thought. He kept his hands on her breasts as he talked. "This is what we know so far. York missed his meeting with one Benito Garcia and his bodyguard, Julio Juarez, both from Colombia. They work for the grandson of a German immigrant and the drug lord vying for territory, Wilhelm Gonzales."

"That name sounds more German than Spanish."

"Right. Wilhelm's grandfather was one of Hitler's SS guards before leaving the homeland after World War II." Chance's thumbs rolled over both her nipples before he cupped her breasts together, his chin hooked over her shoulder while he watched what his hands were busy doing. "He made an honest living, but Gonzales runs a wicked ship, meaning he punishes anyone who gets in his way. Beheadings, torture, you name it. He's set himself up as a dictator in his part of the country, and he's looking to expand."

Suede listened as intently as she could, a difficult task with Chance toying with her body, lighting her up.

"My boss thinks there's a connection, a family tie between Gonzales and York."

"Because they're both from Germany?"

"That and because they're both in the same business. Not every wannabe from the States gets invited into a Colombian drug ring. Then there's your father, Mick..." Chance cleared his throat as he thumbed the tender peaks he'd just driven into pulsating knots that craved the warm, wet recesses of his mouth. "I know for a fact York had a contract on him, and it had nothing to do with you. Apparently your old man's been in touch with a couple nasty players, the Rio Brothers. They're flat out hired-killers, also from Colombia. My guess is York wanted your dad dead, either that or Garcia pushed for the hit. Mick fired back by bringing his own hired guns into Oregon."

Suede was afraid to ask, but she needed to know. "Whom do those brothers work for if they're just hired guns?"

"Viktor Patrone, the Godfather of all Colombian drug trade. He snaps his fingers, and someone drops dead. Except for Gonzales, the only dealers in his country are the ones he allows."

"Which means they owe him a tribute or something." She didn't know the right name for protection money, but that was close enough. Chance knew what she meant.

"Bingo, only the word from my contact down south is Gonzales refuses to pay. That Patrone hasn't offed him yet is a puzzle."

That didn't sound good. "What's my dad thinking? So now, Patrone's moving his cartel north, too?"

"He's trying, but one helluva battle for territory is about to break loose in Portland. This war will get bloody. My brothers are supposed to tie up the loose ends—"

"Which means they're supposed to, what do you say—off everyone involved?"

Chance shook his head, sending ripples down to her toes. "Just the Rio boys. They've got no business bringing their war to America."

"What about that Benito guy? Garcia? And Patrone?"

"Patrone and Gonzales haven't set foot in America yet, and Kruze will take care of Garcia. Kruze knows his bodyguard, Juarez. They went through BUD/S together, that's Basic Underwater Demolition/SEAL in case you didn't know."

"He's a Navy SEAL, too?"

Chance grunted. "No, Juarez is chicken shit. Couldn't handle BUD/S. He rang out, quit the Navy, then moved south to work for Gonzales. That tells me all I need to know about the jerk."

"So your brothers are going up against the godfather's main muscle? All by themselves?"

"We have no choice, Suede. We can't allow mobsters from South America to run roughshod over America. If Patrone and Gonzales want a war, they'll get one."

"But what if Pagan and Kruze get hurt?" How could Chance lay here with her when his baby brothers were running headlong into danger?

"Believe me, they're good at what they do, Suede. I'm not worried. If you had clearance, the stories I could tell you about those guys."

"You need to get me that clearance then."

He nodded, his fingers flexed over her breasts in a gentle caress, his thumbs strumming her nipples. "I already suggested that to my boss."

"But my dad's involved with Patrone? Why? What's he getting out of this?"

"Don't yet know," Chance admitted. "A while back, he filled several Port Authority vacancies with York's men, but they must've had some kind of falling out since then." He dipped his hands underwater. "Now that York's gone, it remains to be seen what your dad does. It's interesting though. York wasn't stupid, yet he ended up stranded on Old Man Mountain instead of being airlifted to safety. He said he didn't know who was behind that debacle, but suspected it was someone more powerful than Patrone."

Suede shivered. "Who's more powerful than an evil drug lord?"

"That's the million dollar question. Wish to hell we knew."

She rolled to her side, her breasts chilled and missing the fiery touch of Chance's talented fingers, but her libido revved on high. Dropping her ass below water she laid her head on his chest and wound her arms around his sides. "You're right. York deserved what he got."

Chance cupped a wet hand to her head. "That he did."

"Are you going to leave him out there?"

"Don't worry. Sullivan's got a good clean-up crew. He'll take care of it."

"But what if someone comes looking for him before then?"

"They'll find exactly what they would've found if it had been you laying out there." Chance pressed a warm kiss to her forehead. "Put it out of your mind. It's done."

"I'm not worried about him. Only you," she murmured through a yawn. "I don't want anyone coming after you. Are you ready for bed yet?" *Because I sure am.*

A sexy chuckle rumbled deep in Chance's chest. "I thought you'd never ask." He toed the drain plug. As the water funneled out of the tub, he lifted Suede to her feet and wrapped her in a bath sheet. "It's been quite a day."

"It has," she purred, her ear over his heart listening to the steady beat of an honest man, "and it's going to be a better night."

Chapter Thirty-Three

"You're kidding me!" Chance couldn't believe what Sullivan just said. "Vera Tennyson is dead?"

"She and her personal assistant fell overboard during the night. Her body's the only one they've recovered so far."

"Mitchell Franks is missing?" Didn't that curious tidbit of intel stink to high heaven? "Are we certain he's who he claimed to be?"

"Already digging into him. Keep your ears on. I'll be in touch."

Chance palmed his phone and tucked it into his front jeans pocket. What was the chance of Suede's mother drowning while Franks merely vanished? In the ocean? Not freaking likely.

He needed to know more about this guy. Seated in his control center, he hit the keyboard and brought up a page of recent German immigrants. Bingo. Franks came to America sixteen years ago.

Interesting. Another few keystrokes sent Chance to a town near Berlin called Stahnsdorf, Wilhelm Gonzales' grandfather's point of origin. Another coincidence?

"I don't think so." Chance began digging into Suede's mother's right-hand man in earnest.

Suede had insisted on making breakfast this morning, what was fast becoming a daily occurrence that Chance liked. Somehow food cooked by a woman always tasted better than anything he threw together. With her, every meal was an art form. With him, it was more grab and gulp. Normally he'd be there at her side chopping onions and peppers for an omelet or squeezing fresh orange juice, but today's urgent call from Sullivan had demanded the privacy of the Montana command center.

There might come a day when he allowed Suede full reign of his place, but Chance was in no hurry to push her into this part of his world. She'd been through enough. He'd rather have her living a normal life for as long as she could, and if she liked to spend it in the kitchen, who was he to complain?

He'd just opened Franks' employee file, the one Pagan had found tucked inside Governor Tennyson's server, when his phone buzzed an incoming. *Speak of the devil.*

"What do you know, Brother?" Chance asked, his sharp eyes scrolling over Franks' stellar resume and credentials. On paper, the man walked on water, but Chance didn't get that drift from Suede. Every time the guy's name came up, she dodged eye contact and changed the subject. They needed to talk.

"I know Garcia's meeting Tennyson at Terminal Eight this morning. That's where I am at the moment. On the wharf. Want to know who leases this terminal?"

A waterfront terminal was a warehouse, plain and simple. This one had to be a cover for one of the two cartels vying for Portland's location. That Garcia was in town spelled trouble, possibly Tennyson's death. "Sure. Spill."

"The name Domingo Zapata ring a bell?"

Chance hissed. This mess just kept getting bigger and badder. Zapata was a lone wolf out of Brazil, a mercenary in every sense of the word and an outright psycho. He liked the blood of a fresh kill, was known to paint his face with his victim's blood, and then leave a selfie behind with the deceased displayed in the backdrop. The man was an animal, loyal to no one but himself.

"Who's he working for, Patrone or Gonzales?"

"My gut's telling me he's not aligned with either."

That made sense. Gonzales had Garcia and Juarez. Patrone had the Rio Brothers. Why would either of them call in an outsider like Zapata when they had plenty of their own muscle? "You think he's solo?"

Pagan grunted. "I think he's working for someone else. T-8 is either his lair or a misdirect. I'm hanging back in case it's rigged to blow. The Feds already sent

Bomb-Boy in." Bomb-Boy, the latest in high-tech bomb-sniffing robots.

"Why's the governor there?" Chance asked.

"Good question," Pagan answered. "Guess he wants a ringside seat."

"Yesterday, York said someone more powerful than Patrone's behind the scenes."

"Oh, yeah? Who?"

"Don't have a name, but Sullivan's on it. Where's Kruze?"

"Tailing Miss Vicki" —Pagan cleared his throat— "if you get my drift."

Wasn't that a surprise, Kruze chasing tail in the middle of an operation? It wasn't the first time. "He's a dumbass if he catches her. What's her stake in this? Do you know for certain she's after a piece of the waterfront?"

A low growl came over the line. "I don't really know anything. She's just eye candy to me. There's no way she can compete with degenerates the likes of Gonzales and Patrone. That little girl needs to pack up her pink pistols and go home before she gets hurt."

And there you have it, the reason Pagan didn't have a woman in his life and probably wouldn't for years to come. He tended to stick them into cubbyholes marked *wife, cheerleader, teacher,* or *mother* instead of granting them full marks for possibly having better brains and more complex thinking than most men. Yes, the two pink-handled Sig Sauers Miss Vicki carried—somehow—in her matching pink underarm holsters were a girly trademark, but they were her trademark, and she knew how to use them. How she reached for them as full-busted as she was and as quickly as she did, defied logic, but apparently, the Sicilian mob's number one go-to-gal managed her boobs as easily as her pistols.

"Don't be so sure of yourself, Pagan. She's got one helluva track record for getting her man. Kruze needs to stay sharp or she'll wing him." Another eccentric trait, Miss Vicki winged law enforcement officers who got in her way, a thoughtful, albeit sadistic reminder of who she was and how good of an aim she was.

Most hit men and women were content making body shots when it came to a gunfight with the law. If a police officer got in their way, so be it. It was no skin off their teeth; they got paid either way. Not Miss Vicky. She went for smaller targets when she encountered the police. Ankles. Wrists. Fingers and toes. Never heads or throats. Never came close to carotid or femoral arteries. Mostly she nicked, winged, or grazed the boys in blue, and wasn't that interesting? An assassin with a soft spot for cops, federal agents, and first responders? Professional courtesy, maybe?

"Not worried about her," Pagan huffed. "I'm hard pressed to think the mob wants a piece of this war, though. They've got their hands full in Sicily. You think she's gone rogue?"

The Sicilian Mafia had recently gone through massive restructuring due to the poor economy and the Italian crackdown on organized crime in their country. They were currently settling in Germany, where prospects were brighter.

"I think she's working an angle we haven't figured out yet. Like I said, keep your eyes open and tell Kruze to lay off the lady. He's supposed to track and watch from a distance, not engage in physical contact." Something about Miss Vicki and her hard-assed rep nagged at the back of Chance's mind. He just couldn't put his finger on what.

"Shit," Pagan hissed. "Bodies. The FBI's pulling bodies out of the terminal. One. Two."

Chance stiffened in his chair. "How close are you?"

"Don't worry 'bout it." Pagan's standard answer when he was in too deep. "I'm up high on a boom across the way. All these terminals have glass windows front side. I could pick one of these guy's ears off if I wanted to, and they'd never know where the hit came from. Damn. Tennyson's puking his guts up."

Chance could imagine his brother lying belly down, feet anchored over the edge of that boom, his eye to his scope and as cool as a cucumber. "The man should've stayed home and minded his business. His wife fell overboard last night."

"She's dead?" Pagan asked without a hint of surprise at that bombshell.

"The ship's captain believes her assistant fell overboard with her sometime during the night. They're still looking for him."

"Hmm," Pagan murmured. "Then why the hell is the governor here, when he's got a state funeral to plan? Does Suede know?"

"Not yet, I just found out. I'll bet Tennyson thought he'd catch York in that terminal. That's why he's there. Want to bet this turn of events screwed his plans?"

"No shit." Pagan grunted. "Tough break, her being born to those two. Never had much use for either Tennysons' politics, but I like her. Be good to that girl."

"Copy that," Chance said. "Stay safe, Baby Brother."

"Nine, Chance," Pagan hissed. "Zapata had nine bodies in that terminal."

"Nine?" Chance closed his eyes at that magic number. "Want to bet those are the Port Authority Commissioners? Most of them were York's buddies. Someone's cleaning house, Pagan, and whoever's aligned himself with York is next." Which meant Julio Juarez and Benito Garcia, maybe Suede, if that someone came looking for York. Chance's stomach dropped.

"Why do I get the feeling all roads lead back to Mick Tennyson?" Pagan asked. "You remembered to set the beacons, didn't you?"

"Yes, smartass," Chance hissed. Man, make one mistake, and his brothers never let him live it down. "I set four topside, some cameras, too."

"You climbed back up Old Man Mountain? At night?"

"It was nearly morning by then, but yeah. I'm not taking chances."

Pagan chuckled. "How's our girl doing?"

"Good. She was there when York fell."

"Christ, you took her on a job with you?"

"There was no choice. I couldn't leave her here alone. She's neck deep in this mess, and she deserved to look her murderer in the eye."

"You should've let her take him out."

"She had her chance, but she chose not to."

"So you did it? In front of her?"

"Not precisely. He slipped." *Kind of.*

"You tossed him over the edge? Like he did to Suede? Gnarly!"

Who said gnarly anymore? "Get a life. I said he slipped. Suede and I both grabbed for him, but we couldn't get to him fast enough."

"You all choked up?"

Chance grunted. "Crying my eyes out. Gotta go. Keep your ears on." He had a breakfast date with a beautiful woman, and he couldn't miss it, not with the bad news he now had to share.

Chapter Thirty-Four

What is keeping that man? Suede drummed her fingertips on the kitchen table. She'd gone all out this morning and made cinnamon roll French toast, eggs over-easy, and browned a half-pound of Canadian bacon. Gallo had already had his piece of bacon, but Chance was late and his food wouldn't stay warm and delicious if he didn't hurry.

"On my way," he called from the direction of his office.

A smile threatened to steal over her whole face at that simple, ordinary statement. In a week, her life had changed from hell to near nirvana. She still had to deal with the real world one day soon, but for now she basked in the glow of Chance Sullivan's home and the comfortable familiarity of living with him.

He rounded the corner, rubbing his palms together. "Smells good."

"I hope you like it," she said, loving the way his T-shirt stretched over his chest. An insatiable appetite for her man began a restless beat in her blood. *Coffee, tea, or Chance? Hmmm...*

Suede jumped to her feet for a hug, but he'd already taken his seat, his focus on the platter in front of him. "For me?"

"What's wrong?"

Still no eye contact and no answer, just a lip-smacking guy grunt and a change of subject, "Let's eat."

She took her seat opposite him, her elbows on the table and her chin on her steepled fingers. "Spill, Sinclair. Something's up. You can't keep anything from me. I'll always know."

He shook his head. "I'd rather eat first."

"I knew it. It's in your voice. Who's hurt? Not Pagan or Kruze?"

His lips pinched as he lifted his head to face her, but there was sadness in those deepening ambers. "It's your mother, Suede. She was on a cruise, and I'm sorry, but... she fell overboard last night."

"She's dead?" Suede hadn't expected that. *Mom? Dead? Does not compute.* "Umm, okay. You're right. We should eat before everything gets cold."

He cocked his head. "Did you hear me? Your mother's gone, baby."

"I heard you, I just..." She lifted her fork, not certain what to feel. Relief? Anger? What precisely should she feel when someone who, by her own admission had never loved her, died? "I don't know what to say. I'm sorry." *I guess.*

Chance flew to her side. It was his warm grip at her waist that got through to her. "It's okay. Let it go," he breathed into the side of her head.

But there was nothing to let go. All Suede could do was nod. She wasn't in shock or denial. It was more like a rug had been jerked out from under her just when she'd caught her balance for the first time in her life. *Didn't it figure? Just when everything was going good, Mom ruined everything?*

Suede couldn't wrap her head around this interesting, awful news. How can you mourn someone who didn't want you? Who never had one kind word to say to you or about you? Suede leaned into Chance, hoping he'd share some of his compassion, because all she felt was—nothing. "I don't know how to feel. I was afraid for your brothers, but my mom?" *She never crossed my mind.*

Nose to nose, Chanced threaded his fingers into her hair as he kissed her forehead. "It'll come, and when it does, I'm here for you."

Suede closed her eyes and breathed in the fresh scent of the wild Montana sky that always came with Chance. "Okay. That's nice." *I guess.*

*****

Pagan was right. Someone came looking for York. Twelve somebodies. Two choppers landed on Old Man Mountain at noon after Chance and Suede finished breakfast. They touched down precisely where York's rig was stranded. Six men all decked out in winter camouflaged tactical gear and loaded for bear piled out of each chopper.

Chance had left Suede with an earpiece so she could reach him without having to come looking for him. For now, she sat snuggled with Gallo in front of the fireplace, reading one of his mom's novels, *My Enemy Tryst,* if Chance remembered right. He didn't dare take his eyes off the camera feeds he'd rigged topside. He hadn't set the beacons to sound alarms though. It hadn't seemed right to alert York's buddies that a covert operator quartered nearby.

So he watched from the privacy of his office as the men scouted the rig, then cautiously entered like SEALs going door-to-door in Fallujah. These guys were just as steady and maybe half as good. They moved with the precision and accuracy of special operators while one brave individual entered the rig, pistol drawn. Three more followed on his six, but all came out shaking their heads. From there, they spread out.

One kicked around the rig and found the men York murdered just beyond the exit. He knelt long enough to determine COD, but didn't search for identification, and Chance knew then that he was looking at a death squad. These guys hadn't come to rescue York. They'd come to kill him.

Several others stood overlooking the falls. They stayed there a good long time, one peering through high-powered binocs, the others using rifle-scopes. Scanning. Searching.

Chance held his breath. If they were looking for York, all they'd see was the pristine scenery he wanted them to see. York wasn't in the pond where he'd fallen. Chance had taken him deep in the woods and buried him in a plot of easy–to-dig bark and peat moss he'd prepared for just such occasions. If Sullivan's crew didn't show soon, the animals would take care of York, but for now, he was out of sight. Suede would never know this part of the op, and someday, he hoped she'd look out across his parcel of wilderness and think 'how pretty' again.

There seemed to be no leader in charge of the guys up top, which meant they relied on earpieces as well. As one, they turned back to the choppers. In minutes, the birds lifted off. That was when it got interesting. Instead of hovering over the site of York's last known residence, both choppers veered directly west and disappeared in a cloud of snow. Precisely ten seconds later...

BOOM! A tremendous reverberation rattled the ground. Chance lost all video feeds. His cabin windows rattled. Those men had just blown York's rig to kingdom come. Had to be Viktor Patrone's work.

It made logical sense. *Kill your enemy. Erase his name from the face of the Earth.* Winners had been doing that for years. It also meant those mercenaries and whomever they reported to, Patrone or Tennyson, now knew Suede Tennyson wasn't with

York. They had no way of knowing about the video. They'd target her next.

Chance jumped to his feet. Sullivan still didn't know who was behind his previous employees' betrayals, and no one knew which side Domingo Zapata or Vicki Hex worked for. Trouble could come at Suede from any player still in the game. With one keystroke, Chance activated the live ordnance concealed within the foundation, walls, and perimeter of his home-sweet-home. Company was coming.

*****

The windows rattled, which in California meant any number of mini-earthquakes, but here in Montana? Suede felt a sudden draft float past her, kissing her cheek like the breath of winter. She looked over her shoulder as the slide and click of heavy metal at the windows darkened the massive room. The interior lighting flickered along the ornate overhead beams. That was no earthquake. The pages of the book in her hand collapsed into themselves as she reached for her pistol. Better safe than sorry Chance had taught her, and after a week like the last, she believed.

"Come, Gallo," she said as she lifted to her feet, one fingertip to her earpiece. "Chance?" she asked, her voice clear and strong.

"Right behind you."

She lowered her pistol when he came from the opposite direction than she'd expected. "What's going on?"

"Visitors up top just blew York's rig. Patrone's men possibly, but I can't be sure. There are too many players in this mess. I activated the cabin. Don't worry. We have nothing to fear."

"But fear itself," she shot back at him as she holstered her weapon. "So what happens when you *activate* the cabin? Does it spring to life into a *Transformer* or something? Sure hope it's not one of the *Decepticons*."

That got a grin out of her grimfaced companion. "Remind me to tell Pagan and Kruze they've got *Optimus Prime* working on their side." Chance ran a hand up the back of his neck and through his already shaggy hair, ruffling it as if he needed to look more like an unkempt bear than he already did. "I built this cabin with five-inch-thick steel plating between the outer logs and the inside framing. No one's getting in unless they bring heavy explosives with them."

She blinked in surprise. "Wow."

Chance nodded. "I also added a couple offensive features in case someone gets in too close. The corner joints conceal remote operated weaponry to ensure no enemy lives past a twenty-yard radius. The porch itself is an electrical trap. One step up and whoever's in that boot is on their way to hell." Chance cocked his head. "Close your mouth, Suede. You're drooling."

That made her smile despite the fact she was now living in a massively armed camp instead of a log cabin. "What if they still get inside? What if they bring a tank and blow past all your defenses? What if they use rockets?"

The cocky, handsome man winked. "Then we go downstairs and escape through the tunnel while my interior traps do their stuff. Trust me. If anyone gets in here, they'd better be wearing Kevlar pajamas and gasmasks." He canted his head. "Any other questions?"

Suede scanned the plush interior that only seconds before had been merely rustic. She ran into his open arms and snuggled under his chin. "Only one," she breathed. "How'd I get so lucky?"

He tipped his head back and laughed. "You've got it all wrong, babe. I'm the lucky one."

Chapter Thirty-Five

Chance relaxed in the easy chair in front of the fire, his stocking feet on the matching ottoman. Suede had gotten a burst of nervous energy and decided to launder the bed sheets from Chance's room, then the blankets. She cleaned the bathroom, tub, and shower stall, then folded what she'd laundered once it dried. With all of her traipsing back and forth, he wasn't sure where she was at the moment, but she had strict instructions not to leave the cabin.

Chance had a direct line to his brothers and Sullivan via his high-tech earpiece, so he'd purposefully stayed out of his office to keep her company, if she'd hold still. He had a remedy for her nerves. "Suede," he called out.

No answer came back to him, and now that he noticed, Gallo wasn't in his customary place by the fire either. The hairs lifted at the back of Chance's neck. He pushed up, his throat dry and his hands on his knees. "Suede?" he called again, every fiber of his body tuned for her sweet voice.

Still nothing.

The easy answer for her silence was that she was intently scrubbing something else and couldn't hear him, and Gallo was with her. Chance needed to see that to be certain, and she needed to cease and desist the Suzy Homemaker routine. It was driving him crazy.

He paused at his nearly shut bedroom door, not wanting to startle her. She was already uptight. Easing it open, his heart caught in his throat. There she was, sound asleep on his freshly made bed. The poor thing. She had to be exhausted.

That lazy scoundrel Gallo lay stretched alongside of her. He lifted his lazy head and gave Chance a, *'Hey. Close the door. We're sleeping here'* look. Chance snapped his fingers. The long-legged kid took his time slinking to the floor, but at last there was room for the real man of the house beside Suede.

She didn't make a peep as Chance covered her with a light blanket, then eased in behind her. He came to rest in line with her body, spooning with his hand on her hip. His early defense warning had been quiet since this morning's rumble, so he grabbed this stolen opportunity to hold the woman he'd fallen for. Who would've thought he'd fall this hard or so fast?

An errant thought wiggled its way into Chance's wandering recollections. *What would Bear think of Suede?* Navy SEAL, Master Chief Petty Officer Barrett

'*Bear*' Knight. The only man Scarlett Sinclair had truly cared for besides her sons.

The name fit him. Bear was a mountain of a man, but as kind and as gentlemanly as could be. He'd not only treated Scarlett with the respect she deserved, but he taught Chance and his brothers things a man needed to know. Like gun safety. Deep-sea fishing out on the wild Pacific. Bear taught them everything, from how to steer his fishing boat to baiting hooks and wrangling rock cod, yellowfin tuna, and calico bass into the boat, all without giving the ever-present dogfish a snack on the way up from the deep.

The youngster barracuda that Chance had snagged one summer afternoon was the highlight of his teenage years. Somewhere in the cabin, he still had a picture of him holding that toothy baby beast and grinning like a fool. You'd have thought he'd nailed the record for largest catch of the day by the size of that grin. It might be time to dust that memory off and frame it. Suede might like to see it. *Yeah. Good times.*

Bear was the one who'd taken the photo. He was the only real man in the Sinclair boys' lives. It stood to reason they'd follow in his footsteps. Chance lowered his nose into Suede's fragrant mass of tangles, breathing her in. Loving this woman with all he had. It might be time to reconnect with Bear. He had to be grieving Scarlett's death as much as her boys.

Chance found it odd that merely holding Suede while she slept brought his tenderest emotions to the surface. Everything about her was feminine and soft, and Heaven knew he'd been a loner for too long. He couldn't help but wonder what he would've amounted to if his mother had deserted him like Suede's mother did her. How does a kid survive without a soft place to land at the end of a bad day? Without a mom who stopped writing her novels the minute her boys showed up because she had to know everything they'd been up to since she'd seen them last? Without a mom with light in her pretty green eyes just because you woke up in the morning? Without love?

He'd managed to survive the six months since he'd lost her, but only because he'd thrown himself into building this cabin. Without working every twenty-four-seven like a maniac, he'd still have the nightmares. Jimmy *Superman* Olsen, Gerard *Hot Shot* Rowe, and Stokes *Gunpowder* Remington would still be visiting him when the cabin was quiet and the work crews were gone. Merrick *Ears* Wong. Kevin *Chill* Frost. Pete *Ducky* Newton... They'd gone through hell together. God, he missed his mom and he missed his guys.

But surviving wasn't quite the same thing as living, was it? Chance knew he'd been hiding out more than just dedicating his time to his brothers' future security. Who was he kidding? He'd become a coward for the first time in his life, slow rolling the commitment Sullivan and his brothers deserved. In truth, the cabin had been ready a couple months ago. It had taken an angel dropping from heaven for Chance to wake up and get his priorities straight.

He lifted a strand of her auburn hair just because he could. Then another, thrilled at this stolen intimate moment. Suede had beautiful hair, a cascade that curled and dripped off her shoulders like a ruddy mountain waterfall in spring, full of glints of red and gold and—life. That moment up top when she'd loosed her goggles and beanie to stare York down would be forever etched in Chance's mind.

Despite great trepidation, she'd been the real hero up there. Right then, she'd looked like some warrior goddess out of a graphic novel, her hair the mane of a lioness, the silky strands whipping into her eyes like tongues of fire. Frightened yet fierce, she'd ruled the day when—like a gracious queen—she'd granted York another chance at life instead of taking the revenge she'd so righteously deserved.

Stretching alongside his queen, Chance let the cares of the world slip away. His nose came to rest at the now bare nape of her neck. His belly expanded with one delicious breath after another. If there were a heaven on Earth, Suede was it. He had no business loving her, but God knew he did. Patrone or Gonzales, or whoever'd sent that death squad, had best go home to Colombia where they'd be safe. If they thought for one second they were coming after Suede, they were Dead. Damned. Wrong.

*****

She heard voices. Pleasant male voices, but none of them belonged to Chance.

"Whatever happens next, I need one alive for questioning."

"We'll see how it plays out, sir. They won't come willingly." *Pagan? What's he doing here?*

Suede shifted to her elbows, listening. She'd slept into the evening.

"Then drag the bastard in kicking and screaming. I'm getting to the end of this bullshit today, goddamn it."

Shhhhhs hissed out of at least two male mouths, and Suede needed to know who was in the cabin with her, and where Chance had gone.

Gallo sat at the partially closed bedroom door with his ears cocked forward. Tiptoeing closer, she listened before she revealed her position.

"Son-of-a-bitch, he ought to be right in the middle of them by now." Whoever that strange man was, he seemed wound as tightly as a spring. Every word out of his mouth was clipped and sharp.

"This is what you hired us for, sir. He'll be fine."

It sounded like a fist hit the coffee table in Chance's front room. "Goddamn it, stop 'sir'-ing me!"

When someone grunted, Suede eased Chance's bedroom door open. Three men were in front of the fireplace, two in the easy chairs, their backs to her, the other seated on the leather couch facing her. She recognized Pagan by his shiny, tousled locks and his broad shoulders. The man seated next to him had to be Kruze. He had the same color hair and build, but the third man on the couch was gray-haired and dressed completely in green/brown/black camouflage like a hunter. He stroked his silvery moustache repeatedly. His bushy brows looked like they'd never slanted up, only down, matching the wrinkles etched into his weathered face. *So where's Chance?*

Suede cleared her throat to make her presence known, then stepped around Gallo's bushy tail and into view. The gentleman in camouflage sprang to his feet. "Ma'am," he said as his eyes scrolled from her face to Gallo and back again. "I'm sure sorry if I disturbed you."

By then Pagan and Kruze were on their feet as well, both headed her way.

"Hey, Suede. How are you feeling?" Pagan asked.

"Where's Chance?" she fired at the three men.

Pagan drew up short. His gaze flitted to Kruze as the stranger spoke up from behind them. "I'm pleased to make your acquaintance, Miss Tennyson. I'm Senator McQueen Sullivan, and right this moment, Chance is two miles south of here scouting an incoming army that's headed your way."

"You're Chance's boss? A United States Senator?" She hadn't seen that coming.

He gave her one curt nod and snapped, "Chance was supposed to read you in. Didn't he tell you?"

Suede shrugged her shoulders, not sure precisely what McQueen Sullivan meant, but for the first time, acutely aware that Chance and his brothers were more than just former Navy SEALs if they worked under the direction of a US Senator. This man had an intensity to him that rivaled the alpha streak in Chance when he'd faced York.

"He told me enough," she replied steadily. There was no way she'd be disloyal to her man by hinting that Chance should have told her more. Suede turned to Pagan, who was nearly at her side. "I thought you were in Portland."

His shoulders came up. "Portland's not that far away. Kruze and I hightailed it out of there this morning after Chance told us you guys had trouble."

"And I wasn't about to sit on my ass in D.C. while all hell's breaking loose here," the Senator growled. "I trust my operators, but there's no sense throwing them to the wolves."

A breath whooshed out of her. Suede swallowed some of the angst she hadn't realized had been building inside her like a pressure cooker. "Are you gentlemen hungry? Can I get you anything to drink?"

By then she was close enough to Pagan that he grabbed her under his arm and hugged her into his side. "No way are you waiting on us. Have a seat by the boss, and we'll fill you in first."

Kruze smacked Pagan's bicep. "Hold up. I haven't been formally introduced." He held out a massive callused hand, his green eyes dark and sizzling with interest. "The last time I was here, you weren't feeling too good. Name's Kruze Sinclair, ma'am. I'm the handsome one."

Pagan groaned, but her brows lifted at that brag. "Hardly," she shot back at Chance's other baby brother. "Chance is much better looking than you, and he smells better, too."

Pagan slapped his thigh and hooted with laughter. "Man, she told you! Told you to shower once you got here."

The surprise on Kruze's manly face made Suede smile. He lifted one arm and performed one of those disgusting smellfies, sniffing at his armpit. "Whatchu mean? This ain't stink. It's perfume. Ladies like it."

Suede coughed, surprised how comfortable she felt with these two men. "Where? On the *Planet of the Apes*?"

"Oh, come on," Kruze grumbled over Pagan's rowdy guffaw. "This is what a working man smells like after a hard day's work. You know you like it."

She fluttered her fingers under her nose. "What I know is you need to step back. My eyes are watering and I can hardly breathe." *Cough. Cough.*

Pagan grinned. "Watch your Ps and Qs around Chance's girl, Kruze. She doesn't take any crap."

A genuine smile smoothed some of the worry wrinkles from Senator Sullivan's stern face. "Chance's girl, huh? Sorry, Miss Tennyson, but you'll have to ignore Kruze a while longer." He nodded to the cushion at his side. "Please, have a seat. We'll bring you up to speed."

Kruze grumbled as he and Pagan took their seats while Suede accepted her position at Sullivan's side. He didn't sit until she did, and Suede couldn't recall ever feeling more at home. Smoothing her hands over her knees, she was more than a little thankful that her jeans and T-shirt weren't too wrinkled from sleeping in them.

"My wife likes to shop," Senator Sullivan said, his sharp eyes skating over her attire. "Hope you like what she sent. Everything looks like it fits."

"Please thank her for me. I'll repay you as soon as I get back on my feet."

"No, you won't. It's on me." The Senator's gaze speared Pagan. "Goddamn, I hope Chance is smart enough to keep this one."

Pagan winked at Suede as his face cracked with a grin. "Yes, sir. He'd better."

Suede meant to argue about her not paying him back, but Senator Sullivan's brows collided and one big hand smacked his thigh. "Will you two stop calling me 'sir'? It's McQueen. Just McQueen, Goddamnit."

She extended her hand to diffuse the stress in the air. "And I'm just Suede. It's a pleasure to finally meet you, Senator Sullivan."

He took her hand in both of his. "You're one helluva surprise, young lady."

"You might not know it, McQueen, but we don't cuss in Chance's home," she told him evenly. "Now where's my man and why's he out there all by himself?"

Chapter Thirty-Six

Chance would've interrupted the conversation back at his cabin, but he had work to do. Still, it made him smile to hear his brothers' and McQueen's acceptance of Suede into their tightly knit, all-male circle. Until today, Chance had resisted the familiarity of first names with the senator. It always seemed disrespectful. Well, no more. From now on, Senator Sullivan would be simply McQueen. If he proved worthy, the tough guy might even earn a nickname. Like Steve.

Ha! Chance chuckled at his humor. He and his brothers would be working for *Steve McQueen. The things that pass through a block operator's mind when he's inches from certain death.*

At the moment, Chance lay hunkered down and camouflaged beneath the snow-laden boughs of a giant mountain hemlock. The hollowed out tree well beneath those boughs created by too much snow falling in too short a time, provided the perfect sniper hide on this late afternoon. Another weather front had moved in, providing plenty of gray shadows that allowed him to get inside the enemy's ranks without being seen. On his belly, he lay within hearing distance while he gathered intel on the small force of assassins making their way up the hillside to his cabin.

Twenty was a larger force than he cared to take on alone, but it wasn't unheard of. He knew this land and winter better than his brothers, which was why he'd taken point and was now lying where he was. They'd been holding up this three-legged tripod called the Sinclair Brothers long enough. He meant for them to sit this one out as long as they could. Besides, he needed them to keep Suede safe.

At rest, these spec ops guys rarely spoke, but the few times they had, they'd used American English, not the Spanish Chance expected. Most were Caucasian males, one Japanese, and one African-American. All were Americans and obviously former military. They looked the part and they moved like it. All were thick-bodied and decked in tactical gear from their armor-plated vests to their kneepads and reinforced work gloves. No doubt about it, this was an army on the move.

The leader wore no identifying rank insignia to set him apart, but all deferred to the one who Chance had tagged 'Grunt,' simply because that was the extent of his communication skills. Apparently, these guys had been pre-briefed and were running a predetermined drill. Either that or they were online with someone back at their combat control team via earpieces.

When he'd first wormed his way under this tree and into their rest stop, Chance needed to know who they were looking for, York or Suede. Not that it mattered either way. The second they hit the kill zone he'd established around his cabin, they'd be history and he'd be glad to bury them alongside York. Let whoever'd had the balls to send them after Suede come sniffing around next. Chance would end him—or her—too.

The mole in McQueen's office might not have revealed this location to York, but someone else surely knew where Suede was. Body recovery didn't require the assets these guys had. Several carried heavy gear bags no doubt full of ammo or grenades, while others toted RPG launchers. One shouldered a LAW, a light anti-tank weapon to breach heavy-duty defenses, or an eight-inch thick wooden door and steel plates.

After gulping down a quick meal of protein bars and bottled water, Grunt shoved to his feet. Tossing the plastic bottle aside, he dragged his M2010 sniper rifle out of the snow and back over his shoulder. Fitted with a quick-attach sound suppressor, a Leupold Mark 4 scope, and clip-on night sights, that rifle alone made this guy a lethal killing machine all by himself.

The rest of the men were equipped the same. Each performed a similar drill, discarding their trash and gearing up, yet none of them were wise to the sniper in their midst. Considering the spec ops training these guys obviously had, Chance made certain he gave nothing away. Not one breath or a whisper.

The men moved out, Grunt leading the way. Interesting. He hadn't sit-repped any CO while he'd rested, leading Chance to think these men operated under the same ROEs he and his brothers did. *Report only when the job's done.*

And if they never reported? Who'd come looking for them? Chance intended to find out. He stayed in the shadows, appreciative of the active weather front moving in over Old Man Mountain and the light snowfall blanketing the forest. Bodies were easier to bury in deeper snow.

"Comm check," Pagan whispered in his ear. "Can you talk yet?"

Chance cupped one hand to his mouth and spoke low, his gaze never leaving Grunt and his men. "They're coming your way. Twenty. All former-military. All Americans. Move Suede into the basement. These guys intend to level the place."

"They can try. Sullivan, I mean McQueen's here."

"Damned glad that was his chopper earlier."

"You know it. What are they packing?"

"Automatic rifles. LAWs. RPG launchers."

"No kidding? Who the hell's behind this? They said yet?"

"Wish I knew. Can't be Tennyson. He wouldn't dare."

"The man's chicken shit," Pagan agreed. "McQueen ever find out who leaked your twenty?"

"Not yet. The real question is who paid the folks on his staff to do it. None of them have the guts to ante up and rat him out. He must be one powerful SOB."

"Or they're scared of him. Which leaves you in the crosshairs. Bastards."

"Is there a reason you called?" Chance had to ask. Pagan tended to take the world of covert operators lightly, instead of seriously. Chance did not. Not since Suede.

"Just wanted you to know Gallo took off."

"He what?" Chance hissed. "You couldn't have led with that?"

"Don't worry. He'll be back."

"No, Pagan, he won't. Christ, he'll come gunning straight for me."

"Sorry, I—"

Chance stopped listening. A crazy damned German Shepherd had just plowed through the ranks of bad guys and straight to him.

✲✲✲✲✲

It was an honest, though bone-headed mistake. Gallo had to pee. Pagan opened the door and let him out. Now Suede sat glued to McQueen's side listening while someone beat the hell out of Chance. Pagan and

Kruze were on their way to get him. They just weren't there yet.

"They won't kill him," McQueen said through gritted teeth, his fists clenched, and his face pale. Gunfire erupted over the speaker amplifying his earpiece, and Suede buried her face in her hands. "He wants you below in the basement. Now's a good time to—"

"I won't go," she declared, her heart high in her throat, choking her. "I need to hear what happens to him."

"Then put this goddamned thing in before we have to move fast." McQueen tossed an earpiece at her.

She'd forgotten hers in the bedroom. Fumbling, Suede tucked it where she could follow every spoken word that came out of the Sinclair brothers' mouths. If only they'd say something! All she could make out was Chance grunting and groaning over Pagan's and Kruze's heavy breathing. The guys pounding Chance hadn't sworn or called names, not the behavior she'd expected in mercenaries. Her nerves stretched tighter as the seconds dragged into minutes. Poor Chance.

Then rapid gunfire. Indistinguishable mayhem. Men bellowing. A dog yipping. *Was that Gallo?*

"Got him." *Was that Kruze?* Suede couldn't tell who was who out there.

"Bringing him in the back way." *Definitely Pagan.*

"What back way?" she asked McQueen, her feet set to fly.

"Motherfuckers shot him." Pagan again, his voice as hard as nails.

"No!" she cried. "How bad? Is he alive?"

"Yeah, but he'll never walk on all fours again."

"Who the hell are we talking about?" McQueen bit out.

"They shot Gallo!" she nearly screamed, relieved and terrified at the same time. "Not Chance."

"Copy that," Chance hissed. "Hang tough, Suede. See you in a few."

"What about you?"

"I'm good," he said, but she didn't believe him. His voice sounded too tight. Too strained.

"This way," McQueen gestured as something tremendously loud and powerful hit the front of the cabin. The impact nearly knocked her off her feet. Suede ran for the basement, her heart pounding in her chest as loud as her feet on the wooden steps. The labored rasps of three men's heavy breathing vibrated in her ear.

At the bottom of the stairs, McQueen strode past her and the shooting range into a hall dimly lit along the baseboards by safety running lights. She hadn't noticed them before. They had to be part of Chance's activating the cabin scheme.

"Where are we going?" she asked, needing to be prepared for whatever Chance needed.

"Here," McQueen barked, jerking his head at the metal door in the hall. "This lock has a sixty second delay, so when I say *'now'*, you pull everyone on the other side in as if their lives depend on it."

She had a feeling the Sinclair boys' lives did depend on it. Swallowing hard, she poised to be all she could be. Seconds dragged into minutes, until a raspy "Here" came over her earpiece. McQueen hit a palm pad in the wall by the door, and... *Whoosh.*

Hydraulics hissed as the massive steel door rolled to the right and three men in snow gear tumbled onto the basement floor, Pagan with a whining Gallo on his chest, Kruze with his arm around Chance's waist. With sweat dripping off their brows and running into their eyes, they'd no more than dropped to their knees when a yellow light flashed overhead and an alarm buzzed. The door began to roll back.

"His tail!" Chance yelled. "Get my dog's tail out of the way!"

"Got it," Pagan replied as he rolled from his prone position and grabbed Gallo's fluffy tail in the nick of time. "Shit. Close call."

"Close call?" Suede shrieked. "You call that a close call? What are you guys, complete idiots?"

Pagan quipped, "No one's a complete idiot," while Kruze shot Chance one of those raised-brow guy looks that pretty much said, *'Women. Sheesh.'*

Enough! Fighting mad now and scared out of her wits, Suede slapped her palms to her hips and shrieked, "It's not funny, Pagan! You boys are grounded!"

If that didn't make her look and sound stupid, nothing did. Chance rolled to his knees with a terse groan, and Suede lost the heat of her convictions. "You're hurt," she cried sinking to the floor with him, not sure if she should smack him for scaring her to death or kiss him for making it back alive.

Sweating and dirty, his face was a mottled pattern of blacks and reds. His lips and his nose were bleeding. "Guys, get my dog to sickbay," he ordered as he staggered to his feet and took her with him.

He tilted to the side, and Suede forgot about everything but holding him up. "Where are you hurt? What can I do?" she asked as she dabbed her shirtsleeve to the cut over his bloodied eye.

"Get out of my way, for one thing," Pagan growled behind her, his arms full of a whimpering German Shepherd. "Not sure the last time I got grounded, Suede, but you're going to fit right in," he muttered as he angled Gallo through the first doorway in the hall.

McQueen stood positioned with his hand on yet another control panel across from the steel door. "Hold onto your seats, lady and gentlemen. It's about to get ugly."

"Not my mountain!" Chance hissed. "The yellow pad, sir, not the red one."

"This?" McQueen asked, looking over his shoulder to where Chance stood leaning into Suede. "For Christ's sake, it's too damned dark in this cellar. I can't tell what's what. Take an action item, Chance.

Install bright whites down here and get rid of that goddamn yellow shit."

Shifting his palm from the red pad to the yellow, he winked at Suede. "Don't look so worried, ma'am. It'll all be over in a minute or two."

He pressed the button and... *BOOM!* A clap of thunder roared, and the structure overhead shuddered like a wet dog shaking itself. She steadied Chance with a palm to his chest so they didn't both fall down.

Once the structure stopped vibrating, Kruze spoke up from the lighted doorway where Pagan had taken Gallo. "Do you think that got all of them?"

McQueen lowered his head as his silvery brows clapped together. "Sure as hell hope so. Your brother won't let me drop the MOAB."

"Guys," Chance growled, clearly in pain. "Let's save the MOAB for another day, shall we?"

What's an MOAB? Suede wondered, but didn't ask.

"I guess," Kruze grumbled as he turned back to Pagan, "but it would've been cool."

Chance leaned heavily into her side, every bit of his big body trembling. "Are you okay?"

"Me?" she bit out, peering up to see past those swollen eyelids. "You're the one who's bleeding, and we've got an army outside ready to kill us, at least we used to, and Gallo's hurt, and—"

He slammed into her, covering her open mouth with his, and that was as close as she came to chewing him out. He swallowed her angst along with the tears that had come out of nowhere. "This is what I do, baby," he growled against her tongue and lips. "If you can't handle it, I need to know now."

"You can't get rid of me that easy, so shut up and kiss me," she growled back, her fingertips dug into the sides of his sweaty head and all of her feminine receptors on overload as she claimed his mouth with a vengeance. She bit his bottom lip so he'd remember whom he was dealing with. This man had his nerve, insinuating she couldn't handle a few bad guys. If he could, she could. But it also made sense to know what that red button did now that the ground had stopped shaking.

"I take it that's a yes?" McQueen muttered from somewhere—else.

Chapter Thirty-Seven

Opting to stay on his feet, Chance dragged Suede upstairs, headed for the shower instead of the tub. Fiercely in need of a long nap, he wanted the grime of an op-gone-bad off his body and down the drain first. He also needed to keep her too busy to look outside the windows and see the carnage his home defense system had wreaked on those men.

The falling snow would soon cover the blood and gore, but McQueen and Kruze needed time to cart what was left of the bodies into the woods. It'd have to be a long shower, and Chance hoped he stayed awake long enough to make love to her when the scrubbing was done.

Damn, Grunt had taken it personally when he'd found a black ops guy on his tail. Those guys would've beaten Chance to death if one of them hadn't fired on Gallo. *No one hurts my dog and gets away with* it.

Chance had come up swinging, kicking, and shooting like a madman then, his second wind a tsunami of righteous wrath. He'd seen red the split second before he'd nailed six of Grunt's men. Around then, Pagan and Kruze stormed the scene, popping lead and enough yellow smoke to mask their dash-and-grab getaway. Damned good seeing them.

But Gallo still laid bleeding and whining on the ground then. Out came the LAW, and the Sinclair boys nearly died together. If it hadn't been for Pagan blubbering like a baby because he'd gotten his mother's dog shot, it could've been the end. But when he stumbled to his knees to cradle the whimpering dog, Chance and Kruze stumbled, too. The rest was history.

The shooter missed, and somehow, they all made it home in one piece. Gallo would live, and Suede got her first lesson in what a future with a covert operative was like. Dicey, at best.

"Slow down. I need to look at you," Suede prompted, running to keep up with him as he dragged her along.

"Trust me, you will," he answered, shoving his bedroom door open, then locking it behind him. He wasn't worried now that Pagan attended to Gallo. An animal lover since birth, Baby Brother had a few veterinarian classes under his belt, plus he'd volunteered at various animal shelters across Mission Bay area before he'd joined the Navy. Gallo was in good hands.

"Chance, please," Suede begged as into the bathroom they went. "I'm serious. Let me take care of you."

"Oh, baby," he growled as he reached over his shoulder and ripped his shirt over his head. "You're going to take good care of me." *If I can last.*

The smile that he loved, half shy and half seductive, blossomed over her face in a heated blush. "I can do that," she said with a sexy nod at his zipper.

"Then get out of those pants, woman," he ordered, his cock at attention despite his condition. He'd left his snow gear in the basement, but the jeans he always wore under that gear had to go. He peeled out of them, his muscles already tight with an overload of lactic acid and fatigue. He needed a shower and a good workout, in that order. Suede was that workout.

"You're bleeding," she murmured as she shed her clothes, then hugged up against him, her fingertips to his collarbone.

He wanted to take a step back from her just to look at her nakedness, but he was doing good just staying upright. "No, I'm not. I'm good."

"Stubborn man," she growled as he tugged her into the shower and turned on the spray.

"Tired is more like it," he replied, his face in the water and the heat of it working its magic. The cuts around his eyes and mouth stung the worst, but they were nothing. His kidneys worried him. Grunt had meant to kill him with his bare hands, and the bastard nearly had. But most of all, Chance didn't want Suede looking at him like she might cry.

Collateral damage came in all varieties, and the emotional impact on families was the worst, the one the rest of the world failed to see. What he'd just lived through, barely, reflected in her eyes. The tropical light was gone, replaced by a swirling storm of pain. Suede was hurting for him. Knowing he'd put that pain there, and would again... That he couldn't change this part of who he was, messed with his mind and his mission.

His battle weary heart cried, '*For God's sake, tell her you love her!*'

But he couldn't. Not yet. Not now. *First things, first.*

Suede stood behind Chance, running her fingers up his back and into his hair. He bowed his head and let her carry on. A soft, warm breast bumped against his back and a slender foot eased between his feet, but for once, Chance was too tired to act on his naturally horny impulses. He'd deflated to half-staff and was glad for the break. Sex with Suede was not in his immediate future. He didn't have the energy, not so soon after battle. Warfare and killing juiced some guys up, not him. That initial spike of adrenaline was long gone.

She worked her own magic up the tight muscles in his neck, her thumbs kneading the knots out and enticing warmth in. While he stood there in the spray, she worked gradually down his shoulder blades. From his rigid traps to his lats and onto his obliques, she coaxed a soothing balm into his battered body. A paid masseuse couldn't have done better.

"Turn around," she said quietly. "Lean against the wall, so you don't fall down."

"I won't fall," he lied, but he might. His knees wobbled, the after-effects of the beating he'd survived.

"You're a stubborn man," she told him.

"We've already established that," he muttered, his eyes closed, so the sight of her lush, naked body wouldn't tempt him. This wasn't going to be one of those nights he outdid himself like a horny teenager in the sack. He was fading too fast for that.

Her fingers smoothed down the sides of his head to the hollow of his neck. Applying just enough pressure, she worked over his shoulders and biceps and all the way down to his wrists. She washed his hair, then smoothed body wash over his shoulders and down his back. Skillfully. The last of his strength ebbed away when she started on his pecs.

"I need to sit," he admitted.

Reaching around him, Suede turned the faucet off. "No, you need to go to bed."

Agreed. He jerked one of the two bath sheets off the table beside the shower stall while she wrapped herself in the other.

Suede took hold of his hand and said, "I'm taking you to bed."

The patience in her tone about did him in. While part of him wanted to tell her no, that he didn't need to be looked after, the rest of his battered body couldn't come up with a reason not to be coddled for the first time in years.

She led him to his side of the bed, pulled the blankets back, and down he went. "Go to sleep," she told him, which sounded like a good idea once his head hit his pillow. "I'm here."

"Isn't that what I'm supposed to tell you?" he asked, his brain already fogged and on its way to oblivion.

"I think it works both ways when you love each other. You took care of me and now I'll take care of you. Go to sleep, Chance."

"Ibuprofen," he muttered before he drifted off. "Four."

She returned quickly with a glass of juice and the tablets. He leveled himself on one elbow, swallowed the meds, and "G'night," was the last thing he said. But he thought, *'How do you know I love you? I haven't said it yet.'*

*****

You poor man. Suede sniffed as she nursed the stubborn man asleep at her fingertips. Bruises covered most of his body, and he was swollen where no man wanted to be black and blue. She'd gently scrubbed him in the shower to make sure nothing was broken. *My goodness, what they did to you.*

Overwhelmed with the entire day, she left him to sleep it off. Pagan, Kruze, and McQueen hadn't come upstairs yet. Too pumped to rest, she resorted to what she knew best for therapy: cooking and baking. Imagine her surprise when she found dry yeast in Chance's refrigerator. Incentivized by that small discovery, Suede mixed up a batch of sourdough bread starter, and set it, loosely covered, at the back of the counter. In three or four days, the bread she'd make from that starter would go great with a big pan of soup. Maybe loaded baked-potato soup if Pagan hadn't eaten all the bacon.

She was cooking with gas now. Banana bread came next because the bananas on the hook were ripe. Then cheesecake and caramel brownies, chocolate chips with walnuts, and shortbread cookies because everyone loved shortbread cookies. No milk remained in the Sinclair fridge, but a hint to the right brother at the right time would surely take care of that. Suede wasn't worried, but she'd have to learn how that drone delivery system worked one of these days. How difficult could it be?

Setting the coffeemaker to brew ten cups, she cleaned the mess she'd made, her nervous energy quelled for the moment. By then, the counter was covered with a good choice of homemade goodness, but the bread pans on the highest shelf in the pantry called to her, and since the yeast wasn't gone yet...

A half-hour later she was up to her elbows in flour and dough. The last sheet of chocolate chip cookies came out darker than she liked, but men didn't notice over-baked anything. They were locusts. Get out of their way and just let them eat.

She'd just greased three bread pans and set them on the counter nearest the oven to warm when Pagan appeared at the kitchen door, his sleeves rolled up and his arms across his massive chest. "If Chance isn't smart enough to keep you, I will," he said by way of greeting.

Suede blew a puff of air to clear the tangles that kept flopping into her eyes. "What if I don't want to be kept? Not all women are domestic, you know."

"Says the woman with flour on her cheeks and butter all over her hands."

She had to give him that. "I guess I should practice what I preach, huh?" A tired chuckle bubbled out of her. "What's going on now? Where are Kruze and McQueen?"

Pagan flipped the closest chair around and straddled it. "Outside. As far as what's next, guess we'll find out soon enough. You like to cook." He made that a statement.

Suede nodded. "Sometimes. It's my release valve. I couldn't go anywhere without an escort when I lived with York, so most of the time, I stayed in." That brought back a raft of ugly memories she didn't want to share. "It was easier. I didn't have to deal with the paparazzi, and in the kitchen, I had total control. So I watched cooking channels and I learned."

His nose twitched. "Smells like you're good at it."

"You're just hungry. Come on in and grab a cup of coffee and a couple cookies while they're still warm."

"They're warm?" That got Pagan off his chair. He didn't settle back down until he had a mug of coffee and a plate full of chocolate chips cookies. "We got any milk around here?"

"That's what I was wondering. There's none in the fridge. How does that drone delivery system work? I'd never heard of something like it before I, umm, dropped in," she said as she punched the raised dough and rolled it onto the freshly floured tabletop.

Pagan chuckled around the whole cookie he'd just stuffed into his mouth. "Works good. Chance and McQueen set it up with the local grocer down in the valley. All we've got to do is call, give him our order, and presto, chango. Within hours, groceries show up on the doorstep. It works with the department store, too. I'll show you once you're finished with whatever you're making now." His nose twitched. "Smells good."

Suede stopped kneading. "Do we still have a doorstep?"

His eyes scrolled to said door. This side of it appeared untouched. "Hope so. If the charges went off like they should've, the porch will still be intact, too. I don't know for certain, but I doubt those guys got this close. Kruze and McQueen would've said something by now if they had."

"Is that where Kruze and McQueen are? Cleaning up the... the forest?" She puffed at the persistent curl that kept dropping into her eyes.

"Don't think about it. They know what to do."

Silence reigned in the toasty kitchen. Suede wondered what Kruze and McQueen were doing with all those bodies and parts. She swallowed hard. Pagan was right. It was better if she didn't think about it. "How's Gallo?"

Pagan cleared his throat. "Sleeping at the moment. He'll be okay. I was just kidding when I said he'd never walk again. Sorry 'bout that. His big butt got in the way, nothing too serious. I doped him up to clean and stitch the wound, but he'll be fine. He's like Chance. He just needs twenty-hours of shuteye, and he'll be raring to go again."

Suede sliced the dough into three loaves, kneaded them into shape, slipped them into the pans, and covered them with a towel before her mind circled back again to what lay in the woods. "Do we just keep adding to the body count in Chance's cemetery then?"

"It's more like a morgue at the moment. Sullivan's already called a team in to remove the bodies. They should be here in a couple hours."

That was good to know. The idea of dead bodies, especially York's, hidden nearby creeped her out. "So what's next, Pagan?"

By then the cookies on his plate were gone. He rapped his knuckles on the table and turned to the door. "That depends on you, Suede." He turned back to her then, his dark green eyes filled with something she couldn't quite read. "You're no different than Chance. Montana's a great place to live, but you can't hide here forever."

That caught her by surprise. "I'm not hiding."

He grunted on his way out the door. "Bet me."

Chapter Thirty-Eight

"Americans," McQueen growled. "And mercenaries. Every last one of them."

Chance nodded. After sleeping the rest of the previous day away, he'd awakened early this morning with Suede's lush body tucked in next to his. Nothing beat the warmth that flooded his soul at the feel of her against his belly and thighs. After smoothing a hand down her shoulder and arm to her hip and getting no response, he'd eased out of bed and let her sleep.

The rest had done him good. His back hadn't been hurt nearly as bad as he'd expected. One eye was black and a couple teeth were loose, but he was as good as ever. Waking up to the aroma of fresh baked cinnamon rolls hadn't hurt, but those cookies she'd left in containers on the counter? Best damned things ever with a good cup of coffee. She must've baked all night long.

Dressed in casual wear, jeans, and a crisp white polo, he now held a cup of black coffee in one hand and Suede's hand in the other. She hadn't slept as long as he would've liked, but she'd wanted to be included in this discussion, so here she was. Right beside him where she belonged. She'd chosen a light pink knit sweater that hugged her ample curves, black jeans, and leather boots, the short kind that met the hem of her jeans. McQueen's wife had done well shopping, but Chance couldn't wait for the day that he took Suede out to get her own things. A man needed to do that for his woman. Buy things for her. Spoil her. Dress her up. *Undress her.*

Everyone sat around the fireplace in the front room, brainstorming with Senator Sullivan about the army that had attacked the cabin and where the mission needed to go from here. Gallo lay asleep on his rug in front of the fire, no doubt drugged with the pain meds Pagan gave him.

McQueen had changed his hunter's wear for ordinary Rider jeans, cowboy boots, and a light blue sweatshirt with *Dallas Cowboys* stamped across his chest. Pagan and Kruze wore jeans, but Pagan had topped his off with a white T, while Kruze wore a white tailored, button-up shirt and enough men's cologne to fog the entire cabin. The boy always did like that crap.

The latest FBI word out of Portland was that Viktor Patrone was in town with a five-man entourage of muscle. Patrone didn't merit diplomatic immunity, so the moment he'd landed, the FBI had climbed all over him. Homeland Security too. They made no bones about inspecting his single piece of carryon luggage, as well as his person. Of course they'd found no guns, not on him or his men. Those items were easy to get on the streets.

"Yes, Americans, but those were *not* Patrone's men," Chance repeated. What had started as a simple one-man show now threatened the status quo of the entire state of Oregon, possibly the nation. It had to be stopped.

"Then whose were they?" McQueen bit out.

"Had to be Tennyson's. He's the only gringo in this mess, and trust me, Patrone would've used his own guys. I'm telling you, it's time we strike back before he does."

Kruze grunted. "And that means what?"

Chance lifted Suede's hand to his mouth and kissed the back of her fingers. "It means Suede and I need to leave our mark in Portland."

"We do?" she asked.

"Absolutely. I've given this a lot of thought. You facing your father will take this debacle out of Montana and put it in Governor Tennyson's front yard where it belongs. Let him clean up his own mess."

Pagan leaned forward, his elbow to his knees and his fingers steepled under his chin. "I get it. That press conference you wanted to hold. The big reveal, right? Let the world know she's still alive?"

"Exactly." Chance angled sideways to face the nervous woman at his side who would soon be center stage, if she agreed. "Look him in the eye the same way you did York. What do you think?"

Suede blinked, then brushed her free hand over her chin, cupping it before it dropped to her throat and back to her chin again. He could almost hear the wheels turning in her head. Her hips twitched against his, and she was nervous. He got that, so he waited. The whole room did. This was her decision, and it was a tough one, especially with her mother's funeral just days away.

He'd asked her earlier if she'd wanted to attend, but she'd said no. "Let her have her day." She and her mother hadn't been close when Vera was alive. To attend the funeral would only prolong media speculation and incite the gossip rags.

At last, she pinched her lips and swallowed hard. "But those guys are all killers."

"I hate to tell you, lady," Kruze drawled, "but so are we."

"I know that, but you're different." The trepidation radiating up Suede's arm to her fluttering fingertips worried Chance. He knew she loved him, but she'd seen him *accidentally* kill the unarmed man she'd let live. That alone could be a game-changer.

"The difference between them and us is we're on the right side of the law," McQueen bit out, then qualified, "at least the moral side of the law."

She cocked her head at him. "Is there a moral side to killing?"

"I'd like to think so," Chance said evenly. "The law can't reach some of the biggest, baddest bastards on the planet. We can. I'm totally good with whichever answer you give, but Pagan's right. We can't hide out here forever. The bad guys already know you're here, and they'll be back. Do you dare take a chance on us Sinclairs to help fix what's broken before it kills more innocent people?"

"When you put it like that..." She stared at Pagan, her lips pinched tight and the slightest tremble to her head. This had to be the greatest leap of faith of a lifetime for her, yet she of all people knew how wicked the world was. If she wasn't willing to share this side of Chance and his brothers, all bets were off. He'd have to break ties with her—somehow. The sooner, the better. The notion pained him, but the thought of her living another unhappy life hurt worse.

Chance pressed her knuckle to his lips for what might be the last time. If anyone needed a safe place to land, it was Suede Tennyson, and God, he loved her more everyday. He had yet to say the words to her, but he knew it to his core. Unfortunately, love didn't solve all the world's problems. That was just the way it was.

"Would I have to talk to him?" she asked.

"To the Governor? No, ma'am," he answered. "You don't even have to see him. This face-to-face will be pre-recorded from here, right where you're sitting in fact. You don't even have to dress up. All you have to do is look directly into the camera and tell the world what happened."

A breath of relief poured out of her until she gulped and said, "But no one will believe me. Not after all the things I've done."

McQueen took that challenge. "Let the truth speak for itself, Suede. Yes, there'll be a media-frenzy, but that's what the press does best. They're no better than jackals nipping at the king of the jungle until they draw blood. Let me deal with them."

"But York was the Lion, not me."

"In name only," Kruze growled. "He was more of a vulture than king of the jungle. Get that through your head right now. He shoved you over a cliff, for hell's sake. What kind of a man does that?"

Suede turned on Kruze, her chin lowered. "That's true, but I'm not him, am I?"

Chance could've kissed her. The longer she stayed with him, the more he detected a lady of class and nobility behind that timid veneer. He was proud of how she'd just put Kruze in his place without resorting to theatrics or threats, and she hadn't dropped an f-bomb in—he had to think—days.

"No, you're more like a robin, Suede," Pagan murmured from across the room where he sat, the reverent tone in his voice capturing everyone's attention.

Suede's head came up, and there was a connection between her and his brother that Chance hadn't seen coming. He cocked his head as a different side of the spoiled brat, baby brother he'd grown up with emerged like a butterfly unfolding out of its dusty cocoon. This Pagan was—sensitive. He didn't look away from Suede, and she didn't break eye contact with him. It was as if they were the only two in the room. *What the hell?*

"You're not as big or as fierce as the eagles, owls, and hawks of the world, Suede, and for sure, you're no lion. Thank God for that. Not everyone needs to be a bird of prey," Pagan told her, his voice uncommonly gentle. "But that doesn't make you any less important in the scheme of things. It just means you see the world in a different light. You have a better purpose than I do. You get to deal with life, not death."

He ran a quick hand over his scalp from front to back, ruffling his deep black hair. It ended in messy spikes. "You don't have to live in the shadows like I do. Trust me, the world needs more songbirds, and you're the robin who'd rather sing in the sunshine and build a nice safe nest for her family than hunt the scum of the world. It's true. You've been fed a pack of lies all your life, but those days are done, and that person you thought you were, never really existed. She was a lie, but I see the real you now. I think you do, too."

Quiet Pagan certainly had a lot to say on this subject, but Suede had leaned forward as if hanging on his words. This was precisely what she'd needed to hear.

"You're everything your parents could never be, because you're made of better stuff," Pagan continued. "I'm sorry for what you've been through, and I know you're scared, but even a mother robin will fight to defend her nest, little sister."

"Oh," squeaked out of Suede, and Chance had to give Pagan credit. Whether he knew it or not, he'd just given her the very thing she craved most, something Chance never could've given her. *Her first sibling.*

"Robins can be fierce, too," she told Pagan in a whisper.

"I know *you* can be fierce," he said with an encouraging nod. "You're brave. The whole world knows you're unstoppable. Hell, you're also the first person to ground me in years, and no, Chance doesn't count."

"Hey, wise guy," Chance shot back good-naturedly. "I do too count."

"No, you don't. Not in my book. " Kruze deadpanned, shaking his head for drama. "He mean something to you, Baby Brother?"

Pagan's face wrinkled as he aimed a wink at Suede. "He does know how to cook."

"So does Betty Crock—" Kruze caught a pillow in the face for that one. But when Suede snuggled back into Chance with her head against his bicep, the battle was over.

McQueen shot Chance a sharp look from across the room. "Goddamn, she's a keeper."

Wasn't that the truth?

Suede cleared her throat. "Excuse me, Senator, but you've got to stop swearing. Scarlett Sinclair wouldn't approve."

Chance nearly choked at that prim reminder after some of the words she'd spit out when she'd first arrived, but McQueen took it well. "You know, I just might do that for you, ma'am. I'm damned, er, I mean..." He touched his index finger to his forehead in a quick salute, his soft blue eyes brimming with respect. "I'm mighty proud to know you."

Chance pressed a kiss to the top of her head and whispered from the bottom of his heart, "Welcome home, Suede."

Chapter Thirty-Nine

Camera. Lights. Action! Despite the weather, McQueen flew a national news crew straight out of New York City and into Montana by the wee dark hours of the next morning. Kruze and Pagan led them inside the cabin through the tunnel, no doubt because of the shredded trees and damage to the front of the cabin during what Chance called *'that little skirmish'*. No TV cameras needed to see that.

Suede had the worst case of butterflies. Dressed conservatively in a gray pencil skirt, a blushing pink button-up silk blouse, and three-inch strappy heels no one in the viewing audience would ever see—courtesy of McQueen's savvy wife—Suede hadn't dared drink coffee with the crew. She had enough nervous energy to buff the ceilings without needing a ladder.

Prior to leaving the safety of Chance's bedroom, she'd wound her hair up high on her head and secured it with a clip, striving to present the image of a strong capable woman instead of a slutty girl-gone-wild.

"Don't worry," Dixie, the pretty make-up artist patting powder on the tip of Suede's nose said. "Once the camera starts rolling, you'll settle down."

Dixie was a free spirit who wore green leggings under a bright orange slouchy sweatshirt with bold black lettering that read ME! COFFEE! NOW! across the front of it. She'd twisted her blonde, purple, and pink hair into a topknot and tied it off with a scrap of frayed black velvet ribbon. She also liked feathery earrings, the black and pink kind that dangled to her shoulders.

"How do you know?" Suede asked, winding a thick strand of hair around her index finger and shifting her backside farther into the kitchen chair.

Dixie's left cheek scrunched. "Easy. You're the expert here, nobody else. Just answer the questions, and once you get rolling, Micah will let you take it from there. You'll see."

If you say so...

"And stop messing with your hair. That makes you look weak. Keep your chin up. Look at Micah until he signals you, then talk to the camera. Tell 'em what you know. You've got this, girlfriend."

Dixie certainly sounded confident.

"Ready?" Chance asked, his hand extended for Suede's. He'd just broken away from where he'd been with McQueen and his brothers at the fireplace.

She had to look twice. Wow, what a sight. The transformation in this guy knocked the wind out of her still tender lungs. Chance had swapped his normal jeans and T-shirt for a navy blue button-up, tan chinos, and dark brown dress shoes. His hair was combed evenly to the side and he'd trimmed his scruff and shaved his neck. Sophistication dripped off him, and, *oh my, my, my*. She girly-fanned her lips so she didn't drool. The man was *Esquire* delicious, and those melted honey eyes? *Mmmmmm, mmmmmm good.*

"Look at you," she breathed, giving his massive body another visual once over since she couldn't molest him with her fingers. Or her mouth. Or her tongue. "You're beautiful."

His cheeks reddened as he clasped her hand. "Nah, you're beautiful. I'm just some guy. Ready?"

Suede sucked in a deep breath and lifted to her feet, wishing they were going dancing instead of to an inquisition. "As ready as I'll ever be."

Dixie whisked the make-up trays out of the way, and it was show time. Suede took her place beside Chance on the couch facing the fireplace. They didn't cuddle, but sat side-by-side like co-workers. He leaned back with one arm sprawled along the back of the couch like he did this kind of thing everyday, while Suede sat at the edge, wringing her fingers and wishing this interview were done.

Micah Watanabe, the anchor for America's largest broadcasting network, sat to her right in an easy chair, just as relaxed as Chance. Dressed in an expensive looking three-piece gray suit, white shirt, and a soft green tie, Micah was a charming mountain of a man. A stalwart Samoan with a mic hidden on him somewhere, he represented corporate America. Trimmed and manicured, suave and polished, he was her dad's kind of people. Not hers.

Suede dropped her lashes, fighting a wave of anxiety that threatened to send her into the restroom where she *would* lock the door and never come out. This was so not a good idea, outing her father and his dealings with York. The reasons to not go through with this interview ticked at the back of her mind, but the worst of them? In too few minutes, everyone would know what happened to foolish young women who thought they knew everything.

"Relax," Chance said, his warm hand blanketing hers where she'd stabbed it under the cushion between them. "You're not under fire here. You can do this. Breathe."

"This is your show," Micah chided Suede while her stomach clenched as if her intestines had just twisted into a hangman's knot that would eventually find its way around her neck. "Don't say anything you don't want to. If I ask the wrong question, let me know. Smile. Now tell me about your dog."

"Gallo?" Her gaze settled on her faithful companion in his place near the fire. That she could do. "He's not mine, but he might as well be. Gallo follows me everywhere. He thinks he's a lapdog."

Micah canted his head. "How so?"

And she was breathing again. Gallo was a safe subject. "Well, look at his big ears, for one. How can you not adore a fur baby with big brown eyes topped off with those fuzzy, floppy ears? He's adorable." *And I love him.*

Chance grunted. "He does think he's cute."

"I understand that pup saved your life?" The leading question came sooner than she expected, but Suede knew what to say. Chance had told her to be honest. Pagan told her to be kind. Kruze said *'give 'em hell'*. But in keeping with her burning need to change from the inside out, Suede started her story at the beginning, with the neglect she'd endured as a child in her parent's various homes, then the abuse she'd suffered at the hands of America's flamboyant tennis star, Lionel York.

Micah listened intently, asking questions to be sure he understood while the camera rolled. What Mitch had done to her as a child screamed for its turn in the spotlight, but she swallowed that nightmare down. This interview was about her father and her ex-fiancé; the two men who should've loved her most but who'd plotted to kill her. A shiver jerked over her shoulders. As bad as they were, the monster that had assaulted her in her own home still lurked like an evil minion in the shadows.

Not now, she told her sorry self. *He'll get his. Someday.*

If that wasn't the most ludicrous thought. It was possible the sharks had already gotten Mitchell Franks. That would be perfect. He was still missing. A girl could hope he stayed that way.

Chance chose that moment to settle his warm palm at her shoulder, giving her strength and bringing her back on task. Suede slammed the door on Mitchell Franks and kept going.

She talked about the abused women's syndrome, and how she'd allowed York to do what he'd done, mostly because of her age and inexperience, but also because she'd been too proud to admit she was wrong and ask for help. All through their relationship, she'd blamed herself for the cruelty he'd inflicted on her. She'd honestly thought it was her fault when she'd *made* him slap her.

She'd also accepted the blame for York's reaction when she wasn't pretty, quick, or sophisticated enough to please his perverse tastes. In short, she was always responsible, never York, an adult male ten years her senior. He never stepped up to be a man because she hadn't known then how to stand up for herself as a woman and demand that he grow up or drop dead.

Micah's cues were minimal. A small smile of encouragement here. A covert wink there. A simple question... "How did you hook up with a celebrity like Lionel York in the first place?"

Oh, that. Deep breath. "After I sued my parents for emancipation, he stopped by my apartment one day. He said I impressed him and he wanted to meet me. That he admired my spunk."

Micah cocked his head. "He just dropped by? Didn't you find that odd since he lives in California? Was there a tennis match in Portland at the time?"

She shook her head. "No, what really happened is that my father made a deal with him to take me off his hands. Dad wants to be president and I was" —she ducked her head into her shoulders— "bad press."

Micah's brows slammed together. His eye narrowed. "A deal? What kind of a deal?"

Suede was beginning to like this man. "York got me, and the Governor..." *I am never calling him Dad again* "...got a clear shot at the White House."

Someone off-camera growled. Didn't sound like Gallo. Might have been Dixie.

"That's quite a..." Micah seemed at loss for the proper word.

"Accusation," Suede filled in for him. "Yes, but when the Governor wants something, he usually gets it."

"You do know that if this is true, the FBI will want to talk with you."

"I would expect them to," she agreed, nonplussed at the qualification for truth Micah had just inserted into her story. After all she'd lived through, an investigation by the FBI was just another speed bump on a long rough road to being a better human being. Let them dig into York and the Governor's emails, their phone calls, and all of their lies like Chance, his brothers, and McQueen had done. They'd find out everything she'd said was true. Until they did, this interview was nothing but her word against the Governor's anyway.

Suede inhaled deeply. She had nothing to worry about. Like McQueen said: *Let the truth speak for itself.*

Micah tapped his index finger to his bottom lip, scrutinizing her. "But how do you explain the change in the Suede Tennyson that America knows today, because frankly" —he crossed an ankle over his knee— "you don't resemble the obnoxious woman you recently were. Your cheeks are pink, and, of course it helps that you're not wearing makeup, but you look and act—different." He couldn't have said anything better.

"Thank you," she said from the bottom of her heart. Suede explained the fear she'd lived with at York's California penthouse. She explained that now she knew he'd drugged her, then baited her to make an outrageous fool of herself, which she did every time. Not content to shift the blame entirely to him, she admitted she'd complied at other times because she'd felt a need to strike back at her parents. That she wanted to look tough when actually, her life was out of control.

"It wasn't all Lionel's fault. I can't remember some of it, but other things, yes, I did it," she told Micah firmly. "I admit it. I acted out. I was lewd, and I deserve the reputation I've got. I have a lot to make up to America for. I'm no role model, and that's why I'm here. I was on the fast track to an early grave." She swallowed hard, not ready for the big reveal yet.

He canted his head. "What was the catalyst behind this new and improved you? There had to be a specific moment in time when you knew you couldn't live the way you were any longer."

This was it. The moment when Chance had said all hell would break loose. Trembling, Suede gathered her courage, faced the camera and declared to her father and the world, "The night Lionel York shoved me off Old Man Mountain. I knew if I survived, I had to change who I was and where I was going. I'd been given a once-in-a-lifetime second chance. Lionel might have shoved me. He might have meant to kill me, but I'm the one who stayed with him and put myself in danger."

Micah's brows lifted. He leaned forward. "You just accused Lionel York of murder. Do you have proof?"

"Y-yes." Her voice quavered. "One of his men took a video of the whole thing. It was snowing, but you can clearly see the moment York put his hands on my shoulders and pushed me backward. It also shows him kicking my... my forehead with the heel of his b-b-boot." She blinked the tears away, but her composure failed as the utter terror of that night came back on her. "I was falling. Trying to hang on, and he... he kicked me."

A semi-hysterical chuckle bubbled out of her. "It's crazy, but even when I was falling, I still thought he was just playing, that he'd reach out and save me. I thought he'd grab my hand and pull me up at the last minute, and... and..." She lowered her head at how dumb she'd been to think he'd kill her one moment, then save her the next.

Her chin came up at the last moment and Suede wiped her eyes. She refused to let York or the Governor reduce her to a victim. She wasn't that person anymore! Never again!

Squeezing Chance's index finger, Suede lifted her head, faced the camera, and told the man who'd fathered but never loved her, "You wanted me out of your life, Governor Tennyson; you got it. You paid York to take me off your hands, but... I'm. Still. Here."

Chapter Forty

Exclusive! Micah's pupils flared. He'd been told this story was well worth the trip, now the investigative reporter rose to the challenge like a Great White after a baby seal. The truth was finally out and Chance couldn't have been prouder. Suede executed that reveal perfectly.

"How did you come into possession of the video?" Micah asked her.

"A good friend—"

"I did it," Chance cut her off, his nerves as steady as a summer breeze off the Pacific in June. "I climbed my mountain and I confronted York. I took the video, so he couldn't hurt Suede again."

"And you are..."

"United States Navy Retired Chief Petty Officer Chance Sinclair, sir."

The briefest hint of a smile raced over Micah's eyes. "I can almost imagine the look in Mr. York's eye when a Navy SEAL showed up for that video."

"Yes, sir." Chance gave him that. This reporter was sharp to have deduced his true military family. "I'd already climbed up the day after Suede fell to see what kind of asshole I was dealing with. That's how I knew there was a video to begin with. I overheard York arguing with two guys." *Who shall forever remain nameless because they're dead.*

"And I bet that once you asked Lionel politely..."

Chance shook his head. "No, sir. I didn't ask and I wasn't polite, but this interview isn't about me, is it?"

Micah took the hint, no doubt because he could edit this interview later until it suited his agenda. "May I see the video?"

This was that turning point from which there was no return for Suede. Chance faced her, not Micah or the camera. "Only if Suede agrees." They'd both viewed the video—between making love, a few tears, and making more love—the same night they'd retrieved it. It was up to her if she wanted America to see her at the lowest point in her life.

"A person falling to her death isn't a very pretty thing to watch," she murmured. The tip of her tongue peeked out just long enough to moisten her bottom lip. "It's an ugly thing, but yes. I have the original. You may have the only copy if you... if you'll promise not to alter it."

Micah damned near glowed at the scoop that had just landed in his lap. "Miss Tennyson. Suede." He swallowed hard. "I give you my word. I wouldn't think to edit the truth. I believe everything you just revealed. You're an amazing woman."

She shook her head. "No, I'm not. I've made a mess of my life, but I'm not done living yet. It's my time now, and I want to prove that bad things happen, but that doesn't mean good things won't happen next. We all make mistakes." Her fingers gripped Chance's index finger like a Chinese finger trap. "All it takes is a second chance. I hope America will understand that I was just a kid when I did those things and give me that much."

Micah leaned forward then, engaged. "Tell me about the fall. Can you bear to share the moment you thought you were dying with all of America?"

A tiny whimper eked out of her. "It was... cold. Snowing. Really windy." She squeezed Chance's finger tighter. He squeezed back. "We were up on the mountain—"

"Old Man Mountain, right?" Micah prompted. "The stone wall directly north of here?"

Her head bobbed. "It's not exactly a stone wall, but yes. We flew in for a photo shoot, but that was another one of York's lies. There was no photographer and no shoot. Then the wind kicked up and the snow started to blow sideways, and I got scared. I hadn't dressed for a blizzard and there was no heat in the rig he'd brought in for us. I wanted to go down, but he said wait. Then he... he..."

Chance untangled his fingers to shelter her against his chest and under his whole arm. Suede shot him a look, and he knew what that small gesture meant to a girl who'd been fighting the world alone for most of her life.

"He wanted to play games, Mr. Watanabe." Her throat constricted with the effort of swallowing. "Mean games. He wanted me to undress up there, but he really wanted me to die in the nude in the middle of nowhere-Montana so the press would think I'd died the way I'd lived—as a strung-out drug addict and a nut-job."

Micah nodded once, compassion gleaming in his dark brown eyes.

"Only I didn't really live that way. He drugged my booze and..." As if she'd said too much, she shook her head. "But that's another part of this ugly story. Anyway, when I refused to get naked, he got mad, and he... he shoved me backward, and I slipped. He stuck his boot in my forehead because I wouldn't just fall off the mountain, and make it easy for him. I couldn't hang on, and I did fall, but I don't remember anything after that until I woke up. By then, I could barely breathe and my ribs hurt, but I was somewhere warm and safe and..."

She lifted Chance's fingers to her mouth. "This man saved me," she whimpered. "Gallo found me in the frozen pond below Mother's Day Falls, but

Chance is the one who breathed life back into me. He wouldn't give up on me, and he resuscitated me, and he carried me here, and if not for him and his dog…" Suede dropped her lashes. Crystal teardrops fell then, and Chance wanted the interview to cease. He cocked his head at Micah, prompting him for a change.

Micah had the good grace to nod in agreement. "You, Suede Tennyson, are a living miracle," he said, his voice filled with tenderness. "Thank you for sharing what had to be the most horrible night of your life."

Her head bobbed as she lifted a finger to her nose. Suede swallowed hard but met Micah's gaze. "It was, but I'm going to prove York and the Governor wrong. Just you wait."

His face lit with a wide, island smile. "I know you will. America loves an underdog. They're going to love you." Turning to the camera, he said, "This is Micah Watanabe broadcasting live from God's Country in Northern Montana. Goodnight America."

"And that's a wrap," Dixie whispered, her eyes shining. "Suede, honey, you rocked this interview. I want your autograph before we leave, and, oh hell." She burst onto the scene, angled around Micah's knees and dragged Suede out of Chance's arm and into a womanly hug.

"You poor damned kid," she cried, stroking Suede's back like she would a little girl. "I get you, sweetheart. So will every other woman who's been kicked to the curb by some low-life dirtbag like York.

You don't need men like him and you're not alone, baby. Not today. Not ever."

Chance stood back and watched Suede absorb the sisterly connection. It wasn't until Micah leaned back in his seat that Chance realized the camera was still rolling. *Good job,* he thought. *America needs to know the real Suede Tennyson. Damn Lionel York and Mick Tennyson to hell.*

When the light on the camera blinked off, Micah put his hands on his knees and pushed to his feet, satisfaction lighting him up from the inside out. "Thanks for the heads up, Senator," he told McQueen over a warm handshake. "We'll edit this take on the flight home, and you can plan on it airing tomorrow night after the five o'clock news. Count on it. Same agreement as last time?"

McQueen put a hand to Micah's shoulder. "Same deal. You be square with me, I'll be square with you." *Whatever that meant.*

"I wouldn't have it any other way. I plan to use the video in its entirety if it's not too graphic."

"Use it," McQueen shot back at him. "The terrorism of a lone young woman by a celebrity bully stops here. Today, goddamn it." He looked to Suede then, shrugged like he'd been caught, then winked, and said, "Sorry, ma'am. I'm working on it."

With her arm still around Dixie's waist, Suede dried her teary face with her other hand. "That's okay. I'm no angel, either."

Micah disagreed. "You've got that wrong, young lady. You're one hell of an angel. I expect to see you change the world one of these days."

A lovely crimson blush kissed her cheeks. "I'd just like to be left alone."

He smiled at that. "See? That's what makes you different. You already know what you want and it isn't notoriety."

She shook her head, her eyes wide. "Heavens, no. I've got plenty of that."

While they talked, Chance scanned the television crew. Micah Watanabe was a rare find in an industry puffed up with pride at its own celebrity status. The people who had accompanied him worked *for* him, not just with him. They weren't network employees, but Micah's own handpicked assistants. Better yet, they were every bit as trustworthy as he was.

Chance knew that for certain. Rick Warren, the cameraman, was former-Army. The sound and lighting guy, Byron Cord, was a former-Coastie, and Dixie Jensen, the make-up artist, was Air Force Reserves. Micah himself had served two tours of duty in the Marines.

"Thank you for this opportunity," Micah said as he shook Suede's hand. "I'd like to come back and do a follow up when the dust settles."

"I'd like that too," she said as she returned the shake. "Maybe then I won't be so nervous."

Chance reached around Suede to grip the big Samoan's hand. "Thank you for taking the time to meet with us, sir. I'll be in touch."

"I know you will. Take care, Chance. See you kids later."

Chapter Forty-One

Pagan and Kruze took over from there, directing the crew into the kitchen for refreshments before they headed back to the East Coast. Chance circled Suede's shoulders with one arm, tugging her ear to his mouth. "We need to talk," he whispered.

She gave him that quizzical look he adored. "We do?"

He nodded at the front door. "I'll help you into your jacket. We won't go far, just out to the porch. No need to change out of those sexy heels." *I've got plans for them once everyone leaves.*

Gallo scrambled to his feet at that magical word. *Walk.*

Once outside on the porch, Chance closed the door behind him while Gallo made his appointed rounds, anointing the snowdrifts and any twig that survived the blizzard or the carnage. Suede rolled her collar up and stuck her bare fingers into her pockets, her breath a cloudy vapor in the cold, crisp Montana morning. She turned her eyes on Chance, and he wondered what secret was so bad she couldn't share it with him.

"Come here you," he murmured. Her hair clip had to go. With one snap he loosed that silken auburn cascade and sent it tumbling over her shoulders and down her back. The instant scent of sugar cookies and flowers hit his nostrils, calming the center of his soul. Combing his fingers through the luxurious tangles, he was convinced he held the best part of his whole world in his hands.

Chance framed her sweet face between his hands and leaned his forehead to hers. "You froze in there. You were doing well at the start, but then you froze. Is there something I should know?"

Her head turned from side to side in denial, but her lashes came down. When a man refuses to look at you, trouble's a breath away and you might get knocked on your ass. But when the woman you love can't—or won't—look you in the eye? Heartache. Plain and simple.

He took hold of her wrist. "The Sinclair family's a little overwhelming, isn't it?"

Suede nodded, still not looking at him. She inhaled in an extra deep breath. Swallowed hard. Shook her head. Swallowed again. Stalled. And that was okay. He tugged her flat up against his chest, his hand at the nape of her neck and his nose in her hair. She'd had enough stress for the day. Whatever was bothering her could wait. She'd tell him eventually. "Know that I will always have your six, baby. Maybe someday—"

"He raped me," she whispered into his jacket.

Chance's heart stalled. "Who?"

The erotic plans for Suede's fancy heels against his ears evaporated. *Doesn't matter who, I'll kill whoever hurt you like that.*

She nuzzled in deeper, her face sandwiched between his breastbone and her lush auburn locks. "Mitchell Franks. He raped me, and I was afraid to tell you and... That's my last terrible secret."

Chance could barely speak. He eased his fingers under her thick tangles, needing to connect with her, then settled for the bare skin at the nape of her neck, holding her gently but firmly. "Your mother's assistant?"

She nodded.

"Tell me about it?" he asked as calmly as he could. *I'll find his sorry ass if I have to drag the ocean, then I'll strangle the shit out of his worthless dead body. I'll cut what's left of him to ribbons!*

A sad whimper lifted between them. "He came to my room one night. I was fifteen and I thought Mom needed to talk with me, but it was just him, and he... and he..."

Strangulation's too fucking good! I'll stake that rat bastard over an anthill and use him for target practice. With my knife!

"He tied me to my bed and he..."

Forget the ants. A bed of hot coals works better, then I'll dance on his shittin' body till he burns!

"He told me if I told anyone, the next time would be worse. That he knew what girls like me liked. That he'd bring a belt and a collar and a..."

Chance could barely hear over the angry buzz in his head. *Christ, I hope that bastard's still alive, so I can kill him!*

"I told Mom, but..." Suede stopped as if the words caught in her throat.

Chance couldn't take the hopelessness pouring off her. He didn't need any more details. He already knew what the high and mighty, self-serving Vera Tennyson did. *Absolutely nothing!* "She didn't believe you, did she?"

The truth poured out of Suede in a sad whisper. "She never believed me. I asked her not to tell him, but..."

Goddamn it to hell! "Your mother betrayed you," Chance said, his voice flat because if he let his anger loose...

"She told my dad, umm, the Governor."

"What'd he do?" *The prick!*

"He held a meeting. With Mitch and me. I had to face Mitch and repeat what I said to Mom, and then..." She swallowed hard, trembling. "And then..."

The universe ground to a deadly stop. Chance had never been so enraged. Very carefully, he set Suede back a foot where she wouldn't get hurt. Then...

"Fucking assholes!" lashed out of him like a whip of lightning.

The sturdy log rail caught the first one-two punch as image after image of an older man hunched over a frightened fifteen-year-old Suede Tennyson rolled through Chance's head like porn he couldn't shut off. He pummeled that son-of-a-bitchin' rail because he couldn't hit Franks. *The lies! The rape! Where were her goddamned parents when this was happening to their only kid? Campaigning? Preening for the media? Fucking the world?!*

The solid pine uprights caught his wrath next. Then the log wall. Kick after well-aimed kick shook the timbers as Chance battered every prick in Suede's life, and there'd been plenty. Mick and Vera Tennyson weren't parents. They were fucking trolls!

"Stop it, Chance, stop!" Suede cried, her poor head shaking. "Please. You're scaring me."

He turned aside long enough to see the tears streaming down her reddened cheeks and dripping off her jaw. Her fingertips fluttered at her lips. Instant remorse stole his need to kill. *Shit, what have I done?*

She was right. He needed to tone it back instead of acting like the monster he knew he could be. Chance stilled, flexed fingers that were no doubt bloody, possibly broken. He sucked in belly deep breaths that still left him oxygen deprived. The need to end the allegedly dead Mitchell Franks in the most painful way possible was a hard beast to rein in.

Rage still held a tight grip as Chance forced himself back to reality. His vertebrae cracked. His jaw ached. He'd cracked a tooth. Both hands were bleeding, not that he cared that he'd hurt himself. It was the image of Suede—*a fifteen year old, for fuck's sake!*—living through what she'd survived. Her whole life had been one nightmare after another. *Fifteen!*

Well, no son-of-a-bitchin' more. Mick Tennyson had a rude surprise coming tomorrow. Vera Tennyson had already died at sea, a fitting punishment for the bitch who'd neglected her only offspring every day of her life. York—damn him to hell!—lay moldering in a shallow grave where wolves, bears, and wolverines could snack on him until spring as far as Chance cared. Franks was missing at sea, presumably dead.

DAMN! How does anyone treat a little girl like that? A child!

He flicked his wrist, sending red drops flying into the pristine white snow capping the rails, and—damn it—he winced at the pain radiating up his forearms. After another measured breath, the world settled back into focus. The red haze that had blinded his sight with temper faded.

He'd only lost his mind like this once before, that after he'd learned of his mother's death. But her death by cancer was a result of natural selection, whereas this young woman's spirit had been eroded her entire life by an acidic home environment. It was no wonder she'd ended up running with a wild crowd.

That was what survivors did. They adapted, and sometimes, they ended up fighting the world when they didn't have to.

DAMN! Another unrelenting wave of rage surged over him like poison he couldn't shake. *All those years...* Yet there Suede stood, her spine straight, still giving life her best shot and still striving to overcome what for most people, would've been a crushing handicap. Still eager to be a better woman. Trying not to curse, the sweet, crazy thing.

Her persistence humbled him. Her light. Her courage. Desperate longing unfurled inside Chance as if a ray on sunshine had finally breached the hard knot in the deepest chambers of his heart, allowing her energy to cleanse his soul. Suede had become everything to him, and he wanted her more than his next breath. God, he loved her.

"Come here, you," he growled as he pulled the woman he adored back into his arms, cupped his hand to the back of her head, needing her scent to calm the frightening beast he'd morphed into. That beast served his needs in battle and it would again one day soon, but this was Suede's time.

Holding her calmed his tremors, and breathing in the light fragrance of her shampoo quieted the blood-rage in his heart to a slow boil.

"I'm sorry," he said when at last he could speak. Even then, his eyes brimmed at all the innocents in the world who'd never stood a chance: the battered little girls and boys, the neglected babies and the elderly that no one knew suffered in silence. The mistreated cats, dogs, and horses. The sad-faced, over-burdened and beaten donkeys he'd seen overseas. Jarheads didn't find them just in third world countries. There were places in America that were just as evil, but shit. This was the last thing he'd expected to happen in a governor's mansion.

"I'm sorry," he told her once again, still striving to be the man she needed in her life, not another bastard. She'd had plenty of them.

"It's okay," she murmured. "I get mad, too. I understand."

"No, not that. Well, yeah. Maybe that too." Chance eased her far enough back that he could see into her pretty eyes, if she was willing to look at him. "But I'm more sorry that I didn't know you then. I would've brought you home to meet Mom and the guys. You could've lived with us where you'd have been loved every day. Spoiled rotten. Kruze would've teased the death out of you, and Pagan would've been jealous because Mom liked you best. I know she would have."

"And you?" she asked, her voice a hopeful whisper. "What would you have done with me?"

"This," he murmured, pressing a fervent kiss to the forehead that York had kicked only days before. Dixie had done a good job with the makeup, but Chance knew precisely where that bastard had left his mark. Bruises on faces healed, but hearts were a different matter.

The purest blues smiled timidly up at him. Suede's nose wrinkled. As her arms circled his waist, her ear came to rest over his heart. "That's the nicest thing anyone's ever said to me."

Chance wanted to talk of their future together. He needed to ask her that all-important yes-or-no question. His heart ached to tell her how much he loved her.

But there were too many wild cards still in play to talk of forever. Vicki Hex. Domingo Zapata. Not to mention the unknown mastermind behind Senator Sullivan's staffing problem. The mysterious person who'd sabotaged York's helicopter retreat from Old Man Mountain. The puppet master who'd had the balls to send his mercenaries into Chance's front yard.

Could those three be one and the same?

Chance intended to find out. But holy shit, the more lowlifes he and his brothers uncovered, the more it seemed climbed out of the woodwork. This thing wasn't over. For now, Chance did what he did best. He breathed deeply. He prayed. And he just held on...

*****

Suede inhaled the familiar scent of her hero, her lover—her kryptonite. She couldn't lie to this guy, couldn't hold back any of the things she'd never told York. With every detail of her assault, Chance only held her tighter. Well, until that moment when he'd gone off the deep end and pounded on his cabin, but even then, he hadn't directed his rage at her. Not for a second. Neither had he questioned nor interrogated her, called her a liar or made her feel as if she had to prove the horrible truth she'd just dumped on him. He hadn't defended Franks' actions either. Not once had he intimated that she'd done anything to deserve the rape. Instead, Chance believed her. He was on her side, and how odd was that?

"You're safe," he whispered at the top of her head, his body still thrumming from his outburst. "With me, you'll always be safe."

"I know." There was a certain luxury in knowing Chance would fight for her. That he'd die for her. No man had ever held her as gently or been as outraged at her pain. She'd always been the throwaway daughter and lover. Never the treasure. Until now.

Tears she couldn't hold back streamed into his shirt, wetting him to the skin, yet he didn't push her off. Instead, his big palms held her flat to his chest like he'd never let her go.

His heart throbbed beneath her ear with a rapid yet steady beat. Her nose sought his clean masculine scent, needing his brand of courage. She nuzzled into his shirt while she reached under his jacket, her fingers craving the feel of power in those massive muscles that even now, flexed protectively around her. Suede couldn't remember a time she'd felt so sheltered or had so much to live for. She'd gone from pauper to princess the moment York tossed her aside, the moment she'd fallen at Chance's feet.

He didn't have to say the words. She knew. He loved her like she'd never been loved before.

Chapter Forty-Two

Hellfire rained down on the elitist governor of Oregon, and Suede was glad to see that Mick Tennyson had no comment for the throng of eager investigative reporters at the governor's mansion the morning after her story and York's video aired. He certainly couldn't deny what she'd said, and after hearing her version of life in his home, America woke up and took sides. Twitter crashed when people all over the world cried out in her defense. Facebook went wild. It seemed the world loved the young woman, who'd not only survived the neglect and abuse by powerbrokers the likes of York and Tennyson, but who'd stood up to them as well.

They called her brave and a fighter. An example to beleaguered women and girls everywhere. Out of the shadows, other women stepped forward with their horror stories of dates, weeks, and months spent living with York's psychotic behavior. Not to be outdone were the dozens of claims of unwanted sexual advances, intimidation, and outright assaults by Oregon's 'charming' governor—and his wife.

By then, Mick Tennyson's political goose was deep-fried. The FBI cuffed him, courteously escorted him from the lavish home he'd never return to, and away he went in a black FBI van. Charges were pending. Micah and his crew caught it all on live TV.

And that deal between Micah and McQueen? To devote sufficient airtime to Suede's unique plight. The investigative report lasted *Two. Hours.* Seemed Micah and his crew spent the time between Montana and New York City delving into Tennyson's and York's shady business dealings. Talk about a scoop.

Suede didn't catch the live program thanks to Chance's lack of a TV, but the recorded version that McQueen sent was just as good. She'd watched it earlier on Chance's laptop from the comfort of his warm body where she'd been tucked in safe and sound. Odd. It was like watching a news story about someone she didn't know.

A smile creased her lips at the scatterbrained look in her father's eyes when he'd been trotted down the steps and away from the home Oregon's taxpayers paid for. He deserved this comeuppance. If he only knew what Chance wanted to do to him, he might have considered himself lucky.

Lieutenant Governor Broderick Bale stepped up to the plate that afternoon as Oregon's acting governor. Suede watched that too, via satellite link, this time from the kitchen where Chance and she were chopping vegetables for a pasta salad to go along with the venison roast in the rotisserie.

As his first official act, Bale held a press conference aimed at the Colombian degenerates in his town. He called out the National Guard to restore order to the streets and docks of Portland. He instituted a curfew, requested the state legislature to revamp the port authority selection process, and he invited Homeland Security to partner with him in making his state safe again.

"Green onions or purple?" Chance asked, a bunch of green onions in one hand, a succulent purple in his other.

"I like them both. You pick," Suede told him. They'd both dressed in jeans. She'd topped hers off with one of Chance's button-up shirts, the sleeves rolled up. He wore a dark blue henley.

By then, Pagan was in the air. Kruze was already in Portland. She didn't know why, but she knew better than to ask. McQueen was back in D.C., but he'd called to make certain she'd seen the news.

"English cucumbers or regular? I've got both."

She finished slicing the first of two sweet peppers, one red and one green. "It doesn't matter to me. Exactly why are we making this dinner?"

Chance's brows lifted. "No special reason."

Shaking her head, she resumed her chore while he tended to his. Her nose filled with the pleasant aromas of—home. The venison bubbling on the rack and the scents permeating the kitchen was nice, but that subtle hint of wind, sun, and Chance that she adored? Priceless.

She drew in another breath, relishing this moment in her life when everything was absolutely perfect. If she could freeze-frame it, she'd keep it in a locket around her neck and save it for the hard days ahead. Because Chance was right. This thing wasn't over, and she suspected the man she feared most would still come for her, or that he'd send someone to kill the Sin boys she now loved.

When chopping and rinsing were complete, the veggies went into a giant bowl with the rotini. The rainbow colored version. Black olives joined the mixture, then Chance's *secret family recipe*, a bottle of store bought vinaigrette.

"Oh, no!" she squealed, surprised he'd ruin a fabulous dish with off the shelf dressing. "You don't make your own?"

"Who me? Make salad dressing? Are you serious?" He winked at her. "I'm a guy. This is good enough—"

"But it's not," she corrected. "I'll make my version next time, then you'll know the difference between good, better, and best."

He tossed the towel he'd dried his hands with into the sink. In two steps, she found herself in his arms and giggling. "Baby, I've already got the best," he growled before he covered her waiting mouth with his, nibbling at her lips like they were on the menu.

They danced right there in the kitchen, and Suede couldn't recall another day so fine. She knew he'd be off to another mission before long, maybe sooner than she liked, but for this one shining moment, she was that storybook princess and he was her knight in shining armor.

"Hmm," she moaned, her cheek against his broad chest, her favorite place in the whole world. "There's something I should tell you."

Sexy maple eyes melted all over her. "What now?"

"I've fallen for you," she breathed.

He grimaced as he dipped her backward, her head nearly to the floor. "That's not funny."

They never made it to dinner, and those jeans and shirts? Suede hadn't a clue where they landed between the kitchen and the fireplace.

They went after each other like hungry savages, tearing clothes off, grinding lips and teeth while they fired each other up. The back of the couch served as a pillow when Chance took her from behind the first time, but now... She moaned as he stretched her arms over her head and straddled her, ruthlessly plundering her mouth, nipping at her lips and chin, her neck, as if dinner wasn't waiting a room away. Feverishly hot, his cock pressed against her belly, inciting her with its hard, slow promise.

She licked up his neck to the underside of his chin, pinned to the blanket she hadn't known he'd previously spread in preparation for this moment. Way up high in the rafters, tiny stars glittered down at her, and she was pretty sure they were leftovers from her last *coming*, because wow. Chance knew how to make her ache for more, more, more.

As usual after their initial frenzy, he'd shifted into a gentler, more deliberate gear, anointing her eyelids as he released her hands and cupped her breasts. Dropping his head, he captured her nipple in his hot mouth. The resounding jolt to her core thrilled her every time.

Buzzing with pleasure, she shifted her fingers from his muscular back down to his taut ass. A shiver rippled up his spine. He speared her with one quick thrust that left her pleasantly full and panting. Arching, she pushed her breast into that amazing mouth, and they were doing it again. Climbing higher and higher. Reaching for the stars. Falling into each other.

Sex had never been so thoroughly intense or so satisfying before Chance. But she wanted him to come first this time. She wanted that final thrust when he growled his pleasure. Not happening. She had no resistance against the fuse he'd lit in her core and... and...

"Come for me," he commanded, like she had a choice. The orgasm rippled from her core to her fingertips, clenching him in the same fierce grip she found herself lost in. Aftershocks took over then, leaving her breathless and her lips on his collarbone, nuzzling and loving the scent of his skin, craving his all male body and the honorable soul that came with it.

Still connected, he eased back enough to rub his nose on her chin before his lips found her mouth. "I fell hard for you, Suede Tennyson," he said, the scent of peppermint washing over her face. "So damned hard. You're the spark in my life. You make me want to live."

It all came down to that, her living through that first terrible night, his making sure she did. "You could've left me," she murmured, hating the way she needed him. Love was a funny, scary thing that had let her down in the past. Could this thing with Chance be real? Could it be as good as it seemed? Sometimes she wondered.

"Not happening, baby. I hold onto what's mine, and..." He ground his hips against hers, lighting her core again. *Did that thing never get enough?* "You're all mine."

A smile broke out of her heart at the way he called her baby. Other guys said baby like she was a thing, but when he said it, she felt like she was his whole world. Threading her fingers through his thick, soft hair, she pressed her lips to his. His answering growl was all she needed to know. This was her mission in life now. To keep Chance happy.

And alive...

Chapter Forty-Three

"No! Don't go!" Suede whined, lost in a nightmare where nothing made sense. Not Chance falling like he was. Not the way he kept sliding down Old Man Mountain when she knew what a good he was. Not how every time she'd almost touched his fingertips, he slipped farther and farther away.

"Grab onto me," she begged him, her knees scrabbling for purchase on stone that had grown soft and spongy with every move she made. "Don't let go!"

His eyes shimmering with regret. "I love you. I always have. I always will."

"Then don't leave me," she cried, scared this was the end. "I can't live without you!"

But he did let go. He did fall. She watched his amber eyes fill with the black dreadfulness of total terror. His arms and legs flailed. His strong fingers grasped at the nothingness between them until he—

Oh, my God! He hit! Her heart stopped beating then. There was no air on this cold, black mountain. No wind. No reason to live. Heartbreak poured out of her soul like a banshee, screaming, "Nooooooo!"

"Baby, wake up. Suede, you're dreaming." She opened her eyes and found her teary cheek plastered flat against Chance's broad chest, her ears craving the thunder of his heartbeat beneath her. One big hand cupped her head, his fingers in her hair holding her tight. "Breathe for me, Suede. God, you scared me, baby, just breathe. You're okay."

She swallowed hard and tried to do as he asked, but her chest seemed tight. Too tight. The image of him falling clung to her like a shroud. Hyperventilation commanded her senses, but before she could scream, he murmured in her ear. "You're safe. I've got you. Take a deep breath and let it go. Honest, you're safe."

"But you... you..." She forced a torturous inhale into lungs that refused to relax, needing this panic attack to let go. "You fell," she accused him, her voice incredibly tight and hoarse at what his death would mean. Without him, she was nothing, and her brain told her that wasn't good enough. *She* wasn't good enough. "I... I saw you fall. You d-died."

"S'okay, baby. It's okay. I'm right here and I'm not dead." He had her completely circled with his body, his arms around her shoulders and torso, his knees drawn beside her curled legs, and his nose in her neck. "Can I get you a drink or something? Another blanket? God, you're so cold."

"N-no," she told him. "I only need you. Just you."

"You've got me. Honest, baby. I'm not letting you go."

"G-g-good to know," she breathed, finally catching a lungful that didn't hurt when she inhaled. "I had a b-b ad dream, a really bad dream."

"Talk about it?"

Wow. Where to start? Drawing in another gulp of air, she gave him what she could remember. The cold. Him slipping. The look in his eyes as he'd fallen. The way her heart shattered when he died. "I can't live without you," she confessed like a fool. What man in his right mind wanted to hear that?

"Not happening, Suede. I'm here and you're safe. No one can get to us. It was just a nightmare."

She rubbed her nose through his crisp chest hairs, sucking air in through her nostrils as she did. This was what she needed, the rich, masculine scent of Chance in her soul, his manly hands on her quivering body, holding her together like only he seemed to know how to do.

"Never let me go," she whimpered, ashamed she'd turned into that lost little girl again, that she needed him so desperately. As strong as he was, he must think her a weakling.

Chance didn't seem to notice. He gathered her onto his lap and settled against the headboard, rocking. Just rocking. Whispering, "I love you, Suede.

I love you. And I've got to tell you, I don't want to live without you, either."

"But I want to be strong again," she cried.

He kept rocking. "Trust me, you are. You are. I just hope there's room for me when you turn into the strong woman you really are."

"Always," Suede promised as she closed her eyes, and cried for all the things that had brought her here. The liars. The betrayers. Her own sins of commission and omission. Her stubborn head. Through it all, Chance never let go, just held on until her tears ceased. At last, her eyes grew heavy until, blink by blink, Suede succumbed to the bliss of being his.

*****

The beacon sounded at midnight, the witching hour. Already awake, Chance had been staring at the ceiling, talking himself out of getting up for the last hour. Suede slept soundly, tired from their lovemaking and her nightmare.

He trailed a finger over her cheek, told Gallo to guard her, then soundlessly slipped out of bed and climbed into a pair of sweatpants, needing to know for certain that what he'd told her, that she was safe, was still true.

Closing his bedroom door, he noticed the roll-down shutters were already sealed and the safety lights along the baseboards offered the only indoor illumination. Whatever had just set the beacons off could be nothing more than a large predator inside the safe zone, and that was okay. Animals ruled this part of Montana, but Chance needed to make sure.

Once in the office, he palmed the wall switch, brought up the overhead light panels and dropped his ass to the nearest terminal. Multiple monitors relayed the outside drama in night vision clarity. On the south-by-southwest view, two wolves lingered at the perimeter of his property, their snouts lifted, testing the night air.

They could've easily set off the beacon. They were big enough. Especially if they were tracking the bull moose hunkered down in the quakies to the west of them. Unless that moose was sick or injured, it'd be a stupid move for those two lanky-legged carnivores to take him on, but starving wolves did crazy things this time of year.

Moose were the freight trains of the north, only they didn't run on rails, and when disturbed, they carved their own tracks and they did it at lightning speed. This guy didn't seem sick or wounded and he was big enough to mow those two wolves down if they got cocky.

Chance's fingertips tapped the keyboard as he brought up a display grid of all views on the big screen overhead. The cameras located with every beacon transmitted individually, but not one inch of Sinclair property went without twenty-four-seven surveillance. All other cameras reported nothing but moonlight and winter. The wolves had since disappeared, but Chance couldn't shake the hyper-vigilance that had awakened him long before the beacons did.

Something was wrong in his universe. He could feel it. One of his brothers in trouble might explain the sense of dread pooling in Chance's gut. Swiveling to the extra cell phone he kept in his office, he tipped back in his chair and contacted Kruze first. No answer. Next call went to Pagan.

"Yes?" snapped out of Baby Brother before Chance could get a word out. *'I'm busy!'* came through loud and clear.

"Status," Chance snapped back.

"I'm on Julio Juarez's six off Harbor Drive near Terminal Twenty. The bastard never left Portland. He's headed somewhere. What do you want?"

Chance checked the time. Oh-two-hundred hours in Montana was oh-one-hundred on the West Coast. Pagan had been assigned to ensure Benito Garcia and his bodyguard boarded his flight and left the States. Why had Garcia left Julio behind? "You need an assist?"

"For this pansy-assed wannabe?" Pagan grunted. "Hell no. I've had him in my sights on and off for an hour now. Could've taken him out any number of times. Is that why you called? To check up on me?"

"No. You heard from Kruze?"

Another grunt. "Don't tell me. He's not picking up."

Kruze's greatest weakness: communication. He tended not to answer calls when he was with a lady, *the dog.* "Don't worry about it. I'll give him five, then ring him again."

"He doesn't need that long. Give him two. He's quick."

And irresponsible.

"I've been checking out our dead buddy while waiting for Juarez to hook up with whoever's he's meeting." Pagan loved hacking computers almost as much as he loved his new fifty-caliber rifle.

"Which dead buddy?"

A crackle sounded over the connection indicating a lightning strike between Montana and Oregon. Then another. Then...

"Chance!" Pagan shrieked. "I'm hit, shit, brother, I'm—"

The line went dead and Chance jumped to his feet. Those weren't lightning strikes. They were shots fired. "Pagan? Come back to me. Pagan!" Not that he expected to reconnect with Baby Brother, but he hadn't expected the cry for help either. "Pagan, do you copy?"

Leaving the command station on a dead run, Chance headed for his bedroom. He could be on the ground in Portland inside of two hours, but if Kruze had been where he should've been, Chance wouldn't need to leave Suede behind. "Answer me," he hissed at the brother he hadn't been able to reach. "Damn you, Kruze, pick up for once in your worthless life."

He stopped at his bedroom door, bile lifting up from his gut. Now that she knew how impregnable this cabin was, Suede would be plenty safe here alone, but the leaving would be hard.

Ending the call to Kruze, he placed a quick call to Woody, the local chopper pilot who worked for McQueen and could get Chance to the West Coast in no time flat. Once he made contact and with Woody's ETA in less than fifteen, Chance turned the doorknob and found the light next to his bed already on. Suede sat at the edge, fingering the buttons of his button-up shirt. What a sight. Long messy spirals cascaded over her shoulders, curling over her breasts like he wanted to, spiking his hunger for her. If he lived to be an old man, she'd always leave him breathless.

"You're leaving," she said, her chin up and her eyes clear.

Good girl. She'd guessed right and was taking this news like a trooper. "Yes. You'll be safe here."

"You're right. Gallo and I will be fine." She pushed off the edge of the bed. Her tongue slid over her bottom lip and Chance knew she had questions for which he could give no answers. "I'll, umm, keep the home fires burning while you're gone. Be safe out there, okay?"

Another point in her favor. She hadn't pried. "Intend to," he said as he opened his closet and lifted three pre-packed gear bags for the trip. Packing beforehand made leaving quicker if not easier. He donned green and black jungle cammies, laced up his boots, and tucked a knife into his boot sheath. Holsters went next. Arming himself for the trip would happen at the front door before he broke cover. Binocs. Rangefinder. Blowout kit. Check, check and double check. Time to move out.

Suede took a seat on the end of the bed, watching. "How long will you be gone?"

"Don't know," he replied, closing the closet door. *Please don't ask.*

"Is anyone hurt?"

"Don't know that, either. The less you ask, the better. It's bad enough that you already know what you know about the SOBs."

"I don't know anything." She patted her leg and Gallo lifted from his mat by her side of the bed and joined her. "Come back to me," she murmured.

Chance nodded curtly, then took a second look. He wanted more time with this woman, especially now when she was soft from having been loved. Her lips were pink and swollen, and, yeah, leaving was damned nigh impossible. But leave he would. That was what he did when duty called.

"Do me a favor while I'm gone," he said. "Stick close to the cabin, but if you go out, always take Gallo. He listens better to you anyway."

She nodded, her eyes big and luminous.

"Don't cry," he told her firmly. "This will be our life from now on. Give it a chance. Give me a chance."

That earned a meager smile. "That's your name. Don't wear it out."

There she was, frightened, but putting on a brave front. Being courageous. In one long stride he had her in his arms, his face at her ear. "Take care of yourself while I'm gone and try not to worry," he ground out.

She nodded against his jaw, her heartbeat a quiet thunder in her chest. "You can count on me. I'll be here waiting for you."

He kissed her deeply. Passionately. Lovingly. Then he walked away, but this time, he didn't look back.

*****

Suede couldn't sleep after she told Chance goodbye. Her eyes wouldn't stop tearing up and her heart hurt like it had never hurt before. Love, she was finding out, was a painful, treacherous thing. As whole as she'd felt in bed with Chance, she felt a resounding emptiness now, as if half her heart had gone with him. Her chest physically hurt as if someone had torn her heart out by its bloody roots.

She couldn't sit still, not with her ears already tuned to the front door, waiting for his return. Wouldn't it be grand if he came through that door right now? If the mission was cancelled? They could go back to bed and all would be right with her world again. Was that asking too much?

Apparently.

When wishing didn't produce the desired, albeit wishful effect, and when the doorknob didn't turn like she willed it to, when Suede heard the rotor slap of his ride away from Old Man Mountain, she did what she did best. She planned for the moment he returned.

He'd be hungry, and she'd spied a large freezer chest in the basement the other day. If it wasn't full now, it would be by the time Chance, Pagan, and Kruze were back safe and sound. That was the only scenario she allowed herself to imagine. Them, home. Joking with each other. Teasing. Eating.

"Come, Gallo," she said as she pushed her sleeves up to her elbows. "We have work to do."

Chapter Forty-Four

Helo rides could be cold sons-of-guns. Chance was glad for the woolen beanie he'd topped off with on his way out the door. His spacious log cabin grew smaller the higher Woody took the chopper until the forests welling up around the massive wooden structure swallowed it whole. There was no sense looking back then. Suede would be safe. Gallo would see to that.

In no time, the dark snake that was the mighty Columbia River wound below. Bright lights to the south meant touchdown on one of Portland's two riverfronts was imminent. Nestled at the confluence of the mighty Columbia and Willamette Rivers, metropolitan Portland boasted a population of nearly two and a half million. It'd be damned hard locating Pagan in that crowd, but Chance didn't plan to search for him. He activated the homing beacon transmitting from the microchip inserted at the base of his brother's skull. Black ops got all the latest and greatest toys, but this particular one was a lifesaver. A man didn't have to be conscious to *'call a cab.'* It had better work tonight.

Sure enough. A steady blink lit the handheld device in his palm. "Take her in as near to Terminal Twenty as you can land without attracting attention, on the water if you need to. I can swim."

"No can do, amigo," Woody drawled. "I never dump my guys in the drink unless I have to. It's the docks for you." He switched the chopper to stealth mode and killed the running lights. Stealth mode these days meant the aircraft was damned near invisible to a person on the ground. "You fast roping in or should I set her down?"

"Rope," Chance replied. "Short rope."

"Copy that." Woody cut to the left and zeroed in on Terminal Twenty, a cavernous warehouse that opened onto the dock as well as at the frontage road on its opposite end. Portland's waterfront was a modern day miracle of conveyor belts, hoppers, and silos for dry bulk cargoes of grains, grabbers, and railway cars on standby for coal and other ores, plus a mixture of loading booms, gantry cranes, and stacking cranes.

Tugboats escorted the dry cargo ship alongside Terminal Twenty-One while the deck crew prepared to unload. Spotlights lit the entire area. That there was still plenty of dock left at either end of the massive ship belied the monstrous length and depth of the terminals. They were built to accommodate not one, but several inventories the size of the mammoth one they were preparing to unload. A small third world country could live inside one of those terminals. Why Zapata rented Terminal Twenty nagged at Chance. It had to be a cover, but for what? Just to stash the nine bodies the FBI had found? Didn't make sense, but then, dealing with a killer like Zapata, rarely did.

Neither Terminals Nineteen nor Twenty had activity dockside tonight. Woody leveled out and hovered closer to Nineteen. "Leave your tips in the tip jar on your way out."

"Stay close. I'll be in touch," Chance said as he stepped off the chopper skid and began his descent. His hands warmed beneath the heavy-duty gloves he wore, but the drop was short and sweet. In ten seconds he was on the ground with the smells of the busy riverfront in his nose: diesel exhaust fumes, fish, and the pungent odor of creosote coated timbers.

Woody's chopper blades barely made a sound as he headed east, another stealth enhancement. Chance ducked low but kept his head on a swivel, quartering the scenery with eyes that had seen too much.

Pagan's alert hadn't slowed and it was stationary, both good signs. The chip monitored his pulse. Its steady beat meant Pagan was still alive and the stationary blip meant he was nearby. Chance jogged the narrow shadow between Terminals Twenty and Nineteen, a path that would put him street-side and directly across from Pagan's location, but could also get him killed.

Moving fast, he cleared the alley, but halted street side, still in shadows. The way across looked clear, but Chance wouldn't venture forth until he could be sure. The storage warehouses, offices, and equipment garages opposite his twenty were quiet and dark. Several big rigs idled to his far left at Twenty-One, the night air thick with diesel fumes.

The swing shift had dwindled to very few men at his right, where five-high stacks of twenty-some rows of shipping containers lined the wharf, no doubt pending incoming transport. He counted five men, four standing alongside the semi, the other seated inside.

No traffic blocked Chance's way forward, but the yellowish light cast from tungsten halogen industrial lights was the problem, that, and the long empty space between Chance and Pagan.

Chance flipped his jacket collar up, pulled a baseball cap out of an inner pocket, and beelined to Pagan's twenty, his eyes and ears on high alert. No one called him out, but the very real probability of ambush niggled every step of the way. His last op in South America replayed through his head. Everything could go to hell before a guy knew what happened.

Hyper-vigilance sucked. It made a man paranoid, jumpy and prone to make mistakes. To over calculate. To second-guess every damned decision. It amplified every wrong scenario in a man's playbook, and it just plain ate away at his confidence.

Flinching at the sound of his boots against the pea gravel underfoot, Chance kept going, his eyes straight ahead, dodging the imaginary army of what-ifs that had plagued him since South America. The tremendous loss of good men that day wouldn't be as painful today if they'd gone down protecting their package. But everyone had died for nothing. Even Gillian Enright.

In the end, he knew he was one lucky SOB to have survived. Still sucked rocks to know he'd failed his men and that woman. Chance shook the ghosts off his shoulders, needing that day behind him, not crapping all over the mission ahead.

Finally across the street and in shadow once more, he followed Pagan's distress call to the opposite end of the alley, dodging trash receptacles and storage sheds sandwiched between the two narrow office buildings.

There he was, face down with one arm stretched forward. Missing? The rifle he wouldn't be caught dead without. As much as Chance wanted to run to his injured brother, he took it slow and steady. Angling sideways, his back against the one building and his pistol up, all six senses reaching into the dark for the bastard who had Pagan's piece, Chance sent another whispered, "Talk to me, Baby Brother. Give me a sign you're still with me."

Pagan's index finger on his left hand lifted. Just barely. *Thank God!*

"Are you hurt bad?"

Two finger taps and Chance blew out a measured breath. One meant yes. Two meant no. "How many were there?"

One tap. Okay, good. One person as far as Pagan knew, but he could be wrong.

"Where from? Your left?"

Two taps. No.

"Your right?"

Two more taps.

"Behind?"

One tap. Some asshole shot Pagan from behind. There was no sense asking where he'd been hit. The list was too long and Chance hadn't the patience. "I'm coming for you."

Two definite taps.

No? "The shooter's still here?"

One tap.

Shit. Then so be it. Chance dug two cans from his gear bag, peered out of the alley long enough to pop yellow smoke in both directions, then broke cover. Grabbing hold of Pagan's waist, Chance had him undercover in the alley in seconds.

"Shit," Baby Brother spat when Chance eased him into the corner of a trash receptacle and the brick building. "I can't sit here."

"You can and you will," Chance growled as he bit the gloved tip of his index finger and pulled the glove off. "I've got my blowout kit. In a couple seconds, you'll be fine."

"No," Pagan ground out, his eyes squeezed tight and pain contorting his face. "You don't understand."

Chance leveled a palm to Pagan's heaving chest. "Trust me. I understand. Sit still and—"

Pagan growled, shoving Chance's hand off. He stuck one leg straight and rolled to his hip. "For Christ's sake, let me roll over. She shot me in the ass."

"She?"

Pagan pointed behind Chance. "Her, damn it."

Oh. Her. Damned if the she-devil in the game hadn't just stepped clear from all that yellow smoke. Miss Vicki Hex. In the flesh.

Chapter Forty-Five

Reveling in her new future, Suede was thrilled that the worst was behind her. She'd worked all night and the Sinclair's freezer was now stocked with a hearty supply of Texas Meatballs, Greek Beef Kabobs, a tender, succulent barbecued venison shoulder, and enough chicken tamales to feed an army. Tension radiated down her neck to her lower back from standing too long, but she'd finally found her niche in the world, and it was definitely in Chance's kitchen.

Gallo whined at the door, poor baby. He'd been patient while she'd finished wiping the counter and loading the dishwasher, but those big brown eyes begged for relief.

"You are the cutest baby boy," she told him as she tossed her cloth into the sink and stretched her arms back, elbow to elbow. Hard work had transformed her worry into action and being busy eased her mind.

Chance was no dummy. Wherever he'd gone, he'd be back before she knew it. No need to fret.

Who was she kidding? Suede shook her head at that idiotic straight-out-of-the-fifties thought. She'd worry about that man until he was home again. "I'm coming," she told Gallo.

Big brown eyes followed her, his tail marking her progress with louder thumps the closer she came. But Chance had taught her proper protocol when opening any exterior door to his cabin. Check first. Deactivate second. When in doubt, stay put. One did not just swing this door open and invite the world in. The fact that no beacons had pinged the earpiece she now wore should've been enough, but she followed the rules.

The monitor beside the door showed a complex grid of outside views. Sunlight bathed the snowy scenes as a mist of lightly falling snow sparkled like fairy dust in the air. "No one's out there but Frosty the Snowman," she told the anxious pup at her feet.

Thump. Thump. Thump.

Suede pressed her palm to the pad beside the door. Chance had made sure her fingerprints and palm prints were in his security system days ago. His faith in her amazed Suede. They'd been together such a short time. She still needed to tell him how he'd boosted her confidence, trusting her like he did. It might seem like nothing to him, but it meant the world to her.

When the system came back with a lime green flash of *'all clear'*, Suede flipped the upper lock first, then the dead bolt. She waited the prerequisite number of seconds for it to slide out of locked position before turning the knob. Gallo was on his feet by then, his nose pointed at the door and ready to burst outside.

Suede opened the door to a pristine winter wonderland that Gallo quickly defiled with his big feet. It took him a series of leg lifts to finish his job while Suede watched from the door. "Don't run away, buddy," she told him.

Gallo cocked his head, those adorable puppy ears flopping and the cutest quizzical light in his eyes. He snapped up a mouthful of powder and tossed it as if he wanted to play.

"You want me to come outside too?" she asked, tempted to let loose and just be a kid for the first time in a long time. Not since Chance and that snow angel baby had she wanted to play in the snow, but Gallo seemed to be coaxing her to join him.

Stepping out onto the snow-covered porch, Suede bent over and grabbed a handful of snow to test its consistency. All powder. No staying power. "This stuff's too light to make a snowman," she told the dog, "but if you watch where you put those big feet of yours, I could make another snow angel."

Wouldn't Chance get a laugh out of that when he came home? Did she dare?

"Come," Suede patted her knees to bring Gallo back into the house. "Let me get changed and we'll play for awhile, okay?"

Gallo lifted his snout to the sky and grumbled, but he came bounding back. "Good boy," she told him at the door. Then, because she was a fast change artist when it came to having fun in the snow, she closed the door and didn't reset the alarm. There was no need. This wouldn't take long.

*****

Chance sucked in a gut full of angst as his weapon snapped automatically on his target. Every sniper's wet dream. Miss Victoria Hex in all her killer glory.

Dressed in thigh-high black leather boots with six-inch heels, her long legs ate up the distance. The matching leather skirt wrapped around her curvaceous hips looked more like a skimpy napkin from a stripper bar. Glossy black hair swung off her shoulders. She came at him like a mean girl strutting down freshman hall in high school, pink pistols holstered under her arms and that rifle in her hands on target. Him.

The too small, black leather jacket clutching her shoulders didn't stand a prayer of covering her catch-me-if-you-can cleavage, her girls highlighted by a bright white tiny T that damn near glowed in the dark and further accentuated by the pink pistols holstered under her arms. Thick dark lashes kissed her high cheekbones when she stared past his rifle and winked. "You going to shoot me with that little pop gun?"

"Damn straight," Chance growled, his weapon on target. "Give me one good reason not to. You shot my brother."

Vicki Hex was an anomaly in a career field filled with mercenaries, psychos, and cruelty. She played by rules. Granted they were her rules and just as cold-blooded as any other murderer's, but the lady had class. And a helluva lot of nerve.

With one last step, the butt stock of her piece landed on her hip, barrel pointed at the sky. Tendrils of yellow smoke licked up her boots and thighs, her long legs spread, her attitude as seductively misleading as the heroine out of a B movie. "I will give you two, Chief." Her index finger came up, along with a long black fingernail. "First, I only winged Pagan. I could've killed him, but I didn't."

A cold finger of premonition streaked up his spine. Calling him Chief was no accident. She knew he was Navy property. What else did she know?

"You did this on purpose," Pagan muttered, his bloodied right hand on his ass. "A butt shot's *not* a wing shot."

That bought him a subtle chin nod and a twitch of her nose. She tossed her head, her hair swirling over her kiss-me-killer-red lips. "But you're still alive, aren't you? To be honest, which I always am, I thought you were someone else. You Sinclair boys are fun to play with, but I'd never kill any of you three. If

I'd known you were sneaking around behind Julio's back, my love—"

"I'm not your love," he bit out. "I don't do skank."

"Quiet," Chance muttered, his weapon steady on the sassy dominatrix in his sights. "Who'd you think he was?"

She shook her head, her index fingers waggling from side to side. "My brother speaks highly of you. What a delicious name, Chance." She licked her lips as if savoring the taste of it. "It speaks to me of long sweaty nights in Palermo. Of many goblets of crisp, golden Marsala." The tip of her tongue made a slow, wet pass over her already glistening bottom lip. "Of, what is it you American's call it, do-overs?"

"Can't do over what never happened," he growled. "Who were you following, damn it? Who'd you mean to kill when you shot my brother?"

A sensual smile curved her mouth as one perfectly shaped brow lifted. "My friend from Brazil has something I want."

"Domingo Zapata? He's here? Now?"

"Stop talking in riddles! What's he got that you want?" Pagan snapped. "A decent scope for that pea shooter you're packing?"

Chance shot his brother a quelling glance to shut up. Why the hell was he baiting Miss Hex?

Lifting her slender fingers to her mouth, she blew Pagan a kiss. "I am sorry I had to shoot you. Poor baby."

"Wait," Chance ordered. "You *had* to shoot Pagan? Why?"

"Yeah, why shoot me? If you're here after Zapata, who's Julio after?"

By then Miss Hex stood at the end of the alley. Another air-kiss drifted Pagan's way. "Why, me, of course."

"Stop talking in circles!" Chance bellowed before he lost sight of her, his pistol still trained on her head. He had a clear shot. He could take it if he wanted to. Mafia hitmen and women enjoyed no mercy on American streets. He'd be doing a public service to end her, but damn. A rock weighed heavy in his gut. Something was different with this particular song and dance. He lowered his rifle and decided to trust. "What's Zapata got that you want, Vicki? Who are you really working for?" *What the fuck's going on?*

Miss Hex pivoted, her butt stock still on her hip. She hesitated, her black eyes sharp and piercing, her lips suddenly thinned as if she had more to say. "You really don't know, do you?"

"I wouldn't be asking if I did." Extending one hand, he went for broke. "Listen, I'm tired of chasing the wind. How about a truce? You share what you know. We'll help you get Zapata and Juarez."

Her chin came up and the calculating glare of a killer on the hunt was back. "Go home, Chief. Try not to worry. I don't miss." Like the smoke, Vicki Hex was gone.

"Damn, she's one crazy bitch," Pagan muttered.

Chance turned on his brother. "Did you hear what she said? She *had* to shoot you, not that she wanted to. Why? You were closing in on JJ, right?"

Pagan chuffed. "Damned straight. If you hadn't called, I'd have had him, too."

"If JJ's after Zapata, and Hex is after JJ..." Chance took a knee beside his brother. "You were getting too close. That's why she shot you, to keep you from killing JJ."

"They're in on this together. They're both after Zapata. Why? And who the hell's with Suede, Chance? You left her alone?"

Icy cold fear slammed into Chance. "Gallo." *My dog. My air-headed dog's the only thing with her.* His hand found his phone. "Pick up," he ordered Suede. "Pick up!" But it never rang. He turned a bleak eye to his brother. "My phone's dead."

"It can't be. It's a sat-phone. We're..." Pagan's brows climbed up his forehead. "Shit. Zapata's in Montana."

Chance already had Woody on the line. "Need you now. Same location. Step on it."

"Copy that. You got our boy?" Woody asked.

"Hurry! We've got trouble back home," Chance explained, his gut twisted with the need to fly.

"Roger that. ETA in ten."

Pagan dragged himself to his feet. He stood panting, his hands on his knees and as pale as Chance had never seen him before. "Sorry 'bout this."

Shouldering his rifle, Chance shook Pagan's apology off, more worried what Hex knew. What Zapata knew. "She's in league with Zapata. That's why she's after JJ. Can you move?" He hadn't yet treated Pagan's wound, and he wasn't going to now. "Where's your rifle?"

"Last I knew, Hex took it." Like the good troop he was, Pagan soldiered up. "I'm good. I can walk. Let's roll."

Together they made it to the pick-up point at the same time Woody dipped low out of the gathering fog the Columbia River was known for. The chopper's skids had no more than kissed the edge of the dock when Chance shoved Pagan aboard and climbed in behind him. "Go!" he shouted over the rotor slap. *Go faster. Suede's alone with nothing but my dumb dog. Step on it!*

Chapter Forty-Six

Getting back outside took longer than Suede expected. After a short nap, a shower, and toast with coffee, the sun made a weak appearance. Buttoned up in the same snowsuit and gear she'd worn when she climbed Old Man Mountain with Chance, Suede closed the cabin's front door behind her and faced her brand new day. The fresh scent of pine filled the air as Gallo bounded down the steps and through the snow.

She stood there drinking in the cold, fresh air, pulling its pine-fresh scent deep into her lungs. Delicious, that was what it was. Utterly delicious. If this day were a cake, she'd take a slice of it now to save for later.

The light snow that had fallen earlier left the evergreen forest at her right dusted, turning the pines festive despite their missing branches and the raw bark on some of their trunks. Wasn't Chance clever to have pre-planned for an attack like he had? It was awesomely scary, but Suede understood. They both seemed to have some pretty lethal enemies.

"Arff!" Gallo barked at her from the shade of a stately pine, his nose in the snow and his bright eyes on her.

"Work first," she told him. "This won't take long."

Energized after her nap, Suede looked the porch over. The snow shovel stood in the far corner at her left, just as buried in fluffy white as everything else. By the time Chance returned, she'd have the porch and steps cleared, maybe a path into the woods as well. He'd warned her to stay close to the cabin. That didn't mean she couldn't get a little exercise.

Funny dog. With each shovel of the white stuff, Gallo attacked, grabbed a jaw full, slapping his paws when it settled to the pile accumulating beside the porch, just generally being a kid at heart. Suede tossed a shovel of snow over him, tickled when he lifted to his haunches and batted it. "You're such a goofy guy," she told him. Setting the shovel aside, she ducked down for a big handful and cancelled the project. Time to play ball.

"Catch!" she squealed, tossing the snowball in an arc over Gallo's head. He pushed off like a deer. His powerful hind feet dug into the frozen ground and up, up, up he went, twisting in the air like a snake to catch that prize. And he did! A laugh burst out of Suede when his powerful jaws snapped his plaything into nothing. Gallo hit the ground perplexed, rooting through the snow for the ball that had disappeared. So funny!

While he pawed the snow, Suede packed another, mentally adding dog toys to the next drone order. She hadn't had this much fun in forever. Every snowball Gallo crunched earned a giggle she couldn't suppress. He looked so cute!

Suede spread her arms and dropped backward onto the snow, sweating, but content with the way her life had turned out. *Snow angel baby, here I come!*

Swooshing her hands over her head, she stretched her legs wide and flapped all fours, smiling at the delightful picture of clouds and evergreen branches overhead. But she should've known Gallo would be up for this fun new game. As quick as a jackrabbit, he pounced on her. Hugging his neck, Suede rolled to her side, giggling. This wasn't Montana. This was heaven.

"You're as crazy as I am," she told him sincerely as a cold, wet nose slid along her cheek. "But no kisses."

By then, the snow angel baby was officially an unrecognizable mess. Excited by who knew what, Gallo tucked his tail under his haunches and launched into a wide lap that took him around the nearest trees, to the opposite edge of the cabin and back to Suede.

"Go, Gallo, go," she chanted, urging him as he gathered speed, his tongue lolling out the side of his mouth. Wasn't that cool, a dog smiling just because of snow?

Out of breath, Suede eased to her butt on the still un-shoveled steps. The marvel of being alive on this fresh and beautiful new day hit her hard. She owed everything to this happy-go-lucky dog. She didn't know what had possessed him that night, but he'd come for her, and because his owner loved him, Chance had rescued her. Talk about Karma.

The miracle of it brought tears to her eyes. "Thank you, God," she said sincerely, from the bottom of a heart that had once been sullied and cynical, full of despair. Suede wiped the back of her gloved hand over her cheek. Nobody got second chances in this life, but here she was, living a perfect day in the most beautiful place on Earth.

"It's time to go in," she called to Gallo before she turned melancholy. Too much introspection encouraged depression. She needed to bake something. Anything! Soon. Lifting to her feet, she slapped her knees and called again, "Gallo! Let's go!"

What she got was body-slammed by a gangly German Shepherd. Suede came up laughing. "You want to play rough?" Smacking his rump playfully, she bucked to dislodge him from her lap. "Get off. You weigh a ton."

But Gallo didn't budge. His feet were spread and his head had lowered. His hackles were up, and a deep growl rumbled from his throat.

"What's wrong, boy?" she asked, jockeying onto her elbows to see around his fuzzy body to the forest.

God, please don't let a bear or wolf be after us. For sure not a mountain lion.

Suede ran a hand over her face, now dripping with melted snow. "Oh crap," hissed out of her. There he was. Standing in the shadows as if he thought she couldn't see him. A man in black leathers. York's right-hand man. Domingo Zapata.

She fisted Gallo's mane to keep him from charging. Zapata would kill man or dog without compunction. "Time to go inside."

Gallo didn't move, but Zapata did.

*****

A red and silver helicopter banked to the left far ahead of Woody's chopper. Could be anyone. A news channel. A private pilot. Julio Juarez. Domingo Zapata.

Hyper-vigilance sat heavy on Chance's shoulder like a demon from hell. Every man-made thing in the sky was a tango and they were all going after Suede. The aftermath of past choices, two in particular, nagged at him that this could all go so, so wrong.

Once aboard the chopper, he'd doctored Pagan's rump with a shot of *Quik Clot* and an antiseptic pressure bandage. The bullet still had to come out, but helicopters weren't known to be optimum surgical sites. Baby Brother might be uncomfortable, but he'd live.

With every mile still to go, Chance's blood pressure ramped higher. If Suede stayed indoors, she'd be fine. But the woman had cabin fever, and who could blame her if she stepped outside? With the house quiet and only Gallo for company, yeah. Chance blocked the thoughts of her taking his brainless dog for a walk. Into the forest. Alone.

"Can't this son-of-a-bitch go any faster?" hissed out of him.

Woody nodded once, but his five-seater was no *Eurocopter X3*, the fastest helo on the market, and he'd already pushed the turbine-powered engine to its limit of one-forty miles-per-hour. Still not fast enough, but those were the breaks. A man made his choices and there Chance was, stuck with the knowledge that his split decision to save his brother might cost Suede her life.

"Stay inside," he commanded her across the distance. *God, please, stay inside where you're safe.*

Chance swallowed hard, his gloves forsaken and his fingernails digging into his palms as they passed over Western Washington and the northern leg of the Columbia River. From liftoff, Woody had set a straight flight. Spokane lay ahead to the northeast. Beyond that the Idaho panhandle and the northwestern most corner of Montana. Chance cursed the day. His parcel of land would be worthless without Suede Tennyson to share it with. Hell, the whole world would fit that category if anything happened to her. She was his heart, his soul, and every last one of his reasons to live.

Pagan's heavy hand clamped Chance's shoulder. "She's smart. She'll know what to do," he called out over the engine noise.

"Yeah, but…" Chance let his fears go unspoken. Gallo. It all depended on a hardheaded dog that had yet to act like the watchdog he should be. The kicker was that Gallo would already be a decent guard dog if Chance had taken the time to train him, to build him into one of the finely-honed EOD dogs he'd worked with, flown with, and served with. But he hadn't.

Grief over losing his mom and his men had weighed heavily on him then. Hell, he'd been buried in it. Stuck. His own injuries had played a role in his melancholy, but they hadn't compared to losing so many of the people he loved. Despite all he'd done to get his head back in the game, there'd been days it was damned hard getting out of bed in the morning. Until Suede dropped into his life, then *BOOM*. He was alive again. He was himself.

"But shit, I've been sloppy," he murmured, not caring who heard or who judged.

"I'm only going to say this once, Big Brother, because Mom's listening, I know she is," Pagan growled in Chance's ear. "You ain't been sloppy. You've been sad, so shut the fuck up about that shit. It's hammer time. You're going in hot and you're getting your woman."

Chance cast Pagan a spiked brow. "We've both been cussing a lot lately."

Pagan's eyes popped. "Shit, I'm sorry man, but I cuss when I'm hurt. Mom would too if she'd been shot in the ass." He lifted his eyes heavenward. "Sorry, Mom, but I know you would."

As usual, Pagan was right on the money. Chance let the past roll off his shoulders and focused on the job at hand. This wasn't about ghosts and it wasn't about losing. He didn't intend to be late this time. Zapata, if he were smart enough, had better stay the hell away from Suede Tennyson.

Chapter Forty-Seven

Suede crab-walked backward, her gaze fixed on Zapata. Playing with Gallo had put her five, maybe six feet to the side of Chance's front porch. Every inch to the steps had turned into a mile, but she didn't dare turn her back and run for her life. Zapata would like that too much.

He had yet to take more than a step toward her, not that he didn't frighten the hell out of her just by standing as still as he was. The inked symbols tattooed all over his face, neck, and bald head were scary enough. Sixes and snakes. Crosses and Spanish words she didn't want to know the meanings of. Other symbols and ink-covered scars decorated the ugly face of one of the cruelest men she knew.

"Stay with me," she urged Gallo, but as tense as he was, Suede doubted he'd listen much longer. He tilted forward, his nails dug into the snow as if coiled to spring. He whined. "Please don't leave me," she begged him. "We need to get inside together. Both of us. You and me. That's the way it has to be."

Zapata cocked his head. Suddenly, as if he'd teleported from the shadows into sunlight, he was out in the open, between her and the forest, standing taut like he'd just launched out of Hell. "Bitch," hissed out of him, his name for her.

Suede Tennyson must've been difficult to pronounce, because he'd never called her by anything other than something derogatory to women. *'Bitch'* was mild. He must be feeling generous. He usually used the ugly 'c' word.

She didn't answer. Just kept creeping backward, tugging at the long hairs on Gallo's belly to make him stay with her.

Zapata scanned the cabin behind her with the sharp black eyes of a stone-cold killer. As if he could scent her from where he stood, his nose wrinkled with its customary disgust. He loathed women, and she loathed him. The man was repulsive, like a two-headed snake that ate its young alive.

At last, her fingertips hit the lowest snow-covered step. Suede backpedalled as quickly as she could, but only got to the second step from the top before Zapata was at her feet. "You alone, heh?"

"Stop!" she shrieked. "Come any closer and I'll detonate the minefield you're standing on. I will! I swear I will!"

Where that bravado came from she had no clue, but the evidence was all around him. There *had* been a recent detonation. Some of it might be camouflaged beneath a few inches of snow, but all he had to do was look around to see the rest of it.

She knew where the red button was that could make it happen again. If she could get to it.

Gallo stood over her now, his fuzzy rump nearly in her face and his hackles spiked along his spine. He'd lowered his head even more, his ears flat against his skull, and his fangs bared.

Zapata's head rotated downward and from left to right as he studied the scene and her. His nostrils flared. "I believe you *had* a minefield. I believe men died here. I can smell their blood," he hissed, ignoring the posturing dog. He carried no weapon that she could see, but Zapata didn't rely on guns. He preferred switchblades, knives, and blood. Lots of red, warm blood. "But you don't know a fucking thing about killing a man."

"L-look again. H-h-hundreds died here," she lied, her throat gone dry and her courage shrinking. The distance to the door seemed an eternity away.

Gallo inched toward him, outright challenging the monster in his territory.

Zapata grunted at the wary pup. With her heart jackhammering, Suede couldn't believe he hadn't already knifed Gallo and grabbed her. The coward in her demanded she turn and run. *Only eight feet to the door. To safety. Once Gallo charges him, run. Leave Gallo behind. He's just a dog!*

But she wasn't leaving her sweet boy, Gallo to face this spawn from hell alone. Chance's dog didn't deserve to die any more than she did. "I don't want to kill you," she had the nerve to tell the assassin at her feet. "But I will."

That same level of disgust shadowed his expression like an evil mask. "Then why do I see tracks in the snow where you and your mutt played like little children, heh?" Extending one arm, he snapped his wrist, and the slimmest blade that he'd mot likely sharpened until his fingertips bled from testing it, appeared out of nowhere.

"Then go for it," she shot back at him, her chin up. She was through sniveling to bullies. "Try me, Domingo. I owe you a bloody death. Let's go together, shall we?"

His gaze narrowed until he peered at her through slits. "Look at you. On your back again." The revulsion radiating from him was palpable. "You have no way to detonate anything."

"I do, too. You just can't see it. It's... it's under my gloves."

Zapata snorted. "Liar. Where is he?"

"Who?" blurted out of her before she had time to think. But she'd been transfixed by the mercurial blackness in Zapata's eyes. There was no light there. No sparkle or glimmer. There'd probably be no reflection in a mirror, either. He was that kind of dark. If Charles Manson was the epitome of evil,

Zapata was the one who'd given him the map and taught him how to get there.

"York. Who else?"

Oh, him. It'd been a while since Lionel had crossed Suede's mind. "He's dead and I killed him," she declared boldly.

Zapata tossed his chin at her, scoffing. "Lying bitch. If you're so tough, show me his grave and maybe I'll let you walk out of here."

Fat chance in hell. Suede knew better. The second she turned her back on him, if she were dumb enough to do that, she'd be dead. "No. It's done and..." *If only I can jump to my feet... If only Gallo will follow me... If only I can slam the door shut before Zapata gets inside! God, give me strength.* "... and you need to go while you still can."

His face wrinkled from the arrow-like indentations alongside his beak-shaped nose to the waves of wrinkles creeping over his bald forehead. "Show me the fucking body!" he hissed, taking another step in her direction, "Now! I want to see it for myself."

Scared for her life, Suede bolted to her feet and twisted, needing that doorknob in her hand Right. Damned. Now!

Just as her gloved hand hit the knob, Gallo roared to life. Snarling. Barking. Vicious. Zapata punched him. He yelped, but before he could attack, Zapata grabbed her jacket collar and yanked her off her feet.

Suede flailed elbows and knees until the knick of the blade in her cheek forced her to cease moving.

"Call your mutt off or I butcher him first and I make you eat his heart," Zapata rasped in her ear, his breath rank with the scent of cheap cigarettes and something that smelled dead.

"G-Gallo," she whimpered, straining to catch sight of her pretty boy's furry face. He still growled, but with her neck twisted like it was, she couldn't see him. "Down. Umm, sit." *Please sit down, so you don't end up dead, too.*

The dog whined, but finally came into view. His ears twitched. Big brown eyes peered up at her, but he planted his butt and obeyed. He looked so worried. "G-good boy."

"Now we go to the grave," Zapata ordered, his arm around her neck as he dragged her backward. Down the steps she'd just crawled up. Back across the frozen landscape and over what was left of the snow angel baby. To the trees. Into the shadows she'd never return from.

"Oh-kay," she whispered, her mind reeling at how to save herself and Chance's dog. *Cooperate. Comply. Wait for the right moment to strike.* She'd heard those words somewhere recently, but her brain was alive with adrenaline, and the last of her logic had scattered to the wind. "I'll show you where York is buried. Just don't hurt my dog."

"That mangy cur is not your dog. It belongs to the bastard Sinclair and his brothers," Zapata snarled.

"You think I'm stupid, that I don't know who lives here? You think I don't know you are alone? I am not dumb like El Jefe. I am not swayed by bitches in heat."

"W-Who?"

"The boss, you dumb bitch." He jerked her ruthlessly into the cover of fragrant evergreens. "You played him long enough, chica. Now you get what's coming to you. I told him to get rid of you five years ago, but he was not so smart. He liked playing with you too much. Like a stupid cat with a stinkin' mouse."

Five years? You wanted me dead five years ago? That made no sense. Suede had only met York four years ago, Zapata even later. "Why me? What'd I ever do to you?"

That earned her a stranglehold, his cocked elbow a vise around her neck. "You made him weak! Now shut the fuck up and do what you're told."

Another jerk on her windpipe and she choked. "Air," she wheezed. "I can't breathe."

Zapata laughed, twisting his other hand, the one holding the knife, yanking her head back and exposing her neck for the slice that was sure to come. "Is no worry to me if you live or not. Soon you need no more air. Am I dragging you in the right direction or is there something you want to tell me?"

Like I don't have a clue where Chance buried York? "N-no," she stuttered, slowly easing her fingertips between his solid bicep and forearm to make enough room to catch a breath. "You... you're... we're almost there."

She rolled her eyes, desperate for a glimpse of Gallo. He followed, but damned if those big brown eyes and his floppy ears didn't make him look as hopeless as she felt. Suede strained to catch any landmarks on this desperate trail of tears she was on. A rock. A crooked branch. Anything she could use to find her way back to the cabin.

But everything was green and white. Only the tracks in the snow could guide her home. She steeled her last nerve, determined not to cry. Zapata wanted nothing more than to break her and watch her fall apart. He'd mocked her in front of York and his men at every chance. *Not going to happen today. I can be brave like Chance, even if you kill me.*

Damned if Gallo didn't pick that moment to take off running past Zapata and into the trees.

"Looks like your dog is smarter than you," Zapata growled in her ear. "What you gonna do now that you're alone, bitch?"

Maybe I will cry after all.

Chapter Forty-Eight

Woody took the chopper in low and silent, a mile from the cabin. High noon, straight up.

"Stay here," Chance ordered Pagan, but didn't wait for an answer as he pushed out of the chopper and dropped to ground level. He sunk into the powdery depths to mid-thigh, then crunched through the crusted older snow until he hit rock bottom. By then he was hip deep and floundering. He'd struck a fallen log beneath the white and nearly fell. It took a moment to catch his balance. Shit. All this snow was a nightmare.

Wind from the rotors whipped it into a whirlwind of ice crystals that buffeted his face and made sight impossible, but Chance scrambled onward, damned near swimming through the white stuff. His thighs and glutes suffered a firestorm of agony fighting the weight of it. He might as well have been running in slow motion, but run he did. Out of breath and tasting copper at the back of his throat, he'd left all but his two pistols and a half-dozen extra mags behind. Whatever happened next would be short and lethal.

Pagan had offered alternatives on the ride home. "We could be wrong," he'd said.

"She probably stayed indoors," he'd said.

"I doubt she even knows anyone's outside laying for her," he'd said.

All plausible, but all wrong. Once again, a woman's life hung in the balance because of Chance's poor choices. Recrimination walked with him every floundering step of the way until at last he stood at the edge of the graveyard, where York and twenty-one other bodies lay. McQueen would soon send in a team to remove them. Kruze and McQueen had wrapped them, so no animals could get at them, but for now they waited in silent, gruesome slumber.

The forest was silent around him, when Gallo came out of nowhere, knocking Chance to his back. Pissed that the dog had left Suede, he grabbed Gallo by the scruff of his neck and shook the worthless mutt. Gallo snapped, his canines bared. Pushing off Chance like a kid off a trampoline, he bounded back the way he'd come. Ten steps away, he whirled on Chance, his snout lifted and growling his peculiar dog-speak. *By hell, he wants me to follow.*

"You know where she is, don't you?" Chance asked as he climbed to his feet.

That earned him another snarl and a shake of the dog's head. Bared canines again. Gallo stood there in the deep snow, poised to run and his ears pitched forward like radar dishes.

"Find Suede," Chance ordered, though it was clear he wasn't in charge.

Whirling, Gallo bounded through the drifts like a damned flying reindeer, while Chance barely managed to keep up.

"N-noooo," Suede's voice drifted from far beyond the graveyard. "I told you it's just a little farther. He's buried close by, but with all the snow, I got lost and..."

"Gallo. Sit. Stay," Chance whispered to his faithful dog. Gallo dropped his butt to the snow where he stood yards ahead, his focus one hundred percent beyond the stand of snow-laden fir trees between him and Suede.

A husky male voice grumbled, but when Suede cried out, "Not that!" Chance was done waiting. His pistols sprang to his hands. The powder made his steps silent. His anger made his intentions certain.

Gallo sunk to his belly, stalking their prey alongside his master like a skilled teammate instead of an untrained mutt. They came within ten feet of the killer without Zapata knowing they were there. The bastard had Suede on her knees facing away from him, her long hair twisted around his gloved hand. With his elbow cocked and knife raised like it was, he meant to cut her throat.

Chance didn't think twice, but before his trigger finger went live, another man stepped into view just beyond Zapata to his right. A Spanish male with darkly tanned skin and sharp black eyes, dressed in black jeans and jacket. A tactical jacket.

"Stop!" he bellowed, his weapon also trained on Zapata.

Zapata jerked Suede off her knees, leaning her back on his thigh. "You pig! You lying pig! I knew you were dirty!"

"He's mine!" a distinctly feminine voice shrieked at Chance's left. "Drop it, Chief."

What the holy fuck just happened? The forest had turned into a damned sniper convention. Chance dropped nothing.

Zapata crouched low in the snow, growling like an animal while Suede whimpered, "Chance?" She still couldn't see him.

"I'm here," he confirmed, though he was still a couple yards away, and retrieving her had just gotten incredibly complicated.

"Back off, Hex," Juarez demanded even though he kept his pistol trained on Zapata, "or you'll die with him."

"You think I'm afraid of you?" she taunted, but neither she nor Juarez lowered their weapons. Juarez still had his sights on Zapata, and interestingly, Hex did, too. Chance also had a clear shot at the back of Zapata's head. He edged up closer behind the killer, but didn't get far before Juarez barked, "Don't do it, Chief."

Son-of-a-bitch, does everyone know I'm a retired naval officer?

"Go to hell," Chance growled, finally close enough. He pressed the barrels of both weapons into the back of Zapata's skull. "Let her go or die where you stand."

"Chance," Suede whimpered. "I lost Gallo. I'm s-sorry."

"No, he's…" *Shit. Where'd that damned dog take off to now*? "Don't worry, Suede. Hang on." *He'll be back, and then I'll kick his ass, the coward.*

Zapata had the balls to jerk Suede's head up higher, her neck fully exposed and his knife under her chin. "She's mine, Sinclair. I smell her blood. There's nothing you can do to save her."

"That's nothing compared to what you're going to smell if you don't let her go," Chance hissed, grinding his cold steel into Zapata's head.

"You don't want to do this, Zapata," Juarez said. "He's got you. Be reasonable. Let her go."

"Don't kill Domingo," Hex spat. "He's mine, I'm telling you. He's mine!"

"What the hell do you want?" Chance asked her.

Juarez cast a terse look at Chance. "There's a bounty on your head, my friend. Dead or alive. You're a legend. That is all she wants. The thirty silver coins."

Counting on Juarez to be the friend Kruze said he was, Chance leveled one pistol at Hex, still keeping contact with Zapata's skull. "Two can die here as easy as one," he promised her.

"But no one *has* to die," Juarez corrected, his weapon still trained on Zapata.

Chance shot him an appraising glare. Bronze-skinned with dark hair cut short and tight, built like a linebacker, Juarez was not the typical hit man. Square from the ground up, yes, but he made intelligent sense in one of the worst situations Chance had ever been in. No one *had* to die. But they sure as hell would if they came between Suede and him.

Chance prodded Zapata one last time. "You heard the man. Drop it and live. But if you so much as flex a muscle or breathe hard, I'll blow you to hell."

The bastard huffed frosty white vapor in defiance with Suede's hair still curled in his fist and his knife at her throat. "Then trade York for this lying bitch," he said, his voice devoid of emotion. "Where is he? You know, don't you?"

"The last time I saw your boss, he was up on my mountain waiting for a bus," Chance lied. "Why? You lose him?"

"Nobody came for him? He left him there?" Zapata asked.

Chance cocked his head. "Who left him there?"

"El Jefe! The lying son-of-a-bitch!"

Chance didn't want to blow Zapata's head off with him standing over Suede like he was, but if he kept jerking her around like he was, there'd soon be no choice. He gave the bastard one last opportunity. "Who the hell's El Jefe?"

Zapata's neck muscles turned to rods of steel, his jaw clenched so tight Chance heard something pop. His knuckles turned white. The man was ready to blow. When he still said nothing, Chance bumped that pistol into Zapata's hard head until he was staring at his boots. "Get up, Suede. Now. Nice and easy. Zapata's going to let you go now, aren't you?"

"Drop the blade, Domingo," she bit out, "and let me go."

She'd just called him by his first name. *Unbelievable.* "You know this guy?" Chance had to ask. This standoff was Laurel and Hardy's *Who's on First* all over again, only without the laugh track.

Suede's mean girl came out to play. Her fists balled and her chin stuck out. "Domingo Zapata was Lionel York's *Deputy Dog.* Where York went, bodies tended to disappear."

"Why are you just telling me this?"

"Because Zapata's been gone a while, and I thought maybe we got lucky and someone killed him."

"I will kill him for this," Zapata spat, his knife still at her throat.

"Who the fuck's El Jefe?" Chance had to know.

Everything happened at once. Suede leaned into the knife at her throat, then jerked her head back. Zapata's too-close nose split wide open. From out of nowhere, a vicious gray wolf landed snarling on the man's shoulders.

Gallo?

"Diablo!" he screamed, his arms curled over his head. But Gallo hung on, slashing and snarling. Anything he could reach, fingers, ears, scalp, the vicious dog snapped, ripped, and tore. Down they went, Gallo growling like a demon, all fangs and claws; Zapata grunting and kicking. Screeching in Spanish.

Suede dropped to her belly. Vicki Hex stepped in close and took careful aim at the whirling mass of pissed-off dog and bloodied man.

Chance didn't think twice. His wrist flicked as his pistol shot the pink SIG from Miss Hex's hand.

With a shriek, she dropped to her knees in the blood sprayed snow, cradling her bleeding hand. "Stop this madness! He's killing him!"

Juarez sent Chance a chin nod, not exactly what Chance expected from a cold-blooded killer, but okay. Juarez's weapon still aimed at the whirling mass of Gallo and Zapata, not Suede and not Chance. Trusting his instincts, Chance roared over the din of a groaning man and a fierce, unrelenting German Shepherd. "Gallo! Off!"

When Gallo shook Zapata's hand like he meant to tear it off, Chance bellowed again. "Off!"

Still as menacing as a damned fine guard dog, Gallo backed away from Zapata. His head remained low, his fangs bared.

"Drop it, JJ!" a man ordered. Damned if Kruze hadn't just stepped out of the trees, huffing and puffing, his rifle trained on Juarez before he jerked the goggles off his head and glared at Chance. "What the hell are you doing here?"

Chance nodded at Suede. "Rescuing my woman. What are you doing here?"

Kruze's killer-gaze shifted from Suede to Juarez, from Juarez to Hex and onto Zapata. Then back to Suede. "Same thing. I came here to save her from this asshole. You heard from Pagan lately?"

Chance could've sworn a hint of a smile tweaked the corners of Juarez's thin lips. "He's safe. I honestly don't know what just happened here, or who's who. Let's bag 'em and tag 'em, until we're inside and can sort this mess out."

Kruze relieved Juarez of his weapons and knocked him to his knees. Oddly, the man didn't resist, not even when Kruze pushed his face into the snow and cuffed his hands behind his back. "Stay the fuck down, you two-faced traitor," Kruze hissed, his knee between Juarez's shoulder blades. Glaring at Chance, he ordered, "He moves, you shoot him."

Chance nodded from where he knelt zip-tying Zapata's bleeding wrists behind his back. It wasn't often Kruze pulled rank on him. Almost made him smile.

But damn, Gallo had gone crazy on Zapata. He was torn up pretty bad. Chance pulled the now subdued killer to his knees, then let him get his feet under him. Once the man was able to stand, he added a leather collar to Zapata's neck, then fastened a chain from the back of the collar to the cuffs. A hog-tied prisoner made for a controllable prisoner.

Interestingly, Miss Vicki Hex hadn't received the same face-in-the-snow treatment Juarez did. Instead, Kruze had her sitting on her butt in a snowdrift while he wrapped her bloodied hand in bandages from his blowout kit. What the hell?

"You about done playing doctor?" Chance asked sarcastically.

"For now." Kruze didn't spare a glance. "Are you able to walk, ma'am?" he asked Hex.

Damned if her cheeks didn't glow when she nodded and said, "Yes. I think so. Thank you."

"Because of our radio silence" —Chance wouldn't let on that he hadn't been able to contact his nitwit brother or that Kruze didn't play by the rules— "you may not know that woman you're treating shot your baby brother today."

At last Kruze pulled his gaze from the Mafia's best girl. "She did? Is Pagan okay?"

"I only winged him," she murmured, her chin tilted up, her dark eyes on Kruze. Charming him like the snake she was.

When Kruze looked down into Hex's upturned face like a lovesick hound dog, Chance barked, "They go in the back way," in case Kruze had forgotten that these three—oh, by the way—were fucking murderers. "Move it. Now!"

Kruze nodded, while he cupped Hex's elbow and assisted her to her feet with a polite, "There you go, ma'am. Watch your step."

What the fuck! "Kruze!" Chance bit out. "Now'd be nice." That earned him a frown, but seriously? Sucking up to the female assassin? *Get your head out of your ass, brother.*

The trek through the trees to the cabin's tunnel entrance went fairly smooth. Kruze led out with Hex and Juarez. Chance followed with a surly Zapata, while Suede and Gallo brought up the rear. It made a dog-owner proud to hear Gallo growl every few feet, no doubt warning Zapata. Damned proud.

Once inside their secure basement, Chance sent Suede upstairs. He didn't want her involved in what had to happen next. Chance wanted answers, and he wasn't above a little rough play if that was what it took. He added manacles to Zapata's restraints and locked him in a cell, while Kruze manhandled Juarez into the cell across the hall from Zapata. Miss Hex had taken a seat on the bench outside the two cells as if politely waiting her turn.

"You think you can make me talk?" the stupid man with the chewed-up, bloody face hissed.

Chance finally looked Zapata in the eye. He was a tattooed freak from hell, black ink covering his face, neck and arms. He'd filed his teeth into sharp points, but the fully dilated pupils staring back at him caught Chance's attention. "What are you on? Coke? Mescaline?"

Disgust stared back at him. "Death," Zapata spat.

"Then you're in luck. You came to the right place," Chance shot back at him. Gallo prowled the hall, but he seemed most interested in Zapata, not Juarez or Hex. Interesting.

Juarez took the bench at the back of his cell, his knees spread and his cuffed hands interlocked between them. His head was up and his dark eyes were clear. Untroubled. *Damned disconcerting.*

"You," Chance hissed. "From the Navy to this. What makes a man sink so low?"

Juarez gave him that same cocky chin lift as before. "Let me out of here and I'll show you."

"Chance," Kruze called out from ten feet away where he stood with Miss Vicki, who seemed damned docile given her bad-assed rep. "A minute?"

"Yeah, what?"

Kruze nodded at the clinic door to his right, his hand clutching Hex's bicep. Her eyes were as clear as Juarez's, another puzzle Chance hadn't time to decipher.

"Stay," Chance told Gallo. Damned if the dog didn't drop his butt at the door to Zapata's cell, his ears forward, his hackles up, and his eyes on the man he apparently hated. Chance didn't blame him, but why the distinction between Zapata and the other killers in the room? What'd Gallo know that he didn't? Was it merely that Zapata had harmed Suede?

Once inside the clinic where man and dog could be treated if needed, Chance kept one eye on Kruze and Miss Vicki, the other on the hall where Gallo sat at taut attention like the Old Guard at the Tomb of the Unknown in Arlington.

"Shut the door, Chance."

Tired of the games being played, Chance complied, but turned in a huff to his errant brother, the one who obviously had an in with Hex. "You want to tell me what the hell's going on?" he barked, his fist curled, ready to knock some sense into Kruze's big, dumb head. "Because I've got to tell you, for two cents, I'd—"

"You can't lock her up," Kruze said, his voice low.

That spiked Chance's temper all the more. "Why not? Because you're sleeping with her?"

Sure as hell, Kruze didn't deny it, but Hex cocked her saucy head and said, "Because I'm a CIA operative, Retired Chief Petty Officer Chance Sinclair, and thanks to you, I may never be able to fire my weapon again."

Chapter Forty-Nine

Suede scrambled into the bedroom and changed out of her snow gear, her body still buzzing like a hive full of angry bees from her narrow escape. What a mess. But Chance was home safe and sound. That was what mattered. If she could only stop shaking.

In the bathroom, she cleaned the thin slice where Zapata had cut her neck. *Chance will kill him for that alone*, she thought as she pressed a butterfly bandage to the nick on her cheek next.

Full of adrenaline, she fast-tracked to the kitchen and set a full pot of coffee to drip. Chance would be hungry. Kruze too. She had no idea if Zapata or his assassin friends would hang around or if Chance planned to feed them, but she set three pounds of peppered bacon to sizzling on the massive built-in griddle alongside the stove, then sliced two loaves of banana bread while the bacon browned.

A double breakfast casserole came next, but omelets had to wait until the men came upstairs. No one liked tough eggs, and she didn't know how long this interrogation, or whatever Chance was doing down there, would take. She half expected to hear gunshots, he'd looked so fierce.

Now she understood hyper-vigilance. Her nerves were strung as tight as the skin on a snare drum. Every little noise seemed too loud and everything startled her until she seriously contemplated dosing her coffee with the expensive liquor Pagan loved.

Speaking of Pagan, where was he? Opting for reading instead of drinking, Suede settled into the corner of the couch and lifted Scarlett Sinclair's novel, *My Enemy Tryst*, from the end table. But as much as she tried, her brain wouldn't focus. She kept reliving what had just happened. Even York made an after death appearance in her frazzled brain. Rest and reading wasn't happening until she had Chance in her arms and could kiss the hell out of him.

Suede set the novel aside when a sound at the front door brought her upright. What now? She jumped to her feet. Did she dare see who was out there? For a secluded cabin in the mountain, this place certainly got a lot of company and most of it was unwelcome. Should she hide like the coward she felt like?

Whoever it was, that person banging at the door wasn't leaving. Where there's a will, there's a way, right?

Before she could get to the door, it shoved open. "Pagan!"

*****

It all made sense now. The rep for winging the boys-in-blue instead of killing them. Her presence in Portland. Vicki wasn't there for a piece of the action. She didn't want in on the drug distribution in the Northwest either. No. All this time, she'd been tracking Domingo Zapata under the guise of her moonlighting job while she'd actually worked deep undercover for the Drug Enforcement Agency. Inside the Sicilian mob, for hell's sake. Could things get crazier?

Yep.

Chance had no sooner called the senator and told him who he had in custody and why, when his cell lit up with a number he dared not let go to voicemail. "Excuse me, but I've really need to take this." *Really.*

Automatically, Chance's spine straightened. He motioned Kruze to shut the door behind him so Juarez and Zapata couldn't listen in, thumbed *'Accept'* and said, "Yes, Mr. President."

"Chief Sinclair, it's a pleasure to finally speak with you." President Adams sounded as if he were there in the basement instead of sitting at his desk in the Oval Office in Washington D.C.

Chance damned near saluted. "Yes, sir."

"Relax, son. How's the fly-fishing in your corner of my country?" This was why Chance voted for

President Adams. He was one of the guys, a down-home boy from Oklahoma, and a true blue American who stood by his military men and women.

"You'll catch more rainbows once the weather warms up, Mr. President."

Kruze came to Chance's side, his arms crossed over his chest, a big question mark in his eyes. *Why's he calling you?*

Chance shook his head. *I have no idea, unless it has to do with Vicki, umm, shit, Agent Hex.* For once he was one step ahead of things, and she was no longer in custody. But he'd shot a federal agent. *My bad.*

"Chief Sinclair, I understand you can't let on exactly what it is you're doing out there in God's country, and I wouldn't ask you to. But could you do me a favor and stop calling me Mr. President? Nobody needs to know who you're talking to. This is just between us guys."

"Yes, sir," still sprang to Chance's lips. His mom had ingrained good manners in him long before the military did.

"Say, you wouldn't have enough room in that high tech cabin of yours for an overnight guest, would you?" The twang in the President's rich baritone was a pleasure to hear, but Chance knew this was not just a friendly call. Not from the Big Guy.

"Absolutely. You name the day and I'll make it happen, sir."

"I just might do that." President Adams cleared his throat. Papers ruffled and Chance could imagine him signing documents while he chatted. "Chance, it's been brought to my attention that you have a friend of mine staying with you at the moment. To be honest, I need you to do me a favor."

"Already done, sir."

"Well, good." Satisfaction radiated all the way from the East Coast. "Put him on the line. I'd like to talk with him."

Chance caught himself before his big mouth asked, *'Him?'* He offered a clipped, "Yes, sir. I'll get him for you," instead of *'Shit. Not him!'* Covering the mic on his phone, he glared at Kruze. "President Adams wants to talk with his friend, and it's not Victoria Hex."

A bottle rocket went off behind Kruze's eyes. "Told you JJ was one of the good guys." It took him less than thirty seconds to bring Julio Juarez to the phone. The damned man suppressed a smile, *the jerk!*

"You have friends in high places," Chance said as he handed his phone over to one of America's best kept secrets.

"I do," Julio said simply. "Mr. President. What may I do for you, sir?"

The conversation was terse and succinct, no more than one "Yes, sir," and an "Understood" before he handed the phone back. "President Adams would like to talk with you, Chief Sinclair."

Umm, okay… "Yes, sir," Chance said, his voice gone hoarse while his brain tried to connect the dots. What kind of work did Julio do that the President of the United States would be personally involved? Shit, was he CIA? Something darker, blacker than the SOBs?

"Chance, it's been a pleasure and an honor to finally talk with you. Agent Juarez has my permission to share several items of interest. Could you make him comfortable until my men arrive to escort him back to work?"

"Yes, sir, I can do that."

"And Chance," President Adams' tone dipped low. "I was sure sorry to hear about your mother passing away. I had the privilege of working with Scarlett during my re-election campaign, and not a day went by that she didn't make me look good. Everyone loved her. You three boys were the brightest lights in her life. She was proud of each of you, but it was clear that you were her favorite. I hope you know that."

A knot wound around Chance's throat so tightly he could barely speak, "Yes, sir. I do know that." *I always knew that.*

"I'll be seeing you." And just like that, the President of the United States was gone.

Chance turned on Agent Juarez, now rubbing his uncuffed wrists. "You bastard. You're CIA?" He nearly said *'too'*, but that would've outed Victoria Hex, and right then, Chance wasn't sure who knew what about who.

Julio extended a hand and a humble nod. "Special Agent Julio Juarez at your service, Chief Sinclair, and yes, I'm like you. For the last couple of years, I've been assigned to an operation no one outside the Oval Office is privy to." Lifting a clenched hand to his mouth, he cleared his throat. "May I please have a drink of water? It's been a long day."

Chance leveled a shrewd eye at the man. "Do you know...?"

"Miss Hex?" Julio asked, a quiet sparkle in his dark eyes. "Yes, but it'd sure be nice if we discussed this somewhere" —he scrubbed his palms up and down his biceps— "warmer."

"You bet." Chance wanted to bat the *I-told-you-so* grin off Kruze's smug face. "Let's head upstairs."

Julio offered his fists. "Put me back in cuffs first. I cannot break cover."

"We can do that," Kruze offered. "Shall I bring Vicki?"

So now it's Vicki, huh? You dog. "Yes, bring her, but keep her cuffed," Chance muttered. "And stop drooling on her."

Kruze's cheeks flushed bright red. "I'm not drooling on her."

"Yes. You were," Julio said evenly, his voice stern.

Damned if Kruze didn't turn redder.

Chance double-checked Zapata's cell to make sure he wasn't going anywhere, then told Gallo to, "Guard." His dog jumped to his feet, growling at the man in the cage.

This had turned into one hell of an interesting day.

Chapter Fifty

"May I get you another cup of coffee?" Suede asked her two unexpected guests.

Julio lifted a palm in denial, but Miss Hex tilted forward, her cup extended. "Yes, please."

Despite her shaking hands, Suede poured a full cup without spilling a drop. Never in a million years had she believed she'd be sitting here with two of the most lethal people on the planet, well, aside from Chance and his brothers.

Miss Hex was as badassed as Chance, only in a skin-tight, black leather kind of way. She was a sleeker version of *Cat Woman* without the psychosis. Vivacious. *She must really enjoy her job.*

For now, the group sitting around the coffee table in Chance's living room seemed oddly comfortable. Miss Hex and Julio had removed their jackets. Kruze had re-bandaged her wounded right hand, but she assured Chance her fingers still worked. She'd be okay. He didn't look like he believed her.

Thank goodness Domingo Zapata wasn't here. *That* would've been too, too much.

"We knew Mick Tennyson worked with Patrone and the Rio Boys, but York and Zapata?" Chance shook his head. "Didn't see that one coming." He still needed to talk with Suede about her connection with Zapata, though. Another thing he hadn't seen coming.

"Zapata's been tight with York several years now, but that wasn't why he was in Portland." Julio was incredibly soft-spoken, but the steel in his voice was hard to miss. As an undercover operative in a Colombian cartel, he had to have seen and done things Suede could never imagine.

Miss Hex took a tiny sip of coffee. "You boys threw us a curveball when York went missing. That really pissed off Patrone and Gonzales, though I doubt they knew you were behind the end of their glorious plan for the Pacific Northwest."

"Glad we could help," Chance said simply. His palm settled over Suede's kneecap. She had no business sitting in on a high-powered meeting like this, but he'd said yes, and Julio had agreed, so here she was. Trying to be helpful and ready to serve. *Refreshments. Only refreshments.*

"Why'd Zapata take out the Port Commissioners?" Kruze asked.

Julio offered a nod to Suede as he replied, "Patrone ordered him to ramp up the heat. Things unraveled fast for Mick, Miss Tennyson. By the time he saw the video on national TV, he already had ten dead commissioners on his hands, a murdered wife, and a missing daughter who'd made him look bad."

"We're certain the missus was murdered?" Kruze asked.

Julio nodded, his dark eyes boring into Suede. "I'm sorry, Miss Tennyson, but yes. She was strangled before she hit the water."

Suede blinked at this graphic news, feeling the first hint of grief, and something else, for her mother. They finally had something in common. They'd both been murdered. "That means Mitchell Franks is still alive." Her pulse skyrocketing.

Chance's hand smoothed over her kneecap as if he'd read her mind. "Not for long, Suede. Not for long."

"But do you know where he is?" She had to know. "Right now? How do you know he's not coming here?" *For me?*

"Because McQueen's office is working on locating him. Pagan will help, too. He's good with computers. You'll see. We'll get Franks before you know it."

"I'll always help you, sister," Pagan's voice rose behind her from the far left hallway. She knew he'd been shot, but he'd refused to let her bandage his wound, which was kind of funny since he'd bandaged her butt. His hair was still wet from his shower, and he looked tired. But he also looked mean. His eyes held hers captive for one long minute before he said, "No one's getting to you. No one."

That promise should've calmed her nerves, but she knew Mitchell Franks, and just thinking about how he knew her made her skin crawl.

"Come sit down, Baby Brother," Kruze offered cheerfully.

That merited a dark scowl. Pagan shot a middle finger at his brother. "I'd rather stand, smartass."

"I thought Tennyson was in league with Patrone, not Zapata," Chance said.

"No one who sells their soul to the devil wins," Julio murmured. "Viktor never cared what Tennyson wanted. He used Tennyson to get a toehold in the States, and he used Zapata to get intel from York. Patrone's goal was always the river and the wider markets he could reach."

"Tennyson will go away for a long time, possibly Leavenworth," Kruze offered.

Julio shook his head. "No, he won't. If he does any time at all, it won't be in the federal correction system. He wouldn't last a day. Patrone has too many men inside."

"Guantanamo?" Chance asked.

"Too warm," Julio answered, not meeting Chance's eye. But that was enough of a clue.

Ah, so Tennyson would end up in the top-secret installation on that little frozen island in the Arctic Ocean, north of Deadhorse, Alaska, then. Chance didn't voice his suspicion, but it made sense. Other men as ruthless as Tennyson were already housed in the top-secret facility. Had been since World War II.

"So why'd you ring out?" Chance asked. "Why not go all the way in Coronado? It's obvious you're a patriot. Why didn't you stick it out and become a SEAL?"

"I made it three days into Hell Week when they called," Julio said quietly. "Patrone had kidnapped my wife and baby son. He wanted an inside man working for Gonzales, and because of my heritage—my father is from Colombia—he wanted me. He said Gonzales would never suspect a loser like me, that my familia would be safe as long as I cooperated and didn't go to my CO or the police. He wanted me in Colombia right away to begin my new life." Julio snorted. "That's what he called it, my new life."

"So you went to your CO and he contacted the CIA" —Chance waved his hand in a circle— "or someone, and you went to your new job as an undercover agent for a drug lord."

Julio murmured, "Something like that."

Suede couldn't stand the suspense. She didn't care if Julio worked for the CIA or the Pope. "Are they okay? Your family? Your baby boy?" *Please say yes.*

Intense brown eyes met hers across the coffee table. "Yes, ma'am, they are now," Julio said softly. "Zapata held them captive until last week, but he doesn't have them now."

"Zapata had them?" She wanted to cry. "All this time?" *God, no.*

Julio nodded. "He had some woman watch over them when he was away, but yes. They've been confined in his house all this time."

Suede leaned forward, wringing her hands, afraid to think what Zapata had done to them. "I'm so sorry."

Julio's eyes narrowed. "Don't be. They're going to be okay."

Somehow, Suede couldn't believe that. No one who'd ever met Domingo Zapata was ever okay afterward.

"Which is why you didn't leave with Benito Garcia. You're not going back to Colombia, are you?"

Julio said nothing, just stared at Chance, unblinking.

"That's... that's years, Julio," Kruze sputtered. "Fuck!"

Julio's lips pursed before he said, "Five long years, brother."

"Why didn't you contact me?" Kruze's anguish was palpable. "I would've helped. My brothers and I would've stormed heaven and—"

"Because I didn't know where they were, my friend," Julio interrupted, "but now I do. Don't worry. They are well. I am going home to them soon."

Kruze shoved back in his seat. "Jesus H. Christ, JJ. I didn't know. I'm sorry. All this time I thought... Shit, I didn't know."

Suede brushed a quick hand over her face, trying to hide her tears. "I'm sorry too," she murmured. But damn. That number five kept coming up like a bad penny. She'd only been with York four years. He couldn't have been behind all this turmoil in her life, not back then, could he?

Julio gave her a tired smile. "We all have our burdens to share, ma'am. It's over."

"Can I ever meet them? Your family?" She blinked, her weepy eyes not cooperative.

"Perhaps someday. I think Bianca would like very much to talk to you."

Chance shook his head, then turned to the feisty dominatrix-turned-kitten at his left. "Why'd you shoot Pagan?"

She turned to Baby Brother then, her lips soft and the cocky, mean-girl light in her eyes gone. "I am sorry," she told him, her voice dripping with sincerity, "but Julio was so close to capturing Zapata, and I knew how much that meant to him. I had to draw your brother to you before he tangled with Zapata."

"So you shot my ass?" Pagan bit out.

"It is a very nice ass," she offered, and wasn't that interesting? Something shimmered in her big brown eyes that looked oddly like—compassion? Suede brushed that errant notion out of her head.

So apparently, did Pagan. He stuck his chin out at Miss Hex and told her, "Yeah, right. You're a cold-blooded piece of work."

"You took one helluva chance. You nearly got Suede killed," Chance growled.

"It was a risk I had to take," Miss Hex said as her eyes scrolled from a surly Pagan to Suede. "I truly hoped you were still recuperating from what York did to you. I didn't expect you to be so mobile so" —she tossed her head— "soon."

"A risk *you* took?" Suede asked. "You're mighty free with everyone else's lives, aren't you, Miss Hex?"

"Please. Call me Vicki." *That will be a cold day in hell.* "What choice did I have? I had to give Julio time to take care of Zapata. As it was, I nearly arrived too late. Chance could've killed them both."

"I would have, too," Chance muttered.

"Guys," Kruze interrupted. "Back off. She did what she thought was best at the time for the mission. We all make choices and trade-offs. It's the business we're in."

Suede had more to say on that subject, but Chance's grip on her arm tightened, so she let it go until later. But she did notice Kruze's eyes rarely strayed from Miss Hex. Interestingly, she had yet to flirt with him, but she couldn't seem to keep her eyes off—Pagan?

"Why were you looking for Zapata?" Kruze asked Miss Know-It-All Hex with her killer bod, her forever-wet lips, and her smudged, sexy eyes.

"For Bianca and Tomas, that is why. Patrone sent Zapata to steal them from Julio. To Domingo, it was just a job and a game, but to me" —she broke eye contact with Kruze to toast Julio with what was left of her coffee— "familia is everything. The minute

Domingo touched Bianca and Tomas, he sealed his death."

"You and Julio knew each other before," Chance said, not asked.

"You could say that. Julio is my brother," she answered with pride and a toss of her glossy black hair as she shot Pagan another coy look.

Suede nearly laughed at the games Miss Hex played. Poor Pagan didn't have a clue.

"We are in the same family business, of sorts. We love our country, but we choose to love it from afar. For now, that is where we are the most effective. That is also why you must never divulge a word you've heard here today. No one must know we are related."

Suede looked closer then. They had the same shaped eyes, though his brows were thicker, and her eyes were a dark blue instead of brown. Everything about Julio seemed sadder, which was understandable. But knowing Miss Hex had her brother's interests at heart all along changed Suede's opinion. Maybe she was okay.

"Are you going to kill him?" Pagan asked. "Zapata?"

"No. He goes to South America with me," Julio told him, his gaze on his sister. "I have one more little job, and then I am done, Vicki. The Presidente of Colombia has an army set to raid the Gonzales compound outside Cartagena today, another positioned to take down Patrone in Bogotá at the same time. It will be a bloody fight, but by the end of the week, only smoke and ashes will be left of those two kingdoms. I'll be free."

Suede stared at Julio, knowing in her heart that Julio's last *little job* was to kill the man who'd terrorized his family for five long years.

Chance lifted his cup. "Here's to good men everywhere, though they ring the bell or not."

Julio's lips pursed as he nodded to Chance. "It has been a long journey."

Suede caught the drift. "I'll never see you again, will I?"

Wrapping one big arm around her, Chance tugged her into his side. "He can neither confirm nor deny, Suede. Just be glad you met him."

She stared at Julio through a sudden veil of tears, swallowing hard at all that he and his family had suffered. This one tiny thing she and he had in common—their suffering—had turned him into another brother. "Thank you. I mean it, really. Thank you so much."

"No, Suede Tennyson. Thank you." He winked, but the man was not prone to smile. He hadn't yet, and she suspected it would be a long time before he did.

Chance cleared his throat. "You never said, JJ. Why was Zapata in Portland? Who besides York and Patrone is he working for? Who exactly is El Jefe?"

Julio stared back at Chance for a long minute as if choosing his next words carefully. "Mitchell Franks."

"Mitch?" hissed out of Suede's mouth before she could stop it. "Mom's personal assistant? *That* Mitchell Franks?"

Chance's grip tightened on her shoulder to keep her from jumping to her feet. *OhmyGodohmyGod,ohmyGod,ohmyGodohmyGod.* "Zapata was undercover for Patrone, but working for Franks at the same time?"

"The bastard," Kruze hissed.

Which one? Suede thought, shaken to her core. *They're all bastards.*

"Patrone is very sly in his business dealings, but Mitchell Franks is" —Julio looked at Suede as if he knew precisely what Mitch had done to her all those years ago— "evil."

Her heart thundered. It was as if Franks was in her bedroom assaulting her again. How many times would he have his way with her? Would these awful flashbacks never end?

Chance leaned forward, his hands on his knees. "*Is* worse or *was* worse? He's dead, right?"

Julio's head moved from side to side. "I cannot confirm that, Chief." His gaze dropped to the coffee table, a sure tell he wouldn't divulge what he knew.

Suede brushed a hand through her hair, frazzled and not finished with the conversation. *Mitch, really? He's alive. I knew it. That bastard!*

Julio glanced over his shoulder at the sound of rotor slap outside the front of the cabin. "Ah, my ride. Before I go, there is something you Sinclair brothers must know." His gaze circled the room, from Chance to Pagan standing behind him, to Kruze. "You are all wanted men. There is a bounty on all Senator Sullivan's men."

Chance grunted. "There's been a bounty on our heads since we became SEALs. Who wants us dead this time?"

Impossibly, Julio's eyes turned darker. Blacker. "Mitchell Franks."

"Shit," Pagan hissed. "That's why he infiltrated Sullivan's office."

And just that fast, Suede knew where Franks was. She'd seen him in action. She'd felt his hot mouth on her body when he'd pinned her to her bedroom floor and savaged what was left of her innocence. Like any narcissist, he'd liked to brag about her exploits. As if they were merely lovers, he'd told her then how much he knew about her family, her parents. At the same time, he'd boasted how much better his family was than hers. He'd told her how much they owned, and how far his reach in the international community had expanded since he'd come to work for her mom.

Like everyone else who'd crossed his path, he'd used her parents to serve his end. But he'd talked too much, and Suede knew precisely where he was now. She'd tried to forget every last second with that degenerate, but she remembered now.

"It's been an honor, sir," Chance said respectfully as he lifted off the couch and extended a hand to Julio. They gripped each other's forearms and slapped each other's backs, but Suede was having none of that.

When it was her turn, she tugged Julio in for a hug. "You're a good man, Julio," she whispered against his neck. "I'll never forget you. Know that you're always welcome here." She didn't have to look at Chance to know he agreed.

Julio hugged her back and whispered, "You take care of yourself, Suede Tennyson. It's your time to heal. Be smart. Stay home and cook. Let Chance take care of Franks."

It was as if he'd read her mind. "Of course. Chance knows how to do that, not me." *But I do know how to shoot.*

Julio's eyes narrowed like he didn't believe a single word she'd said. "I will keep my eyes on you, Suede Tennyson."

She smiled, fluttered her eyelashes, needing him to let it go. Secrets like this were better kept. Not shared.

Miss Hex and Julio put their jackets on. Pagan and Kruze moved in. More backslapping. More handshakes. Suede smiled at her smart man when he shook Vicki's uninjured hand instead of hugging her. Chance knew better than to play with fire.

Kruze went below and returned with Zapata in chains. Kruze had tossed a lightweight jacket over the man's head, but Suede didn't care if Zapata froze to death on the flight out of Montana. He still wore his leathers. Let them keep him warm on what she hoped was a freezing ride to wherever. Hell, strap him to the pontoons or whatever those things were called that choppers landed on. Let him freeze his balls off.

She stood with the Sinclair boys as Julio and his sister climbed into the small helicopter waiting in front of the cabin. "Is that one of those baby birds you told me about?" It looked small enough. Well, smaller than choppers she'd seen in California.

"No, ma'am, that is a UH-1N from the President's elite squadron." He waved as Julio turned and waved after helping his sister aboard.

"Want to bet there's a cage inside for *Do-ming-go*," Kruze ground out. "Manacles."

"I hope it's refrigerated," Suede said, shivering.

Chance's hands landed on her shoulders, warming her even as he offered the strength of his body for her to lean against. "Just breathe," he whispered. "I know you're thinking of Franks and you're worried, but your panic will pass. Trust me on this."

Chance was wrong. This panic would never pass. Mitch would keep coming after her. He'd send more men with bigger guns next time. He'd never quit until she was dead.

"I have to use the bathroom," she whispered, her feet set to run and her mind already making travel plans. She owed Scarlett Sinclair that much. She wouldn't let Chance lose his brothers.

His fingertips skated down her arm as Suede pulled away. "Hurry back."

"I will," she promised. *When Franks is dead.*

Chapter Fifty-One

Suede didn't join them in the living room after the chopper took off. While Chance and his brothers debated strategy for nailing Franks, he watched her take a basket of clothes down the hall to the laundry room, her eyes furtive. Suffering. All this talk about Franks had dragged up bad memories, and Chance needed to end the son-of-a-bitch to give Suede the peace she deserved.

Pagan had finally joined them and stood leaning over the back of the couch. He needed that bullet removed, but Pagan was no baby when it came to pain. As quickly as that bullet was out, Chance wanted him on Franks' virtual trail.

Gallo had followed Suede down the hall and that was good. She needed her furry companion right now, plus Gallo wouldn't let anything happen to her. He'd proved himself a hero today. Chance was proud of his dog.

By the time she returned, the basket was full of folded laundry, probably from another load, but she didn't pause more than a couple seconds to say, "I left my cold weather gear in the basement. It needs to be washed. Do any of yours?"

"Sure," Kruze piped up, but Chance disagreed. "We can wash our own things."

"It's okay. I won't be long."

He understood. When Suede was nervous, she needed to keep busy. "Come sit with us when you're done. I want you to hear these plans."

She nodded, but didn't meet his gaze, and that hurt his heart. Damn Franks. He'd done this to her.

"Once I find him, I'm gone," Pagan said the moment Suede was out of sight. "This one's on me, Chance. I'll end him and I'll send pictures."

"You want to bet Julio's going to end Zapata before the day's done?" Kruze interjected.

"He damn well should," Pagan hissed. "Shit. I'd have offed him on sight if he hurt my woman."

"You were right," Chance admitted to Kruze. "Julio is one of the best."

Kruze shrugged one shoulder. "I wasn't sure for awhile. He's good at what he does."

"At what he did," Chance corrected.

Silence reigned for a moment. "What a mess," Pagan said at last. "Who the hell is Franks that he's got this kind of power over men like Tennyson, York, and Patrone?"

"And Gonzales," Kruze added.

"I need to get that round out of your ass," Chance grunted as he pushed up from the couch. "Let's get it done, then I need you to track that rat bastard down. We'll end Franks, with or without Sullivan's say-so."

"Consider it done," Pagan growled.

Kruze jumped to his feet. "I'll get started on his paper trail. If there's one, I'll find it."

"Where do you want to do this, your room or the clinic?" Chance asked Pagan.

He nodded at the west hallway. "Already took the first-aid kit to my room."

Chance flicked on the light as he followed Pagan's limp. Nothing happened. "Looks like I've got a short. Damn it." Another thing to worry about. Light bulbs.

"Fix it later," Pagan grumbled. "My butt cheek's killing me."

It took less than an hour to prep and perform that minor surgery. Another to give Pagan a couple shots, tetanus and antibiotics, then clean up. By the time Chance finished, Pagan looked gray and weary. "Why don't you sleep for awhile, then we'll start hunting Franks?"

Baby Brother rolled from his belly to his side, drowsy from the painkiller. "You might be right. Morning's soon enough, isn't it?"

"You bet. If you're lucky, Suede will fix some of those blueberry pancakes for you."

"And bacon," Pagan hissed, his eyes already closed. "G'nite."

"'Nite, brother."

Chance had just cleared Pagan's door when Kruze met him in the north hall, his eyes wide and his tanned face pale. "Chance."

With that one word, acid hit Chance's gut like a kick of nitrous. "What?"

"She's gone. Suede's gone and I can't find Gallo. I've looked everywhere. The computer monitor was lit when I went to our office. The door was unlocked. I scanned the latest searches and I thought maybe you'd already been hunting Franks, so I dismissed them. But then I... I..." Lifting his arm, he swiped a hand through his hair. "I backtracked one of your searches, only they weren't yours, not unless you've got a bank account in LA I don't know about and some guy in Spokane who sells passports. I think Suede's going after Mitchell Franks."

"Like hell." Chance raced downstairs. She couldn't get far, not in this snow, but he couldn't believe she'd taken Gallo. What'd she plan to do, let him loose when she'd gotten to where she was going, which had to be the valley. Or the nearest cab. Maybe a bus. Shit!

Then double 'shit!' None of the light switches worked down here, and now he knew why the west hall lights weren't working either. The main electrical panel was still open. Suede had cut the electricity to this section of the cabin, including the basement security door. "Why didn't you tell me," he hissed as he flung open the massive steel door and stared at the frigid world. "I'd have gone with you."

One pair of snowshoes was missing from the hooks outside the rear exit. She hadn't come down here to gather up their jackets for the laundry. She'd come down here to leave.

"Found Gallo. He's in here," Kruze muttered from the clinic door. "She leashed him to the exam table."

Chance stalked to the clinic where Gallo lay surrounded with dog toys, a big rubber bone clasped in his mammoth paws, and a smile on his face. That meant Suede was alone.

"I'm going after her," Chance growled as he one-eightied and jogged upstairs to command central. "Get hold of Woody. Need him here ten minutes ago."

At his heels, Kruze made the call and muttered, "Yeah, the sooner the better. That long? No, do it. Just get here."

While Chance fired up his laptop to dig into Suede's hare-brained scheme, Kruze filled him in. "Woody said it'll take thirty minutes at least. His bird's cold and he needs to refuel, but he'll be here."

"Shit!" Chance hissed, torn between waiting on Woody and going after Suede on foot. Shocked didn't begin to describe his state of mind. Pissed. Furious. Maybe a touch of pride that she'd done this. But shocked? Not. He should've known she wouldn't let Franks get away with all he'd done to her and her family. He should've known she'd go after him.

"She's got my pistol," he told Kruze. "She's going to kill him."

"She'll never get it past airport security."

True, that. Suede was smart. Wherever she was headed, she planned to arm herself once she got there. Chance shifted gears. He wanted eyes on the sky, that bank in LA, and the guy in Spokane who sold illegal passports. Now!

While Kruze hammered at his keyboard, Chance did what he should've done days ago. It all came down to why York had chosen Chance's parcel of land to end Suede's life. Chance needed to know now what he hadn't cared about before. *Who the hell are my neighbors?*

It took seconds to bring up Google Earth along with the county's property assessment website. A little hacking know-how brought his corner of Montana into geographical relief, boundary lines and property owner's names included. Bumping that information up against his boundaries identified his neighbors. He'd vetted this portion of Montana thoroughly when he'd bought this land, but hadn't thought to double-check which properties, if any, had changed hands since. Now he knew. "That asshole's my neighbor."

"Be specific," Kruze said without looking up. "I know lots of A-holes."

"No wonder York dumped Suede here."

"Who are you talking about?" Kruze barked, still intent on his search. "Which asshole's your neighbor?"

Chance turned on his brother. "Mitchell Franks."

*****

It took no time at all to catch a bus out of the little town in the valley. Apple Valley, how quaint. It smacked of all the things Suede had left behind. Warmth. Family. Love.

She was headed west to Spokane, Washington, now. Like Julio needed to end Zapata, she needed to end Franks. Chance would put himself at risk for her, but not this time. Her mean girl was back in the game and her plan was foolproof. Franks had taken too much this time, and Suede meant to tell him so, right before she shot his fucking head off.

Maneuvering through the snow was the hardest part of the trip into town. Dressed in the winter gear she'd used when she and Chance had confronted York, she'd borrowed a pair of snowshoes and sneaked out of the basement door while Chance was busy upstairs with his brothers. Poor sweet Gallo. She'd leashed him to a table leg in the clinic. That hurt as much as leaving Chance. Gallo had treats to keep him busy, but Chance would be angry.

He might never forgive her for this breach of trust, but she wouldn't lose another person she loved to Franks, and yes, the loss of her mother now hurt like a knife lodged in her chest. Suede didn't understand the grief that kept surfacing like waves, but that single thread she shared with her mother—of being murdered by bastards—now pulled her relentlessly onward. To do good. To finish what Franks had set in motion five years ago. To pay

Chance back for all he'd done. Suede meant him to be proud of the gifts he'd given freely, not ashamed for saving her life.

As the wintery scenery rolled by her bus window, she smoothed her hands over her stomach to calm her jittery nerves. This *was* the right thing to do. It was.

At the Spokane airport, she paid the cab out of the funds in her now depleted personal bank account, as well as the one York had set up for her. As odd as their relationship was, he'd always made certain she had one hundred thousand dollars at her disposal. She'd withdrawn every last cent while in Apple Valley and kissed her dreams of a happy life with Chance goodbye. He deserved better, and maybe someday, he'd find that special lady who could give it to him. It surely wasn't her.

Suede didn't expect to survive this confrontation, and that was okay. A tear eked out of the corner of her eye, but she dashed it off her cheek so it wouldn't attract others. The darn things worked on gravity. They only needed one to prime the ducts. Franks. That was her sole mission now and she would not fail.

The flight to Costa Rica was pricier than she'd expected, but okay. She only needed a one-way ticket. Off the southeastern shore of the country, on the Caribbean-side near Puerto Veijo De Talamanca, several tiny islands lay, some only a couple acres of isolation, others large enough to have been small countries. That was where Mitchell Franks was. She knew it.

He was probably sitting on his beach, laughing at all he'd gotten away with. Well, not for long. She hadn't brought a weapon with her, but she had enough cash. Guns were plentiful on the streets of Puerto Veijo. Housing was cheap in Puerto Veijo, and people were poor. She knew a few of those poor people. They'd help her, and soon Mitchell Franks would be as dead as her mother.

Oddly, that didn't bring the peace she expected. Her heart ached. No. It was breaking. She'd never loved anyone the way she'd loved Chance, and it hurt, physically hurt, to be separated from him now. She couldn't catch a deep enough breath, and she honestly thought she might be having a heart attack. Who was she kidding to be so brave all of a sudden?

The grief he'd told her would surely come had arrived. Her feelings for her mother hadn't mattered before, but they mattered now. But what had gone wrong between Vera and Franks? Was her death his attempt to get back at the Governor? Was he that cruel?

"May I get you a blanket?" the kindly flight attendant asked.

Suede looked up into the soft brown eyes of a pretty Hispanic woman. They were the same deep, chocolate brown as Julio's. He, his wife and son had suffered at Zapata's hands, and all because Mitchell Franks was the wicked spider at the center of this treacherous web. He'd ruled not only Zapata, but Governor Tennyson and two evil Colombian drug lords as well. Yet here she was, going after a powerful man.

Suede's resolve turned to concrete. She *could* do this. She *would* do this.

"Yes, thank you, I am a little cold," she told the attendant. *And I'm not turning back until Franks is dead.*

Hours later, the flight touched down in the Costa Rican city of Puerto Limón. Since the only items to her name were the essentials she'd purchased prior to this self-appointed mission, Suede carried one small suitcase off the plane and half a bottle of water. The cash she'd withdrawn in Montana was concealed in a wallet beneath her baggy shirt, along with the passport she'd bought illegally in Spokane. That was right, Spokane. Thanks to her exciting life with Lionel York, she knew how to circumvent the law when needed.

Disguised beneath Jackie O dark glasses, one of Chance's blue baseball caps, his baggy shirt, and plenty of *'I-don't-give-a-shit'* attitude, she ambled out of the Jetway tunnel, popping bubble gum and with a burner phone stuck to her ear like the majority of her generation.

After passing through customs and only sweating up a tiny storm over that illegal passport she'd paid a bundle for, she caught a cab to the bus station, then boarded the bus to Puerto Viejo, sixty some miles south on the coast. From there, she had no idea how to get out to Franks' island, but she wasn't worried. Puerto Viejo was known for its surfing, nightlife, and college-aged men and boys. She had money and looks. She'd be on that island in no time.

Suede opted for a room at the *Otel del Sol*, Hotel of the Sun, where she'd previously spent a few days. York had left her there while he traveled for business, which she now knew meant drugs. *What a world I lived in,* she thought. *I thought I had it all, but all I had was ignorance to fall for every trap laid for me. Never again.*

Her room faced east as if Karma were one step ahead, giving her a final view of the beautiful Caribbean where she'd most likely die. But first things, first.

Suede had only hours to procure a weapon and a boat for hire. She showered and wrapped her wet hair in a braid, then wound it high and tight to fit under Chance's cap while she prowled the streets and back alleys. She had one shot at killing Mitch. She intended to make him love her first. Well, at least lust for her.

Chapter Fifty-Two

Sunrise spread across the Caribbean like a tropical cocktail. The soft rosy hint of a Cosmopolitan began in the east, then spread west like a Banana Daiquiri splashed over a top-shelf, strawberry margarita. Finally, the all-too-brief lightshow ended with the vivid hues of an orange Screwdriver drowned in the wide-awake blue sky of Curacao, on the rocks, a hint of Pina Colada at the rim. In other words, the day was too pretty to spend on murder. But by sunset tonight, murder she would.

The loveliness of the sky combined with the fresh sea breeze off Suede's second story balcony where she stood looking down at tourists, surfers, bare-chested college boys on their way to the beach or coming home from a late night party. Life unfolded slowly here, even the traffic moved slower. She'd ordered room service for breakfast, a glass of orange juice and a plate of focaccia with marinated vegetables, but her stomach refused to settle enough to allow her to eat.

Despite the natural splendor on her horizon, her mind had awakened in Montana with the promise of Chance Sinclair's strong male body at her back, his nose in her hair, and his hand on her hips, maybe between her thighs. His other hand cupping her breast. Or splayed to her belly. If she were home now, she'd be covered in warmth and the scent of her fully aroused man. He'd wake her gently, teasing her body to play, and she'd be willing, wet, and ready. A delicious orgasm would break over her like a waterfall, triggering his release as she shattered in his capable hands. *God, I love him.*

Yet here she was. Alone again. Her nose twitched, full of the scents of the island, but missing the ones she loved best. Peppermint. Pine. Chance.

Her heart ached with missing him, but today was the day she saved him and his brothers. The only day.

Her newly acquired pistol rested at the bottom of the bag she intended to take to the island with her. In less than an hour, she'd betrayed the man she loved in order to kill the man she hated. The rented boat of the frat boys she'd met last night waited at the dock. The clock was ticking.

Yet Suede stayed at the rail of that balcony a moment longer than she'd planned, wondering for the first time if Chance drank alcohol. She knew Pagan did, but she'd never seen Chance with a can of beer or a glass of wine in his hand, and for some reason, she very much wanted to know the answer to that question.

But that was life for you, wasn't it? Full of unrealized expectations at every turn, giving nothing back it couldn't rip away from you in a heartbeat like the eternal trickster it was. Leaving you not only bereft, but humiliated, plundered, and sometimes morally bankrupt. Desperate for true love. Lonely.

"I do love you," she told Chance, "but I have to do this. I hope you'll forgive me someday. I hope you'll understand." *I hope you'll love me anyway...*

Enough. She had work to do. Suede strolled out of the hotel and down to the dock like a tourist, checking out the street vendors and their colorful wares as if she had all the time in the world. The smells of pineapples, oranges, bananas, and a myriad of other fresh produce filled the air, but this was a day for work, not play. You'd never know it to look at her. Suede had transformed herself back into the snooty diva she'd been with York. A lace wrap-around angled over her hips, covering just enough of her black string bikini that didn't cover much of anything. The truest kohl eyeliner accented her charcoal smudged eyes. Deep red tinted her naturally lush lips and gloss made them shine. She hadn't done much with her lashes, not as thick as they were, but added mascara and a hint of blush to finish the package. Men needed to want her, at least they needed to want to fuck her. Like Franks and York had.

Sparkly flip-flops slapped at her feet and her toenails were now as glossy red as her lips. The too-big-for-her face, black-rimmed sunglasses completed her disguise. A bag hung loosely off one shoulder as if she simply carried sunscreen and a towel in it, stuff that most women her age would take to the beach.

Like she knew they would, her frat buddies whooped and wolf-whistled when they saw her coming. They wanted her because, well, that was what men did. They wanted what they couldn't have.

"Not today, boys," she told them as she dropped over the side of their boat and took the bench near the back by the engine. They didn't argue, not at the price she'd promised to pay them. They were to drop her off on a specific island off the coast, then return to the hotel where an envelope waited for them. In the envelope, a check with five digits in front of the decimal point. Was she desperate that she'd pay them so much for a simple boat ride? Yes, but that was the only way she could be sure they'd deliver her safe and sound to—Franks.

It took less than forty minutes of wave-bumping salt spray in her face to arrive at her point of destination. By then her mouth had gone dry and her heart thumped, but adrenaline did that, didn't it? Recklessly, she jumped off the landing dock at the rear of the boat and into the water, her bag held high over her head so her weapon stayed dry.

One of the boys called, "Good luck!" before the wake of their getaway rolled over her, lapping at her chin.

Suede strolled to the sandy beach, dripping wet. Tossing her wrap around over a nearby bush, she set her bag at her feet, then took stock of her last stand. Giant palms stood like sentinels along the sandy strip of white sand. Sea shells glistened like lost treasures on the isolated shore where waves rolled in relentless rhythms of give and take, Mother Nature's way. She'd never given much to Suede though, had she? That was a sad thought on a sad day, to know that the one thing Suede treasured most, she'd lose before the sun set.

But her life was worth the trade. Chance needed to live. If Patrone was in deep with Mitch, then all roads led here. To this beach. To this island. To this one last—Chance.

"Let's get it done," Suede murmured, forcing her mind off what she'd done to the man she'd left behind. Dropping to one knee, she lifted the pistol from her bag and chambered a round. Even as small as it was, the pistol was too heavy to conceal in her swimsuit. It stayed in the bag.

The beach was bare of any signs of human visitation, but a path wound under the giant palm at her right and into the heart of the island. A dog yipped up ahead, so she donned her wrap-around to hide the scar on her thigh and followed the noise. The path led her straight to a plantation style home, complete with a wide veranda, baskets of palms and fuchsias dripping over the railings as if some genteel southern boy lived here instead of a monster.

A standard-sized Schnauzer sat at the top of the two-steps to the porch, his bright, black eyes following her every move, his ears perked forward. Like Gallo's.

The sight of that faithful companion stabbed a place in her heart Suede hadn't realized existed before. Pain on top of pain washed over her. Man, the collateral damage—to her—was stacking up. She loved that furry baby she'd left behind.

By now Gallo had to be wondering where she'd gone, and why she hadn't taken him with her. She'd given him one last hug and told him, but her sweet boy's big brown eyes had been full of smiles right up to the moment she flipped the switch in the electrical panel to kill the power to the circuit. He'd growled when she'd opened the heavy security door once she was sure the alarm wouldn't sound, a questioning kind of grumbly growl that had seemed to ask, *'Why are you leaving me behind? I'm your best bud! I should get to go too!'*

"Because I love you, too," she'd told him now. Those words didn't convince her heart though. Love *did* hurt, but this pain was different than the version of parental love she'd grown up with, even worse than York's. This was a bittersweet wash of guilt and regret for destroying something precious and rare. For not trusting the only man in the world who'd trusted her with his brothers. His dog. His heart.

Chance had to be hurting as much as she was at this separation and that realization was eye-opening. Her heart pounded with what she now knew to be true. No one had ever loved her like Chance did. With every step, the sweet love she'd found in Montana tugged at her to turn around and run, to not do this despicable thing. To return to the cabin where she belonged.

But that wasn't happening. Not today.

All at once, the Schnauzer bounced off the steps, wagging his nub of a docked tail and happy to see her. Didn't that throw her killer instincts off? Suede dropped to one knee to pet the neatly trimmed and very polite fellow. She almost felt welcomed, until Mitchell Franks opened his screen door and stepped into view. Dressed in a cream-colored, short-sleeved shirt, khaki shorts that came to his knees, and boat shoes, he looked just as she'd hoped. Relaxed and unsuspecting.

Fine-boned, and maybe five feet nine inches tall, she'd never realized what a short man he was until now. How feminine he seemed. He'd seemed so much bigger the nights he'd raped her. She swallowed hard, fighting memories when she needed to focus on the job ahead.

With his light brown hair combed on the right, his face clean-shaven, and his fingernails no doubt manicured and spotless, he hardly looked the part of an evil mastermind. His head canted to the side, his eyes gobbling her up like they always did. "Suede? What are you doing here?"

Lifting to her feet, the strap of her bag securely over her shoulder, she shrugged. "Where else should I be? I have nowhere else to go. Isn't this what you wanted? Me to come here? Me to be with you?"

He said nothing, just watched her approach with his dog trotting at her side.

Suede let her gaze sweep over the neat patch of freshly mowed grass. The well-cared for beds of pink, purple, yellow, and orange flowers beside the steps where he stood. The two stately palms. The elegant arbor off to her right that led to what looked like a well stocked koi pond. "I remembered you telling me that your parents left you this island. Nice place. So close to where York did business, too."

Franks' hands perched on his hips. "Nice try. I saw you on television."

Of course you did. "So?" She stopped her casual stroll. "What's that supposed to mean?"

One perfectly trimmed brow lifted. "It means I know you've got a boyfriend who's a Navy SEAL, and who most likely killed York. That's why he isn't answering my calls."

"Tell me another lie, Mitch. You're the reason York nearly died when you cancelled the chopper that was supposed to retrieve him, so don't tell me you've been trying to reach him. Did you also plan for no food to be in that rig? Did you hire that for him, too?" She had him there and she knew it.

Both Franks' brows lifted then. "It seems I underestimated you." His hand swept backward, beckoning her up his stairs and into his home. "Why don't you come inside and tell me what else you *think* you know?"

Removing her dark glasses, she wrinkled her nose, hesitating. Appraising the situation. Entering his house would get her—perish the thought—up close and personal with her target. But could she go through with this crazy scheme?

Again his gaze scrolled down her long legs to her painted toes and back up again, stopping at her ample cleavage before they lifted to her eyes. A crafty smile twitched his thin upper lip. "The Suede I see now is an amazing beauty and an intelligent woman. Come. You must be thirsty after your..." His eyes darted behind her. "How *did* you get here?"

"By boat. The town's full of college boys eager to please, if you know what I mean."

A smirk pinched one of Franks' cheeks. "That shy-girl act still works for you, doesn't it?"

She let the strap of her bag roll off her shoulder, the bag landing in the sand at her feet, needing him to believe she'd brought nothing but 'shy-girl' stuff with her. "Yeah, but you knew that years ago. Sex is my drug of choice now." *With Chance, not you, you pervert.*

Her ruse must've worked. His back stiffened as if he'd just gotten hard and knew he could have her, if he could only get her inside. Franks tried a different tactic then. Taking a seat on the top step, he called his dog. "Here, Meine Liebchen. Let the lady alone."

Obediently, the dog pranced to his side and dropped to its haunches.

Meine Liebchen? What a stupid name for a cute dog. "Nice dog. I like *her*," Suede said pointedly as she folded to the soft sand, cross-legged and wanton, playing this game of one-upmanship to the bitter end. She gave him a peek at what he could have—in his dreams—before she draped the warp-around over her scant bottoms and covered herself. "Is your dog German too? Like that Wilhelm guy in Colombia? Like York?"

Her dead mother's personal assistant nodded, but the smile on his thin lips didn't reach his cold, gray eyes. On hand settled on top of *Meine Liebchen's* round head. "This bitch is straight out of Stahnsdorf, Germany. I have a friend there who raises them. The breed makes the best companions in the world. You should get one."

"I used to be your best companion," Suede murmured. "I believed you when you helped me file for emancipation. I thought you wanted to help. Why'd you dump me on York?"

Franks folded his hands in front of him, his elbows on his knees, and that poor innocent but loyal dog at his side. "You'd gotten unstable, Suede. Surely you knew that. You were prone to inventing stories that never happened, telling lies—"

"Like you raping a minor? A child?" She bobbed her head, going for sarcasm. "Was that just a story?"

His brows narrowed. "I only gave you what you wanted, what you still want. I'm right, aren't I?"

"Possibly..." She trailed a long red fingernail in the sand near her bag, drawing a heart for the man she might never see again, for Chance. "But why kill my mother?" *My Mom.* Lifting her hand, she coughed into it to hide her sudden emotion, her throat gone dry at the thought of him strangling Vera Tennyson, then dumping her body into the ocean. Her heart seemed determined to break for the woman Suede was positive had never loved her. Why this intense awakening of a family connection now? What purpose did it serve anyone?

He stretched one leg down the steps, shaking his head. "Vera never had any use for you. You know that. Why do you care now?"

Suede didn't. Not really. Did she? "Just wondered." *But I do care. I just don't know why.* "Not like it matters now. She's gone and Dad's going to prison."

That dropped Franks' gaze to his shoes. "Since you're here..." He drew in another breath. "Oh, what the hell. I might as well tell you. Your mom always was a pushy bitch, Suede. You knew that. Hell, the world knew that, but lately she'd gotten nosy. Nosier." His gaze arrowed past Suede to the trees and the ocean behind her. "She found something she had no business finding, then she made a federal case over it. She made personal accusations that hurt. Hell, she'd turned into a fuckin' Rottweiler, hell-bent on ruining me." His hand went to his chest as if he had a heart in there.

Suede kept her eyes on him. The man seemed genuinely sad, but she knew better. "I get it. You offed her just like you offed York when you didn't need him anymore. No big deal."

"Ah, but I didn't '*off*' York as you so eloquently put it. Where is he? Do you know what happened to him?"

"You're right. I killed him," she lied. "That SEAL you saw me with on TV taught me how to climb that mountain of his, and he taught me how to shoot. Only I didn't need a gun to end Lion. I shoved him off the same cliff he shoved me over. Guess he'll never do that again."

"Then what?" Franks asked, his voice soft and low, leading her on. "Did you kill that SEAL too or do I have to worry about him showing up to rescue you?"

She hadn't thought this far ahead, but whatever it took, she was in this game to win it. "Yes-s-s-s-s," she hissed, her head down and her eyes closed at the thought of harming Chance. "I had to kill him. He thought he owned me..." *Chance, please forgive me.* "I hate bossy men. I hate most men, but you..." It was her turn for regret. "You're different."

"Look at me, Suede," Franks ordered.

She tipped her chin up, wiped her eyes, and obeyed despite what she'd just said about bossy men.

He sat there staring at her, patting the step at his side. "Come here. Let's finish what we started five years ago."

Five years. He made it sound like she'd willingly entered into a tryst with him that night he'd snuck into her bedroom and assaulted her. Revulsion crept up her throat at the thought of what he'd done to her tender body, how he'd trussed her up like a prize before he taken her hard and fast. The pain of that awful invasion still burned like a coal at her core.

Was this man insane or had he really, in his demented way, thought he'd loved her? Was that what had driven him to toss her to a wolf like York? Had he done that to punish her because she'd spurned him? Somehow, it all made creepy, scary sense.

As if tempted to obey, she lifted to her feet. She would've gone to the bottom of that step... She would've taken her bag with her and drawn her pistol on him and blew his brains out. She would've, but—

Two strong arms snared her just as she stood. Some guy with a heavy Spanish accent asked, "This the girl?"

Suede jerked to get away, but he held her fast. "Let me go!"

"Why yes, Viktor. That's the high and mighty Suede Tennyson. It's damned time you showed up."

Franks tipped his head to the man. "Where are your boys? They were supposed to be on guard."

"She's alone if that's what you're worried about. Check this out." Viktor ran his hand up her thigh, revealing the nearly healed scar. "This gal's got spunk."

Franks waved an impatient hand dismissively. "Whatever. Bring her in. I don't want blood on my doorstep."

Chapter Fifty-Three

Infiltration. A noun. The ability to gain access to an enemy camp without the enemy's knowledge. A skill set to acquire information or inflict bodily harm or death. Chance rolled the angst of his neck, as focused as he'd never been during all the infils of his nine-year Navy career. Bodily harm ranked high on his to-do list this morning. Damned high.

His brothers had his six like no other operators before, and they'd geared-up as only SEALs did. Plenty of ammo. Several pistols. Enough extra magazines to get the job done. Knives. High-tech listening devices and the latest spy gear. Good stuff like that.

Leave it to Kruze to have friends in low places. The fisherman who'd dropped them a mile offshore was another one of his old friends. Swimming to shore took less than thirty minutes, and now they stood wary. Thrown off balance. For all their badassed reps, the Rio boys lay dead on Mitchell Franks' pristine private shore, their necks broken courtesy of who, Chance didn't know and could see no sign of. It spiked his instincts to Threatcon Delta: *Attack is imminent.*

"Heads on swivels," he growled, not that his brothers didn't already know that.

But wasn't it interesting? If the Rio boys were here, the Godfather himself, Patrone was most likely here as well. Then who in Colombia was El Presidente going after? Who else, besides Suede, was Franks entertaining? Had JJ lied? Was Wilhelm Gonzales here, too? Was this another betrayal and an ambush like that other South American op?

Chance sucked in a gut full of I-don't-fucking'-give-a-shit. Patrone. Gonzales. Juarez. Franks. Didn't matter who stood in his way today. He'd smoke them all to rescue Suede.

Oddly, thoughts of the CIA agent who'd disappeared before that op gone horribly wrong in South America came to mind. Why, Chance had no idea, but the truth was that CIA Agent Card had never resurfaced after the bungled mess that had taken most of Chance's team and most of his heart. *Wonder where he is,* Chance thought. Not that he cared. Still... Card was one of those unanswered questions that plague him yet today. Probably always would.

Rolling his shoulder, Chance shrugged thoughts of Card off and focused on Suede. It wasn't hard to locate her. All they had to do was follow Franks' annoying voice straight ahead. The pig had her inside his island home, tied to a wooden chair, her hands bound behind her back, her ankles strapped to the front chair legs, and her knees spread. If seeing Suede in a string of a swimsuit and restrained like she was didn't spike Chance's rage into the red zone, nothing did. He needed to kill something. Franks and Patrone would do.

Chance knew damned well why she was here. What rape victim didn't want to cut the balls off her attacker? *But Suede baby, you don't have the heart. You couldn't kill York. What makes you think you can kill Franks?*

Yet Franks hadn't shut up since Patrone dragged her, kicking and screaming, inside. Dressed like an islander in beach attire, Franks was everything Chance expected. Thinning, light brown hair. The pale blue eyes of his German ancestry. Pasty complexion. Nervous. He was that wimp on every grade school playground who never made the cut to play ball when the bigger, more athletic boys handpicked their teams. Wimps like him proved their lack of real power by bullying younger kids and girls. Like Suede.

Patrone himself was barrel-chested, maybe six-foot three, wearing white linen slacks with a pale yellow polo shirt that hung over his expansive waist, and the comfortable, high-priced leather shoes of a gentleman. He reminded Chance of Anthony Quinn in the old gangster movies. He radiated the calm

Franks didn't, the kind that came from knowing he was the most powerful man on the continent.

"I'm picking up chatter," Kruze whispered from the earpiece snugged deep in Chance's head. He and Pagan had since circled the building and secured the perimeter. "Let's give it up for Benny."

As if on cue, Benito Garcia made his entrance behind Suede. An elegant Hispanic male with a neatly trimmed pencil-thin moustache, the barest hint of a goatee on his chin, he wore a bright blue sports jacket, white shirt, and tie. The guy looked like he was going dancing.

"Ears up," Chance ordered, meaning the listening/recording device Kruze handled. If possible, they'd acquire as much evidence as possible to the twisted scheme that had nearly brought Oregon down and America to its knees. If the Sinclair boys' unapproved trip to Costa Rica turned into a political nightmare, President Adams would need solid ammunition to defend his men—if he'd still claim them.

Kruze came back to him with, "Already on it, brother."

"Two down in back," Pagan affirmed, meaning he'd located two more tangos and had taken them down silently. Like a pro.

"We do this slow. We do this right," Chance hissed, though every nerve in his testosterone-charged body told him to rush the place, smoke Franks, Patrone, and Garcia. Rescue Suede. Kiss the hell out of her. Spank her ass until she couldn't sit down for a week. Exfil to safety. In that order.

Easing one boot flat to the porch, Chance settled his shoulder blades to the wall beside the door in seconds. Pagan took the opposite side, limping a little, but just as pissed as Chance that they were now on an illegal operation in a foreign country. McQueen wouldn't like this, but Chance hadn't asked permission. The senator could like it or lump it, fire him or arrest him for all Chance cared about protocol. Suede would be home by the end of the day, damn it.

"This," Franks declared from inside, "is what your mother found. Like mother, like daughter. Sit back and enjoy the show."

Kruze hissed from the side window. "Shit. Porn. He's making Suede watch porn of... son-of-a-bitch... of her. Him and her. The bastard filmed what he did to her when she was a kid. Even I can't—*shit!*—watch this."

Chance peered through the screen door. "I see it." His instincts screamed, *'Take him out!'* but his right hand came up automatically in a fist as if he needed to tell himself to follow orders.

"And you want to know what your bitch of a mommy did then?" Franks bent forward in front of Suede, his hands on his knees, berating the woman who'd turned her cheek to him. "She cried. Do you believe that? Vera Tennyson cried like a little girl. For you! She got all weepy and sad, said she'd failed you, wah, wah, wah. That you were worth more than anything or anyone in her world, and she'd let you down. Said she should've known you wouldn't lie because you were always a good kid." Lifting his eyes to the ceiling fan overhead, he raked a hand over his sparse hair, flattening it to his scalp. "Fucking bitch said she never deserved you. Isn't that the joke of the century? Look at you now, ten times the whore she was!"

Suede's head came up then, and Chance's heart sank. Her cheeks were wet with tears and she was that little girl again, belittled by her parents, tossed to wolves the likes of York, yet believing every last word out of Franks' lying mouth. Chance wasn't buying any of it. Franks only said those things to hurt Suede, leading her on to believe that her mother had ever loved her? Cruel. Damned cruel.

"She cried? F-for me?" Damn it to hell, the catch in her voice sounded so pitifully small.

"Oh, boo hoo, yes." Glaring at Suede, Franks pursed his lips. "She was going to the police to tell them how I'd lied, and, shit. She went crazy on me."

"But why not just threaten her like you did everyone else?" she asked, her voice soft and sad. "Why kill her?"

"Because I had bigger fish to fry!" Franks slapped Suede's face then. Her hair whirled over her shoulder as her head jerked to the right, and it was all Chance could do to hold fast and wait.

"York was off the reservation by then. Zapata said he liked York, and shit, once you aired that damned clip of yours on national news, it didn't matter, did it?" He struck her again, forcing her head to her other shoulder, her mouth bleeding now and her chest heaving. "I killed the bitch, and you made sure your daddy will never see the light of day. We're alike, Suede. You and me. We're exactly alike."

Patrone's head canted, as if he'd just heard something he didn't understand. Suede whined, "We're... we're nothing alike."

"Not taking much more of this," Pagan warned.

"Wait," Chance ordered his brother, though it killed him to let Franks batter Suede. But this was why she'd come to this island. To go in too soon, to rescue her now, would undermine all she'd given to this desperate task. She'd already proved she was willing to do whatever it took to end Franks. She understand, because Suede Tennyson was tougher than Mick or Vera. Tougher than York any day, and— *by hell, she might just be tougher than me.*

"Want me to spell it out for her?" Garcia asked as he fiddled with his cufflink. "You get more with honey, you know. Might work. I do have a softer touch, least that's what the ladies say."

"I'll kill him," Chance whispered at the insinuation.

"Not if I kill him first," Kruze murmured.

Franks stretched backward, his palms on the small of his back as if his spine ached. "Yeah. Go on. Give it a try, but don't cut her. I just had this carpet replaced."

"Zapata should be here. He'd convince her." Patrone dragged another wooden chair, spun it backward, then straddled it ringside. To watch.

"But no blood," Franks bit out even as he rubbed his bloody knuckles. "It's messy. I won't have it."

"Ah, yes, our tidy boss hates the messes he leaves behind, which is why we are here today." Garcia rolled up one sleeve, very slowly, then the other as he circled the scantily clothed woman in their midst. At last, he took a knee between Suede's spread legs. Placing one hand high on her thigh, he cupped her chin with the other. "Ah, so this is the mess we must clean up today, the mighty Suede Tennyson. You are not so pretty now, eh little girl?"

She had the nerve to spit in his face. "Get your dirty hands off me."

"You taught her well," Kruze muttered.

But Chance knew better. He hadn't taught Suede anything. She was already hardened when she'd come to him. If anything, he'd hurt her by loving her. By softening her up. By giving her hope.

"She is a spitfire," Patrone chuckled. "Need a towel, my good friend?"

Garcia swiped his face, then grabbed Suede's throat, his fingers dug in under her chin, forcing her to face him. "Let me tell you what you came all this way to find out," he hissed, his eyes dropping to the plump swells of her breasts before they scrolled back up her neck to her eyes. "Mitchell Franks did your daddy's dirty work for years. He covered up for his whores, his lies, and for his murders. He paid off lawyers and judges, police chiefs and pimps, but when you told your mommy and daddy that he raped you?" Garcia's head tipped to the ceiling as he laughed. "Ha! What a lie. You liked it and you know you did. But then he knew you had to go, so pffft! He sold you to the Lion. You were easy to manipulate back then. What happened to that sweet little girl?"

His gaze tracked down her taut neck to the swell of her breasts again. "Still, maybe we can do a few things with you before we kill you. Things that may convince you to stay. To join us."

Chance wanted this over. *Hold on, baby, he prayed. Get them to talk.*

"So Mitch blackmailed my d-d-dad?" Suede stuttered.

Franks jumped back into the game. "You call it blackmail. I call it getting what I deserve."

"B-but why infiltrate Senator Sullivan's staff? What good did that do?"

That brought Franks up short. "How do you know that?"

She peered up at him, her face wet with sweat, tears, and blood. "I know a lot about you, Mitch. Your plan to distribute Colombian drugs out of Portland's docks. The way you used Zapata to get inside York's business when Mr. Patrone thought Zapata was working for him. The way you used others to undermine Mr. Gonzales' plan to bring fascism into the heart of America. You were just using them too, weren't you?"

Don't out Julio, Suede, Chance prayed. *You can do this. I know you can. Just don't out Julio or Vicki when you do.*

Benito Garcia lifted to his feet, his face screwed into a grimace as he turned his back on Suede and accused Mitch. "You did what? You do not trust my boss? You sold Wilhelm out? Your *familia?*" His disbelief rang out shrill, loud, and clear.

Franks tipped back on his heels, both of his palms forward as if to placate his friend. "Just business, Benny. It was just business. Trust me. Don't take it personally."

"I did trust you!" Garcia shot back at him. "Wilhelm trusted you. He thought we had a deal to take over all the Pacific Coast business! Together!"

Patrone's chair scraped and he was on his feet now, his dark brows furrowed over darker eyes. "What's this about Zapata? You stuck maggots inside my organization like you did Sullivan's? Who do you think you are to spy on me?" he asked as he thumped his broad chest.

Chance lifted his hand to signal his brothers to go in, until Franks said, "Don't go soft on me, guys. You both got your share of the blackmail Mick paid, and you'll get more. Trust me. This is business, and we're in it for the long haul. So I made a few decisions without you. Get over it. We can do this, right?"

Garcia didn't look any more convinced than Patrone, but they both calmed. Their brows came down. Their fists relaxed. Chance stilled his trigger finger. Whether she knew it or not, Suede made a damned fine operator under pressure.

"I think it is time we call Wilhelm," Patrone said quietly to Garcia. "I want to hear what he knows."

Garcia tugged a cell out of his inside jacket pocket. "Exactly my thoughts, amigo."

"And you," Patrone turned on Franks. "Go get my boys. Tell them I have need of them. Here. Pronto."

Franks shot the Godfather of Colombia a crusty, injured look. "*Me?* You want me to run '*get your boys?*'"

"Si," Patrone said, his voice soft and lethal. "I no longer think American soldiers are coming like you said. I think you lie. This woman came here alone or I would've heard otherwise by now. So go. Get my boys. Be quick."

Suede interrupted the pissing contest. "So you... you blackmailed my dad? That's what this was all about? Just money?"

"Just money," Garcia scoffed, still swiping at his bloodied collar, his phone to his ear.

Franks seized on the distraction. Rolling his neck, he hunched one shoulder like he had a neck cramp. "No, it was about your father becoming President of the United States, you shithead!" He'd gotten close enough he could've spit in her face. "We could've had it all, but once you pissed York off and he tried to kill you on *my* property, mind you. *My land in Montana, the asshat!* Once he crapped on me, I had to get creative, didn't I? I knew Mick was still tight with some of our frat buddies, and I'd already planted spies in all their businesses. I improvised. I made decisions! Never expected Sullivan was in so deep into the black ops until then, but finally I had him by the—"

"But you spied on a United States Senator? Really?" Suede asked, her tongue sliding over her bloody bottom lip, facing her tormentor yet again. That she'd deliberately circled back to the crime Franks had committed against McQueen told Chance plenty. Suede knew precisely what she was doing, baiting Franks while outing him to Patrone and Garcia at the same time. Damn, she was good.

Good girl, keep them talking, Chance urged mentally. *God, I love you, Suede. Just do what you're doing a little longer. I'm here. I won't let anything happen. I promise.*

"Why not? Nobody can pin this on me or them. They sure can't hurt Johnny."

Mental note-to-self: pay a visit to this Johnny-asshole. Whoever he is. At night. Make it hurt.

Suede's head dropped then, and Chance worried she'd passed out until she whispered, "It was you all along, Mitch. You used my mom and my dad. You used me, and now you're using these poor gentlemen to take over the drugs in America. You don't care about Mr. Patrone or Mr. Garcia any more than you did York or me. Do you think they're stupid, too?"

Good touch, calling Patrone and Garcia 'poor gentlemen'.

Chance jumped when Franks backhanded her and screeched, "Poor gentlemen! These guys?"

Suede lifted her chin and kept taunting him. "You're the one who wants to be president, Mitch. Of America. Of Colombia. That's why you needed Mr. Patrone and Mr. Garcia here, just when the Presidente of Colombia sent his army to kill them. They're here now doing your dirty work for you just like you did for my dad. It's Wilhelm Gonzales you want dead, isn't it? That's what this is really about. That's why he wasn't invited to this little party. He's probably in front of a firing squad in Cartagena right now, isn't he? But you needed Mr. Patrone and Mr. Garcia alive. Why is that?"

Way to go, baby, Chance thought. *Give him just enough rope...*

She lurched forward against her restraints, the same as when she'd broken Zapata's nose. "What are you going to do now, Mitch?" she hissed, the fire in her eyes smoking hot. "Drown Mr. Patrone and Mr. Garcia when you're finished with them, just like you drowned Mom? Leave them on a mountain without food or rescue like you did York? Rape their children like you did me once they're dead and they can't protect their families?"

Both Patrone and Garcia had stilled at her steady declarations. The room went deathly quiet.

"Do you think I care for one goddamned minute what happens to my long lost uncle!" Franks shrieked. "Wilhelm's a prick! He always has been. And York! York was just plain stupid. He wanted a piece of the action, so I gave it to him. Too bad it wasn't all he thought he deserved, the arrogant bastard. Now shut the fuck up!"

It was the damnedest thing to watch this feisty five-foot-nothing lady take on three crime lords. In. Their. Own. Territory.

Franks cocked an arm to hit her again, but Patrone pre-empted the strike when he struck a knife into Mitch's kidneys. Jerking a beefy elbow around Franks' neck, Patrone twisted the blade until the man stopped squirming. When he dropped wheezing to the floor, Patrone wiped the blade Franks hadn't seen coming on the leg of his pristine, white slacks. He turned to Garcia. "If what this woman says is true, Wilhelm's in trouble. Call him. Now."

Suede's head came up, fear glittering in her eyes. "Wilhelm Gonzales is Mitch's f-family? H-his uncle? Is that true?"

Patrone knelt at her side, his big hand on her bare knee. With one hand at the back of her head, he nodded. "I'm sorry, Miss Tennyson, but yes. Now tell me. Who are you? Really?"

Since she was facing away from Chance, he couldn't read her eyes when her shoulders heaved and she cried, "I'm just me, Mr. Patrone. I'm the unwanted kid of two politicians who loved themselves more than anyone else. I'm Suede Tennyson, and I'm so tired of men throwing me away. I... I'll do anything you want if you please, just let me live."

Her bottom lip quivered and Patrone almost looked like he cared—until the blade slithered out of his sleeve and nestled in his palm like a pet snake.

Chapter Fifty-Four

"Go," Chance hissed, and from where he stood at the far window, Kruze took Garcia down with a headshot. Patrone jumped to his feet and whirled to embrace his demise, courtesy of Pagan. From the window opposite Kruze, he'd emptied both Sigs into the guy's broad chest. Between bullets flying and the risk of ricochets, Chance walked calmly to Suede. Cutting her restraints, he had her under his chin where she belonged in a minute, shivering but safe before Patrone's hefty body hit the floor.

"I knew," she whispered, her poor eyes swollen again, her lips ragged and bleeding. "I knew you'd come for me."

"And now that I've got you, I'm going to spank your ass so hard you won't be able to sit down for a week," Chance promised, though he knew better. He was no woman beating asshole, and this strong, intelligent, beautiful creature had an entirely other kind of discipline coming.

While he dug out the extra large T-shirt he always carried and worked it over Suede's tender shoulders, his brothers hurried through Mitch's place, lifting laptops, portable drives, every last one of the porn clips, and as much other intel as their backpacks could carry. The four of them exited Franks' island home on a dead run while Kruze hung back and covered their six.

"W-wait," Suede muttered as they neared the shore. "There's a dog. A big black Schnauzer. Meine Liebchen. We can't leave her."

Pagan took off for the dog before Chance said a word. With his back to them and his rifle still trained on the trail behind them, Kruze hit the shore, his phone to his ear, already contacting his friend to come get them. While they waited on Pagan's return—*which had better be quick*— Chance gave Suede a quick once over. Bloodied lip. At least one black eye come morning. Maybe a couple loose teeth. Other than that, she'd be fine.

Breathing hard, Pagan strode out of the jungle with a Giant Schnauzer prancing at the end of the leash in his hand. "Bastard had this pretty girl locked in a crate. She's coming with us."

Great, Chance thought. *Now I've got two dogs.*

Once safely at sea, they settled in for the ride back to Puerto Veijo. Pagan sat facing Chance and Suede, the dog at his side and talking a blue streak to her.

The animal sat watching him and not at all distressed. He ran her through some simple commands—sit, stay, shake, bark—none of which Gallo could do. Yet.

"This is a smart dog," Pagan said. "Glad you remembered her."

Suede nodded. "She didn't deserve to die."

Pagan cocked his head at Chance. "Did you hear what I heard back there? Wilhelm Gonzales is, umm, was, Franks' uncle? Do you believe that shit?"

"Kind of makes you want to stay far away from the whole fam-dam-ily tree, doesn't it?" Chance said.

Pagan shook his head and grunted. No. Makes me want to end every last one of them."

"And who the hell is Johnny?" Kruze asked from where he stood aft, watching their wake and guarding their exfil, his rifle still aimed at the shore.

"Not sure," Chance hissed, "but we need to do a little research, boys." *Because I'm paying Johnny a visit.*

"I just want to go home," Suede murmured.

Chance leaned his nose into her cheek. "Montana or—"

BOOM! His head jerked up as Mitch's legacy blew up behind them. Sky-high. The center of the island was nothing but a writhing ball of orange and black conflagration surrounded by a sandy beach. The evidence that the Sinclair boys had ever set boots there was gone.

"Nice touch. Which one of you planted explosives?" Chance asked, his binocs to his nose, watching the curls of bright flame and black smoke rise skyward.

"Not me. Wished I'd thought of it, though," Pagan replied.

"Me too." Kruze had his bincos up. "There. On the beach. Look! It's—"

"Julio," Chance finished. "Son-of-a-bitch. He's been there all along. He's who neutralized the Rio Brothers."

Sure as hell. Julio stood extra tall watching them hightail it across the Caribbean. He lifted his right arm and waved, then clicked his heels and performed a regulation military salute that brought a sheen to Chance's eyes. "He was there all along," he told his brothers, his voice gone husky. "He set those charges. He had our six. Julio's finally free."

"This was that one last job," Kruze muttered, a catch in his voice, too. He climbed the boat railing, gripped one of the fishnets overhead for balance, then waved and bellowed, "I see you! Brother, I see you! Fair winds and following seas!"

"He's as good as any SEAL I know," Pagan said firmly. "Let's go back and get him."

"No," Chance answered, the wind in his eyes making him tear up again, damn it. "He didn't need our help today. He won't need it tomorrow. He'll be okay."

"His family is safe now," Suede whispered from where she nestled, one hand on Chance's chest, her tired head on his shoulder.

He cupped her cheek, barely able to refrain from kissing the hell out of her poor mouth. "You did good, real good, baby. Don't ever do it again."

"Promise," she murmured. "You get the bad guys. I'll cook and clean for you, take care of your dog, important stuff like that."

And you'll take care of our sons and daughters because I'm knocking you up the minute we get home. He pressed her head under his chin, his eyes watery, and his heart so damned full that his chest hurt. But this was a good kind of pain, not the ragged kick in the gut he'd gotten when he'd found out she'd gone after Franks. No, this level of pain felt more like torture. Like love. It hurt so damned good.

This was why he did what he did, because of love for his country and his God., for his brothers and the men who served with him. And now—for the rest of his life—for her.

"I love you, Suede," he told her. Finally.

"I know," she whispered.

When Chance laid a kiss on the top of Suede's head, Kruze and Pagan had the good sense to turn their heads. "Let's go home," Chance told his woman. "Let's go home."

Chapter Fifty-Five

Chance licked her again, sending Suede into a writhing frenzy just before she screamed and toppled over the edge into her third orgasm of the night. He hadn't spanked her, though she had it coming. No. Chance took his temper out on her by pleasuring her until he drove her crazy. Three orgasms, huh? *Let's go for four.*

Burying his face between her thighs, he kissed her core, so damned satisfied that she'd fallen into his world and had given him a reason to live again. To want to live.

"You're killing me," she panted, her hair a delightful mass of tangles and curls, some of them hiding her face at the moment. But that was what happened when a man dominated his woman in their bedroom. He'd turned her upside down, over and under. Different positions with all of them ending with him inside of her. The best was yet to—*come.*

"I shaved just for you," he teased. "One more time?" He'd shaved because his scars no longer mattered, and he could finally stand to look at himself in the mirror.

"I can't," she whined in that spoiled, petulant little girl tone she pulled out of her bag of feminine tricks when she wanted her way. "It's too much. I won't survive."

"Yes, you will," he promised as he climbed up her sweat-slathered body. Stopping with his knees at her hips, he swirled his tongue in her navel, then licked a slick trail up her delicious body, between her voluptuous breasts, up her slender neck, and ended at her kiss-swollen lips. He liked her like this, swollen, sweaty, her lips bitten and mashed. Her chin was a little chafed from what was left of his whiskers, and his scent was all over her, from her top to, well, her bottom.

Clenching the cheeks of that sweet ass, he gave her no time to argue, but lifted her hips and plunged headlong into his bride-to-be. If he got his way and talked her out of using birth control, she'd be barefoot and pregnant in weeks. Maybe months, but soon, damn it. Real soon.

"Marry me," he told her, not asked. But he thought, '*Please, please marry me!*'

By then he had her outrageously aroused. What else could she say but, "Yes! Oh, God, yes!"

For a second he wasn't sure if that was an answer to his proposal or her reaction to another breathtaking orgasm. He had to ask, "You will?" even as she sighed in his arms.

Suede nodded, her eyes closed, her body clenching his. "Oh yes, I'll marry you. I love you. You know that."

"I do," he answered, so damned overcome with happiness that tears swamped his eyes. Lowering his forehead to hers, Chance covered her mouth with a heartfelt kiss. Deeply in love, he could no longer see life without the resilient, intelligent, incredibly sexy woman in his arms.

When they'd come home to Montana after that fateful day in Costa Rica, he'd laid the law down, though why he felt as if she'd wrapped him around her little finger that same day, he still didn't get. It wasn't supposed to work like that, but it had. He'd meant to tell her no more operations for her—EVER. Instead, she ruled him, day and night, just like she was ruling him now, though Suede might not realize it. But everything he owned was hers and everything he did, he did for her.

He thrust extra deep this time. Extra hard. Did an extra good job at the intimate mission he was on. When she bucked and groaned against him, he knew just what to do. The second her scream "Chance!" split the air, he smiled and plunged over the edge with her. Flying with her. Holding her tight and never letting her go.

They shattered together, and he couldn't help thinking that each time they went to the stars together like this, each time they fell back to Earth wrapped in each others' arms, they also absorbed a part of each other. He'd never be just *Chief Sinclair* again. He finally was that *more,* that real man he'd been searching the world for.

"I love you, Suede," he growled as he took her mouth one last time. So sweet. So giving. So damned fine. A man wanted to linger in her body and never leave, but that wasn't humanly possible. He rolled off and to her side, anchoring her with his heavy arm just below her cushy breasts, one leg over her thighs, and his nose tucked in the warm recess of her neck. Chance took a long, deep breath of the future Mrs. Sinclair.

"Whew," she huffed, the pulse in her neck pounding as hard as his. "We have to disagree more often."

"You like make-up sex?" he asked, pulling the heady scent of her into his soul. They hadn't really disagreed. Her trip to Costa Rica was more a mission he hadn't seen coming, yet one that he should've expected. He would've done the very same thing.

"So babies," she whispered. "You really want children right away?"

"Yes," he declared as he dragged his lips up her neck to nibble at her ear, his scruff catching strands of her hair along the way. "Unless you'd rather wait. I want a family, but I want you with me in this life raft we call marriage. If this isn't the right time, tell me. I really can wait." Yeah. She owned his balls.

Suede rolled to her side, facing each other, her luscious breasts aligned to the planes of his pecs. "You, Chance Sinclair, are the best thing I've ever fallen into."

He cringed, hating when she minimized her near-death. "Will you stop saying that? I'm no Prince Charming, and you didn't just fall. You were pushed."

"But I did fall for you," she insisted, "and just like in the fairy tale, my Prince Charming kissed me and—"

"Not the same thing. I pinched your nose and re-inflated your lungs. Damned near broke your ribs doing CPR—"

"And you prayed."

She had him there. "Okay. I prayed." *God, how I prayed.* "But I cursed God, too. He should've taken better care of you from the start. Giving you decent parents would've been nice."

"But He did take care of me," Suede murmured, her nose rubbing his scruffy cheek like a cat scenting her territory. Up his sideburns she went and into his hair, following the ridge of one of those scars she claimed were medals of valor, not proof of mistakes made. The woman was born to be a military wife. She certainly said all the right things. "If I hadn't fallen off your mountain, I wouldn't be here now, would I?" Her big blue eyes blinked as if she'd just asked an obvious question. "And you wouldn't have fallen for me."

He had to smile. They'd both done a lot of falling. But a SEAL can be stubborn. "Gallo found you, not me."

"And why'd you have a dog to begin with? Huh?" She knew the story, yet he let her lead him into temptation with those wet lips and innocent dewy eyes. His cock sprang to attention. Again.

"My mom," he admitted. "The pup was Mom's idea and—"

"And now, he's yours," Suede finished with a sly wink. "Trust me. Your mother knew what you needed, so she sent you a furry guardian angel."

"In her will," Chance clarified, just to be difficult. "That's how guardian angels work? They show up late, don't listen, and leave hair all over the place?"

"Whatever," Suede retorted. "It doesn't matter how they come to us, they just do."

"How do you know so much about Mom?"

Her lashes came down. "Because of you. Because of Kruze and Pagan, too. I don't think Scarlett Sinclair knew how to raise anything but good and honorable men."

"You're biased." He scooped her up onto his chest where he could reach both of her sumptuous breasts and thumb her nipples until he'd turned the tips of them as hard as diamonds. He watched her blue eyes turn dark as she straddled him. "All I know is that this guardian angel" —he thrust upward, connecting with her. Sliding home— "is going to scream my name one more time tonight."

"Me?" she teased, angling her hips and her core to where he needed her to be. "I'm not a—"

"Oh, yes, you are," he growled. "You fell from heaven, didn't you?"

"That makes me sound like a fallen angel."

He chuckled. "Not if you fell for me. Now answer the question. When can we start making babies?"

Closing her eyes, she tipped her head back, giving him an eyeful of her naked self, her long tangles falling down her back and whispering over his thighs like wind through the pines on his mountain. Her plump breasts as round and as soft as clumps of grapes on the vine. "I honestly don't know, but I'd like to go back to college and get my degree first. I'd like to have you all to myself for a while. Too long?"

Arching his back, he filled her to the hilt, growling, "That's what every man wants to hear, *'baby, you're too long.'*"

She slapped his chest. "I didn't say that, but now that you mention it..."

"I can wait for you, Suede. But soon, make it soon." He cupped her breasts, thrilled at the tender weights in his palms. But come to think of it, "I didn't know colleges offered degrees in culinary arts."

"Who said I wanted that?" she asked as she leaned into his hands. "I love to cook, especially for you, but that's not what I intend to do for the rest of my life."

"And what would that be?" he asked, egging her on.

"Besides doing you?" She had the nerve to giggle. "I've always wanted to teach math. Advanced algebra. Calculus. The whole nine yards."

Soooooooooo not what he expected. Chance pushed her gently away from him then, far enough that he could see past her curtain of tangled hair and into her eyes. Her being a math geek actually explained a lot. Geeks weren't known for being socially adept, which Suede was—now—but at fifteen and sixteen? Probably not. No wonder she'd fallen for the likes of Lionel York. She had no experience knowing one creep from another.

Chance had to ask. "How many boyfriends have you had in your life? Before York."

Her shoulders lifted. "Umm, one. Why?"

He arched his hips upwards, wanting her to know how much he adored their unique connection. "Did you and he ever...?"

That earned him another smack. It stung, but that smack also told him plenty. "I'd say that's none of your business, but" —she shrugged— "once. After the homecoming game. At least he tried."

Son-of-a-bitch. This sweet, inexperienced little thing had gone from being raped by Franks, traumatized by York, to finding true love in Chance's bed. What a sad, wild ride that had thankfully, ended with happily-ever-after. He rolled her over, taking her by surprise when he trapped her thighs between his knees. Pride in this courageous woman and all she'd survived welled up, bursting his heart. "I love you, Suede Sinclair."

Starlight blossomed in those deep Pacific blues at the new name she'd soon have. Her fingers skimmed his temples on their way into his hair. "And I love you, Chance, but I want to contribute more than cinnamon rolls to the Sinclair family. I hope you understand. I love you with my whole heart, but I have to be productive, too."

He let the need to explain how *productive* she could be go. This was a serious subject for Suede. He could read it in her eyes. "Math, huh? I may have a job for you when you're ready."

"You do? What?"

He had to smile. "I know this dumb jock whose mother left him and his brothers a few million. The idiot travels a lot. He needs someone he can trust to handle his estate while he's gone. Pay his bills. Budget. Invest. Feed his dog. Cover his ass. Kiss his face. You know. Financial stuff like that."

Suede dug her fingernails into said ass. "Like this?" she teased.

Smoothing her hair out of her eyes, he kissed her forehead, his knees still outside her thighs, but his randy cock making his intentions known to her belly. "Absolutely," he growled. "You interested?"

"You want me to manage your finances?"

He bumped his nose to hers. "*Our* finances. Yours and mine. I told you a long time ago, baby. What's mine is yours. I get that you need to contribute, that you need to feel empowered in your own right, and I'm thrilled that you do. You'll go far. I wouldn't be surprised if you own your own business on Wall Street someday, but until then..." He landed a kiss on the tip of her nose. "Work for me. Cook for me. Never let me go."

Shimmering pools of liquid blue stared up at him. "Never let *me* go," she corrected.

Shifting his weight, Chance angled his knees between her thighs and with one thrust, sank into her body. "Never," he breathed. "I found you fair and square, and I keep what I find."

"Me too," she whispered in his ear as her hands slid up his back to his shoulder blades. "I finally found what I've been looking for."

If that didn't tear his heart out, then she made it worse. "It's you, my love. You're my last and my only... Chance."

The End

Epilogue

Some eighteen hundred miles east of Montana, Pagan took a knee outside one of two eight-paned rear windows of a townhouse in D.C. proper. Like row houses, the homes adjoined but their facades were different. Some were painted in federal blue with stark white trim, others in earth tones with dark brown accents. Gray stone and red brick decorated others, lending to the appearance of America's individualistic spirit.

Yeah, right. This 'burb' was nothing but a cookie-cutter tract of over-priced housing for the upwardly mobile near-misses and abject failures in the frantic District's business world. It was for wannabe politicians who'd never gotten elected, for men and women resigned to teach because they weren't good enough for higher aspirations. The faded paint and shabby lawns did look half decent by moonlight though.

This particular home was special. John Wesley Mills lived here with his cat, and didn't that figure? Johnny-Boy was a cat person. Gallo wouldn't like that on principles alone. Neither would Lucky, the good girl who used to go by that awful moniker, Meine Liebchen. Who in their right mind names a dog something that translated means *love of my life*?

Pagan wondered at people like the recently deceased, Mitchell Franks.

Dark had fallen hours ago, but Pagan had time. He now knew the intimate details of Johnny-Boy's alter ego. A lackluster insurance salesman who barely made his quotas by day, he dabbled in illicit drug distribution by night. Didn't fall too far from the proverbial tree that had taken root in South America a long time ago. Well, not really that long ago, but back in the 1940s, when Nazis there thought they were safe from the reach of justice and truth.

His ancestors, two brothers, Richard and Zimmer Franks, both SS guards, had settled in beautiful Bogotá, Colombia, after the war. It was a nice place to live—then. But as sure as crusted dirty snow follows the freshly fallen, pure white flakes of a wintery storm, deceit and misery followed the Franks brothers.

Richard, the younger one, despised the lack of sophistication in his new country. In less than months, he fled to the United States, took on a new history, that of a used car salesman, but kept his old name. Zimmer, the older brother, was made of tougher stuff. After ingratiating himself to the governor of Bogotá, he began two businesses, one legal, one not. He married well and entrenched himself in wealthy Colombian society. The downside to his success was his only heir, a daughter, who in turn had married Diego Gonzales, the local crime lord. Not because she'd wanted to, but because Zimmer needed her to.

It was an arranged marriage of epic proportions, two criminals uniting their kingdoms and expanding their grasp, all accomplished in the time it took for innocent little Amanda to say two words: *I do.*

Zimmer had long since lost track of Richard. He'd always acted as if he had a broomstick stuck up his ass anyway, and there were times Zimmer thought he'd detected homosexual tendencies in his brother. That perversion wasn't tolerated in their mother country, and Zimmer wouldn't tolerate it in Bogotá. Richard had sent letters to his brother, but Zimmer burned each and every one.

A staunch believer in all Der Führer stood for, Zimmer set his aims high and his means low to acquire those aims on behalf of the Third Reich. He'd not only organized SS operations while in the Homeland, but architecturally designed several of the finest crematoriums. He was good at it, this death thing. That was how he did business. Efficiently. He said what he meant, and he followed those few words with lethal enforcement. That was how a strong man ruled the world. A few beheadings, here. A dismemberment or two, there. All in a day's work.

Eventually, at the age of one hundred and one, Zimmer passed away in his sleep, but not before he'd trained his grandson, a darling, blond youngster to take over the family business.

Wilhelm Gonzales immediately executed every person in the city who owed his father or his grandfather as little as one peso. That was also the day Wilhelm learned he was not alone in the world. A long lost relative surfaced in his fair but troubled city, another blond and blue-eyed man who reminded Wilhelm of his proud German heritage. That man was Richard Franks' grandson. Mitchell.

As for Johnny? Mitchell's sister, Celia Franks, had married Collier Mills, a Maryland banker. Not an important banker, but a hard working nine-to-fiver who was never good enough for the rapacious, conniving dreams of one of Hitler's right-hand man's progeny. At least, that was the story John told his friends down at the local German tavern about his father.

Pagan had done his homework well, not only online, but at the tavern as well. Men on the downside of life tended to gripe about the father's they hated, especially after a few beers. And Pagan liked to listen.

John Wesley Mills had just earned rank in the local fascist chapter, a group with violent tendencies toward murder, chaos. The usual. First lieutenant now, he had bigger dreams for America, dreams that paralleled Zimmer's dream. Beheadings. Dismemberments. Hangings. Terror. The tactics worked in South America. Why not here?

Hence Pagan took a knee, not to pray, but to rack the slide of his Sig Sauer P226 MK25, complete with SR09 suppressors. X-ray sights. Elite ammo. He didn't plan to use its twin, but kept it holstered for now, loaded and just as ready. Like a brother who'd come bail your ass out of trouble if things went sideways.

But that wasn't happening tonight. Donning black nitrile gloves that matched his leather jacket and his mood, Pagan ghosted into Mills' home without the OTS doorknob making so much as a snick. But the second—the very second—he entered Johnny Boy's space, his nostrils flared wide at the coppery scent of freshly spilled blood in the air. Damn. Johnny Boy wouldn't have killed someone in his home tonight, would he?

When a silent shadow slid down the loft steps at his left, Pagan crouched low, his piece forward, ready to fire. He leaned into the act, anticipating it, needing to end this lowlife for the sake of the woman his brother loved. This was no sanctioned hit. Neither had it been vetted through the SOBs. This was personal. Johnny was the last living descendant of the treacherous Franks brothers. He and their warped ideology needed to die.

Primed, all Pagan had to do was press the trigger, light up the night, and leave without waking the neighbors—until he realized he'd caught Miss Hex.

"Freeze," he growled, lifting to his feet and into view.

She halted, her right arm across her chest, her fingertips still on the handle of the pink-as-a-newborn-baby's-butt weapon she'd just holstered, her voluptuous breasts crushed and plumped inside the cups of her black sports bra in the process. "Oh, hi Pagan. What are you doing here?"

"You ended John Mills?"

The woman smiled. She knew she was eye-candy galore, from the peaks of those girls to the tips of her designer boots. That she managed two underarm holsters with the size of her *assets* amazed male snipers everywhere. Not that they minded. They just liked to watch while she put those babies away.

"Course I killed him. Why are you here? To kill me?"

"Hardly." He holstered his piece to prove his word, his heart thumping at the heady scent of cherry blossoms wafting from Miss Hex's sexy body. How could she smell so good, yet be so lethal? "You knew one of us Sinclairs would be coming for Johnny Mills. You should've let us end him."

Her deep brown eyes widened under delicate brows that made her look extraordinarily innocent, which she was not. "I had a job to do and I did it, and yes, thank you for asking. My fingers mended nicely, no thanks to your brother. Why are you here?"

Pagan's mouth went dry at the sight of all that exposed skin. Her belly. The creamy swells of her breasts above the bra. Her long neck. Of course she'd dressed in black leather shorts that creaked when she walked, but those legs...

Every drop of blood in his brain fled south. Hex was a tits-and-ass, *'play nice with me and I won't kill you'* kind of gal. A brazen alpha, he had no doubt she'd dominate any partner dumb enough to get too close. At the end of the day, she was Kruze's type, and didn't that reminder of who she'd probably been with—as in *slept with*—pump a gallon of bile into Pagan's already churning gut?

He stepped away from Miss Hex, then took another step back for good measure, not sure why the thought of Kruze with this woman irked him. "Fine then. It's done. Goodbye."

She took a step toward him. "Would you like to double-check my work? I'm not proud. I'll show you. One shot. He never felt a thing. Never knew I was there."

Pagan shook his head, as much to shake the notion of actually sharing the same air with this tantalizing, but off-limits woman, as to distance himself from the scent of her. Cherry blossoms made him unfocused and weak, two traits that could get a sniper dead. "No thanks. Gotta go."

"But Pagan," she breathed, her perfect lush lips drawn into a pout that made a man stop and take notice and wonder what those lips would feel like. What they'd taste like. From there, it was only a hop, skip, and a jump to what her other parts would taste like.

His tongue licked a quick lap over his bottom lip before he bit it. He squared his shoulders, intending to leave, damn it, but Miss Vicky wouldn't shut up.

"You and I had a common enemy. I got here first, that's all. You would've done the same. Friends?" She extended slender fingers, the nails painted pink, but reaching for him. Daring him to accept—something. He was pretty sure it wasn't friendship.

Tugging his gloves off, Pagan stuffed them in his rear pocket, then made contact quickly. Succinctly. Barely squeezing those feminine bear traps. But sometimes, in the cosmic scheme of things, it only took... One. Touch. That single brush of skin against skin. The melding of lifelines to lifelines. The matching of fingerprints on fingerprints.

A spark sizzled up from her palm and hit his brainpan like a bolt of greased lightning. It was a different kind of energy. Brighter. Crazier. So. Damned. Hot.

She pulled back with a hiss, a glint of shock in her eyes. "Pagan? Did you just...?"

As her words trailed off, he leapt into defensive mode. "Shock you? No. The carpet's full of static electricity, that's all." *Liar.* He'd felt something and he knew it. Pagan just didn't know what it was.

Rich black mane swished over one leather-clad shoulder, rivaling the leather for shine even in the dark of a dead man's house. Vicki Hex, the Sicilian mob's number one killer, cocked her pretty head and said, "I like you Pagan Sinclair. You're... different."

Was that an insult or an attempt to be funny? He wasn't sophisticated enough to play with the likes of Hex, and he didn't want to look like a fool. "I gotta go." Damned if his voice didn't sound rough and ragged instead of suave—like Kruze's had he been here.

She moved in closer. "Let's go have a beer. Talk. Maybe we can work a few jobs together. I'd like that, wouldn't you?"

He shook his head, not ever—EVER—working with Hex, not in this kill-or-be-killed career they'd both chosen. It seemed wrong offing bad guys with a truly beautiful woman at his side. "No," he told her, his lower back sore, and his balls aching from standing at attention. Least that was why he thought his balls ached. Couldn't be—*that.*

Her lips pinched. Again with the hair swish and the coy fluttering of lashes. God, her eyes were black tonight. Deep and dark. Sultry and full of steamy promises. He didn't dare blink for fear this was all a dream. *A dream come true...*

"Aw, you're turning me down?" she asked.

Are you turning me on? "Yes," he damned near shouted. "Work. I've got work..." *Or something.* "...to do. Now goodbye."

Miss Hex knew no boundaries in her specialty. In less than the time it took Pagan to draw in a belly full of air, she was in his face, her girls plastered against his pecs. His gaze automatically fell into the tempting valley between those breasts. Soft. They had to be soft and warm. Femininely fragrant. Tasty.

Umm, yeah. About that... Pagan knew damned well his brother had bedded her, at least once. That was his big brother's style: Love 'em and leave 'em.

Suddenly, Miss Hex's elbows were on Pagan's chest. Her fingertips were teasing the curled hair behind his ears, and her lips were within kissing range.

"I need a cut," he told her, not sure why that trivia blurted out, but okay. *Not on my best game here*, he thought. *Mostly, because I got no game.*

Her lips pinched and Pagan closed his eyes, not because she might kiss him, but because this was a dream. He'd wake up any second now, and he didn't want to embarrass himself when he did.

Instead, the softest lips caressed his firmly closed mouth like butterfly wings, brushing over his skin, asking. Her tongue flickered like a whisper and a promise, wetting his lips just enough to start a fire in his gut.

"Come on, big guy. Just one beer?" Miss Hex coaxed, her breath a heady hint of whiskey sour and forgotten good intentions.

The beer could wait. Circling her, he cupped the nape of her neck with one hand, and the leather clad cheek of her ass with his other. Tilting her head, he took her mouth hard, mashing her lips, thrusting his tongue into the slick warmth of her mouth while he imagined that other slick warmth, and what it would feel like to know her in every sense of the word.

She growled, but not in disgust. Giving back with passion and heat, her boots lifted off the floor. She wrapped her long legs around his hips, pressing her core to his belly. If this was what she wanted, she was going to get it. Here. Now. He had both hands full of ass, and a hard-on from hell in his pants. "I'm not doing this here," he told her open mouth.

Her fingers slid up his jaw into his too-long-for-military hair, smoothed over his skull and set off every last milliliter of testosterone in his body. "I know a place."

Suddenly he was nitroglycerin, unstable and ready to blow. Until his brain re-engaged. He set her feet to the floor, not sure what just happened, but not—NOT—going down this road with one of Kruze's girls. Not in this lifetime.

There'd be no kids in her future, and Pagan wanted a family like the one he'd been raised in. A family required a real mother for his future sons and daughters, not some killer dominatrix with a leather fetish and a delectable, but well-used, ass. Pagan didn't do one-night stands, and he didn't do easy. If nothing else, the woman he married would be respectable.

Disgusted at his lack of control and morals, he uncupped his fingers from said ass, inhaled deeply to clear his head, then settled Miss Hex's boots back to the floor. With his heart jackhammering up his throat, Pagen stepped away from the hottest temptation of his life. He'd done crazy a time or two in his life, jumped off a couple bridges, drove too fast, hitchhiked, and downed too many fifths of Irish Whiskey, but this was his future on the line. Yeah. Miss Hex had no hold on that, and he wouldn't—absolutely would not!—give her one now.

She stood there with her feet spread, breathing hard and her plump girls heaving beneath that tiny T. Hex was a gorgeous mess of long, black hair, her just-kissed lips still wet from his tongue. "Pagan, I—"

He reached for those lips and ran the pad of his thumb across the bottom one, walking away from an offer of free sex that would've been out of this world. But so damned wrong. "I'm not that guy," he told her gently before he changed his mind. "I don't do women like Kruze does. I'm not made that way. Sex has to mean something. Sorry."

Her nose wrinkled. "Kruze? What's he got to do with this? With us?"

"There is no us, Victoria. I've got" —he ran a quick hand over his head, not sure what he'd just heard or why he'd called her by her full name— "Jesus, I've got to go. Bye."

Her fingers hit his wrist, clutching him before he got away. "I'm... I'm sorry. I..." She seemed tongue-tied. "I didn't know."

That got his pride's attention. "You didn't know what?"

Her eyes flashed then. "Never mind. Go. Just go."

He couldn't help but nod. If he lived to be one hundred, he'd never understand how a female mind worked. "Fine then. Bye."

Turning back at Mills' rear doorway, it hit Pagan hard. Something was wrong with this picture, but damned if he knew what it was or how to fix it. And no, turning back was not an option. She'd read weakness into a dumb-jock move like that. To Hex, this was nothing but a game. A kill-or-be-killed game, and he didn't play with love that way. He just plain didn't have the heart for it. Yet he couldn't stop his big mouth from asking, "Are you sure you'll be okay?"

Victoria stood there in the dark, alone, her arms crossed over her magnificent chest, but her chin down, her hair hiding her face. "Yeah, fine. No worries," she replied without looking up, her voice unusually tight. "Tell your brothers 'hi' for me. Later, Pagan."

"Will do." And that was that.

Pagan shut the door behind him. He had a flight to catch. Like the way it ended or not, this mission was over. He was on his way home to Montana—until his wide shoulders turned all by themselves. Until his palm rotated Mills' POS doorknob like it had a mind of its own. Until he found himself facing the door he'd just closed instead of the fast getaway he'd planned.

"Oh, hell," he cursed. "What's one beer?"

Thank you for reading Chance's story!

If you enjoyed this book, be sure to check out the sexy guys and gals of Irish Winters' series, *In the Company of Snipers* on Amazon.com.

Other Irish Winters' books:

King of Hearts, Deuces Wild Series, #1

Joker Joker, Deuces Wild Series, #2

Smoke, Hearts and Ashes Series, #1

Ash, Hearts and Ashes Series, #2

These ebooks are also available on Barnes and Noble, iTunes, and Kobo.

Coming soon!

Seth, In the Company of Snipers, #17
One-Eyed Jack, Deuces Wild Series, #3
Assassin, An SOBs Novel, #2

YOU ARE THE KEY TO THIS BOOK'S SUCCESS!

Please tell other readers why you liked Chance and Suede's story by leaving an honest review at the retail site where you purchased it.

Recommend it to your friends. Lend it.

Most of all, enjoy it!

The best way to keep up with my new releases, giveaways, and actionable intel is to sign up for my spam-free newsletter at IrishWinters.com.

About the Author

Irish Winters is a best-selling author who, when she isn't writing, dabbles in poetry, grandchildren, and rarely (as in extremely rarely) the kitchen. More prone to be outdoors than in, she grew up the quintessential tomboy on a dairy farm in rural Wisconsin, spent her teenage years in the Pacific Northwest, but calls the Wasatch Mountains of Northern Utah, home. For now.

She believes in making every day count for something, and follows the wise admonition of her mother to, "Look out the window and see something!"

Connect with Irish online:

On Facebook

https://www.facebook.com/IrishWintersAuthor/

On Twitter

https://twitter.com/irishwinters1

www. IrishWinters.com